# The Tobacco Wives

## A Novel

## Adele Myers

## HARPER LARGE PRINT
*An Imprint of HarperCollinsPublishers*

THE TOBACCO WIVES. Copyright © 2022 by Adele Myers. All rights reserved. Printed in the United States of America. No part of this book may be used or reproduced in any manner whatsoever without written permission except in the case of brief quotations embodied in critical articles and reviews. For information, address HarperCollins Publishers, 195 Broadway, New York, NY 10007.

HarperCollins books may be purchased for educational, business, or sales promotional use. For information, please e-mail the Special Markets Department at SPsales@harpercollins.com.

FIRST HARPER LARGE PRINT EDITION

ISBN: 978-0-06-321135-3

Library of Congress Cataloging-in-Publication Data is available upon request.

22 23 24 25 26   LSC   10 9 8 7 6 5 4 3 2 1

# The Tobacco Wives

The Tobacco Wives

For Dietra

For Dieiro

# The Tobacco Wives

# One

My mother woke me in the dead of night again. I felt her standing over my bed, the heat of a flashlight on my face.

"Maddie, get up."

I tried to wake, but stay asleep too, fighting with myself in some in-between place. She paced back and forth, arguing under her breath with an imaginary someone.

I wondered what the matter was this time. Surely it couldn't be worse than what she did last Sunday.

"Get up, and come with me," she'd said that night. It was four in the morning and her green eyes were wild. She'd rushed me onto my feet, the wood floor cool and in need of sweeping, gritty under my toes. "I need your help," she'd said, her voice urgent.

I still had a sore spot on my arm where she'd grabbed

me in that moment, dragging me into the living room. I thought maybe I had left my sketchbook and dress patterns out, that I was in for it. Then I saw the living room and understood it wasn't my mess she was worried over; she'd made one of her own. Momma had stacked up clothes and Daddy's model airplanes, paintings, and pictures. There were novels with their spines bent back and photographs ripped into little pieces, an unruly pile smack in the middle of the room.

"We have to get rid of all your father's things . . . all of them."

Momma had hauled the outdoor trash can inside, the heavy metal one, leaving a wet, brown trail on the carpet.

"Why?" I asked, tears in my eyes at the sight of Daddy's belongings strewn around so careless. "Why would we do that?"

My father's undershirts were stacked on the worn cushion of his favorite wingback. His hat lay on the floor next to the wooden kit he propped his foot on to shine his shoes. I loved the gasoline smell of his shoe polish and the brisk sound of the brush when he buffed his boots to a high gleam. I reached out to rescue it, to save the memory of my daddy, but Momma gave my hand a smack.

"I'm the mother and you do as I say."

The mother. She always said it that way. Like she needed to remind me—or maybe herself—of her place.

When Daddy died last fall, Momma took to her bed for months. At first I thought she'd come down with a bad flu. I wiped her brow with cool washcloths and set steaming mugs of honey lemon tea at her bedside. I sat with her through the long days, making sure she was still breathing. But she wasn't sick, least her body wasn't. Finally, she came out of hibernation, and over the last few weeks, had barely slept at all. She was real alert when darkness came, pacing, scribbling notes in a steno pad, and waking me to join her.

Flashlight in hand she'd jolt me out of bed in the middle of the night to tell me that she had to move on, that she had to find a new husband to pay the bills. She couldn't very well court a suitor with reminders of Daddy lying around the house, now could she?

I'd started hiding things from her after the fire. Not just possessions, feelings too. On the night we burned what was left of Daddy's belongings, I'd hidden his pin and Grandpa Sykes's pocket watch in my sewing satchel, where I kept my sketchbook, fabric swatches, and patterns. All the secret things I didn't want Momma getting her hands on were in there, including my stash of cigarettes and all my money: six dollars and change I'd earned sewing house dresses and mending hand-me-downs for the neighbors.

"Your father left us, Maddie!" Momma had shouted the night of the fire, grabbing her wedding photograph. The edge of the metal frame scraped her arm, causing a red line to bloom up through her skin.

"Momma, you cut yourself."

She didn't seem to hear me. There was no talking to her when she got like this.

"Three years I waited for him to come home," she said, tossing the picture in the metal trash can with a clank. "Three years of waiting for him to make good on his word. 'I promise, honey' he said, 'when this war is over we'll move out of Haywood Holler, get away from the smell and find a nice house up on Pine Mountain.' I promise. Hmph. Well promises are cheap. Now we can hardly afford this place."

Momma always complained about the smell of the paper mill. "I'll be damned if I'm gonna live out the rest of my days next to that stench," she'd say. Our whole town stank like rotten eggs from the heat and chemicals they used to pulp wood chips into paper, but Daddy had worked there. All the other daddies too. Didn't that count for something?

"You don't know what you're talking about," she'd

said, when I told her the good outweighed the bad, that without the paper factory, Daddy wouldn't have a job. But she didn't listen to me. She sure didn't listen the night of the fire. "He can't help his plane got shot down. He didn't want to die," I'd said, trying to defend Daddy, trying to pull things from the pile, trying to make sense of it all. "He was going to make a better life for us and all, Momma. He was answering the call of duty."

She sneered at this, her face turning ugly. "He didn't get called up, Maddie. He volunteered. I begged him not to go and he left us anyway."

Momma's words were a hard slap. Daddy told me he got drafted. I'd wondered at the time why he didn't have a draft card. Most men showed theirs with pride, but not daddy. He acted funny every time I asked, and now I knew why. He never got one. Still, it was hard to believe. Why would he leave me? Her I could understand, but not me.

Momma shook my shoulder again, startling me out of my dark memory. "Are you getting up? Put your coat on over your nightgown," she said, brandishing the flashlight like a gun.

She had never laid a hand on me. Momma loved me, I knew that, and I loved her too, but something in her died with Daddy. She wasn't who she used to be, and neither was I. It was like we didn't know how to act, now that there was just the two of us. Like we didn't know how to fill the space he'd left behind.

"Maddie, are you even listening? Dammit girl, you're always off someplace else."

She was right about that. I got away from here in my mind anytime I could, any way I could. Sketching helped. Sewing helped the most. When I was stitching or hemming, dreaming up new designs, the hours would just disappear. All my problems would melt away. I didn't have to think about Momma or the empty chair at the dinner table. It was just me and the needle making the thread go where I told it to go.

I squinted. "Can you get that out of my eyes?"

"Don't get smart with me," she snapped, and pulled back the covers with a cool whoosh. The mountain nights were chilly in June, even though most days it warmed up to scorching by noon. She threw her suitcase and my navy peacoat on the bed.

"Why do I need a winter coat? Where are we going?"

"Get your kerchief on and your saddle shoes, the new ones. I'll finish packing," she said.

She yanked dresses from my closet and threw them in the suitcase, just grabbed them by the hems and pulled, the wooden hangers falling with a clatter. I'd cut and sewed every last piece of my wardrobe myself, and here was Momma casting my dresses about as if they were rags. I wanted to shout at her, tell her to be careful, but I knew better than to say anything when she was like this.

I escaped to the washroom, locking the door and turning on the light. Momma's new rule to stop using electricity didn't make a lick of sense to me. Batteries for the flashlight cost more than the light bill. Not to mention she didn't mind spending a pretty penny on lipstick and rouge.

I studied my face in the mirror, smoothed my auburn curls. My hair was thick and shiny, but always a bit wild. I was forever trying to tame it, to wrestle the whole mess into a victory roll like Rita Hayworth, but there was no use. My hair was just like Daddy's. My eyes were too. Ice blue, just like his.

"Maddie!" my mother shouted, banging on the door so hard it shook on its hinges. "We're leaving. And what did I tell you about the lights?"

I fumbled with my kerchief, folded it in a big triangle, and lined it up along my hairline. It was damp from last night's rinse.

"Coming!" I answered, tying it at the base of my neck and tucking in the tail.

Momma had loved to run her fingers through Daddy's thick red hair. It was striking, she said, a color all his own. When he left for basic training, she made him promise to save a few locks when he got his buzz cut. She wanted to keep them in an envelope with my strawberry-colored baby ones. Then Daddy stopped writing and the telegram arrived. After that, my hair became a painful reminder. "Cover your head," she had said sharply. "You look just like him."

Momma was waiting for me outside the washroom door. "Put this on," she said, handing my peacoat to me.

It was going to be itchy against my bare arms, but I did as she said. "Where are we going?" I asked her again.

"You'll see," she said. She placed the suitcase on the floor and fastened my coat, her pink nails clicking against the buttons. "It's for the best. Really it is." She paused and looked at me sweetly, a bit of her old self coming through. She held my face in her hands and kissed me on the forehead. "You'll see, baby."

I followed Momma out back, the screen door slamming behind us. I could barely see the stone path to the driveway.

Our yard still smelled from last Sunday's bonfire, but sweet too, because she'd thrown the dried eucalyptus on last.

The sounds of night were loud and powerful around

me, an owl hooting in the distance and the big pines swaying with the wind, making that rushing-hushing sound I so loved.

The car was already running in the driveway, and Momma told me to sit in back so I could stretch myself out and sleep.

"You're wasting gas leaving the car running, Momma," I said. "You won't let me turn on a lamp, but you'll gladly burn up a gallon of gasoline without a second thought. It's not fair."

"Life's not fair, Maddie. Get in."

She heaved the suitcase onto the passenger seat up front and got behind the wheel.

"Wait!" I said, before sliding into the backseat. "I have to go to the bathroom."

"Good lord, girl, you just came out of there. Hurry up."

I ran back into the house and felt my way down the hall to my bedroom. I pulled my blanket aside and slid my hand between the mattress and box spring, tugging my sewing satchel from its hiding place. I checked the secret pocket for Daddy's pin. The metal was cool and smooth except for the raised words LIEU-TENANT SYKES, 82ND AIRBORNE. It looked brand-new, not a scratch on it.

Right before Daddy shipped out, at the end of

October of 1943—I remember the month on account of my birthday being November first and we celebrated early—he put the pin on me and let me order him around.

"At your service, Lieutenant Madeline Sykes." He saluted me. "Private Daddy Sykes reporting for duty. Your wish is my command."

I giggled as he marched up and down the living room and let me take a tiny sip—my first ever—of his frosty Budweiser. I was only twelve at the time, but it was just a little foam, and we were careful to make sure Momma didn't see.

The horn honked. I quickly tucked the bag under my coat and ran back to the car before Momma could wake up the whole neighborhood.

"Are you ready now?"

"Yes," I said, slamming the car door and scooting across the backseat. "Are you going to tell me where we're going? I can't be seen like this." My nightgown was so thin you could practically see through it.

"Quit complaining." Momma lit a cigarette and shifted the gear to D with her same hand. "Anyway, you can change later."

Now that we had an automatic, Momma loved to drive. We got it when Daddy came into good money before the war, a used Buick, light blue like the Tar

Heels. He had left the paper mill six months before he shipped out to work on the Blue Ridge Parkway roads project. The days pouring asphalt were hot, but the pay was good. He wanted to make sure we had a reliable car while he was gone.

As we drove out into the night, I thought maybe we were just going to ride around the Parkway again. We'd driven on the smooth, new road before, always in the middle of the night, the only ones snaking around hairpin turns until we got to the top of Beaucatcher Mountain. I felt bad about using more than our share of gas on these drives, but when I reminded Momma about the rationing, she said *this family's sacrificed plenty.* Then her voice went from harsh to soft. *It helps me feel close to your daddy,* she'd said. *Driving up here.*

The last time we'd done it, we'd reached the highest overlook just as the sun was coming up. Momma pulled the car over onto the gravel shoulder and we walked to a rock at the edge overlooking the valley.

"Isn't it beautiful, Maddie?" Momma said. There were tears in her eyes. "I'm sorry, honey. I haven't been myself lately. Your momma's not perfect, but she sure does love you. You know that, don't you?"

She hugged me tight, the smell of tobacco and lemon drops on her breath. "Sure, Momma," I said and hugged her back, but not as freely as I used to.

This time we weren't going up the mountain, we were headed down. My ears popped as we zigzagged our way to the bottom, leaving the Blue Ridge Mountains and Haywood Holler behind. I rolled the window down and leaned my head out, the wind pounding against my ears, making that noise that comes and goes, comes and goes. It smelled of pine and the air was damp, misty. I took my kerchief off and closed my eyes, the wind whipping my hair against my face.

Momma seemed different when she drove, happy even, almost like her old self before she started arguing with Daddy about shipping off. She used to hum while she cooked dinner. I loved to watch her float around the kitchen with a spatula in one hand and a cigarette in the other. She'd let the ash get so long, I was sure it was going to fall in my supper. Daddy said it wouldn't hurt me if it did.

"Hell, it's good for you, Shug. It'll put hair on your chest." He laughed.

"Daddy, that's disgusting!"

"Jack, really?" Momma said, turning to smile and point her spatula at him. "What am I going to do with you?"

"I'll show you later," he teased, then walked over and smacked her on the behind.

The radio station cut in and out as we made our way

down the mountain. Momma flipped around a bit and finally locked into a new channel. A woman was speaking, her voice high and clear, like a bell.

"Say, what's that lovely scent, Jane?" asked the radio actress.

"Oh, it's MOMints, the new, mild cigarette that's coming out soon. It's made right here in Bright Leaf."

"Made in North Carolina *for* North Carolina," said a second voice, this one low and sultry. "My doctor suggested I try them. Did you know that according to a statewide survey, more doctors recommend MOMints for their female patients than any other cigarette brand? Only MOMints are made with North Carolina bright leaf tobacco and mint oil to calm our fragile nerves, which means they're great for expectant mothers—and also for brand-new ones, just like you, Carol! Here, you must try one!"

There was a pause, followed by the sizzle of a match being lit, and then a long, slow exhale. The first actress sighed with pleasure.

"Oh, Jane, you are absolutely right. A MOMint is exactly what I needed!"

"New MOMints," said the two voices in unison. "Coming soon. Because every woman deserves a moment to herself."

After a beat of dead air, an announcer came on and

read news about the troops coming home. "Eastern North Carolina's boys will be among the last to return," he began.

*Return.* What a sad word that turned out to be.

Momma quickly flipped the channel. I was glad she did.

"Maddie, roll up that window and lie down," Momma said. "You best rest up before we get there."

She still hadn't told me where we were going, but I knew we were leaving home, heading east.

I didn't get it. I didn't get it at all. School had just let out for the summer and I was hoping to earn some extra money working. Mary Landis had four little ones and needed someone to help with the youngest a few hours a day and do some repairs on the clothing. If I did a good job for her maybe she would suggest me to her friends. I could make curtains and hem skirts and take in dresses. And Mr. Evans at the paper store had let me put a sign that listed my services in his window. I had gotten a few small jobs from that already. Just this week, I had talked it all over with my friend April. She was going to work in the diner covering the lunch rush and would earn tips on top of her hourly pay. We'd both have money to spend during the summer and could go to the movies or buy magazines. And I'd give some to Momma, of course, to help with the bills.

As I thought about my plan, I wondered where we were going and why I was the only one with a suitcase. I was about to ask Momma again, but before I could get the words out she turned the music up loud.

*When your heart aches, when you fear it*
    *may break,*
*believe that it isn't so*
*The sun will still rise, wipe the tears from*
    *your eyes*
*And smile pretty, my darling dear.*

# Two

Aunt Etta was the best professional seamstress in all tobacco country, just about anyone would tell you so. She learned the basics from her mamaw when she was just a girl, then she got really good by studying *Vogue* magazine and the works of her favorite designers, Coco Chanel and Claire McCardell. Aunt Etta told me all about how Coco Chanel thought women should be able to dress like men if they wanted, and how Claire McCardell thought that clothes should be practical. "If not for them, we'd still be wearing corsets," she had told me.

I was eight when Momma and Daddy first let me visit Aunt Etta on my own, and every summer since, they would send me to Bright Leaf for three glorious weeks in August. We'd drive halfway there to the Texaco station off the highway near Monroe, where we'd meet Aunt Etta. I still remember how I could hardly sleep the night before that first trip. I rose early to the smell of pancakes and Daddy standing over the stove, flipping golden brown flapjacks in his undershirt and work pants.

"Morning, Shug," he said, ruffling my hair and pointing for me to sit. "Excited?"

Before I could answer, Momma appeared in the doorway. "Well, you two are up early. I don't suppose there's any coffee left for me?" She was always saying things like that, acting like we were leaving her out. We couldn't help it if we loved going to Aunt Etta's. She was Daddy's aunt and all the family he had left. To me, she was like a grandmother, though I'd never known any of my grandparents, so I am just guessing. She taught me to sew and helped me develop my talent. Truth is, once I started spending summers there on my own, there was no place else I'd rather be.

I woke up in the backseat of our Buick and the first thing I saw was that big red Texaco star. I knew then that we must be meeting Aunt Etta. This was the first time at the Texaco since Daddy died. Before Daddy had gone off to war, he always drove and always insisted on paying for Aunt Etta's gas and giving her money for our sweet tea too. He was a gentleman like that. Plus,

Aunt Etta had often taken care of Daddy when he was a boy, and he liked to find ways to show his gratitude.

This would be the first time seeing Aunt Etta since she came to stay with Momma and me for the week after Daddy's service, and I felt a fresh wave of sadness. I wondered if it would always be like this, the pain rearing its head with every first.

I stretched my neck, looking around the gas station. It hurt something awful from sleeping in the backseat. There was no sign of Aunt Etta or her car either, just Momma and the same station attendant as ever, grinning and smoking a cigar.

Gus always gave Momma an oil change for free. She'd say oh, she couldn't possibly, but well, if you insist. Then she'd remind him to check the wiper fluid and antifreeze. Oh, and could he spare one of those ice-cold Pepsis and a few peanut butter crackers?

Men were forever giving Momma special treatment, watching her in that hungry way. I tried to tell her that she shouldn't be flirting like that, but Momma just said I didn't understand the way the world worked.

"A lady has to use her assets. You best learn that if you want to go anywhere in life." I thought Momma's flirting was disrespectful to Daddy when he was alive; it bothered me even more now that she was on the hunt to replace him. Not a year since he had passed and she was already fixing for some strange man to sleep on Daddy's side of the bed. She shouldn't be doing that and I told her as much the last time she brought a fella around, but she just shushed me and said I was gonna ruin her chance at happiness.

Now Momma was over by the gas pump, making eyes at Gus, and throwing her head back to laugh at whatever dumb joke he was telling. I knocked on the window, hard. They turned to me, and I waved at her to come over. She tapped Gus on the shoulder and giggled again, then walked over to my side of the car.

I rolled down the window. "What's going on, Momma? Is Aunt Etta coming to meet us?" I said, slinking down in the seat so Gus wouldn't see me.

Momma examined her pink nails for a moment and then said, "Well no, not exactly. We're driving the whole way ourselves this time."

"But why are we going now, when it's her busy time? I'll be in her way."

Aunt Etta sewed for lots of folks in Bright Leaf, rich and poor alike. But she really made her money in June and July sewing custom dresses and gowns for the women she called *the tobacco wives*. The wives were married to the richest, most powerful men in Bright Leaf, the ones who owned the fields, the drying barns, the cigarette factory, practically the whole town.

All June and July Aunt Etta cut and sewed, fitted and flitted from mansion to mansion, getting the wives ready for their summer festivals and garden parties and galas.

On occasion, I would get a glimpse of these women from afar when Aunt Etta took me into town. It was a thrill to see them strolling down the town's sidewalks in their wide-brim cartwheel hats and fitted suits or shirtwaist dresses, their hourglass silhouettes like Hollywood starlets.

My first summer staying with Aunt Etta, I'd actually met one of them. I'd never seen a tobacco wife up close before, and this one—Mrs. Winston—was even doing her own shopping. Most of the wives sent their maids to buy their produce and select the best cuts of meat, but not Mrs. Winston. Aunt Etta said she was very particular about the meals she served on her long mahogany table. She had a reputation for being the best hostess in town.

That day in the butcher shop, Mrs. Winston wore a shirtwaist dress, short white gloves, and a green hat with yellow and white sunflowers on the side. Her skin was porcelain white and she moved with elegance and grace, like a trained dancer. When she reached the front of the line at the counter, she spoke to the butcher like he was a personal friend. *I'll have that roast on the con-ah, darlin'*, she said in an accent so honeyed that it drowned out the *r*s in *corner* and the *g* on *darling* too.

Mrs. Winston caught sight of us then, tucked her pocketbook neatly under her arm, and made her way over to where we stood.

"Good morning, Etta. Don't you look lovely today. And who is this precious angel traveling with you?" she said, bending down and placing her hand under my chin. A bracelet with charms hanging from it jingled lightly. The air above her wrist was scented with rose-water.

Aunt Etta introduced us, and I smiled and blushed. After a few minutes of small talk, with me answering Mrs. Winston's questions as politely and carefully as I could, she glanced at her watch.

"Will you look at the time?" she said. "I'm late for Garden Club, but it was wonderful to see you both. I do hope you enjoy your visit, Miss Maddie." She undid the smart gold clasp on her purse and pulled out two crinkle-wrapped pieces of butterscotch, which she pressed into my hand with a wink. Then she was gone.

It was a rare treat to encounter a tobacco wife in real life. I was used to admiring their magnificent clothing hanging on the racks at Aunt Etta's house, ready for an update or repair, or still in fabric pieces on the work-table like a fancy jigsaw puzzle just waiting to be put together. There were evening gowns and smart Sunday suits with shoulder pads sewn in; broad-brimmed hats for day; sequined fascinators for Friday and Saturday nights; floaty tea party dresses with wide bell skirts; and even swimsuits. Last summer, all the wives wanted polka-dot bathing suits just like Ava Gardner, and my clever aunt stitched up every last one. Even the ladies who were past their prime were asking for an "Ava two-piece." Miss Gardner was a North Carolina native, so her fame must have felt especially personal to the women of Bright Leaf. It made sense that they would claim a kinship with her, that they would feel as if they had the right to imitate her. She might have been an international movie star, but she was still one of them, practically speaking.

Come August, the busy season was over and Aunt Etta could get back to working on uniforms for the factory workers at the tobacco plant, mending things for regular folk, and planning for the tobacco wives' fall and winter parties. That's when I would show up.

It was the same every year. When the last bell rang in June, I'd race out of school, glad for freedom and the warm days ahead. There was always something to do in the Holler—swimming at the quarry with April, bike riding, trying out a new dress pattern, or reading a Nancy Drew book on the porch. Before Daddy joined the service, he surprised me and Momma one summer with a Monopoly game. We'd spread the board out on the table after the dinner dishes were cleared and the three of us would play for hours in the cool evening air. Momma always picked the car for her game piece and I was the thimble, of course. Daddy alternated between the cannon and the top hat. Momma bought the most expensive properties. Boardwalk and Park Place were her favorites. Poor Daddy always seemed to land on them and he'd have to pay dearly. Momma got a real kick out of that.

But for the most part, the long summer days were spent practicing my stitching and sketching. Always in the back of my mind would be Aunt Etta's encouraging voice. When I had first started helping her, my job had been to pin the uniform patterns on fabric for her to cut out. But slowly I graduated to hems and darts, then cutting the pieces myself. Two summers ago, Aunt Etta trusted my hand enough to let me trace, stitch, and finish whole factory uniforms on my own. I felt proud to sew those uniforms, especially for the women. Their faces would just light up when they came to Aunt Etta's house to pick them up. They were so proud of their work. *Can you believe it*, they'd say, *me, making my own money? I might splurge on a jar of Pond's*. There was talk about what would happen when all the factory husbands came home from the war, but for now the ladies far outnumbered the men.

Last year Aunt Etta finally said I was ready to assist her with the tobacco wives' projects. My skills still needed polish, she told me, but that would only come with hands-on experience. I needed to work with silk and lace, chiffon, and the other finicky fabrics the wives tended to favor. So that summer she decided to get a jump start on the holiday season and had me help her with two Christmas party gowns. I suspected she wanted to give herself time to redo them if I didn't live up to her standards, but she was so pleased with the results that she loaded me up with remnants to practice at home. If I kept at it over the winter, I would handle a serious commission on my own next summer.

I did keep at it. Even after Daddy died and Momma took to her bed and everything was left to me, I'd sit up in the evenings and practice my sewing the way Aunt Etta had taught me. It was a relief to pick up a needle and feel the fabric between my fingers. This was something I could do. Momma retreating into herself was almost a relief. I didn't have to worry about the strange things she was saying or what she might do, I had time to think of my daddy and how much I missed him. Grieving, I guess you'd call it. I had time too to think of who I was and what I wanted to be. I kept that in mind as I practiced my basting and gathering and topstitching. I even taught myself how to make a French seam over the winter. My aunt would be proud.

Had Momma told Aunt Etta how hard I was working? Did Aunt Etta believe I was ready now? Is that why we were going to Bright Leaf?

Momma opened the car door, moved my suitcase to the back, and patted the empty passenger seat beside her.

"Come sit with me," Momma said, handing me a Pepsi and a pack of crackers. "Come sit next to your momma."

I scooted up front fast so Gus wouldn't catch sight of me in my nightgown.

Momma may have been up driving through the small hours of the morning, but she looked as fresh as if she had caught eight hours of sleep. She'd combed her hair and put on lipstick, a pretty coral that flattered her fair skin. Before we pulled out onto the highway, she rolled down her window and gave Gus a little wave. Momma could do that—make an entrance and an exit as well.

The sun shined down on us, low and hot. The farther east we drove, the warmer it got.

"Here, honey," she said, handing me some sunglasses, the round white ones with green lenses that I loved. Momma had so many pairs that she could wear a different pair every day of the week. Another of her indulgences despite the war. She was wearing her pink bug-eyed ones, the style that all the ladies in the magazines wore. "Push the lighter in for me," she said, flipping her cigarette case open with one hand and removing a long, slender cigarette.

I waited until the lighter popped out and held it for her. The metal glowed orange red, and even though I knew it would burn me, I was tempted to touch it with my finger. Momma took a slow, satisfying draw and I breathed in the ashy smoke, that sweet earthiness filling my lungs.

Momma's blond curtain of hair flowed behind her as she took another draw. She was happier than I'd seen her in a long time, and it was hard to believe it had been only a few hours since her harsh midnight awakening.

"Isn't it a glorious day?" she asked, glancing over at me.

"I guess."

"What's wrong, honey? Aren't you excited to see Aunt Etta?"

"I am, but why didn't she meet us? Why am I going now, instead of in August like usual? Why did we have to leave in the middle of the night?"

"We'll be there in two shakes," she responded, ignoring my questions.

I could calculate our distance from Bright Leaf by the smell of the different tobacco varieties. When I rode in Aunt Etta's car, she left the windows down so I could learn our location by the scent of the fields. About sixty miles out, there was the skunky smell of the heartier tobacco breeds for cigars, but when we were fewer than thirty-five miles from town, it was replaced with the sweet morning glory scent of the Bright Leaf plants.

It was on one of these long-ago drives that Aunt Etta taught me about tobacco's many uses. It wasn't just for cigarettes and cigars, she'd said. Farmers and gardeners misted their plants with tobacco-soaked water to keep moles and gophers away. Doctors often prescribed a combination of shredded tobacco with Desert Sage to ward off asthma attacks; and, of course, we all used tobacco poultices to calm a croupy cough or beat back a bad cold.

"There are a million ways to use it," she explained. "And thank the Lord for that. Tobacco means money for all of us. Without it, we'd be a bunch of dirt-eaters around here."

**The sight** of Aunt Etta's little house, standing picture-perfect on her tree-lined street, usually brought a smile to my face. It stood proud and happy with its clean white wood and lemon-yellow shutters. The windows, always sparkling clean, were set off by painted boxes with the most colorful flowers: petunias, geraniums, nasturtiums, and begonias. If the house were a face—and I liked to think of it that way—the windows would be its eyes, the flowers its lashes. It was warm and welcoming, greeting you with a smile, just like Aunt Etta did. But there was something else too. When I stepped through the door I felt different, somehow, as if here I could be another Maddie. There were possibilities in this small bright house, a quiet promise that things could be better. That I could be something.

Not today, though.

Everything felt wrong. It was awfully early when we arrived, the grass still wet with morning dew. The *Bright Leaf Journal* lay by the front door, waiting to be unrolled and read over breakfast.

Momma pulled the car into the driveway and parked by the side door. She pushed her sunglasses up on her head like a hairband and checked her coral lipstick in the rearview mirror. My stomach was jittery, my nerves were busy.

"Grab the suitcase. Your coat too."

She'd forgotten to turn off the car, and I told her so.

"Oh, I'll just leave it running. I can't stay long." She

stepped on the parking brake with one high heel, then stood on it with both feet, struggling with all her might before it finally clicked into place. "I shouldn't have to do these things myself," she muttered.

"Momma, what do you mean you can't stay long? Aren't you coming in?"

She swung her car door open and left it that way. Then she flicked her wrist at me, shooing me to get out. I threw a glare at her as she pranced across the gravel drive in her high heels, then grabbed my suitcase, sewing satchel, and coat from the backseat.

Aunt Etta appeared in the doorway, pulling her bathrobe tighter. She glanced back inside, then turned to us, hands on her hips.

"Surprise!" Momma held out her arms and nodded for me to speak.

Then it hit me. Aunt Etta had no idea we were coming. No idea *at all.* I offered a meek "hi."

When Aunt Etta's shocked expression didn't change, Momma said, "Maddie darlin, go wait by the car while I talk to your aunt." I did as she told me but watched them through the screened-in porch—Aunt Etta with her arms crossed, Momma doing most of the talking and raising hers in the air, gesturing toward me. They raised their voices too, but I couldn't make out what they were saying. Tobacco wives season was important to Aunt Etta. June and July were strictly off limits for visiting so she could focus on her work. Now I felt silly, thinking that she'd wanted me here when it was clear that she wasn't just surprised; she was downright upset. After a few minutes, Momma came out, wiping tears from her face.

"Now you have fun," she told me.

"Aunt Etta doesn't want me here, does she?"

"Of course, she does. You'll be a big help to her. She'll see."

"Momma! Where are you going? Why are you leaving me?"

"Don't you get ugly with me," she snapped, like I'd done something wrong. "I told you that this was for the best, didn't I?"

"You didn't tell me anything, Momma! You haven't explained why I'm here and when you're coming back."

"I'm not sure, Maddie. As long as it takes."

"As long as what takes? What about me, Momma? How long will I be here?"

"Stop complaining. You'll be fine here, Maddie, I don't know what you're worrying about. You're a sturdy little thing. You'll always be fine, not like . . ." She trailed off without finishing her sentence. She didn't have to. I'd heard it all before—her life was hard and she needed someone to look after her. "I don't need you distracting my suitors," Momma continued, "or fussing at me for enjoying a little companionship. I think I deserve that, don't you? *I lost my husband for God's sake.*"

"And I lost my daddy!" I reminded her.

"See, that's what I mean. You've got such a mouth on you, always talking back. You still have me, don't you? You have your aunt. That's more than I've got."

I told her she had Aunt Etta too, but she said it was different. Blood mattered, and I was blood, she wasn't. It didn't occur to her that she was my blood and that she was leaving me here like I was some orphan.

"Now go on," she said, forcing a smile. "Scoot. Have fun and mind your aunt."

Momma waved to where Aunt Etta stood watching in the doorway. "Thanks so much. I'll call when I can, but long-distance is real pricey. You might not hear from me on the regular."

She struggled to release the parking brake until it finally gave with a thunk and Momma backed out, tapping the horn and blowing me a kiss like all this was just nothing. Her taillights disappeared around the corner, and I had no idea when she'd return. All that remained was a slick of shimmery oil where she'd left the Buick running.

# Three

Aunt Etta's cat-shaped wall clock ticked in time with the swing of its tail and eyes—back and forth, back and forth.

"Did you eat?" Aunt Etta asked, motioning for me to sit at the kitchen table. "Of course you didn't," she answered before I could.

"I had some crackers."

She shook her head and said something under her breath.

"I'll make some eggs. You're in luck because I got two this week."

The war was ending, but a lot of the soldiers were still overseas, so the rations and shortages continued—eggs, sugar, and meat too. Doing without was the least we could do.

I laid my head down on the table. I hadn't really slept, not good sleep anyway.

After a while, Aunt Etta touched my back, and I sat up. She put a plate of scrambled eggs, a napkin, a fork, and a tin of salt in front of me.

"Here you go, baby. You'll feel better with something in your stomach."

I felt a pang in my chest at the sight of the eggs, cooked just the way I liked them.

Aunt Etta pulled out the chair next to me and sat. "Oh, honey," she said, wrapping her arm around me. "It's okay. It'll be all right." She smoothed one of my curls.

"I'm sorry, Aunt Etta," I said. "I didn't know Momma was just leaving me here without even asking you. It's your busy time."

"You're sorry? You've got nothing to be sorry about, Maddie. I'm happy to see you, and you're always welcome here, you know that. But you're right, I didn't know you were coming."

I took a bite and wiped my mouth with my napkin. "It seems Momma wants me out of her hair so she can find a new husband."

"Hmm." Aunt Etta shook her head. "Can't say I'm surprised."

I sprinkled a touch more salt on my eggs.

"Your mother didn't have an easy time as a girl," Aunt Etta said. "You know she lost her father very young. Many's a night she and your grandmother went to bed hungry. Losing your daddy's been hard on her, opened up old wounds."

I swallowed hard. "I didn't know about that," I said. "I mean, I knew they didn't have much money, but not that they didn't have enough food to eat."

"Well, it was long ago, and life got better for them. But some things you never forget." Aunt Etta patted the top of my hand. "Now it'll be fine for you to stay, but we have to have a talk."

"Okay," I replied, sitting up taller. She looked real serious.

Aunt Etta told me how everything was different at this time of year. It was much more demanding than what I was used to, so I needed to be prepared. Today I would join Aunt Etta for a fitting with her most valued client, Mrs. Elizabeth Winston, the lady I met that one time when I was a little girl. Mrs. Winston, or Mitzy as, according to Aunt Etta, everyone called her, was one of the most powerful women in Bright Leaf. Aunt Etta made most of her money for the year sewing for Mrs. Winston and her friends, so we couldn't afford to disappoint or upset them.

I was nervous and excited at the same time. I told

Aunt Etta about the practice I had put in since last summer. It wasn't right to brag, but I couldn't hold back about my work with embroidery and eyelet, and how I had set a sleeve all by myself.

"You have been busy! I better watch myself or you'll be taking over my best customers."

I started to laugh, but it turned into a yawn.

"What time did your mother wake you up?" Aunt Etta asked.

"I don't know. It was pitch-black."

"I swear . . ." Aunt Etta tsked.

She stood and opened the cabinet over the sink, took a mug out. "Do you drink coffee?"

"No, ma'am." Momma liked her coffee first thing in the morning. *Don't talk to me until I've had my coffee*, she always said. *Thank goodness it was only rationed for a year.* I took over as chief coffee maker after Daddy left, measuring out the grounds and turning on the percolator every day before school, though I never drank any myself.

"Well, how'd you like to start?"

It smelled delicious. "I'd like that fine," I answered, perking up.

She poured me a cup and handed me a bottle of milk from the refrigerator. I knew enough not to ask for sugar. The coffee turned from black to a color close to sand, and the mug clinked as I swirled the spoon around and around. Aunt Etta said the coffee would help me stay on my toes.

I took a sip and pretended to like it. "What's Mrs. Winston like?" I asked.

"Well . . ." Aunt Etta hesitated, then tightened the belt on her robe. "I guess you could say she's like the first lady of Bright Leaf. She's married to the president of Bright Leaf Tobacco, and a real do-gooder, in charge of organizing fundraisers and charity programs for the community. She's always been very outgoing—a social butterfly—even as a little girl."

"You knew her when she was little?"

"I sure did." Aunt Etta nodded. "I helped make her christening dress, as a matter of fact. You know, my mother sewed for Mitzy's mother, so we go way back."

"Great-grandma Lottie?" I asked.

"The very one."

"Wow," I said. "So you've known Mrs. Winston her whole life. How old is she now?"

"Well, a lady never reveals her age. Not once she passes thirty. Let's just leave it at that, shall we?"

"Has she always been rich?"

"She grew up rich, but once she married Mr. Winston, she became *wealthy*. There's a difference."

"How do you mean?"

"The rich have lots of money, but the wealthy don't ever have to even think about money."

Imagine, living like that. Not having to hold your breath every time the checkout girl rings up your groceries, not having the shame that comes when you have to put something back. Not having to worry. "That sounds real nice," I said.

"Yes and no. Money solves a lot of life's problems, but it sure can't buy happiness. There's something to be said for earning your keep. She's got a lot of things, but she isn't what you'd call self-sufficient."

"She seemed independent enough to me," I said, taking another sip of coffee. "She did her own shopping when I saw her that one time."

"She means well. You'll like her. And she did indeed take a liking to you—" Aunt Etta cut herself off. "Want a little more?" she asked, lifting the coffeepot off the kitchen counter.

"No thank you."

"Mitzy is friendly, but it's important to remember that she's not our friend, she's our employer. As close as I am to her, I always keep that in mind. I mostly listen, don't talk too much about myself. It's better that way, more professional. Do you understand?"

"I think so. Okay then," I said, taking another small sip. It really did smell better than it tasted.

"Don't look so worried. Just be yourself, honey. You'll be fine. Now, why don't you go freshen up? Wear your best dress and shoes. We'll get the Murphy bed down later."

**Years ago** Aunt Etta transformed the lower level of her home into her professional workspace and studio. Women came here with ideas—pages torn from magazines or crude sketches on brown paper bags—which Aunt Etta turned into meticulously crafted garments that made them feel beautiful. Even factory uniforms were constructed with care to flatter every figure, thanks to Aunt Etta's capable hands. She made house calls for the tobacco wives, but the factory workers, middle-class women, and wives of lesser executives came to her.

The downstairs was a magical place where bolts of colorful fabric were arranged like a rainbow, and spools of thread peered out of a glass cabinet, just waiting to be chosen. There were machine needles and hand needles, gauges and measuring tapes, scissors and sheers. And, of course, Aunt Etta's collection of *Vogue* magazines. She kept everything neat and orderly, with pride of place given to her collection of antique thimbles. When she was a girl, she bought her first one with some money she had earned mending, then people started giving them to her as presents. Aunt Etta was very well liked, if the number of thimbles was any indication. She had dozens and dozens, and no two the same. Some were hand painted with flowers and birds, others with monuments from all over the country. My favorite was the guardian angel. When I held it in my hand, I could feel the angel's flowing gown and outstretched wings carved into the pewter. Aunt Etta said that thimble would likely have been a christening present from long ago. How sweet, the idea that a little baby would have an angel to watch over her.

I loved falling asleep among the fabric and notions, dreaming of the endless possibilities in a bolt of cloth. Waking to the sunlight streaming through the large bay window felt like its own blessing. The house had been built on an incline, so there was plenty of natural light, and the door that led to Aunt Etta's small back-yard made it easy for her customers to come and go. It also came in handy when I wanted to sneak a cigarette out back while the dog day cicadas chirped.

Lost in my thoughts as I walked down the stairs, I nearly jumped out of my skin when I found someone standing at the bottom of the steps.

"Maddie May! What on earth are you doing here?"

"Frances!" I yelped, and asked her the exact same thing.

"Oh," replied Frances. "I just needed to borrow a few slices of bread. You know how it is. I was in the middle of cooking my breakfast and realized I didn't have any left for toast. I'm always popping over here when I've forgotten something. Lucky for me, I'm close enough to walk. Good luck, huh; that I have a friend who will let me have some bread when I need it?"

Frances was talking awful fast.

"But you! A surprise sunrise visit from across the state is something else entirely. I'm guessing you didn't just come for breakfast. What are you doing here?"

"Momma dropped me off this morning," I said, trying to calm the wobble in my voice. "She said she needs *time to herself.*"

Frances shook her head and made a whistling noise, then wrapped her arms around me.

"Hey now, it's all right," she said. Her short hair tickled my face. "It's good to see you, Maddie May. Always good to see you."

Aunt Etta had known Frances since grade school. She was funny, always knew what to say to make you laugh, but mostly, she was very, very smart. She was the first to call me Maddie May, when I was just a tiny baby. Daddy told me that. He also told me that when he was a little boy, Frances would let him quiz her on any topic, and if he ever asked a question she couldn't answer, she would buy him an ice-cream cone. He only ever stumped her once, though, and Daddy was rewarded with a chocolate burst from the Good Humor man. Daddy thought the world of Frances and claimed that she would have been a millionaire if only she hadn't been born a girl. That might have been true, but she made a good living as the lead executive secretary at Bright Leaf Tobacco Headquarters. Aunt Etta always joked that Frances really ran the downtown office. "She wears the pants in that place, that's for sure" was what she actually said.

"Maddie," Aunt Etta called out as she came down the stairs. "Are you almost ready?" Frances and I looked up.

"Frances! What are you doing here?" Aunt Etta asked, glancing over at me as though I was in on some big secret.

"I was just hoping to steal a few slices of bread," said Frances. "For my breakfast."

"Is that all? Well, come on up and I'll get some for you."

As Frances climbed the staircase, Aunt Etta reminded me to hurry up and change into my best outfit. We couldn't afford to be late or untidy.

I hoped Momma had packed my yellow dress, the one I sewed last summer with the embroidery around the collar and the hem. It was by far my nicest. I was glad to see it when I unbuckled the case, but my stomach flip-flopped at the discovery that Momma had packed practically everything I owned. *I'll be gone as long as it takes,* she had said. Surely she'd be back to fetch me before school in the fall.

I heard Aunt Etta and Frances moving around upstairs, speaking quietly. I couldn't make out what they were saying, so I walked over near the stairway to listen.

"I'll just have to make do," Aunt Etta said. "What choice do I have? I just wish I knew when Grace was coming back for her."

"It'll be fine, though. Maddie May's always been such a good girl. She won't give you a moment's trouble."

I stepped back into the workroom and changed my dress. I didn't want to make things difficult for Aunt Etta, but I didn't have a choice either. There was nowhere else to go.

"Maddie?" Aunt Etta called a few minutes later.

"Coming!" I grabbed my satchel and took a deep breath.

The coffee must have worked. I was wide awake.

# Four

Like all the wealthy tobacco families, the Winstons lived a good few miles away on the north side of Bright Leaf. Since gas was rationed and Aunt Etta only used her car on special occasions, we would cover the distance by bus, the same one we took to town when it was too hot to walk. And boy, was it hot. Not even nine o'clock and already the air was thick and heavy with gnats as we walked to the bus stop. August here was scorching, but I didn't expect it to be this sweltering in June. In the Holler this time of year, the morning grass was cool against my feet, the evening air chilly enough for a sweater.

"The heat's gonna be bad today, but at least we're not working the fields," Aunt Etta said, motioning to the near distance where the tops of the tobacco plants swayed in the warm breeze.

The morning was quiet and the road was empty. Lucky for us the bus soon rumbled to the stop, kicking up dust. The door swung open with a squawk.

"Morning, Etta. Morning—" The driver paused for a minute, studying me. "Maddie, isn't it?"

"Yes, sir," I said. "Morning."

"Morning, Ed," Aunt Etta said, settling herself into a seat and motioning for me to sit next to her. The seat was cracked in places and pinched the backs of my legs.

"How about this heat?" the driver said. "'Bacca sure loves that sun. More sunshine, bigger leaves, and you know what that means." He chuckled. "I'm hoping it'll be a strong season for all of us. I for one would be relieved if we had a bumper crop."

Aunt Etta nodded and then said, "How is Gladys getting on, Ed? I've been meaning to ask."

His face went from sunny to serious. "Well, she's hanging in there as best she can." He glanced from the road to the rearview mirror as he spoke. I could feel the sadness in him as he talked about his wife.

Aunt Etta shifted in her seat, then took two embroidered handkerchiefs from her purse; she handed one to me and dabbed her neck with the other. I patted the back of my neck with the folded cloth, feeling the sweat roll down my back.

"Is she home now?" she asked.

"Yes," he replied. "She came home last week." Sadness changed to worry as he talked about having to take time off work for her treatments, and now a trip to New York. Then his voice got real quiet. "It was way worse than they thought. She's got the cancer in her throat, and they have to remove her voice box."

"Oh no," my aunt said, leaning forward in her seat. "I'm so sorry, Ed. That's just awful. Please tell her I'm wishing her a speedy recovery, will you? The girls at the factory must miss her terribly."

"Oh, they do. They've been wonderful, bringing by casseroles and sitting with her in the evenings, reading to her to help pass the time."

"That's good to hear. They're all such nice girls." Aunt Etta folded and unfolded her hands. "My friend Frances has an extensive library. If you'd like to borrow some books for your wife, I'd be happy to ask her."

He smiled and said thank you, but Mrs. Winston had already brought over more books than they could read in a month of Sundays.

"She and Mr. Winston both have been so good to us. They said there'd be a place for her on the production line until the men came back, but I don't know that I want her doing that anymore. Never liked it much in the first place, to be honest with you. I do just fine as the breadwinner, but no, she wanted to help the war effort. I told her that factory wasn't no place for a woman."

The bus slowed and a woman sitting several rows behind came up to the front. She wore a khaki factory uniform, and her graying hair was pulled back and secured with a net.

She leaned against a pole to steady herself as she lit a cigarette. "Ed, if I were you, I'd ask the Winstons to get Gladys an office job when she's ready," the woman said solemnly, returning her matches to her pocketbook and taking a long draw. "Factory work is hard on the body—especially if you're feeling weak."

The driver tipped his hat at her and pulled the lever to open the door.

The bus got quiet after that. Aunt Etta and I were the only passengers left, and nobody said a word as we trundled on toward town. I pulled down the window to try to get a breeze going and instead got a face full of oven-hot air. Rows and rows of shoulder-high, green tobacco plants blurred together like one of those cartoon flip books. As soon as I tried to look at a row, it turned into the next, the next, the next.

The fields were dotted with men and women dressed in Bright Leaf Tobacco coveralls. Some were white, but most of the laborers were Black. There were also dozens of smaller bodies in the distance—children toiling alongside the adults. Many were barefoot and dressed only in short pants, the sun baking the tops of their shoulders while they wielded hoes twice their size. Some were just little bitty things, probably years younger than me.

My only farming experience was helping Frances weed her strawberry beds last summer; she had given me a shiny penny for every clump of quack grass or chickweed I pulled. At the end of that day, when I complained about my sore arms and back, she said, "You don't know sore 'til you've topped and hoed tobacco from dawn to dusk. You best keep up your sewing, Maddie May, and your studies in school."

"Are they picking already?" I asked Aunt Etta, pointing out the window.

The workers were moving between rows, pulling the tops off plants with a sure flick of their wrists, then throwing the petals on the ground. I could just make out the lonely trail of red flowers they left behind them.

"No, they're topping and suckering for the next week or so. Then they'll start picking. You remember what topping is, don't you?"

"Isn't that when they break off the flowers at the top of the plants?"

"That's right," said Aunt Etta. "Getting rid of the flowers sends more energy to the leaves, makes them bigger." I knew topping made sense for the farmers, but I thought it was sad to cut off the prettiest part of the plant like that.

I closed my eyes and took a deep breath. No other tobacco compared to Bright Leaf, the way it smelled of ripe peaches and fresh cut grass.

"Put that window back up, Maddie. This heat's about to kill me."

I did as she said, and she closed her eyes against the heat. Looking at her smooth and unlined skin, you'd never guess she was in her fifties. Once, when Daddy bragged about her looking so young, Momma said it was because she was chubby. The extra flesh on Aunt Etta's face stretched out all the wrinkles, said Momma, like a balloon full of air.

It was just like Momma to say something like that. She was jealous of Daddy's relationship with Aunt Etta and it showed. I'd never once thought of her as fat. She was a big woman, sure—with broad shoulders and strong capable hands. But she was easy in her body, knew how to dress it with style, and always looked put-together. As far back as I could remember, she'd worn a different version of the same outfit every day, a bias-cut shirtwaist dress that was sharp and crisp even in the most wilting heat. Because she favored neutral shades like gray, cream, or navy, she dolled them up with a colorful pincushion she wore on her wrist like a corsage. She'd collected and constructed hundreds of them over the years, and never left the house without first sliding one of the pretty, pumpkin-shaped pieces over her right hand. Frances would pretend to tease her about them. "Well get a load of you. Guess somebody's going to the prom after all."

I felt the dirt road level out beneath us. Steam rose up off the smooth black tar, now that we were passing through town. Maples and sycamores lined the road like soldiers. The houses stood a ways apart, their yards showing off pink azaleas and rhododendrons in full bloom.

We passed an imposing, cream-colored mansion with a fancy, wrought iron porch swing. It looked like a fairy tale—pretty as a picture and just as perfect, the swing moving back and forth, just barely, in the breeze. What if I lived in that house and could swing on that porch anytime I wanted?

*Quit it, Maddie. Stop your daydreaming. Fairy tales don't come true and you don't belong here. These people will know it soon as you walk in the door, so you better get rid of any highfalutin notions you have. You're here to help Aunt Etta and learn how to become a dressmaker. Don't you forget it.*

I didn't like to talk so harsh to myself, but it had to

be done. Everything was swirling around me and I had to keep my head level. But gosh, it was all happening so fast. Just last night I had been sleeping in my own bed and now this rickety bus was taking me to a grand old home with maids and everything. Aunt Etta said the Winstons' house had more rooms than you could count, and we'd be working in the upstairs parlor, one of her favorite rooms on account of the gorgeous, embroidered drapery panels. They were floral bark cloth, which I had only heard about. She didn't have to tell me that I wasn't to touch them, but she did.

Rich or wealthy made no difference. It always meant *don't touch*.

"Come on, honey. This is our stop." Aunt Etta elbowed me. She grabbed a shiny metal pole and pulled herself to standing, the seat creaking as her weight shifted. I carried her sewing box as we made our way off the bus.

The air was cooler outside and helped me feel less nervous.

As if reading my mind, Aunt Etta said, "Wait until you feel how nice and chilled it is inside the house. They've got the only air conditioner in Bright Leaf." She went on to explain how the light-colored sidewalks and trees also helped account for the difference. They didn't pull as much heat and kept the air circulating.

We walked past a large brick house and two drive-ways that curved so you couldn't see where they led.

"Here we are," Aunt Etta said, stopping at a road to our right.

It took my breath, the sight of it. The house, of course, but the trees too. Beautiful and noble, there must have been twenty huge elms flanking the drive-way leading to the house far in the distance. Taller by far than any I'd ever seen, their smooth trunks, closer to gray than brown, were so thick that a grown man couldn't get his arms around them.

The bleach-white house stood at the end of the end-less driveway, tall columns reaching from the front porch to the roof four stories up. As we made our way up the drive, the road beneath our feet turned from pavement to small, smooth bits of gravel that glinted in the sun like jewels. I bent down to pick up a sparkly gold piece and placed it in my satchel.

At the end of the trees was a tiny box of a building, no bigger than a coat closet. A man appeared and waved to us. He wore a black jacket and slacks, his white shirt crisp and bright. He removed his hat as he greeted us.

"'Morning, ladies."

"'Morning, Isaac. This is my niece, Maddie."

He nodded and smiled at me.

"This your nephew's daughter?"

"Yes she is," said Aunt Etta.

"What a fine young lady, and so grown. You what, about seventeen years old?"

"No, sir," I replied. "I'm fifteen."

"Well, your aunt sure loved your daddy," he said. "Thought he hung the moon."

"Oh, yes, Jack was something special all right," Aunt Etta said.

They both went quiet. People always stopped talking when Daddy's name came up.

"Well, nice to meet you, young lady," Isaac said, returning his hat to his head. I liked his voice. You could hear the smile behind it. For a split second, I wished I could just wait out here with him while Aunt Etta did the fitting. This way I wouldn't risk embarrassing myself, or worse, Aunt Etta.

"Maddie's going to be working with me for a while."

"Oh, Mrs. Winston will love that," said Isaac. "That'll really lift her spirits."

What a surprising thing to say. As if a wealthy woman like Mrs. Winston would need her spirits lifted.

"We best go on now," Aunt Etta said, leading the way toward the house. "Wouldn't want to be late."

"Heavens no!" Isaac shouted after us.

A stone path led up to the house, bright green grass cut as short as an officers' high-and-tight on either side.

Potted red azaleas framed the black front door. Aunt Etta tapped a large brass *W* against a metal plate.

I'd barely had time to smooth my dress when a young woman opened the door and waved her hand for us to come on in. When we crossed the threshold, the air felt nice and cool.

"Thank you, Ruth," Aunt Etta said to the young woman. She had vivid green eyes, light brown skin, and an abundance of wavy black hair tied at the nape of her neck. Her crisp blue uniform was covered with a minute maid apron, with pleats running across the hips and front. I felt like a child next to her, but she couldn't have been much older than me. Eighteen, maybe nineteen at most.

"This is my niece, Maddie," Aunt Etta said. "Maddie," she turned to me. "This is Miss Ruth. She pretty much runs the place," she whispered.

Miss Ruth giggled. "Nice to meet you, Maddie," she said. "Y'all can go on up to the parlor."

I followed Aunt Etta through the marble foyer that led to the staircase—two staircases, really, one on either side that climbed up to meet in the middle at a balcony. As we walked upstairs, I ran my hand along the glossy banister.

"Don't touch that," she warned.

At the end of a quiet hall was a set of heavy double

doors that opened into a light-filled space. In the center of the room sat a three-way mirror and a raised, round platform. It was carpeted, like the ones in the department stores. Chairs and chaise lounges covered in delicate florals were arranged in small groups around the room, and a pink gingham bench sat in front of a vanity. One wall was painted green, and the others were covered with wallpaper, cheerful stripes of white, pink, and yellow, the same yellow as the roses that sat on the coffee table. There was a silver teapot and floral teacups, a small silver bowl with sugar cubes, a tiny spoon resting next to it.

On the green wall hung a life-size painting of a woman in a wedding dress, the white skirt of her gown filling the whole bottom of the gold frame. I guessed it was Mrs. Winston. Her waist was impossibly small, and she rested one side of her lovely face in a petite, gloved hand. She smiled without showing her teeth. Aunt Etta pulled me by the sleeve. "Stop gawking. Here she comes."

Heels click-clacked down the hallway, accompanied by a faint jingling that grew louder until it stopped just outside the parlor. The knobs turned, the doors opened, and the air around us changed, as if a sweet and smoky breeze had entered the room.

"Etta! Thank goodness you're here," Mrs. Winston

said, beaming. Her eyes widened when she noticed me standing there. "Surely this isn't?" she said, blowing cigarette smoke into the air. "Surely this grown-up young lady can't be your niece!"

"Yes, she is," Aunt Etta said. "The very one. This is Maddie. My great-niece, really. My nephew Jack's daughter. She's staying with me . . . for a while, assisting with fittings. I hope you don't mind."

"Mind?" she repeated. "Of course I don't mind. In fact, I'm tickled pink." She walked over to me and took my hands in hers. "Oh, and I am so very sorry about your father, Maddie," she said, lowering her voice. "What a brave man, and what a terrible loss for you. It's wonderful you're here with Etta now, though. I'm so glad to have a chance to get to know you."

She pulled back to get a better look at me, her tiny fingers tucked into mine. "Who could forget that hair? Just beautiful! Half the ladies in town would kill for those auburn curls. The color is to die for," she said, releasing my hands and giving my shoulders a gentle squeeze.

I'd been self-conscious about my hair my whole life. In grade school the boys had chased me around chanting "carrot top," and one of the older girls at school had nicknamed me Raggedy Ann. Daddy told me not to pay any mind, that they were just jealous. "Red hair on your head means fire in your heart," he said. I liked that, but I still wanted to have a silky pageboy like Virginia and Betty. Momma did her best to straighten my unruly mop, but it always curled right back up. Then Daddy died and suddenly my red hair didn't seem like a curse. It made me feel close to him, like a piece of him was with me always. But Momma was jealous of what I had with Daddy, even in death, and for the months since, she'd made me feel there was something wrong with me. It wasn't right, a mother making her daughter feel bad about her looks. April's mother was always fussing with her in the nicest way. She'd smooth her cowlick and make sure she brushed her hair one hundred times before bed. Not mine. "Cover your hair" was the advice I got. But with Momma gone, I didn't have to wear a kerchief. Mrs. Winston was right. My hair was beautiful and I'd be proud of it, I decided.

"You must tell me every little thing about yourself, Maddie," Mrs. Winston cooed. "I want to hear all of it! Have you already completed your schooling for the spring?"

"Well, Mrs. Winston," I began.

"Please, dear. Call me Miss Mitzy. Everybody does."

"Yes, ma'am. I mean, Miss Mitzy. Well, I just finished year ten."

"She's a good student," Aunt Etta said, removing a

tin of pins from her sewing box and handing them to me. "Real talented in art, sewing, and writing, anything creative."

I thought about Mrs. Sellars, my art teacher. She had pulled me aside during the last week of term for a serious talk. "You have real potential, Maddie," she said. "It would be a shame to waste it." She handed me a brochure for the North Carolina College of the Arts. They had a fashion apprenticeship, one of the best in the country. "Promise me you'll at least talk to your mother about it."

I said I would, but of course I was lying.

Momma didn't approve of college for girls—a waste of time, she called it—and even if she did approve, we didn't have the money.

The last time I saw Daddy, the night before he left for Germany, the two of us ended up having a talk about college and other important things too, a real serious heart-to-heart. We'd gone for an evening stroll after supper, the October mountain air cool and crisp as we made our way down the dirt road from our house.

Momma had acted a mess during dinner that night. She had sobbed through the first part of our meal, then fussed at Daddy for abandoning us by the time she served the meat. Daddy had been clever about it, though: he'd distracted her by turning the conversation to the new GI Bill that had just passed in Congress and how it guaranteed all sorts of wonderful benefits to veterans, including a free college education.

"You just wait, Grace," he had said, grabbing Momma's hand. "When I get back from the front, I'm going straight to Duke or Carolina for engineering, and then I'll give you the rich girl's life, I swear."

"Is that right?" Momma had replied, suddenly perking up. "A college education . . . for free? Are you sure?"

"I'm positive," Daddy had said, grinning at me. "After Maddie's last report card, I have a feeling I won't be the only one in this family going to college. What do you think, Shug, should we go together? Will you tutor your old man if he needs help?"

Momma had bristled at that. "Don't be ridiculous, Jack. She isn't going to college, unless it's to skip class and find herself a fancy husband." She was just getting started. "You go get your BA Jack, and Maddie here can go out for her MRS."

"Momma!" I'd cried.

"I'll tell you another thing, Madeline—the pedigreed boys, the ones most worth having, do *not* go in for girls who act smarter than them. So you'd best keep that report card to yourself if you ever meet one."

Daddy didn't disagree with Momma in the moment,

but he had plenty to say when we went on our private walk. He'd told me that things were changing for women. They could get jobs now, take care of themselves if they wanted to. They didn't have to rely on men, especially men who didn't treat them with respect.

"Look at Aunt Etta," he'd said, elbowing me lightly so I'd look at him. "She's smart, like you. She supports herself."

I said I guessed so, but Momma was always preaching the opposite—that women were supposed to act like they couldn't do anything without a man.

"Your mother didn't have the opportunities you have, Maddie," Daddy had said. "Best bear that in mind."

"Maddie," Aunt Etta said, bringing me back to the moment. "Mrs. Winston asked you a question."

"I'm sorry," I replied. I had a bad habit of getting lost in my thoughts. "I'm going to be a professional dressmaker," I said boldly. Remembering Daddy's encouraging words had given me a boost of confidence. "Like my aunt. Maybe I'll even go to college one day. The North Carolina College of the Arts has a fashion apprenticeship."

"Well, aren't you a pip!" Mitzy said. "You know, I do believe talent like that runs in the family. Your aunt's mother used to sew for my mother. Did you know that?"

"Yes, ma'am. She was just telling me about Great-grandma Lottie this morning."

"Oh, what Charlotte could do with a needle and thread." Mitzy sighed. "I remember a darling dress she made for me. It was the softest velvet—pale blue it was, with a Peter Pan collar. I couldn't have been more than eight or nine, but I felt so grown-up."

The dress sounded lovely. I hadn't much practice with velvet. It was slippery and thick, which made it hard to handle.

"Maybe you can make something for me one of these days," Mitzy said, smiling at me.

"I'd like that," I replied. "I constructed two gowns by myself last summer. I adore sewing formal wear." Aunt Etta frowned and shook her head slightly. I guess I wasn't supposed to say that. I'd never talked to her about the fashion apprenticeship either and here I was going on and on like Mitzy was an old friend. *Just listen, Maddie. Don't talk too much.*

"Did you?" Mitzy pivoted to catch my eye. "I'm so impressed." She studied me for a moment, a faraway look in her eye. "You know, Maddie, you actually remind me of myself at your age. I dreamed of going to college too."

I wanted to know more but knew better than to ask.

She sighed and shook off the thought, returning to gaze at herself in the mirror. "I only have an hour before my Garden Club meeting, Etta. We're making arrangements for a luncheon at church. Won't that be fun? I do hope we'll have enough time to finish this."

"We'll make it enough time," Aunt Etta said. Then she pointed for me to stand next to her at the bottom of the platform and gestured for a few pins.

Mitzy removed her blouse and skirt, then stood there in just her slip and high heels, the sunlight glinting off her charm bracelet.

"You won't need a slip with this," Aunt Etta said. "I lined it. Thought it would be cooler for the Summer Solstice."

"Oh, that's clever," said Mitzy. She loosened the straps, letting her slip fall to the floor.

I tried not to notice, but she was standing right there in her bra and girdle, her skin pale and almost flawless. Mitzy must have seen me looking at the pink marks and stretched out skin that peeked out from the waistband of her girdle, because she covered it quickly with her hand. Then she asked me to be a lamb and hand her a cigarette and her pink lighter, there on the table. "And could you close the doors too?" she added. "I wouldn't want David to walk by and catch sight of me indecent."

Her cigarette smelled like peppermint, and she left behind a ring of red lipstick on the light green filter when she lit it. It made me think of that rhyme from when I was a child. *Ring around the rosies, a pocket full of posies, ashes, ashes, we all fall down.*

She took a draw on her cigarette and picked a tiny bit of errant tobacco off the tip of her tongue. Then she placed it in a crystal ashtray and lifted her arms over her head as Aunt Etta helped her into a chiffon party dress.

"Please turn for me, would you?"

Mitzy spun around to face us. The dress suited her to a tee. The pleating gathered at her waist perfectly, and the keyhole neckline exposed just enough of her décolletage without being risqué. Then there was the fabric itself, a fresh and elegant peach blossom that showed off Mitzy's delicate complexion. She was every bit as glamorous as one of the models in Aunt Etta's *Vogue* magazines. She positively glowed.

Aunt Etta pulled at the seams underneath Mitzy's arms. "You've lost more weight," she said, gesturing for me to hand her the pins. She held one in her teeth and fastened the seam with the other.

"Maddie," Mitzy said. "You'll have to meet David." She twisted on the platform to catch my eye, and Aunt Etta almost stuck her.

"Hold still, please," Aunt Etta told her.

"Is David your son?" I asked. Aunt Etta gave me a sharp look.

"No, dear. I don't have any children of my own—I mean, not yet anyway. But David might as well be mine."

She explained that David's mother, Annie Taylor, lived next door to Mitzy when she was a little girl. Annie adored children and loved spending time with Mitzy and her sister, Ashley. She seemed so much older then, but over the years Mitzy and Annie became the best of friends, and when David was born, Mitzy became his godmother. Annie tragically died of pneumonia when David was a toddler, and Mitzy promised herself she'd always look out for David like Annie had looked out for her.

"You remember David's mother, my friend Annie?" she asked Aunt Etta.

"Of course," Aunt Etta said. "Lovely young lady, God rest her soul."

"After Annie died, David began spending every summer here," Mitzy added. "His father is a very important man, a former colonel in the army. He travels extensively—and is overseas now actually, assisting with troop withdrawals. Always threw himself into his work, even more so after Annie passed. I used to worry about David, going off to boarding school so young, but he's grown into a fine young man. He's starting college in the fall. Studying business at the University of North Carolina at Chapel Hill."

"A fine young man," Aunt Etta repeated. She studied her client in the mirror, then motioned for another pin. "I just need to bring these seams in a quarter of an inch," she said. "The length is perfect, don't you think?"

Mitzy turned this way and that, the gown's skirt floating around her legs as she examined herself from every angle.

"What do you think, Maddie? Will this do for the Summer Solstice?"

"Excuse me, ma'am?"

"The Summer Solstice Celebration. The big party on Sunday evening, in the town square. Oh, it's such fun, isn't it, Etta?"

"Oh yes, it's quite an event."

"There will be speeches and exhibitions. I don't know how interested you'd be in that. But there are also games like ring toss and spin can alley. Mint iced tea and cotton candy too, of course. Oh, and there's a Ferris wheel where you can look over all of Bright Leaf!" Mitzy flushed with excitement as she went on. "You know, Maddie, the whole town comes to the

Summer Solstice. So that includes you. You must come! David will be there, and you can meet him. He's been working day and night on a big paper that all the incoming students have to complete over the summer, but I insisted he take a break for the party. Oh, and Rose will be there too, of course—she's such a hoot. Rose is married to Dr. Hale, but she's not very much older than you, really. You two will have plenty to talk about."

I felt my face redden. A party. This lovely lady had invited me to a party. Such kindness. And she didn't even know me.

"You know, your aunt is like family," she said, smiling toward Aunt Etta, "so that means you're family too. Really, you must come!"

Aunt Etta smiled back and nodded. "I don't see why not," she said. "Frances and I always go. Of course, Maddie should come."

"That sounds marvelous, thank you," I said politely, although the thought of mingling with friends of the Winstons sounded terrifying. The clock on the wall went off, tiny doors opening and little birds sticking their heads out cuckooing, startling me.

"Have you never seen a cuckoo clock, dear? Feel free to take a closer look. It's one of my favorite pieces in the house, a wedding gift from my mother I'll pass along to my daughter . . . when she gets married." There was a beat of awkward silence as Mitzy gazed at the clock and rested her cigarette hand on her stomach. Most women her age had three or four children by now, and she seemed to want them. Maybe everything wasn't so perfect as it seemed . . .

"No I haven't," I blurted, shaking off the notion. "Aunt Etta has one that's a cat and its tail swoops back and forth, but I've never seen one with a bird."

Mitzy seemed to have recovered from the awkwardness and laughed gently. "Goodness, we best make sure to keep these cats and birds away from each other."

I grinned. I liked this Mitzy. I'd never met anyone quite like her.

"Now, back to business. Are we done here, Etta?" she asked, examining her reflection in the mirror. "I really should be on my way. The girls will be waiting, and the gardenias won't arrange themselves, now will they?"

"Yes, all done."

"Thank you for this beautiful dress—both of you. I'll be proud to wear it," said Mitzy as she removed the garment, careful not to disturb the pins. Then she pulled her slip back over her head. "Say, are you going into town today, by any chance, before you go home?" she asked.

"We're stopping by the factory," said Aunt Etta, handing Mitzy her blouse. "I have patches to pick up and uniforms to repair."

"Would you mind terribly if I asked you to drop off a few books of raffle tickets for me?" Mitzy asked. "You can give them to any worker you see there. Mr. Winston and I are obliged to buy dozens of them to support the town, but it's more appropriate for the workers to win the prizes."

"Of course, we'd be happy to," Aunt Etta agreed. "That's very generous."

"Well, it's the least we can do," Mitzy said. "Our employees work hard to keep the factory going, everyone chipping in and doing their best. Especially in these last years. The way the women rallied round. It was a sight to see. I guess they'll be happy to go home to their families once all the men come home. It will be a relief to them, no doubt."

"Yes, ma'am," Aunt Etta said. "A relief. I'm sure."

# Five

I took in my surroundings as our bus approached town. Funny how just a few months could make such a difference to a place. When I visited in August the crop had already been cut, dried, graded, prized, and auctioned off. But June was the height of the cutting and curing season, and the town square buzzed with activity. I wanted to ask Aunt Etta all sorts of questions about Mitzy, but it was such a short trip to Bright Leaf Tobacco Headquarters that I didn't get a chance.

The driver dropped us off in front of the main building.

"We won't stay long," Aunt Etta said, removing a handkerchief from her handbag and dabbing her neck. "This heat is exhausting me. We'll just make a quick stop in Factory One where there might even be a surprise for you."

"A surprise? In the factory?" I raised my eyebrows.

"You'll see." Aunt Etta winked.

It was much hotter here than in the Holler and the coffee had worn off, so I was done in, that's for sure. It felt like days had passed since Momma dropped me off that morning.

"You remember Frances works there?" Aunt Etta said, pointing to the tallest building. "That's her office, on the far right." I craned my neck to get a look at the tippy-top floor.

She reminded me what the other buildings were: the warehouse, the drying barns, and two tall brick factory buildings, one for the finest cigarettes and one for the lesser varieties. Twin chimneys towered above the factories like powerful sentries, dense black smoke spewing from their mouths. Train tracks ran right up to the warehouse, where men with shirtsleeves rolled up hauled barrels from the train cars, their muscles bulging.

I knew parts of the town square well and had even dropped off uniforms at the entrance to Factory One for the last few summers. I always stopped at the General Store for penny candy before hopping on the bus back to Aunt Etta's. But I'd never been inside the cigarette factory.

"We'll deliver the raffle tickets for Mitzy to Factory

One," she said. "While we're there we can pick up the uniforms that need updating. You can help me sew on patches for the new mint cigarettes."

"I heard a radio advertisement about those," I said. "In the car on the way here."

"Likely you did," Aunt Etta said. "MOMints, they're called, and there's a lot more advertisements in store. I made dresses, all different shades of green, for Mitzy and some of the other wives who will appear in a magazine advertisement."

My eyes went wide. "*Vogue?*" I asked.

"More like *Life* magazine."

"Wow," I said. "That's exciting." Mitzy's cigarette I'd seen earlier had a green filter. That was smart. Green dresses and a green filter for the mint. I couldn't wait to try one.

"It's a big deal all right," she said. "It's the first special cigarette for women. And the first time women are running the factory lines. They're real proud and want their patches."

All employees at the Bright Leaf factories were required to dress in nearly identical uniforms, with special patches sewn onto the breast pocket like a badge. The patch announced the type of work performed and was a point of pride for many of the employees, especially the ones who had hard-scrabbled their way up out of the fields to the better jobs on the manufacturing line.

A group of men stood outside the factory entrance, smoking.

"Who's this pretty young thing?" the smallest of them called. "Are you spoken for, doll?" The other men snickered.

"Get back to work, Lloyd," said a tall fellow with leathery skin. "She's too young, even for you." He punched baby-faced Lloyd lightly on the arm as the rest of them laughed.

Aunt Etta peered into the door's small window and knocked. We were buzzed through, and once inside, a woman sitting at a high wooden desk asked Aunt Etta to present identification and sign a ledger book.

"She with you?" she said, referring to me.

"Yes, ma'am. She's my assistant."

*Assistant.* I liked the sound of that.

The lady came out from behind the desk to stand beside us, a cigarette in one hand and a weighty ring of keys in the other. She was a slim, dark-skinned woman, with a shock of gray hair and glasses hanging from a chain around her neck, and an air of authority that suited her. She led us down a long hallway and, reaching a locked metal door, made a performance of searching for just the right key. "There you are," she said, holding open the door for us without crossing the threshold herself.

No sooner had Aunt Etta and I stepped onto the factory floor when my eyes began to water. The air reeked of mint. My throat burned like nobody's business, and the inside of my nose felt like it had been painted by a lit match.

"What is that?" I shouted over the whirring of the machines. "What's that smell?"

I had asked Aunt Etta, but it was a man working next to us who yelled back.

"Darlin', that's the smell of money," he hollered over the racket. His smile revealed a mouth full of yellowing teeth.

"Corn mint oil," Aunt Etta said, wiping her eyes. "You get used to it."

We walked between rows of clanking machines and conveyor belts, each one manned by a worker, some standing and some sitting on high stools. They wore matching khaki jackets with green cuffs and collars— the women in skirts, the men in slacks. The wooden floor was worn in spots, where workers had scuffed their feet or scooted up their stools.

I don't know what I'd expected, but it wasn't this. Factory work's hard, everybody knows that, but it was painful just walking through here. How the workers could spend all day and every day here was beyond me.

Get used to it? No thank you.

Women's fingers flew across the conveyor belts, pulling out cigarettes here and there and throwing them into baskets on the floor.

"They're inspectors," Aunt Etta shouted over the noise. "Looking for stems or loose filters."

One of the women smiled at me, her fingernails worn to the quick, a few of them taped up with blood seeping through. "Doris here is one of the fastest, isn't that right, Doris? Nine hundred thousand a day?" Aunt Etta said.

"What?" Doris yelled, her fingers flying.

Aunt Etta shook her head, waved her off like *never mind*.

"She can't hear a lick," she told me. "Ten-hour days in here'll do that to you."

Farther down the line, workers in white gloves scooped up cigarettes, lining them side by side in metal trays. They scooped and stacked, scooped and stacked, the motion almost graceful. When they saw Aunt Etta, they smiled, a few of them pointed to their jackets and gave her a thumbs-up. I puffed up a little, knowing that last summer I had cut and sewed some of their uniforms myself.

The break room was at the end of the long line of machines, a small wood-paneled area with a flimsy door. Inside were fold-out chairs, a cigarette machine, a sink, and a water fountain. A bin of cigarettes—light green, all of them broken or misshaped—sat on a long table next to books of matches. Maybe I could sneak one when Aunt Etta wasn't looking. I'd been smoking since I was twelve, all my friends too. The adults likely knew, but there was an unwritten rule that girls didn't do it in public until we completed schooling or got married, whichever came first.

A large advertisement for MOMints was tacked up on a cork bulletin board in the break room. In it, a man in a white doctor's coat wearing a stethoscope around his neck proudly held up a pack of the new cigarettes while a gorgeous blonde next to him held one between her ruby red lips. JUST WHAT THE DOCTOR ORDERED, the caption read.

Three young white women had arranged themselves in a small circle of chairs, nestled against a wall. They waved to Aunt Etta but kept talking in low voices. One of them looked familiar.

"If they're gonna have fans anywhere, it should be in the stemming room," said the familiar-looking ashy blonde.

"You're nuts, Maryanne," snorted the redheaded

girl in the middle. "Stemming is the absolute last place they'd set up a fan. There isn't a single man working in stemming anymore."

"So what?" said Maryanne. Then it came to me; I'd helped Aunt Etta with her uniform fitting last year. "Why should it matter who's in there? Shouldn't they just put the fans where we need them most? And I still don't see why they won't give us work gloves. All the men in packing have them."

The third woman, a stunning Elizabeth Taylor look-alike, held up her hands to her friends, as if to say *calm down, enough's enough.* Angry red welts covered her long, tapered fingers and crisscrossed along the inside of her delicate wrists.

"Oh, stop your bellyaching," said the wounded movie star. "They're paying you well enough, aren't they?"

"If you count mine plus Clyde's, sure, but he makes twice as much as me for the same job."

"Twice as much?" I blurted out. "That's not fair." Aunt Etta's eyes flashed, and I mouthed *sorry.*

"See," said the redhead, nodding toward me.

"Well, we won't be making anything once the men get back," said the beautiful girl. She sighed.

Aunt Etta set the raffle tickets on the counter with a thunk as a familiar voice rang out from the factory floor.

"Save me a dance at the Solstice, honey," I heard someone say over the whir and clank of machines. "I sure can cut a rug."

My face lit up. "Anthony's here? That's the surprise?" Aunt Etta nodded.

Before anyone could answer, the one and only Anthony LaRue bounced into the break room with a uniform draped over one arm, and a sewing box in the other.

"Anthony!" I exclaimed, glancing from him to Aunt Etta and back.

"Wow, Maddie!" he cried.

His arms may have been full, but Anthony still managed to plant a quick peck on each of my cheeks, Europe-style.

"Well, aren't you a sight for sore eyes," he said, placing the uniform on a chair and his sewing box on the floor. "And I do mean sore eyes, honey," he said, leaning in so close I could smell the Wildroot Cream in his hair. He lowered his voice and elbowed me playfully. "Have you walked through Mentholatum-ville? Whew, honey! That'll clean your clock."

The women giggled. "Oh, Anthony," said the redhead.

Aunt Etta shook her head, but her eyes twinkled as she folded him into a hug.

He winked at me over her shoulder, deep dimples punctuating his slim face.

If my summers in Bright Leaf were a cake, Anthony would be the icing—icing with sprinkles and sparkly candles.

The summer after I turned twelve, Aunt Etta said she'd met a fellow at the fabric store, a boy a little older than me whose father had been an accomplished tailor before he joined the army. Anthony, his name was, and he would be helping her. He was talented, but not old enough to keep his father's business afloat, even what little business there was with so many men at war. "His family could use the money and I could use the assistance," was how she put it. I didn't much like the idea of some boy nosing in, but that changed the moment I met Anthony. That first day he bounded into Aunt Etta's kitchen like a golden retriever, planting kisses on each of my cheeks like we were old chums. We'd been thick as thieves ever since. He even called me long-distance after Daddy died. His family didn't have that kind of money, but he said "where there's a will there's a way, honey. And with a friend, there's always a way."

"Excuse me," said the Elizabeth Taylor look-alike, nodding for me to make way. "It's back to the salt mines for me."

"Sorry," I said, stepping out of the doorway.

After the woman had left, Aunt Etta said, "Anthony, have you rounded up everything we need?"

"You work here now?" I asked.

"Lord no. These girls have the factory running like clockwork," he said, winking at them. "I just keep their uniforms in tip-top shape."

The two remaining ladies shook their heads, laughing.

"Say, that reminds me, Maryanne," he said to one of them. "Tell your sister her new uniform is ready. I built in an elastic panel for the skirt so she can wear it right up until the baby arrives."

Maryanne averted her eyes. Her whole demeanor changed, her shoulders falling and rounding like a shell closing up. "She won't be needing that anymore," she said quietly. "Last week she lost—"

Aunt Etta pulled me by the arm to the bulletin board across the room. "Maddie, let's see if there's a flyer about the Summer Solstice," she practically shouted.

I stared at the announcements tacked up on the cork, pretending to read them while straining to hear Anthony and Maryanne. They whispered and I saw Anthony wrap his arms around her when I stole a glance. Her poor sister must have lost her baby. What a terrible feeling that must be, losing a pregnancy. Just the thought of it made me shudder.

"I'm ready now, ladies," Anthony said in our direction. He blew a kiss to Maryanne as she left the break room.

"Bye, Miss Etta," she said, her voice small.

"I've got the patches right here in my . . ." Anthony said, patting his vest. Instead of a jacket, he always wore a vest with a colorful pocket square. "Oh no," he exclaimed, "what did I do with the patches?" He rummaged around in his sewing box, then hit himself on the forehead with the heel of his hand. "My sister must have them. She was holding them for me on our bus ride in this morning, and I must have forgotten to take them from her. I hope you won't mind going next door to get them. She's working in Factory Two today." Anthony's sister Clarice was four years older than he was, and as reserved as he was gregarious. *I have to pry the gossip out of her*, he always complained. I'd met her only once, when she came to pick up Anthony. She said very little but had the same sparkly eyes and slightly mischievous look as her brother.

"I'm not on the list to get into Factory Two," Aunt Etta said as she gathered her sewing box and handbag. I hung back to let her and Anthony leave the break room first and quickly stuffed a few MOMints into my dress pocket.

"I'll make it quick," Anthony shouted as we followed

him across the noisy factory floor. "Just pop in and get them if you don't mind waiting."

We left the building through big double doors that closed with a heavy thwack. I took a deep breath, grateful to be away from the painful sting of mint. My arms were dusted with brown specks that didn't rub off easily.

Anthony led the way to Factory Two, which turned out to be a long walk. The red brick building towered over us as we crossed pathways linking the many factories and office buildings. Bright Leaf Tobacco Headquarters was far larger than I'd realized.

Factory Two was about the same size as the factory we had just left, and it was surrounded by a tall, forbidding fence covered with yellow and orange signs:

**AUTHORIZED PERSONNEL ONLY**
**NO TRESPASSING**
**RESTRICTED AREA**
**VIOLATORS WILL BE PROSECUTED**

I didn't know there were so many ways to say "Keep Out."

"You'd think they were keeping all kinds of state secrets locked up behind this gate," Anthony said as he approached the guards manning the entrance and showed his badge. "I'll be back in two shakes!" he shouted back as he crossed the threshold.

"What do they make in this building here, Aunt Etta?"

"Nothing you want to be smoking. The off-brand, no-name cigarettes come out of Factory Two. Recon ones."

"Recon?" I asked.

"Short for reconstituted," she explained, lowering her voice. "They sweep up the discards and dust, whatever falls to the floor in Factory One, and bring it here to make a slurry. It's boiled in vats as big as swimming holes, then cooled to make cigarettes they'll sell for cheap without a brand name."

"That sounds awful," I said.

"I certainly wouldn't smoke them," Aunt Etta said. "You shouldn't either. But don't go around talking about it, all right? Most folks don't know about recon. It's a nasty business and hard on the workers—but a real moneymaker as it turns out."

I shook my head in disgust. It really did seem terrible.

"Oh, Maddie, would you wait here?" Aunt Etta said. "There's someone over there I want to say hello to." On a nearby bench sat a petite blonde holding her jacket in one hand and a button in the other.

"Sure," I said.

At least a dozen men carrying large brown paper bags entered the gate while I waited. When Anthony reemerged with a khaki bundle under his arm, the two fellas who'd teased me earlier—Lloyd and his tall friend—were right behind him. They were rough-looking, the pair of them, the type Momma would have called a *couple of characters.*

"Here you go," Anthony said, handing the patches over.

"Thank you," I said.

"Happy to help," Anthony replied.

"Now, hold up just a second," said Lloyd, his voice all syrupy and suggestive. "I'm *very* happy to help too. In fact, I'm sure I can help you *real* good, doll. I'm partial to fiery redheads." He leaned in close, his eyes traveling down my body.

My stomach churned.

"Lord knows this one can't give you what you need," he added, gesturing to Anthony with his thumb. His leathery-faced friend cackled right along with him until a third man shouted for them to knock it off and get back to Factory One.

Anthony continued as if he hadn't heard, but I knew he had. "Maddie," he said. "It's so good to see you, but I better skedaddle. The ladies will have a hissy fit if I don't get to their alterations today."

"Of course." I smiled. "You should get back to work. I'll see you later though . . . I hope."

"I'll try, honey," he said, clasping my hands. "But I hardly have a minute to myself lately. I'm taking on every bit of work I can to help Momma with the bills while Daddy's overseas."

"Oh," I said, my face falling. "That's too bad."

"Cheer up, buttercup," he said, lifting my chin. "If you're going to the Summer Solstice I may see you there. If I get caught up, I may just take the night off." He kissed me on each cheek once more and quickstepped it back toward Factory One.

I walked over to Aunt Etta, who was still talking to the blonde woman.

"Go on up ahead, Maddie," she called. "I'll meet you at the bus stop."

**It had** been a very long day and I was dizzy with exhaustion by the time we arrived home. *Running on fumes*, Daddy would have said. My summers with Aunt Etta were busy, but we mostly stayed to ourselves, working on gowns and uniforms during the day and playing Crazy Eights with Frances in the evenings. Aunt Etta assured me that we'd spend the next four days like usual, then after the Summer Solstice, appointments with the wives would resume. Aunt Etta would be working non-stop over the next month to get their gowns ready for the Summer Gala, the biggest social event in Bright Leaf. Every July, Bright Leaf Tobacco hosted this black-tie affair and fundraiser, *a veritable fashion show of tobacco wives*, Aunt Etta called it. The grand evening of dinner and dancing benefited a different cause every year. This year it would be the servicemen's wives and children.

As we approached Aunt Etta's house, we spotted Frances coming from hers. She walked toward us carrying a covered dish. "Perfect timing," she said, raising it in the air with a smile. "I made beans and cornbread."

"Wonderful," Aunt Etta said. "I'm famished. Thank you, Frances."

"Thanks," I said, but the idea of beans made me want to gag. Thanks to the war rations, I'd eaten enough for a lifetime.

I held the door for Frances and Aunt Etta, and we stepped inside. Aunt Etta placed her sewing box next to the Kelvinator and opened the freezer door to cool herself. "Oh, this heat's about to kill me," she said, fanning her face with her hand.

"I hope you ladies are hungry," Francis said. "Maddie May, why don't you get washed up and I'll fix you a plate."

Aunt Etta's washroom always had the nicest soap—lavender, lemongrass, rose petal. As I scrubbed my hands with the soft, waxy bar, I noticed ugly black flecks taking over the pretty violet suds. Streaks of dark gray foam covered my hands like gloves. I washed off as best I could and headed back to the kitchen. Steam rose from Frances's dish as she ladled a generous helping of pintos into a deep bowl. I didn't want to hurt her feelings, but I'd lost my appetite.

"Would it be okay if I went on to bed now?" I asked. "I didn't sleep much last night and it's been such a long day."

Frances's face fell for a moment. "You're not going to eat?" she said.

"She can take her supper downstairs," said Aunt Etta.

"You do look like you need a good night's rest, Maddie May," Frances said sympathetically.

"I do," I replied. "Thank you both."

Frances covered my bowl with a cloth napkin and gave my arm a gentle squeeze.

I walked down to the basement, put my food on the work counter, and sat in the leather club chair by the door that led out back. It was my favorite piece of furniture in Aunt Etta's house, sturdy but comfortable. I slipped off my shoes to discover my socks had a ring of brown around the top. My calves, my ankles, even between my toes, were caked in a sticky brown dust that smelled of tobacco. We couldn't have been in the factory more than fifteen minutes and I looked like I'd been there all day. I rubbed off the film as best I could, then grabbed my satchel and went out the back door.

The grass still held the heat of the day, surprising my bare feet. I took a stolen MOMint from my pocket and fished in my satchel for matches. This was my smoking spot, the hollow place between the prickly pine and the back of the house. The drag whoosh of the matchstick lit up the darkness for a quick second, and I took a much-needed first puff. The draw of clean mint was heavenly. These were going to be a big hit. I sighed out the day and took in the quiet. Cicadas chirped and a pair of bird silhouettes glided across the sky. This morning felt like ages ago. This time yesterday I was slipping on my nightgown, not knowing it was my last night at home for who knows how long. I pulled again on the cigarette—longer this time—and the lit end crackled orange-red before fading.

What Aunt Etta said this morning, about Momma going to bed hungry, hurt my heart. I thought I knew everything there was to know about Momma, but I was wrong. Her worries about money and her anger at Daddy made more sense now.

I took another long draw and examined the cigarette's light green filter. It was pretty. The ladies would love them.

Now that the shock of Momma up and leaving me had worn off, I quite liked the idea of being here for tobacco wives season. I hadn't realized how small our lives had become, me and Momma. I blamed it on her, but the truth was, I'd withdrawn too. Since Daddy died I had avoided my school friends, everyone except for April; we'd always be close. But the other girls, the ones from school, looked at me different after Daddy passed. You'd think that losing a parent would bring you even closer to girls who also had a daddy serving, but it didn't. They seemed scared of me, like I had a disease they might catch if they got too close. They all had fathers away and I was proof of how the war could change everything.

"Maddie?" Aunt Etta's voice echoed from inside the house. "Maddie?"

Quickly, I stubbed the butt out against a nearby brick.

"Yes, ma'am?" I shouted, rushing inside.

She stood at the top of the steps holding a large white box. "I have something for you. It was sitting by the side door. Might be something your mother forgot to give you."

"Oh. Okay, I'm coming." I couldn't imagine what it could be. I hurried up to take the package. "Thank you."

I took the box downstairs. I ripped through the brown paper to find that it was covered with textured ivory wrapping paper and tied with yellow grosgrain ribbon. Tucked under the extravagant bow was a card of fine stationery, addressed by hand.

*Dear Maddie,*

*I saw this in a shop window on my way home from Garden Club today and simply couldn't resist. It will be perfect for the Summer Solstice Celebration—the first of many, I hope. Nothing would please me more!*

*Love,*
*Miss Mitzy*

I gave the ribbon a tug, then removed the lid to discover a sky-blue dress with a shimmery bodice. The tissue paper whispered as I pulled the dress from the box. It had white lace trim at the collar and a thin blue belt sewed right in at the waist. The silk Georgette skirt gave it a lovely sheer iridescence. My heart swelled at the sight of it.

I rummaged around the room and found a new box of velvet hangers stashed under the daybed. I separated one from the rest of the pack, and carefully placed Mitzy's gift over the hanger's plush shoulders.

I climbed on a stool and hung the dress from a hook screwed into the ceiling, the kind you would normally hang potted plants from. Then I lay on the chaise lounge admiring it, thrilled and yet curious about Mitzy. Why was she being so generous when she didn't even know me? I reread her note as the full skirt spun in a slow circle around the hook above me.

*The first of many, I hope.*

*Nothing would please me more!*

# Six

"N othing," a man boomed into the microphone. "Nothing brings the citizens of Bright Leaf together like our annual Summer Solstice Celebration." He paused before throwing the crowd a big smile. His full head of dark hair was slicked back, his mustache pencil-thin, and his cigar thick, held like a pool cue in the crook of his fingers.

I shifted in my seat and massaged my hands. My fingers ached from sewing all those uniform patches. The patches were too thick for the sewing machine, so Aunt Etta and I did them by hand. The task took us the better part of the last four days, even with a stitching awl.

"Thank you, all of you, for joining us to celebrate the longest day of 1946. Tonight we celebrate fourteen hours of glorious sunshine that feeds our fields and fills our hearts and pockets!"

"Amen," a man yelled. The crowd broke out in applause and whistles.

"Is that Mr. Winston?" I whispered.

Aunt Etta nodded solemnly.

He held his hand up, signaling for everyone to quiet down.

"Thank you. And you, and you, and you."

He pointed to the corners of the crowd like he was raising a thumb and finger pistol—to the rows of workers on metal bleachers across the square, to the men in suits and their wives seated behind him on the stage, to the group of spit-shined kids sitting on the grass down front, and to all the people, including me and Aunt Etta, sitting in row upon row of white wooden chairs.

"What's wrong with his legs?" I asked Aunt Etta.

"Polio," she whispered. "Came down with it in high school."

His forearms bore the weight of him on a pair of metal crutches. His hips leaned to one side and his pants legs hung slack, as if empty beneath him. One of the most powerful men in Bright Leaf couldn't stand without help.

"And a very special thanks to a very special lady," he said, pivoting to his left and gesturing to Mitzy.

Louder clapping and whistles burst forth from the crowd.

"We love you!" a woman shouted. Mitzy half stood, waved, and made a face like *aw shucks.*

Mr. Winston wasn't nearly handsome enough for her. At least I didn't think so. Momma would have said they were a perfect match: one rich and the other pretty. *Find a rich husband,* Momma liked to tell me. *That's what I should have done.*

"You ladies be sure to stop by Elizabeth's Garden Gazebo," Mr. Winston said. "You'll see the prettiest roses this side of the Mason Dixon and," he continued, gazing at his wife, "the plans for the new Elizabeth Winston Day Care Center and School." The crowd went crazy, especially the women; dozens of them stood and clapped.

"Maddie," Aunt Etta said, "soon as the speeches are over, make sure to go see Mrs. Winston's garden display. It gets crowded quick and I know she'll want to see you in your dress."

"By myself?" I whispered.

"Yes," Aunt Etta said. "Frances and I have to catch up with some of the girls from the factory."

I frowned. I didn't expect to be on my own tonight. Hopefully I'd see Anthony somewhere in the crowd.

Mr. Winston motioned for everyone to sit down. "She's a keeper," he said. "Thank you, doll. Now, kids, don't you miss the interactive Field of Dreams Exhibit. Got to start them young," he chuckled, taking a puff of his big fat cigar.

"And the Ferris wheel!" shouted a young boy sitting upfront. His mother smacked him on the back of the head.

"And the Ferris wheel," Mr. Winston, said, grinning with his cigar between his teeth.

I scooted in my seat to get a better look at Mitzy. She sat closest to Mr. Winston with her ankles crossed and her hands folded in her lap, beaming as she watched him speak. Her shoes were a shade darker than her peach dress. A pink organdy hat and matching gloves finished the look. I never would have thought to pair those colors, but they worked beautifully on her. A strand of pearls rested against her collarbone and her charm bracelet circled her thin wrist.

I looked down at my full silk skirt with its matching fabric belt and a confused sense of shame came over me. The dress Mitzy had given me was gorgeous, but it made me feel so out of place. Aunt Etta and I were seated among the wealthy folks—Mitzy had seen to that—and when I spotted Frances across the courtyard with women in simple day dresses, cookie-cutter silhouettes without pleats or pockets, my cheeks burned.

Any extra use of fabric was prohibited during the war and was still frowned upon. Who could afford more than the one-and-three-quarter-yard limit for a dress anyways?

I knew I was lucky. Thanks to Aunt Etta, I always had clothing made from finer materials than we had the means for. When I was little, she sewed for me herself, but as my skills improved, she let me take my pick of fabrics from her workroom. I'd make at least two school dresses over the summer and take cloth home for two more. I didn't dare select the most expensive weaves; they weren't practical anyway. Now, who was I to wear something so extravagant? Mitzy's gift suddenly felt undeserved, selfish even.

"Gentlemen," Mr. Winston shouted from the stage, snapping me out of my worry. "We have a special treat for you as well. In the History Corner, you'll find a fine-looking group of photographs of our own distinguished patriarch, Mr. Augustus Hale—one of our beloved Bright Leaf founding fathers—paired together with a collection of Augustus's early writings, all of which are displayed on the very desk where he worked. Thanks to the generosity of Mrs. Cornelia Hale . . . Cornelia, where are you, Cornelia?" From the front row, a slender woman in a purple dress and hat raised a purple-gloved hand and turned slightly, a pained smile on her lined face. A few folks clapped politely.

"Thanks to Mrs. Hale, her late husband's achievements will become a permanent part of our town's archives," Mr. Winston continued. "Please remember to stop by and have a look at the life and work of this brilliant man to whom all Bright Leaf citizens owe a great debt of gratitude." Mr. Winston waited for the crowd's claps to fade before continuing.

"Finally, I would be sorely remiss, ladies and gentlemen," he said, "if I didn't acknowledge another prominent Hale, Dr. Robert Hale. Robert where are you, my friend?" Mr. Winston reached into his jacket pocket for a pack of cigarettes and held the mint green box in the air. "Dr. Hale helped develop the formula for Bright Leaf Tobacco's next big seller, MOMints! Robert, take a bow!"

A short, stout gentleman rose and nodded as he raised his palm. He wore tiny round eyeglasses, the kind without earpieces, perched on his prominent nose. His brown hair was combed neatly with a deep side part and his heavy eyebrows gave him a serious, stern look. He looked vaguely familiar.

"All of you ladies be sure to try these tonight," Mr. Winston said. "We're giving out free samples in the warehouse and they're especially good for our new mothers."

A pretty brunette seated directly in front of me whispered to her friend as she bounced her fussy baby on her knee, "I'm just dying to try those. Can you believe it, a cigarette just for women?"

"I know," her friend agreed. "It's an exciting time for us girls."

"Before we kick off the festivities," Mr. Winston said from the lectern, "a word of prayer. Reverend."

Everyone bowed their heads as a man in an ill-fitting brown suit took the stage.

"Dearest Jesus, our savior in Heaven, we praise you for this day. We thank you for the blessings you've bestowed upon our fair town, for the sun and rain, for every seedling and leaf that puts food on our tables and roofs over our heads."

He raised his arms skyward, as if holding up the clouds. The orange-red sun was barely visible just above tobacco fields in the distance. I closed my eyes and sent up a silent prayer of remembrance for Daddy, with a P.S. to keep Momma safe. We didn't always get along, but she was my momma and I loved her. It'd been five days and still no word. It worried me.

"Lord, we praise you. We thank you for our country's victory overseas and entrust you to bring our local boys back safely. We beseech you to bless our fields, factories, and workers. We bask in your truth and light. In Jesus's name, Amen."

"Amen," a chorus of voices echoed.

"Thank you, Reverend," Mr. Winston said, clasping his hands. "Now I know we're all champing at the bit to start celebrating. But in honor of our country and our brave soldiers, please rise for the national anthem."

I stood, looked for the flag, and placed my hand over my heart.

"It's hot as Hades out here." Aunt Etta stood and adjusted her wrist corsage. She'd fashioned fabric flowers on an elastic band in place of her usual pincushion.

Just as we got to "the land of the free and the home of the brave" line, our voices were drowned out by three airplanes overhead. One led the other two in a triangle formation as they screamed through the sky. All around me people cheered and craned their necks as the planes raced low overhead, leaving white trails behind them.

I covered my ears and a flood of memories swept over me; Daddy placing his prized model airplane, the Northrop Black Widow, on our bookshelf, pride in his eyes that he'd soon be *a gunner in a life-size one of these babies.* Momma, standing outside the principal's office to collect me, the telegram clutched tightly in her hand.

The cloudless sky and bracing cold on our way home to a house that would never again have Daddy's booming voice in it. The pit in my stomach upon waking every morning, the loss of him hitting me fresh as I opened my eyes each day.

Everything and nothing changed after he died. I resented all who outlived him. Mr. Evans at the paper store, with his big old mustache and his copies of the *Saturday Evening Post*. Why was he not taken instead of my daddy? April's father had come home with a medal, and not a scratch on him. It wasn't fair. Why were all these people still present in the world when my daddy was gone forever?

"Enjoy yourselves tonight!" Mr. Winston shouted. "But not too much. It's another full day of sunshine tomorrow!" He waved and hobbled offstage as the band broke into "Tuxedo Junction."

"I'm going to find Frances and a nice cool drink," Aunt Etta said, fanning herself. "Go on to the warehouse and find Mrs. Winston's display. Tell her how pretty it is, which I'm sure it will be." She retrieved a printed ticket from the handbag dangling on her forearm and pressed it into my hand. "Here, it's a special pass from Mitzy. Otherwise you'll have to wait in that long line."

I looked around the crowd for Anthony; if I could find him then I wouldn't have to go alone.

"Oh, and Maddie," she said, squeezing past me to pursue a server carrying a tray of mint iced tea. "We have a big day and an early start tomorrow. An appointment with two rather difficult wives," she whispered, then went back to her normal voice. "So if it gets late and you can't find me, just go on back to the house. Lots of people will be walking home, so it'll be plenty safe. Best be in by nine. Nine fifteen at the latest."

That seemed awful early. Momma always let me stay out as late as I wanted, as long as she knew where I was. She said I had a good head on my shoulders, so she never had to worry about me.

I sighed and made my way toward the Tobacco Warehouse. Overhead, the Ferris wheel lights formed a bright yellow star that towered above all the buildings, even the Bright Leaf office. The band shifted gears to play a slow number. Women led their husbands by the hand onto the dance floor while a singer crooned—"*She was just a neighborhood girl, and I was just a neighborhood boy . . .*" The song made me think of home, in a good way. Momma had said she might not call on the regular, but she'd call. Yes she would.

The doors to the warehouse stood wide open to reveal an enormous space. A lady working the entrance noticed my ticket and waved me to the front. Dozens of folks were waiting and here I was skipping ahead like I was royalty. Then I was given a flyer with a map of the Warehouse displays printed on it: "Field of Dreams, Miss Bright Leaf, Heritage Circle, Garden Gazebo, From the Desk of Mr. Augustus Hale." Barrels full of MOMints cigarettes stood just inside the entrance. I took a pack and placed it in my handbag, though I was tempted to smoke them all right now.

The cavernous room already hummed with bodies; beautifully dressed men, women, and children–all north-side-of-town types—weaved their way from attraction to attraction. I needed to get my bearings, find a spot to stand off to the side. I didn't much care for crowds, but at least back home I knew everybody at our little county fair. I didn't belong here, among this sea of wealthy strangers, all of them laughing and talking, arm in arm, while I stood here not knowing what to do with my hands. I scanned the room for Anthony, but he was nowhere in sight.

At the Field of Dreams Exhibit, I slipped in behind a meandering family of five, the three children cracking open boiled peanuts and dropping the shells on the weathered floor. The little towheaded boys watched the farmer's every move as he walked them down a path that brought to life all the steps in tobacco farming. He pointed to signs at each station with his walking stick.

There were twelve backbreaking steps in all. Planting seeds, transplanting sprouted seedlings, weeding, suckering, cutting, bundling, stringing, curing, grading, weighing, prizing, and auctioning.

"Can I dig that up?" one of the boys asked. Another stomped on top of one of the seedlings.

"Get off a there," the man cried, pulling the boy by his collar. "Don't you boys have any respect for the plants that feed ya? No digging, ya hear? But you can push that button." The man pointed with his thick, unsteady hand to what looked like a radio at the end of the exhibit. The boys raced toward it, pushing each other, and smacking it at the same time.

"Five, five, can I get five? Five oh. Five. Five and a quarter, do I hear five and a quarter, ho? Five and a quarter, five and a quarter, do I hear six? Oh." On and on it went, the boys giggling and trying to talk fast like the man's rolling voice coming from the radio's speaker.

On the wall behind the exhibit, a line of eight framed photos hung, each one showing a different man standing behind a microphone next to long piles of tobacco. On the bottom of each frame was a metal plaque engraved with a name, a date, and the highest single-day auction tally of the pictured man's career. There was a ninth frame, but it didn't hold a photo at all and the metal plaque was blank. Instead, it displayed a cream-colored piece of paper with some shaky calligraphy on it. THANK YOU TO INTERIM AUCTIONEER MRS. ASHLEY SMITH FOR YOUR SERVICE DURING THE WAR it read. *Mrs.?* I'd never heard of a woman auctioneer. Aunt Etta said it was one of the most important jobs in tobacco. *The farmers' livelihood is in the auctioneer's hands.* It was fun to watch too. Buyers, sellers, and spectators gathered round waist-high piles of tobacco arranged in long rows from one end of the warehouse to the other. The auctioneer held court, all eyes on him as he walked between the rows, reeling off prices at a dizzying speed. Only the buyers, the warehouse owner, and the ticket marker could make out what he said. To the rest, it sounded like too fast singing, music-like with its own rhythm and pattern.

I slowly made my way through the crowd, passing two beauty queens wearing MISS BRIGHT LEAF and LITTLE MISS BRIGHT LEAF sashes. A towering stack of boxed chocolates with the letters *M&M* on them stood behind the pageant winners, the crowns on their heads glittering like shiny automobile hood ornaments.

"New sweets for your sweetie!" the older one called out. "New chocolates! Candy coated and won't melt. The boys coming home love 'em."

Next to the tower of chocolates sat an open book

with pictures of Miss Bright Leaf winners from previous years. I flipped through the last few years and marveled at how beautiful they were, with names to match. Three of them were named after pretty flowers—Rose, Violet, and Daisy.

"Try a chocolate," said Little Miss Bright Leaf, holding out a dish. I took a few and found them crunchy and delicious.

Mitzy's Gazebo was right next to the history exhibit, where the main attraction was the story of Bright Leaf tobacco. Aunt Etta had told me the story many times. Daddy too. In 1839, a twist of fate led to its accidental discovery, which ended up being one of the most important breakthroughs in North Carolina agriculture. Tobacco had always been a major crop for the region, but not until the development of the bright leaf variety did the market for it really start booming. As the story goes, Stephen was a slave on the farm of a wealthy planter near the Virginia border. He worked as a blacksmith, and his other job was overseeing tobacco curing. On one occasion, due to the warmth created by the fire, Stephen fell asleep during the process. A few hours later, he woke up to find the fire almost completely out. To try to keep the heat going, he rushed to his charcoal pit (part of his blacksmithing operation) and threw hot coals on the fire, which created a sudden, immense heat. The heat from the charred logs cured the tobacco quickly, leaving it with a vivid yellow color, and bright leaf tobacco was born.

Both Aunt Etta and Daddy made sure to tell me that the plantation owner took the credit for the bright leaf variety, that the slave didn't get any mention at all until many years later. I said that wasn't fair, and Daddy agreed with me. "That's the way the world is, honey. There are those who have and those who haven't. It's those who *have* that get to tell the stories." When he saw the look on my face he added, "Things are changing, Maddie, there's no doubt about that. And you can be part of changing things for the better."

That's what was running through my mind as I made my way over to the other side of the history exhibit. A group of men had gathered around Mr. Augustus Hale's writing and they were gawking over the framed photos and documents. They took turns sitting in the leather desk chair, putting their hands behind their heads and leaning back like they owned the place.

"You keep busy there, d'ya hear?" one of them said, his friends egging him on. "Time is money and don't you forget it." He was likely a factory worker, but for the moment he was the boss, all bluster and clout.

"Buy low and sell high," someone piped up.

"Plant low and cut high, is more like it, Stan." The men all laughed at that.

I walked to the other side of the Gazebo where, in an area called Heritage Circle, men dressed in old-timey clothes were caning chairs and sharpening knives on a large spinning stone.

"Maddie! Over here!"

I looked up and saw Mitzy standing with two other white women, both of them watching me expectantly. She lifted her hand in a delicate wave.

I walked over to her and she pulled me in for a little squeeze. "Don't you look lovely!" She held my hands and stepped back to get a better look. "Maddie, that dress is the perfect style and fit for you. I'm so pleased."

"Thank you so much, Miss Mitzy. It was so kind and generous of you." I meant it, too.

Mitzy beamed back at me, then said to the women standing with her, "Ladies, this is Maddie. Etta's niece I was telling you about. Doesn't she look darling?"

"She looks like a doll," said the gorgeous blonde, smiling as if she was onstage. I recognized her immediately as one of the former beauty queens I'd just seen in that book. "That light blue is just beautiful with your flaming red curls," she added. She reminded me of Momma, the way she held herself as if men were always staring. She was a stunner all right, with platinum hair that fell just below her shoulders in sleek waves. And that outfit! Elbow-length gloves and a strapless silver princess gown with a tea-length skirt, every inch of it covered in sparkly paillettes. It was a flashy choice for an outdoor party.

"Maddie, this is Rose, Dr. Hale's wife and one of my Garden Club friends," Mitzy said.

"Hey there, sugar." Rose's clipped drawl gave her away as a North Carolina transplant. Alabama or Louisiana born, I bet.

"And this is my sister. My *older* sister, Mrs. Ashley Smith," Mitzy said. Her sister rolled her eyes. Mitzy and Rose giggled.

I wondered if this Mrs. Ashley Smith was the same woman mentioned in the auctioneer plaque. Though from her quiet demeanor and simple gray dress, I never would have guessed that she was an auctioneer. She didn't say much, almost as if she preferred to fade into the background.

"It's nice to meet you both," I said, trying my best not to show my nerves. I felt like a mutt next to show dogs. A well-dressed mutt, but a mutt nonetheless.

"Maddie's helping Etta with the Gala gowns this year," Mitzy explained. "She's going to study fashion design at the North Carolina College of the Arts."

I blanched. I'd said I hoped to go to college, but I certainly had no concrete plans, yet.

"This young lady is very ambitious," Mitzy bragged. "Just like I was at her age."

Ashley furrowed her brow, but just barely.

The way Mitzy boasted about me, someone she'd just met, was odd. Telling these ladies my business. Sending me this dress and giving me the special ticket. *There's no such thing as a free lunch*, Daddy always said. It was all a little unnerving.

"Nice to meet you too, Maddie," Ashley said. "If you'll excuse me, ladies, I have to go check on my boys, make sure they're not breaking something."

"Give the little darlings a kiss from Aunt Mitzy, would you?" she said.

Rose gave Ashley a friendly push on the shoulder. "You're just trying to avoid my mother-in-law, aren't you? You saw her making her way over here and want to bolt, same as me." Rose looked toward the purple-clad woman approaching us.

Ashley laughed politely but didn't deny it.

"Go on, then," said Rose, smirking. "Before she turns you to stone. You can escape her, you lucky thing."

The woman who had donated her husband's writings came toward us at a snail's pace. She was holding the arm of a boy about my age, the feathers on her hat shaking with each deliberate step.

"At least David's with her," Rose said, staring at the slow-moving couple. "That's something."

"Come now, Rose," said Mitzy. "Cornelia isn't so bad. Her bark's far worse than her bite."

"Easy for you to say," said Rose. "You're not stuck in the doghouse with her."

Mitzy just laughed.

"Will you look at this? I swear that old witch is losing her mind. She's all decked out in mauve *again*. I bet she's even dyed her damn girdle."

Rose turned to me and whispered, "They say that this mauve is a new color that's all the rage in Paris. You can't get it in America, even in New York City. But Cornelia used her *textiles connections*"—there was a wink in her voice when she said that—"to get her hands on the pigment. Her poor maid's fingers are permanently purple from all that dye!"

I'd never been spoken to like this before, like I was in on a secret. It was thrilling. Momma didn't have any close girlfriends. She didn't trust women, especially the pretty ones.

"She says the mauve dye is a business venture," Rose added, removing a chic cigarette case from her evening bag. "Then again, she says everything is a *business venture*." Her voice was dripping with poison. "The old crow is losing her marbles." With that she tapped her temple with one long red nail.

Cornelia pursed her lips and wrinkled her nose like she'd smelled a rotten melon as she approached us. She whispered something to the young man helping her, who let go of her arm and gave her a warm smile.

"What a lovely shade of lavender," Mitzy said.

"It's mauve," Cornelia said.

"Oh yes, of course, *mauve*. How silly of me."

In addition to her mauve hat with mauve feathers, Cornelia wore mauve gloves with black piping and a mauve skirt with a fitted mauve jacket. Even her earrings were light purple stones.

"Cornelia, this is Maddie, Etta's niece, who's helping her with Gala gowns this year," Mitzy said. The old lady nodded at me and I smiled back. She reminded me of a strict old teacher I'd once had, all straight back and no nonsense. She meant business.

"I hope you won't mind, Cornelia, if I thank you again for your generous contribution to the History Corner!" Mitzy spoke in an upbeat voice, as if the grumpy old lady could be tricked into mildness by a display of sheer enthusiasm. "I so enjoyed seeing Augustus's desk and papers when we were setting up the Gazebo. It was like stepping back in time. He was such a wise counselor to us all, God rest his soul. Such lovely handwriting, for a man. That surprised me."

"Humpf," Cornelia said. "That's because it's my handwriting, not his."

"Yours, Mother?" Rose gasped, her eyes wide. "You must be joking. You were a secretary?" She couldn't contain herself. "Scribbling his notes like a . . . a girl Friday?"

Cornelia scowled and slowly removed her gloves, one finger at a time. She held the pair tightly in one hand.

"As usual, Rose, you are sadly mistaken in your interpretation. I didn't merely take notes for Augustus, and I certainly wasn't his *girl Friday*. I conceived of and recorded my ideas in those ledgers, and as men are wont to do, he took the credit. In fact," she said, waving her gloves to the ceiling, "we wouldn't be standing here in this warehouse had I not insisted we build it alongside the rail line."

Her eyes met mine with such intensity, I had to look away. "Do you have any idea how much money Bright Leaf saves every year because of the proximity of the warehouse and locomotives for loading and unloading tobacco?"

I raised my eyebrows and froze for a moment, unsure whether I was supposed to answer.

"David!" Mitzy gushed, saving the day. "There you are, dear boy."

Cornelia grumbled under her breath and shook her head. Her hands trembled as she opened her purse. She placed the gloves inside and closed it with a snap.

I glanced over my shoulder, relieved to be free of Cornelia's steely gaze. The grin on David's face suggested he had witnessed the outburst. He was a head taller than me, at least, and had dark lashes framing light brown eyes and a dusting of tiny freckles across his nose and cheeks.

"Hey, handsome," Rose cooed, rushing over. She took a draw on her cigarette through its long, silver holder and pulled David next to me. "Maddie, don't you and David look cute next to each other! Are the boys chasing you yet? I'll bet they are with that gorgeous red hair."

A wash of heat rushed to my neck as I shook my head no.

I thought of Momma, chasing after a new husband back home—or wherever she was—and stood up taller. I didn't have one iota of interest in doing the same.

Mitzy jumped in to properly introduce us. "David, darling, this is Maddie, Etta's niece I was telling you about. Maddie, this is my wonderful and thoroughly perfect godchild, David Taylor." Mitzy went to hug him but stumbled instead. She grabbed his arm for support, and her face went white as a sheet.

"Are you okay, Mimi?" David asked, concern knitting his brow.

"Yes, dear, I'm fine," she said, taking a deep breath and smoothing the hair at her forehead. "I—I think maybe I turned around too fast. Don't worry about me. I'll go sit down a minute," she said and then lowered herself into a chair in front of the Gazebo. "Why don't you two go off and get better acquainted? Oh, I know! You should take a ride on the Ferris wheel."

I clasped my handbag and swallowed hard, fishing for an excuse. This was too much. Being paired off with some boy I'd just met.

"I'll keep an eye on Mitzy, don't you worry, David," Rose assured him. Looking at me, she said, "Y'all go on and have yourself a big time."

Cornelia cleared her throat. "Well, I guess I'll go and find my son. See if he has a moment for his mother."

"Robert's over there," Rose said, waving to two men looking at the knife display. "I'm sure he'd be *delighted* to see you." Dr. Hale stood next to Mr. Winston, his foot propped on a stool to reveal a lily-white calf that looked like it had never seen the sun. There was something familiar about this man with his tidy hair and small round glasses. *Built like a fire hydrant* is how Momma would have described him. He and Rose made an odd pair.

Cornelia mumbled something under her breath and ambled away, leaving David and me to ourselves.

"Shall we take a walk, Maddie?" he asked quietly. "It'd be my pleasure."

I exhaled, thinking about how Momma would've been delighted to see me strolling with a boy like David. "That depends," I replied.

David tucked his chin and squinted. "Sorry?" he asked, obviously perplexed that I didn't jump at the chance to go for a walk with him.

"It depends on whether this walk includes a stop for one of those mint iced teas I saw earlier," I said.

A relieved grin crossed David's face. "I suppose that can be arranged," he answered, offering me his arm.

Together, we made our way back to where I had entered the warehouse. Squeezing sideways past a long line of people waiting to get in, we stepped out into the town square. The chairs had been replaced by tall tables where people stood drinking iced tea, mint juleps, and wine. David quickly caught the eye of a passing server, who unfortunately only had iced tea with lemon on her tray.

"Will this do?" David asked, reaching for the glass.

"No," I said. "It was mint tea that I wanted."

"All right then," he said, withdrawing his hand from the waitress's tray with a chuckle. "The lady knows what she wants, and it's not tea with lemon." The waitress giggled at his teasing remark.

"What's wrong with a lady knowing what she wants?" I asked David as we continued on toward the Ferris wheel.

"Nothing," he said, although he looked startled by my pointed question. "Nothing at all. It's refreshing actually."

"If you don't know what you want, you'll never find it," I said. "I'd rather wait for what I want than settle for something I don't."

David offered me his arm and leaned in close to my ear. "I like the way you think, Maddie," he said, his voice low and face so close to mine that I could smell his earthy aftershave.

As we walked past an army of children gathered around a cotton candy machine, their eyes wide as the sugar spun into fluffy pillows of pink, blue, and yellow, David started coughing. He shook his head and dropped my arm.

"Excuse me," he said as he coughed into his elbow.

"That's all right," I told him.

His eyes started to water.

"Are you okay?"

He nodded and took a handkerchief from his pocket.

"Excuse me," he said again, his voice labored and raspy. He pointed to his chest. "Asthma."

"Oh, I'm sorry. Is there anything I can do?"

"Yes!" he gasped. "How about a new pair of lungs?"

I wasn't sure that he was joking until he recovered his breath and gave me a playful grin. I smiled back, relieved.

"Do you want something to drink?" I offered, looking for a waiter.

"No," he said, folding his handkerchief and returning it to his pocket. "Thank you, but I'm fine. I've had it since I was a kid. It sounds worse than it is. Really."

"If you're not feeling well," I said. "If you're not up to riding the Ferris wheel, that's fine with me. I really should find my aunt anyways. She wants me home early tonight." I stood on my tiptoes to peer across the square.

David broke out into a wide smile, revealing a small space between his two front teeth. "If I didn't know better," he said, studying me, "I'd think you were trying to get rid of me."

"What? No, of course not," I fumbled. "I just, well, you just seemed unwell is all."

He cleared his throat and offered me his arm. "I assure you that I have made a complete recovery and would be ever so grateful if you would grace me with your presence on the Ferris wheel," he said in a funny, formal voice.

"Indeed, kind sir," I said, matching his joking tone. I looped my arm through his.

We strolled past a cluster of folks—ladies in their summer best and men in seersucker, each one enjoying a long cool drink with a slice of lemon or maraschino cherries. It was nice and all, but I could feel eyes on us. Was everybody wondering why a girl like me was walking with David? Or was I just imagining it? I didn't have much experience with boys. The ones in the Holler weren't that interesting, and, truth be told, I preferred to spend time with my sketching and sewing.

But I was going on sixteen and practically a woman, so why shouldn't I be walking arm in arm with a handsome man? Most girls back home were spoken for by seventeen or eighteen. Anybody worth having was married by nineteen, with a baby on the way by twenty. At least that's what Momma said.

I had better things to do. I wouldn't end up like Momma, leaning on a man to pay the bills. You couldn't count on someone else to take care of you. I'd learned that the hard way.

**Three girls** in jewel-colored dresses and short white gloves giggled as they came toward us. A beautiful brunette strode over and stood right in front of David, blocking our path.

"David Taylor," she said, tilting her chin and making eyes at him. "Don't you look handsome this evening?" She didn't so much as glance at me.

"Why thank you, Vivien," David said. "You look lovely as well."

"Oh, well aren't you the sweetest." She gave him a coy little pat on the arm.

"Vivien, this is Maddie," he said. "Maddie, this is Vivien. Our families go way back."

"I haven't seen you around here before," Vivien said, giving me the once over.

"I'm visiting my aunt," I said. It was none of her business what I was doing in Bright Leaf.

"Your hair's real pretty," said the least attractive of the three girls. But before I could thank her, Vivien jumped in and changed the subject.

"Mother and Daddy always ask about you, David," she said sweetly. "My brothers too; they're naughty as ever. Mother would love to see you, I'm sure." Then she turned her attention to me. "David's been my mother's favorite since he escorted me to my debutante ball."

"Oh," I said, shifting my handbag to my other arm.

"That's nice."

"Tell her I said hello, would you?" David said. "It was good to see you, Vivien, but we should go. Maddie and I have an important date with the Ferris wheel, isn't that right?" he said, threading my arm through his and grinning.

"Oh," she said, stepping aside, her spark dimmed. "Well, y'all have fun."

I felt a whisper of satisfaction at the look on Vivien's face. Suddenly it felt pretty nice walking arm in arm with David, the two of us dressed in fine garments.

"So, how long will you be in Bright Leaf?" he asked as we made our way toward the Ferris wheel. I took in its bright lights against the darkening sky. The heat had broken and a slight breeze kissed my cheek. It was a lovely evening.

"I don't know really. I guess I'll leave whenever my mother decides to come back for me," I said, then bit my lip. It probably wasn't a good idea to be telling people about how Momma just up and left me.

"Oh boy, I know that feeling. My father never knows when he'll be home to collect me, either. Could be two weeks, could be two months. He's in the military, stationed in London now, working on the Marshall Plan. Doesn't know when it will be passed, until then it's just wait and see."

I started to ask him where his mother was, but re-called Mitzy saying that she had died when he was a little boy. Losing a parent. Not really what you want to have in common with someone.

"I basically live in the Winstons' guesthouse, just behind their home," he continued. "I spend every summer and most of my breaks from boarding school here. Christmas, Thanksgiving, all the holidays. My father sold our house in Bright Leaf when I was little and bought a place in Virginia, close to my school, but he's always traveling for business, and even when he is there it just doesn't feel like home."

He must have seen the look of surprise on my face. "My father is a good man. He is. He's just better at business than he is at being a dad."

"Hmm," I said softly, considering him.

"Mimi—that's what Mitzy likes me to call her—and Mr. W are kind of like my second parents. Mimi dotes on me like I'm her son."

"That's nice," I said.

"It is. I also help Mr. W with accounting during the summers. I'm good with numbers and he has his sights set on me joining the tobacco business after college."

"Is that what you want to do?" I asked. "Be an ac-countant?"

David paused. "No, actually it isn't," he said. "I'm

interested in engineering, building, creating things versus counting money."

We walked in silence for a few moments before he spoke again.

"It's funny, Mr. W hasn't ever asked me that," he said. "What I want to do, that is. I didn't realize that until just now."

"I haven't met Mr. Winston," I said. "But I liked his speech earlier. Mrs. Winston seems real nice."

"The Winstons are good people. Mimi is definitely easier to talk to. Mr. W is a decent guy, even though he comes down hard about some things. My dad says he's always been like that—that he runs his company and his home the same way he led the high school football team. You wouldn't know it now, but Mr. W was a star quarterback before he got sick. The best player to ever come out of the Bright Leaf Warhorses. If it wasn't for polio, he would have made the professional league."

"Really? Wow." I pictured his legs strong and sturdy beneath him, passing the ball across a field while Mitzy cheered on the sidelines.

"Yeah, it can't be easy," David continued. "But he doesn't let it stop him. I respect that. Of course, he's lucky to have Mimi—she's always looking out for him."

We had reached the line for the Ferris wheel. It wasn't as long as I thought it would be.

"Mimi pretty much acts like mother and teacher to everyone in the whole town. It's her calling, she says, makes her feel useful. Bet you didn't know it was her idea to open the school and new day care center. Every Bright Leaf employee can send their kids there for free, thanks to her."

I thought about the pots of money you'd need to build a school. "That's very generous," I said quietly.

We'd made our way to the front of the line. The ride operator reached for my hand and helped me into a seat that swung back and forth. David stepped in right behind me, and I grabbed the side as it rocked even more with the weight of both of us. I felt the sensation of floating on water, navigating smooth waves that settled under me. There was a bang as the metal bar snapped into place, and a jolt as we moved up into the sky.

My hair flew around wildly as we rose up up up. The music and people talking below faded as we climbed higher. David's leg touched mine, and I could feel my heart thumping in my chest. The fabric of his trousers was smooth, a fine lightweight wool. I looked at my dress, still fresh and beautiful, not a wrinkle in it. We looked like we belonged together, and for a moment, I let myself entertain the thought. It was strange that a dress could make you feel like you fit in, that it could fool others into believing it too.

Who was I kidding?

I may look the part, but that's as far as it went. There were people who drove right in through the gates of these big old houses, and there were people who took the bus—to work. *The haves and the have-nots*, as they said in Sunday school. I knew which group I belonged to.

When we'd nearly reached the top of the Ferris wheel we jerked to a dead stop. The seat rocked in a high arc and the girls up ahead of us shrieked.

"This is marvelous," I said, our legs dangling impossibly high above the ground.

"Yeah," he agreed.

"It sure is beautiful up here."

"It is. See over there," David said, leaning across me and pointing. "That's the site of the new school. They're breaking ground in a few weeks, right after the fundraising Gala."

"Wow, that sure is something."

"You can see the Winston mansion over there—the white one—and that's Cornelia's house, one, two, three, four, five houses down. It's hard to see from here, but it's a big blue Victorian."

"What's that over there?" I asked, pointing to something that looked like a small building floating in the middle of the tobacco fields to the east.

"Oh, that's an amazing spot." David smiled at me. "It's one of the oldest covered bridges in North Carolina. We should go see it sometime."

"Maybe," I said, wondering what Aunt Etta would want me to say. Was it rude to say no? Too forward to say yes? I know what Momma would tell me.

"Maybe?" he echoed, surprise registering on his face.

"Yes, we'll see," I said. "My aunt has a lot of work, so helping her is my priority. I may not have time for socializing."

"No time for socializing?" he repeated and threw me a queer look. "Most of the girls around here do nothing but socialize. That's admirable. A strong work ethic. I like that, although I hope I can persuade you to take a break sometime."

I gave him a tight grin and blushed. "Oh look, there's my aunt Etta's house." I pointed. "And Frances's house. It's two down from my aunt's."

"Frances is . . . ?" David asked.

"Oh, she's my aunt's good friend," I replied. That's always how I described her—my aunt's good friend.

As the Ferris wheel swooped back down, I could see people gathered around a circle of showroom cars and tractors next to the warehouse. They opened and closed doors, turned headlights off and on. Kids ran around kicking the tires and trying to slide behind the wheel.

Behind one of the cars at the end of the lineup, a lady's silver dress shimmered in the big lights. I squinted and saw it was actually two women, one in silver and one in peach. The one in peach was bent over the bumper of a Buick Super, heaving into the grass. The other woman stood behind her, holding her hat and rubbing her back. The sight of a lady like that throwing up at a nice party shocked me. She must have been very ill to have gotten sick in public.

Once we reached the bottom, we began rising back to the top of the wheel.

"Have you ever been up this high?" David asked.

I turned to him and said, "I haven't, no. Have you?" I looked back down, but the women were gone. I could have sworn it was Mitzy and Rose, but it happened so fast I wondered if I'd imagined it.

"Once. I rode in a military airplane with my father a few years ago . . ." he said, trailing off. He looked at me and then scrunched his face. "Oh, gee Maddie, I'm sorry. Mimi told me about your dad. That was a dumb thing to mention."

"That's okay."

"No, it was really stupid of me. I didn't mean to make you think about him."

"It's fine," I said. "I think about my daddy all the time anyways—even when people are careful not to say anything."

David looked straight at me then, his eyes filled with kindness. I could tell he wanted to say something else but the Ferris wheel had glided back down to the bottom and jolted to a stop, shaking us out of the moment. The man helped me and David step down from the car, and as we walked away from the ride, I noticed the clock in the center of the square—9:10.

"Oh no," I said. "I was supposed to be home by now. We have an early appointment in the morning." I couldn't believe how time had gotten away from me. I didn't even get a chance to see Anthony. "It was nice to meet you," I said, but before I could rush away, David touched my elbow.

"Let me walk you home," he suggested.

"Oh, you don't need to do that," I said. "But thank you for offering."

"It's dark out," David said. "I'd feel much better if I could see you home safely."

"No thank you," I replied, more firmly this time. "I know the way and can manage myself."

"I'm sure you can," he said. "But sometimes it's nice to have company."

"That's true. I'm in a hurry though. Another time," I said, smiling. I liked his persistence.

"Another time then," he said. "But only if you promise." He pointed at me as he backed away. "I'll tell you what. How about you let me show you the covered bridge sometime?"

"Okay," I said.

"Promise?" he asked.

"Promise," I agreed, then began walking briskly across the town square.

# Seven

The gravel crunched under my feet as I walked, the sky almost fully dark and dotted with stars. Aunt Etta's house was about a mile down the road, but if I went through the field I'd be there in half the time. I checked over my shoulder to make sure no one saw me then cut across the grass to the rows of tobacco plants. It was a straight shot all the way across, about a foot-wide path between the rows. The clouds shifted overhead, giving me a little more moonlight. The sea of tobacco plants looked scary at night, but I could run. It wouldn't be that bad if I ran.

Aunt Etta had warned me about the fields. She said just walking through could give you a touch of what old folks call the green monster. The nicotine could seep into your skin from the leaves and make you sick. The field workers got the green monster—nicotine poisoning—all the time, especially during topping and cutting.

I was wasting precious seconds debating with myself about whether to take the shortcut or if I could still make it in time if I went the long way when I heard the rumble of a car and men hollering out drunkenly. One of them threw a beer bottle onto the road, and the smash of the glass spooked me enough that I took off between the plants. My feet pounded the hard dirt and the tobacco leaves smacked my legs as I ran, stinging my skin. I stopped once to catch my breath and looked around me, realizing I had lost my bearings. Which way did I come from? The path looked the same both ways. Nothing in the sky gave me a clue, and the plants all around me stood so tall I couldn't see over. I had to get to Aunt Etta's quick. I didn't want to *give her a moment's trouble,* as Frances said, or give her a reason to ask me to leave. I closed my eyes and stilled, willed myself to know the way. *Always trust your gut* was what Daddy would say. Look around you, get your bearings and listen to that little voice inside you. It won't let you down.

I calmed myself and picked a direction. The ground felt different the closer I got to the end of the row, lumpy and slippery under me, and I saw that thankfully, my intuition was right. Aunt Etta's house was just on the other side of the road. There were no cars coming, so I dashed across the street. It was dark and mouse-quiet as I got closer, but then I noticed a car parked in front of the house. Three people stood next to the long white sedan, one of them Aunt Etta. Frances was there too, I saw, and the cautious lady auctioneer, Mitzy's sister, I'd met earlier that evening.

Aunt Etta saw me first. "Maddie! What are you doing out here? You were supposed to be in bed by now."

"I know. I'm sorry."

"It's almost nine-thirty, child. What happened? And what have you done to your beautiful dress?"

I looked down and there on the silk skirt were dirty brown streaks and smudges. I could have cried.

"I'm sorry, I—I took a shortcut through the fields and got lost is all."

"Let's just get you inside, Etta," Frances said. "You can sort this out once you've had a chance to sit down."

"I'm fine," my aunt insisted. "I felt faint from the heat, but it's already passed. Honest to goodness, y'all are making such a fuss over nothing."

Frances opened the front door, turned on the kitchen light, and sat Aunt Etta down at the table. Ashley offered to pour her a glass of water.

"Thank you, dear," Aunt Etta said, motioning to the cabinet over the sink.

"Do you have any Goody's Powders, Etta? You should take one before bed," Ashley said as she sat the water in front of Aunt Etta.

"I believe I'm all out," Aunt Etta said, taking a small sip.

"I have some at home," Frances said. "I'll go and get them now. Be back in a jiffy."

"Is there anything else I can do before I go?" Ashley asked. "I'd stay longer, but I left the boys with my neighbor. The two of them just got over being sick—and after being cooped up for so long, I'm afraid of what they'll try to do with all their extra energy."

"I'll be just fine," Aunt Etta assured her. "Don't worry. I'll be bright-eyed and bushy-tailed for our meeting tomorrow morning."

"Oh, I forgot. I can't make it," Ashley said. "I'll be at the warehouse working on the opening estimates for the auctions."

"What a shame," said Aunt Etta. "I'm so sorry you won't be able to join us. The other ladies will certainly miss you."

"The truth?" Ashley's already quiet voice was now barely above a whisper. "I'm delighted I won't have to deal with all that Gala gown drama."

Aunt Etta pretended to hold a key to her lips, turn it, and throw it over her shoulder. "Your secret's safe with me. Thank you so much for the ride home, I'm feeling better already."

"You're more than welcome," Ashley said, removing her keys from her handbag as she excused herself.

Aunt Etta sighed and took a sip of her water.

"Are you okay?" I asked, trying to keep the worry out of my voice.

"I'm fine, hon. Nothing for you to fret about. I just got overheated is all. Everyone made too much of a fuss." Sweat beaded on her forehead. Her face was still flushed.

Ashley's car sputtered to a start, followed by the engine fading away.

"Oh, would you look at that poor dress," Aunt Etta said. She asked me to stand so she could examine the skirt. "What did I tell you about the fields?" she said, shaking her head. "It's a wonder you're not the one who's sick."

"I know. I'm so sorry. Is it ruined?"

"I don't believe so, but you'd better soak it right away so the stains don't set." She heaved herself up from the table and retrieved a coffee can marked BAKING SODA. "Here," she said. "Use the bathroom sink."

"Thank you," I said.

"You get right to bed, Maddie, after you take care of that dress, do you hear?" Aunt Etta called as I walked down the hall. "We have an early morning appointment with Mitzy and two rather difficult wives." She'd already told me that several times, and her reminding me again made me feel like a little kid.

"Yes, ma'am," I replied before closing the washroom door behind me. I sighed and leaned my back against the door. Being around rich people was downright exhausting. Always on your best behavior, minding your p's and q's. Back home I could just be myself, say what was on my mind without worrying about making a mistake. Here, it was like walking on eggshells.

Now that I was in the light, I could see clearly how the skirt and bodice were banded with light brown streaks. I ran cool water, sprinkled soda in the sink, and pushed the dress under. I held it there and watched it turn dark blue, ballooning up in places between my fingers. My head throbbed when I moved it from side to side. A wave of nausea rose, then subsided, leaving me sweaty and unsteady. I should have listened to Aunt Etta about the fields. I wished I could just go back home, but tomorrow was another day with more people—apparently *difficult* people—to impress.

I couldn't sleep when I got all wound up. It's been that way since I was little. "Don't you worry, sweet girl," Momma would say, before Daddy's death, on the nights she was feeling affectionate. "We'll get you off to dreamland soon enough." She'd draw me a bath and bring me a small dish of vanilla ice cream. We'd giggle as I settled myself under the bubbles. We were doing the unthinkable. "No one in the whole wide world eats ice cream in the tub," Momma told me, sitting on the closed commode in her bathrobe, cigarette in hand. The feel of the hot water and cool ice cream going down was thrilling. "It's the height of luxury, at least by Holler standards," she'd said. "But just you wait 'til we move to Pine Mountain. We'll have an even bigger tub and butter pecan ice cream. Or the most expensive, pistachio."

Why did everything have to change?

I didn't want to believe it when Momma said that Daddy had enlisted. But it was true. Those GI benefits meant more to him than we did. Daddy had outright lied to me about getting his draft notice. *What good news* it was, he had told me. He'd have a regular paycheck and good money too. It wasn't President Roosevelt who put Daddy's name on the list. Daddy signed up of his own accord. Why did he have to go and take that risk? Look where that got us. I was staying with Aunt Etta, who did not need an unexpected guest, and Momma was off doing God knows what with God knows who.

For the first time since Daddy died, I let myself blame him. Not her, *him*.

We could be in Momma's dream house by now, to-gether as a family, if he hadn't gone off and enlisted. She wouldn't be off gallivanting, and I sure wouldn't be here in Aunt Etta's way, trying not to take up too much space. I wouldn't have to put on airs around Mitzy and her friends or worry about saying the wrong thing to that David boy. My cheeks wouldn't hurt from all this grateful smiling.

It wasn't right, none of it.

# Eight

Aunt Etta overslept. We both did. She rushed downstairs, her hair a mess, wearing the same clothes she had on last night, hurrying me out of bed.

"Get dressed quick, Maddie," she said. "We have to catch the next bus or we'll be late."

"Yes, ma'am," I said, springing out of bed.

"Will you please grab some of the nice patterns—*Vogue* or Butterick? I set aside a stack for this morning's appointment."

"Yes, of course."

As fast as I could, I slipped into a dress on top of the stack in my suitcase, and grabbed a bundle of patterns, including a *Vogue*, the cover featuring two ladies in gold and silver evening gowns, each one holding a glass of champagne and a cigarette.

We made it to the bus with hardly any time to spare.

After greeting Ed, we took our seats and slumped down to catch our breath.

On the ride across town, Aunt Etta kept scratching her neck.

"I was eaten alive at the Solstice," she said. "Did you get bit?"

"No, I don't believe so," I said, examining my legs as we bumped along the dirt road.

"Two other wives will be at Mitzy's house this morning," Aunt Etta explained. "They're on the committee for the Gala Fundraiser. Mitzy and the other two like to plan their gowns together, to coordinate, for all the photographs and all.

"I've already got a jump start on designs they tend to favor. Actually, Mitzy's is all but finished, but she's asked me not to let on to the other women. One of them can be quite demanding, so just follow my lead."

As we passed through town, I watched the early morning bustle through the window. Bright Leaf sure was a lively town this time of year.

"Is it Miss Cornelia?" I asked. "I met her last night."

Aunt Etta turned to meet my eye. "You don't miss a thing, do you, june bug?"

"She was pretty crabby when Miss Mitzy introduced me, that's for sure."

Aunt Etta squeezed my arm, her hand clammy

against my skin. She laughed and said that knowing how to read people was an important part of being a dressmaker.

"She's a tough customer, but don't worry, I know how to handle her. She'll never forgive us if we're late, though. We'll have to double-time it," she said as she fanned herself. "Are you hot?"

"It's pretty warm in here but not too bad," I said.

But when we got off the bus, instead of hurrying, Aunt Etta walked at a slower pace than usual, huffing the whole way to the Winstons' stately house.

Finally, we reached the imposing front door, and Isaac took us inside.

"They're waiting in the downstairs parlor," he said, leading us into a large sitting room.

"Etta! Maddie!" Mitzy put down her teacup, dabbed the corner of her mouth with a cloth napkin, and stood. She was cheerful and perky in her flowered dress with a full skirt. Her hair was stylishly flipped up at the ends. Was it possible I had seen her bent over sick just the previous night?

Next to her sat Cornelia. Same pursed look as last night, but with a different mauve ensemble. Rose wore a yellow and white polka-dot dress with black patent heels, her tiny waist cinched tight with a matching patent belt.

"I'm afraid we're late," Aunt Etta said. "We'll get started right away to make up for lost time."

"Hmmph," Cornelia muttered, narrowing her eyes at me.

"Excellent," Mitzy said. "But first, Maddie, I'm dying to hear what you thought about the party! Did you have fun, sweetheart? Here, please help yourself to some tea and cookies. Tell us what you saw and did!" Mitzy took the sewing box from my hands and gestured to a pair of chairs between Cornelia and Rose, all the while chattering about how nice it was to have young people around, how young people really brightened up the place. Young people this. Young people that.

The place seemed bright enough already to me, but I did what was expected, put on a smile and told her about the Field of Dreams Exhibit and the cotton candy. When I got to the Ferris wheel, Cornelia interrupted.

"Some of us have other plans today, Elizabeth. Can we please get down to business?"

"Yes, yes, of course," Mitzy said. "We better not waste any time. I may need to leave a bit early, actually. I was a little under the weather last night and Dr. Hale is going to try to squeeze me in for a quick checkup around ten."

"All right, let's talk turkey!" Rose exclaimed. "I'm

hoping for something very glamorous this year, a real showstopper, Etta. What about you, *Mother*, will you be wearing mauve?" she asked with a cheeky lilt in her voice.

Cornelia didn't answer.

"Mother?" Rose repeated, her eyes Betty Boop-round.

"Are you talking to me?" growled Cornelia.

Rose laughed. "It's been almost a year since the wedding, Mother. I thought you'd be used to me calling you that."

"Can we get on with it, Etta?" Cornelia huffed, but when she turned to look at my aunt her eyes went wide with alarm. "Sweet Jesus, Etta. Look at your face! And your neck!"

I turned to look and saw that Aunt Etta's cheeks were tomato red and puffy. A rash marched up her throat.

"What is it?" She brought her hands to her chin, patting her face.

Mitzy felt her forehead with the back of her hand. "Etta! You're burning up."

"Am I?"

"You're practically on fire. And that rash! Here, drink some water."

"That's a measles rash," said Cornelia with confidence.

"Measles?" repeated Mitzy. "That would be highly unusual. Adults rarely contract measles, unless they didn't have them as children. We've all had them, haven't we?"

The three wives nodded. Even I nodded. Everyone did, except Aunt Etta.

"You did have measles as a child?" Mitzy asked, astonished.

Aunt Etta said she had not. She was never sick. Hadn't gotten sick as a child and didn't get sick as an adult either. Never missed a day of school and never missed a day of work.

"I told you," Cornelia said. "Measles."

"They are going around," Rose said. "Both of Ashley's boys had them last month. Poor things couldn't go out to play for weeks. Little buggers spread germs like you wouldn't believe!"

"Well," Mitzy said. "Only Dr. Hale can say for certain. You should go see him right away. He's expecting me soon. We'll go together."

"She's right, Aunt Etta," I said. "Just to be sure you're all right."

"I'll call Robert now," said Rose, smiling at me. "One of the benefits of being a doctor's wife."

"Now, y'all are overreacting. That won't be necessary," Aunt Etta said. "I'm fine, really, just a little flushed is all." She started to get up but lost her balance and slumped back in her chair ungracefully.

"Please, Aunt Etta?" I said and began to gather our things.

"Oh, all right," she said, sighing.

I didn't expect Aunt Etta to give in quite so easily, but she was clearly startled by her unsteadiness.

"Might as well check things out to be on the safe side. But, Maddie, you stay here with Cornelia and Rose. You can share our ideas for the gowns while I'm at the doctor's. I do hate to delay things for y'all," she said, turning toward the women. "Maddie is perfectly capable of walking you through the sketches and taking down your feedback. She's quite experienced with formal wear."

*Our ideas? Quite experienced?* I'd seen Aunt Etta's sketches and the muslins, but they certainly weren't *our* ideas, and I wouldn't call making two gowns last summer *quite experienced.*

"No," I said quickly, louder than I meant to. "No, I should really go with you, Aunt Etta, to make sure you're okay."

"You're to stay here and carry on with our work, Maddie."

I could tell by her tone there was no arguing with that, but my stomach flip-flopped at the thought of being alone with Rose and her *mother.*

"You'll need help, Mitzy," Rose interjected, gathering her handbag and returning her teacup to its saucer before anyone could object. She didn't want to be here with Cornelia any more than I did. "Besides, Robert will be thrilled by a surprise visit from his sugar."

"Well," Cornelia said as she stood and tucked her purse under her arm. She glared around the room, her steel-gray eyes landing on Mitzy, then Rose, then me. They were a remarkable color. "Clearly we will not accomplish anything today, and I for one do not intend to entrust the biggest social event of the season to a child. Isaac will drive me home before you head on your way to Robert's office."

"We really should go straight to the doctor," Mitzy said, "but if you insist, we can bring you home first."

"I do insist." Cornelia smoothed her dress. "Good day," she said with a huff and started to make her way to the door.

"Maddie, I'm sure this rash will turn out to be nothing," said Aunt Etta. "I probably just got overheated. I should be back before lunchtime. I'll leave my sewing box here. Look through our sketches while I'm gone. Remember, we have five appointments over the next few days."

"Yes, ma'am."

"Please help yourself to the tea and cookies," said

Mitzy. "The cook and our housekeeper are off today, I'm afraid, but David usually pops in around this time, and he can show you to the kitchen if you're hungry. There's a powder room right through that door there if you need it. Oh, and if you're bored, you can look at these." She handed me a stack of glossy magazines and a manila folder. "Oops," she said, taking the folder from the bottom and placing it on the credenza underneath a painting of pink dogwood blossoms. "That's just Richard's boring old plan. The magazines are the fun part."

Then just like that, they were gone.

All of them.

I put the magazines on the side table next to me and sat still for a while, my hands in my lap prim and proper. It was so peaceful and strange to be in this beautiful room, filled with all the finest things. I could hardly believe that just a week ago I was in my nightgown in the backseat of Momma's Buick. She hadn't called yet, and while I was still upset, the whirl of the Solstice party and appointments with Aunt Etta had really taken my mind off things.

I looked inside the teapot and smelled the sweet, steeped leaves. I took two cubes of sugar and let them melt on my tongue, the sweetness flooding my mouth. It had been ages since I'd tasted cane sugar. I guess rations didn't matter to the Winstons.

I picked up a *Life* magazine from the top of the stack and it flipped open to a page that was marked, the top right corner folded down. "INTRODUCING NEW MOMINTS!" the large headline read, and below was a picture. "DR. ROBERT HALE, MD, MOMINTS INVENTOR AND SPOKESPERSON FOR BRIGHT LEAF TOBACCO COMPANY, AND HIS WIFE."

The couple featured in the advertisement looked familiar and then I realized who they were. Of course! The man was the doctor Mr. Winston had introduced at the Solstice party, and the beautiful blonde was Rose. She was way out of his league, looks-wise, but men didn't have to be handsome if they had a fat wallet. That much I knew. Still, I shuddered at the thought of her kissing him, like a princess kissing a slimy frog.

*"I recommend that all you expectant mothers smoke new MOMints. They calm the nerves for a smooth, easy pregnancy and delivery. And after baby arrives, they help you get your girlish figure back in no time!* the advertisement read. That was smart, talking about getting your figure back. Every woman I knew worried about that.

On the page opposite the advertisement was an article about Mitzy that filled the whole page. It featured a striking photograph of her standing next to the window in this very room. She wore an emerald-green strapless ball gown with a full skirt and elongated fitted bodice. In her delicate hand she held up a cigarette with a light green filter. DOCTOR KNOWS BEST the headline read, and just below it, *Mrs. Richard Winston, who will appear in national advertising for new MOMints cigarettes along with other Bright Leaf tobacco wives. "We urge all you ladies to 'turn over a new leaf' and try the only cigarette made especially for the fairer sex," says Mrs. Winston.*

Under the *Life* magazine sat the June issue of *Harper's Bazaar*, a copy of *Bright Leaf Society*, and a handwritten list of a dozen other magazines and news-papers. I recognized Mitzy's neat penmanship from the note that had arrived with my dress.

She really was like the first lady of Bright Leaf. Now she'd be famous across the state, maybe even the whole country. She was pretty enough to be a model, that's for sure. Rose too. Just think—I was going to help with their gowns. It was all so exciting.

I picked up Mitzy's half-smoked cigarette from the ashtray on the table, crossed my legs, and held it near my mouth. The cigarette was still slightly warm and smelled strongly of mint. I walked over to the large picture window where she had stood and struck a pose.

"I urge all of you ladies to turn over a new leaf," I said. I pretended to blow smoke into the air. "New MOMints for women. They're simply divine."

"Ahem." A deep voice startled me.

I froze, then spun around to find David standing in the parlor doorway, clearly amused.

"I hope I'm not interrupting your conversation with . . ." David glanced around the room. "Yourself?"

"Oh, um." I dropped the cigarette butt on the floor and hurriedly picked it up, then placed it in the ashtray.

David looked taller today, and just as handsome as yesterday.

I cleared my throat. "I was here for a meeting for the Gala dresses, but everyone's gone," I said. "My aunt is sick and Miss Mitzy had a doctor's appointment already scheduled, so she took my aunt along too. She insisted that Dr. Hale check her because it may be measles. My aunt, that is. Not Miss Mitzy."

David crossed the room toward me. "I'm so sorry, Maddie," he said. Then, gesturing for me to sit on a nearby chair, he parked himself on the edge of the sofa next to me. "She's in good hands with Dr. Hale, though. He's the best doctor in Bright Leaf. He's been treating my asthma since I was a kid. He takes extra special care of all the tobacco executives' families and their most valued staff."

I bristled at the word *staff.*

"Let's go into Mr. W's study," David said. "He has Coca-Colas in there, and boy is it hot today. I could use a cold drink."

I followed David down a grand hallway, my shoes tip-tapping against the marble floor behind him. At the end was an alcove with an extra-wide door that David opened for me. The room was dark—not a window to be seen—and cooler than the rest of the house. Glass cabinets lit from inside held stacked boxes decorated with painted crests and gold foil. A few were open, displaying fat rolled cigars lined up tight. A black telephone sat on the corner of Mr. Winston's desk next to a wood and leather pen stand.

"Here, have a seat."

I sank into the soft leather of the desk chair, which rolled backward so fast that I let out a little yelp. David grabbed the armrests to keep me from ramming the cabinet behind me.

"Sorry," he said, trying not to laugh. He leaned in to pull me toward him and back to the desk. "I should have warned you about the wheels and the slick floor. Mr. W had everything in his study specially designed so he could roll around without his crutches."

David's hand grazed my wrist as he straightened my

chair, and I felt a little jolt. He cleared his throat and directed his attention to a cabinet across the room.

"Would you like a Coke or a sarsaparilla, madam?" he asked, removing a bottle of each.

I giggled. "Thank you, sir. Sarsaparilla please, I haven't had it since I was a little girl."

David popped the top and handed me the frosty brown bottle. "They've been hard to come by with the war, but Mr. W finds ways to get what he wants," he said.

"So I see," I said. I took a sip, enjoying the tickle of the fizz on my throat. The feeling made me think about Daddy, who used to take me and Momma to the drugstore for sodas after church. I quickly brushed away the memory before my emotions could get the better of me.

"David, I'm wondering, do you think the Winstons would mind if I called to check on my aunt?" I asked.

"I'm sure that would be fine," David said. He walked behind the desk and moved the telephone closer to the edge with a thunk. "I'll dial Dr. Hale's office for you and put you on with his secretary. She's really nice and should be able to help you."

"I sure do appreciate this," I said. "Thank you."

The dial clicked as David pushed his index finger around and around. A moment passed before I heard the faint sound of someone speaking at the other end of the line.

"Hi there, Miss Lucille. It's David Taylor. I'm here with my friend Maddie. Her Aunt Etta came in earlier to see Dr. Hale. She's wondering if she could find out how everything is going."

A pause.

"Oh. Etta's friend is there?" he said. "Yes, Maddie's right here. Yes, of course. Here she is." If Frances was there, it must be serious.

"Hello?" I said.

"Maddie," Frances said, her voice fast and frantic. I heard her take a sharp breath.

"How is Aunt Etta?" I asked nervously.

Frances hesitated, and for the first time, I felt a real sense of panic. I knew all about that blank space between words. It meant: How much should we tell Maddie? How do we give her the bad news?

"I don't want to lie to you, Maddie. Etta has a high fever. Dangerously high. I'm . . . we're all concerned. Dr. Hale is going to have her admitted to the hospital and we're hoping the fever will break in the next forty-eight hours, but we'll just have to wait and see."

*Dangerously.* It was hard to get past that word.

"Is it measles?" I asked, my voice small and suddenly young.

Frances rallied at the fear in my voice. "Yes, it is. Leave it to Etta to go her whole life healthy as a horse then come down with measles a month before the big Gala." She tried to laugh, but it came out a strained little squeak. "And you know your aunt. She's more worried about those dang dresses than she is about her health. She's making a list of all the gowns that are nearly finished and where to find her best fabrics and muslins for the others. The most pressing matter is rescheduling with Cornelia and Rose, which she wants taken care of tomorrow. She had me write everything down for you."

"For me?" I gasped. "But, but why?" The thought struck me that Aunt Etta could be making a last-minute will. David watched me, alarmed. *What's wrong?* he mouthed.

"Well . . . Etta has decided she wants you to take over her work for the time being. Just until she's better," said Frances. "Isn't that exciting?"

"Wait—no! All by myself?"

"I know you must be nervous, honey. But Etta believes you can do this—and so do I. She thinks it'll be for only a couple weeks, but really, we just have to wait and see how the next forty-eight hours go for her. Still, you have to prepare yourself, Maddie May." Frances took a breath, then lowered her voice. "Etta has to quarantine for two weeks after the fever breaks. Then it all depends on her recovery."

I burst into tears at that. I couldn't help it. I didn't even care that David was watching.

"Can I talk to her?" I asked.

"She's still in with Dr. Hale's nurse," she said. "But take down the telephone number for the hospital."

I didn't dare touch the fine linen paper stacked on Mr. Winston's desk, so I reached into the trash for a discarded envelope and took a pen from the holder. I jotted the number down and blew on the bright blue ink to dry it, then tucked it into my satchel.

"Okay, Frances," I croaked. "Thank you." I scrubbed my wet cheeks with one palm as the room around me blurred through a film of tears. Then an idea occurred to me.

"Frances, what about Anthony? Do you think maybe he could help me with some of the gowns? Perhaps he could come to the appointment with Cornelia and Rose tomorrow?"

"Oh, there's a thought," Frances said. "Let me talk to Etta and see what she thinks."

"Okay," I said. "Thank you, Frances," I said again and replaced the receiver with a click.

"I'm sorry," I whispered to David, wiping my eyes with a long swipe of my forearm. "I just don't . . . I can't do this."

"Everything will be all right," he said with a cough.

He took two handkerchiefs from his pants pocket. One he used to dab at his mouth, the other he handed to me.

It didn't take long for fear to turn into anger. Aunt Etta never gets sick. Well hardly ever, and even if she does, she just soldiers on. But this. It wasn't fair.

"You think you can count on someone," I said, panic filling my chest. "That maybe there's one single adult in the world you can count on, someone who won't go off and get themselves killed or leave you so they can find a new husband or go and get some little kid's illness. It's not fair." I sounded like a pouty child, but I was so upset, I couldn't help myself.

"You're right," David said quietly. "It's not fair." The way he simply agreed with me was deeply comforting.

"My mother always tells me 'life's not fair,'" I said, wiping a tear from the corner of my eye.

"My dad says that too," David said, shaking his head. "They're right, I suppose, but when I'm upset that's the last thing I want to hear."

"Me too," I agreed. "It's as if they're saying it's not okay to be angry or sad."

"Exactly." David gazed at me for a moment and then reached behind the desk to open a glass cabinet. He removed a red velvet tray lined with cigarettes of varying shapes and sizes. "Take one," he said, holding it before me like a waiter offering an array of desserts.

"Are you sure?" I asked, glancing toward the doorway. "These look special."

"They are special," he said. "And you're having an especially hard day. Here, try this one. It's my favorite." I took the slim, unfiltered cigarette from him and placed it between my lips. He held his lighter for me, our eyes fixed on each other as the spark caught and I drew in surprisingly sweet, woody smoke.

"Cinnamon?" I asked, examining the cigarette and trying to regain my composure. There was an intimacy, thrilling and yet unsettling, when he lit it for me. It was as if we'd just kissed.

"Yes," David said, lighting one for himself. "Mr. W tests all kinds of flavors. Chicory, cloves, butterscotch, licorice." I scrunched up my face.

"I hate licorice," we both said in unison and laughed.

"You either love licorice . . ." David said.

"Or you hate it," I completed his statement.

We shared a smile and my worries subsided momentarily. David glanced at the clock on Mr. Winston's desk. "I'm sorry about your aunt," he said. "She's in the very best hands with Dr. Hale, though. I'm sure he'll take excellent care of her."

"Thank you," I said. "That makes me feel a little better."

"And that was a great idea to have Anthony help you," David said.

"You know Anthony?" I was shocked. They didn't exactly travel in the same social circles.

"I do," David said. "His father was my father's tailor, and he used to bring Anthony along to his appointments at our house. We were young then—seven or eight I believe—and they'd send us off to play. Anything to get us out of their hair, I suppose. But when I turned eleven, I went off to boarding school."

"I didn't know that," I said. "Anthony has been helping my aunt for years and he's very talented."

"I'm sure between the two of you, you'll do a bang-up job filling in for your aunt," David said.

"I hope so." I was feeling a little calmer now.

"I have to get back to work on my paper," he said. "But I hope I'll see you again soon."

"That would be real nice." I smiled and thanked him for the cigarette.

After David left the room, I sank farther down into Mr. Winston's leather chair. Daddy had a deep, comfortable chair like this. I missed him so. I missed Momma too—or at least I missed the Momma I had before Daddy died. We'd made plenty of good memories together in those days. It hurt to think about our trips to the library every Saturday morning, and how she'd bake my favorite gingerbread with lemon sauce for every Sunday lunch during the winter.

I scooted up to the desk and stared at the telephone. Would the Winstons mind if I tried to call Momma? Would they even know? They're so rich, I mean *wealthy*, surely they wouldn't care. I lifted the receiver and dialed. The disk of circles turned around and around, clickity clack.

I sat up and listened intently. I had to tell Momma about Aunt Etta. I needed her to come back right away and help me. She didn't know the first thing about sewing gowns, but at least she could stay with me at Aunt Etta's. I couldn't do this alone.

The dial returned to its resting place and I heard a click, then a beep and a woman's voice, but it wasn't my mother's.

"Operator, may I help you?" she said.

"Oh, I must have misdialed," I replied.

"What telephone line are you trying to reach, dear?" said the switchboard operator.

"WNC-0204, ma'am."

"You dialed correctly, dear, but that number has been disconnected."

# Nine

I sat there in silence, trying to process everything. Momma had up and left me with the one person in this world who loved me, and that person was gravely ill and I had no way of helping her. Worse, now I was in charge of the most important dresses for the most important women for the most important event of the season. Ever since Momma woke me in the middle of the night, it's like I've been moving between dream and nightmare.

I looked around Mr. Winston's impressive study, taking in the rich, luxurious decor and finishes. I'd never been in a man's private study and I felt like an intruder. Picking up my satchel, I walked back to the more welcoming parlor to wait. I thumbed through Aunt Etta's *Dressmaker's Bible,* as she called it. Her soft leather sketchbook, it's spine cracked from years of use, was a treasure trove of sketches and design ideas, detailed notes on each and every client, and color names and numbers corresponding to her ring of fabric swatches. My stomach lurched at the list of appointments paper-clipped to the inside of the cover. Five wives, no *six*, this week, many names I didn't recognize. I closed the book and stared into space, too overwhelmed to even think about the task ahead of me.

After another hour or so passed, I heard the clacking of heels approaching. Mitzy breezed into the room, smiling as if everything was just peachy keen.

"Maddie," she cooed, pausing to consider me from across the room. "You poor dear. You must be worried sick." She placed her pink clutch on a chair and sat next to me on the sofa. "Don't you fret, sweetie. Everything is going to be just fine."

On the table in front of me sat the empty teapot, sugar dish, and cookie plate from this morning. I'd devoured everything while waiting for her to return. I had even gulped down the milk that had been laid out for the tea. It was warmish with a film on top from sitting out all morning, but at that point, I had stopped caring. I felt bloated and ugly, but I still sat up straight and tried to smile.

"You look like you need a hug, dear," she said. She turned to face me and spread her arms wide, motioning with her fingers moving as one, as if she were wearing mittens. I did as she asked and she squeezed me so tight I thought I'd cough up a cookie.

"I don't want you to worry about a single thing," she murmured. Her body was so close to mine that the crinoline beneath her skirt tickle-scratched my legs. "Your Aunt Etta will be just fine. I had a good talk with her, and she loved my little plan. Maddie," she said with a wide sparkling smile, "you'll stay here with me until Etta is well enough to have you back, or until you've finished the gowns for the gala."

Panic filled my chest. Stay here, in the Winstons' house?

"Now, at first, Etta said she wanted you to stay at her house alone, and then her friend Frances offered to have you come to her house, where she could be with you in the evenings. But I simply wouldn't hear of it. You're going through such a hard time with your mother—" At that she covered her mouth and cleared her throat. "Well, I just think you'd have a much better time staying here with me! It will be such fun, don't you think? We'll get you all set up and the wives can come here for their appointments and fittings. We wouldn't want things to get delayed for the big Gala, would we? And this way I can keep an eye on your progress, and what they're wearing too," she said with a wink.

"Thank you. That is very kind of you." I wanted to feel grateful, but I just felt strange. I could just as easily stay at Aunt Etta's by myself, and I'd be much more comfortable there. Maybe this would be fun for Mitzy, but for me, it was a bit dreadful to think I'd be staying in this museum of a house, where I couldn't even touch the banister for fear of leaving a handprint. And I couldn't explain it, but all Mitzy's enthusiasm was . . . off-putting. She behaved as though Aunt Etta's illness was a gift, as if I were a house guest instead of a charity case. There was something dishonest about it all, about her—a need underneath all that cheerfulness that made me want to run.

"Our home is yours, Maddie," she continued, with a little squeeze of my shoulder. "You can sleep in the Princess Rose Suite, and we'll set up a glorious work-room for you on the third floor." She stood and rested her index finger on her lips for a moment. "We can get a brand-new Singer sewing machine! I've always wanted to have one in the house. Perhaps I might want to do some sewing of my own, little blankets or hats," she said with a tinkling laugh, then clapped her hands and twisted her hips back and forth, her skirt flaring around her in a happy little swish.

My uncertainty must have shown on my face be-cause she stopped her dance and frowned, folding her hands in front of her. "What's wrong, dear? Don't you want to stay with us?"

I felt a pang, a tiny warning inside.

"Of course I do. It's just so generous of you." I forced my face to light up. "But . . . I'm terribly nervous about Aunt Etta. She's never sick, and it sounds serious."

"I know, honey, it is worrying. But she's in good hands with Dr. Hale."

"Then there's all that sewing. What if I'm—" What if I'm not up to it, was what I wanted to say. But I couldn't get the words out.

Mitzy softened.

"Here, lie down, dear." She patted the sofa cushion. "You must be exhausted from all the commotion." Then she undid the smart gold clasp on her purse and pulled out two crinkle-wrapped pieces of butterscotch, which she pressed into my hand with a wink. I thanked her but didn't say what I was really thinking—that I wasn't a little kid and it would take more than candy to fix things.

"I just know that Etta will make a full recovery," she insisted, stroking my forehead like I was a toddler. "Tomorrow you can get everything organized after your appointment with Cornelia and Rose."

Mitzy pulled open the small drawer of a nearby end table and retrieved a cigarette case and pink-and-gold lighter. She flicked it open, puckered, and her cheek-bones became momentarily more pronounced as she drew in a deep breath.

"You just rest here awhile, and I'll arrange a special dinner for us. I already telephoned Cook to come in after all." With that, she click-clacked her way out of the room.

**I assumed** it would be just the two of us at dinner, so I was startled to see Mr. Winston in a majestic high-backed chair, his metal crutches leaning against the wall behind him. He looked different with his spindly legs tucked under the table. Larger somehow. I guessed it was the way his bullfrog face bloomed pink against his buttoned-up collar, how the flesh on his neck pressed against the edge of the stiff white fabric.

Mitzy strode over to him and gave him a flirty peck on the cheek. "Good evening, Mr. Winston."

"Good evening, darling." His gentleman's voice had a refined quality, different from the twangy accents I was used to. "This must be the young lady you've been talking up such a storm about." He smiled at me kindly, then took a long swallow of his drink.

"Yes, I've just been dying for you to meet her! Maddie, dear, come over here and say hello to the man of the house."

Before I could make my way to the head of the table, Mr. Winston waved me off.

"No need for formalities, Elizabeth. Just have a seat, Matleigh. Both of you girls have a seat and get comfortable. Is David joining us?"

"No dear," Mitzy said. "He's taking dinner in the guesthouse so he can work on his paper." She glanced at me apologetically. "Richard, it's Maddie, not Matleigh. Her name is Maddie. Short for Madeline, I suppose?"

"Yes, ma'am," I said.

"Of course, of course. My apologies, ladies. I've had a real bear of a day—and like the beast that I am, I won't be able to think properly until I've been fed." Mr. Winston shook the ice in his glass, took another sip, and put a cigar in his mouth.

Mitzy laughed, but I could tell she was uneasy about something.

Mitzy's place was opposite him at the other end of the long table, with a considerable distance between them, four empty chairs on each side. A place setting was waiting for me right next to Mitzy. As she took her seat, she picked up an ivory-colored napkin from the table and shook the cloth open with a flick of her wrist. I copied what she had done, which prompted an encouraging smile.

Mr. Winston checked his pocket watch and sipped his drink.

Mitzy scooted herself up to the table and rested her forearms on it, her hands clasped in front of her. "Thank you so much for coming home early to have dinner with us," she said.

"Anything for you, my sweet. But I'm sorry to say, I can't stay long. We have an emergency board meeting tonight." He reached for a roll and ripped it roughly in half.

"Again?" she asked, adjusting her silverware so that it lined up perfectly.

"I'm afraid so," he replied.

I took in the neatly arranged plates and forks in front of me, glasses and knives and spoons of every size too, arranged just so. There was more china and silverware at this table than we had in our whole kitchen back home. The tablecloth and dishware were ivory, the plates featuring delicate clusters of painted flowers. The rim of each glass was circled with a thin line of gold.

"That's the second meeting this month. Are the women at the factory making trouble again?" asked Mitzy, reaching for her water glass.

"Something like that," Mr. Winston replied. "Nothing I can't handle, my pet. Now, let's not give ourselves indigestion by talking business during dinner. I don't want you getting yourself worked up—especially not about factory nonsense. You let me worry about production, and you focus on selling MOMints with that pretty little face of yours."

Mitzy blushed and replaced her water glass. "Well, if you decide you'd like a woman's perspective, Ashley would love to attend a board meeting," she said. "And you know all too well that Cornelia hasn't stopped grumbling about being passed over for Augustus's seat. She fully expected to inherit it. Ashley and Cornelia are very smart, so if the ladies are grumbling . . ."

He chuckled at this.

"No, dear. Having women in the factories is a large part of the problem. We certainly don't need any women in the boardroom."

Mitzy shifted in her seat.

Aunt Etta had described Mitzy as one of the most powerful women in Bright Leaf, but here she was, staring at her plate like a scolded child, every bit as dependent on her husband as Momma was on Daddy.

I reached for my water glass and took a sip. It was nice and cold, even though there wasn't any ice in it. I placed it back down, and Mitzy cleared her throat.

"Maddie, sweetheart, replace the water glass where it belongs," she whispered. "Up here, at two o'clock.

Where two o'clock would be on a watch face." She seemed to have recovered from Mr. Winston putting her in her place.

I'd eaten in nice restaurants on occasion. I knew what a salad fork was. But I'd never seen a table set like this. She must have noticed me gawking at the elaborate display because she proceeded to explain it to me.

Mr. Winston puffed out his chest. "Nobody knows her way around table settings like my Elizabeth," he said. "You're learning from the best." Buoyed by his compliment, she explained every single item at my place setting. When she finished, she said, "I do want to warn you, Maddie—there's one thing you'll see on my table that isn't strictly traditional. You may have noticed my dinner setting includes a cup and saucer. Usually, those aren't placed until the dessert course, but Richard likes his coffee right after he takes his last bite of the main course, isn't that right, dear?"

He smiled, his mouth full of bread, and said, "She knows just how I like things."

While Mitzy explained the table setting, two uniformed servants scurried in and out of the room, replacing our "just-for-show" plates with identical piping-hot china dishes filled with food.

My plate was warmed to such a blistering temperature that the woman who set it in front of me warned

166 · ADELE MYERS

me twice not to touch it until it had cooled. My mouth watered at the sight of steak, a baked potato, fresh creamed corn, green beans, and sautéed apples too. I felt a little twinge of guilt though. What if the soldiers didn't have enough to eat and here I was, eating this grand meal? I glanced at Mitzy. She prided herself on being so generous, but she sure didn't seem to be sacrificing much for the boys overseas.

I waited patiently as my plate cooled down, listening to Mitzy chatter on about table settings, when suddenly, she jumped out of her seat and yelled.

"Oh my Lord, oh, I burned myself," she said, flapping her hands and looking frantically around the room.

The young woman who had delivered the too-hot plate looked almost as pained as Mitzy. She grabbed the butter dish and placed the cold yellow stick directly on the burn. I stood and dunked my napkin in water, holding it at the ready.

"Sweet Jesus, Elizabeth! What have you done to yourself?" Mr. Winston twisted in his chair this way and that in an effort to retrieve his crutches, but they eluded his reach. I thought about grabbing them for him but worried that my good intentions would make things worse. He didn't seem like the kind of man who wanted help from a girl. Mr. Winston made one last failed attempt to pull himself to standing before Mitzy noticed what he was up to and warned him, in a sharp tone, to stay seated.

"We don't need you to injure yourself too, Richard," she tutted. This was clearly the wrong thing to say, and Mr. Winston's face flushed bright with humiliation. When she realized what she'd done, Mitzy could only stammer and backpedal. "There's no use in getting a better look to see what a dunce I am. I ought to know better."

Mitzy held up both of her palms for us to examine, displaying a matched set of angry, crimson welts. Everyone in the room winced and made soothing remarks, even Mr. Winston.

"How stupid of me." She sighed. "Now please, eat," she said, gesturing toward me and Mr. Winston. "Don't let your supper get cold on account of my clumsiness."

"Well, I guess you'll be wearing gloves for the big Gala this year," Mr. Winston said with a chuckle, the mood softening. "We can't have you looking like you've been stemming tobacco."

I thought of the woman I'd seen in the break room at the factory, the beautiful woman with blisters all over her wrists and palms, and then I did something Aunt Etta had warned me not to do.

I said what I was thinking.

"Maybe if the women stemming tobacco at the factory had gloves, their hands wouldn't look like that either." I'd shocked all three of us. Even the servers stopped what they were doing and stared. "I could do it . . . make gloves for them," I kept going. "I could sew them myself."

I clamped my mouth shut then, not sure how or why I allowed myself to say such things.

Mr. Winston put down his knife and fork and leaned up in his chair. This was the first time all night he looked me right in the eye.

"That won't be necessary, Matleigh," he said, clearing his throat. "The men will be back soon enough, and then all the little ladies currently in my employ can get on back home where they belong."

With that, he wiped his mouth, slapped his dirtied napkin on the table, and turned to the man standing in the corner of the room. "Have Isaac bring the car around," he said, "I have to get back to work."

What on earth had gotten into me? I stole a glance at Mitzy, but the scowl I had been expecting turned out to be the tiniest hint of a smile.

With the man's help, Mr. Winston pulled himself up to standing and steadied himself on his metal crutches. He slipped them around his forearms and clattered toward the door. Mitzy began to stand too, holding the stick of butter in one hand and the wet ivory napkin in the other.

Mr. Winston made his way across the room and leaned down to kiss her. "Don't wait up, darling. It's going to be a long night." Then he looked toward me and said, "You'll take care of her, young lady, won't you?"

**Mitzy seemed** more concerned about disrupting dinner than she did about the burns on her hands. "I'm so sorry, Maddie," she said again, after we'd finished eating. "I completely ruined our meal."

"You don't have to apologize. Gosh, Miss Mitzy, dinner was wonderful, the best I've had in a very long time . . . but your hands!" I said. They looked sunburned and swollen, as if they might blister. How someone could have such throbbing pain and still play the hostess was beyond me. As to whether she was being brave or foolish, well, I couldn't figure that out either.

"Aren't you sweet," she said. "But don't worry about me, dear. I'll be fine. Really I will." She shifted in her seat and examined the bright red welts on her palms more closely. "It's nothing that a little Smith's Ointment can't fix right up. I have some upstairs. Why don't you follow me up and I can show you to your room?"

We stopped at the parlor so I could retrieve Aunt Etta's sewing box and my satchel, then made our way up the grand staircase. I trailed Mitzy as she climbed each stair with care. From this angle, her feet looked smaller than mine. Her ankles too were slim and delicate, like her wrists. Small boned, some would say.

"My bedroom is just down that hallway there," Mitzy said, catching her breath when we got to the top. She pointed with her whole hand, still wrapped in a damp dinner napkin, and smiled at me sweetly. "Your room is right through this corridor here. The Princess Rose Suite. I do hope you'll like it."

"I'm sure I will," I said, excitement building. As we approached the door—cream colored with a coral rose hand painted in the center—it occurred to me that I would have my own bedroom and bathroom, like in a fancy hotel. I couldn't believe it. I'd always wanted to stay in a hotel, but there was never any reason. Never any money, either.

"Would you mind, dear?" Mitzy held up her hands as she pointed to the cut crystal doorknob that looked like a jewel.

"Oh! Of course," I said. The doorknob was cool to the touch and turned easily with a click. I held the door for Mitzy then followed her inside. I gasped. It was like stepping into a real-life fairy tale.

When Mitzy described the Princess Rose Suite, I had pictured an all-pink room with ruffles and a canopy bed, a girly dream-come-true like the ones I'd seen in the Sears-Roebuck catalog. But this was better than I ever could have imagined.

I stood in the center of the room, taking it all in. The colors were feminine, but refined—ivory, pale yellow, the palest pinks, and hints of green. You could see the care that had gone into selecting each item, like the ivory armoire with three oval mirrors, the one in the middle full length. Or the vanity table laid with a small vase of salmon-colored roses, a silver hairbrush, and three glass perfume bottles with tassels hanging from their necks.

"May I?" I asked, gesturing to the perfume.

"Of course, dear. Why don't you try them all?"

I walked to the vanity and smelled each one—the first was lemongrass, the second smelled sweet, like honeysuckle, and the last was rosewater. I sprayed the rosewater on my throat and wrist, breathed it in so deep I could taste it. Rosewater was Momma's favorite, but this was different from the bottle on her dressing table—fresher, more alive, the smell of honest-to-goodness rose petals.

"You just make yourself at home, Maddie," Mitzy said. She breezed around the room, inspecting the surroundings. "Richard wanted to put air conditioners in all the bedrooms," she said as she opened a large bay window across from the bed. "But I much prefer natural air, don't you?" Before I could answer, she crossed the room to inspect the rest of the suite. "There are fresh towels and some lovely scented soaps in the bathroom."

I stood in the center of the room, mesmerized as she described what would be mine for days, maybe weeks. Staying here suddenly struck me as a glorious vacation, the silver lining to a dark cloud. I couldn't wait to tell April about everything, about how I was whisked away to Aunt Etta's, then ended up here in this . . .

Aunt Etta.

Here I was, whooping it up in luxury and there she was, dangerously sick, lying in a scratchy hospital bed with only her worry for company. But what could I do? Aunt Etta was getting the very best care. It would be only for a short time. I'd do my best for my aunt. I could help her like she helped me. Yes, that's what I'd do.

"If you need anything at all, just ring downstairs," Mitzy said. "The house phone is there on the bedside table and reaches Ruth and Isaac directly. No outside calls, I'm afraid, but if you'd like to call Etta tomorrow, you can always use the parlor telephone downstairs."

With that, she wished me good night and excused herself to tend to her hands and turn in for the evening. We'd both had quite an eventful day and could use a good night's rest.

I waited until the sound of her footsteps had faded before letting out a little squeal and throwing myself on the enormous bed. The focal point of the room, it was large and luxurious, covered with pillows and surrounded by curtains that poured from the high ceiling to the floor behind the headboard. Sheer drapes that framed the large bay window floated as the early evening air breathed in and out.

I tested the firmness of the mattress with my hand, then bounced gently up and down. I brought a pillow to my nose and let myself fall back and close my eyes, letting my feet dangle over the side. A light breeze rolled over me and I opened my eyes to see above me a crystal chandelier stirring gently, making the slightest tinkling sound. My heart felt full, brimming over, excited. I sat up, hopped off the bed, and grabbed my satchel to explore the rest of the room, half in disbelief that there was yet more to be discovered.

Double doors led to a bathroom and a boudoir the size of my bedroom back home. On the vanity in the bathroom was an open hatbox brimming over with soaps, shampoos, a tin of rouge, and a new set of Mason

Pearson tortoiseshell combs. A stack of pale blue towels sat on the edge of the bathtub. A white cotton nightgown hung on the back of the bathroom door. Mitzy had insisted that I not only borrow it for one night but also keep it even after collecting my clothes tomorrow. *Consider it a little gift, from me to you,* she said. Everywhere I looked was alive with attention and detail. I sighed and admired the deep, claw-foot tub. A bath would be heavenly right now.

I slipped out of my clothes and ran the water as hot as I could stand, dropped a few rose-shaped bath soaps under the tap, and eased myself in. The fragrant bubbles blossomed as they spread themselves out on top of the surface. I sank under the steaming water up to my neck, then lowered myself farther so that my ears and mouth were just under the suds. My hair fanned out and floated around my face. Being here was like a dream, a sweet-smelling, far-from-the-Holler dream. Sitting in this tub made me feel like a movie star.

Closing my eyes, I listened to each breath flowing in and out, and talked to myself in soothing tones. I'd make Aunt Etta proud. I was nervous, but this was only temporary, after all. Everything would be fine.

I sat up to wash, satisfied and at peace, and noticed that there was dirt or tobacco—something—under two of my fingernails. A straight pin would do the trick. I reached for my satchel and as I pulled it toward me, all the contents dumped onto the floor. On top of the pile was the envelope with the hospital telephone number on it, and when I lifted it to see if the pins were underneath, water droplets fell on the paper, smudging the number.

"Shoot," I said, examining it quickly while I could still make out the numbers. I'd best memorize them. But as I held it, repeating the digits out loud, the weight in my hand revealed that the envelope I had pulled from Mr. Winston's trash wasn't empty after all. There was something inside. I turned it over to see the word CONFIDENTIAL stamped in red on the front, along with Mr. Winston's name written in black ink and an embossed name and address in the upper-left corner. *Dr. Robert Hale, M.D.* it said, along with a Bright Leaf address. My mouth fell open and I glanced around the bathroom, as if I'd been caught stealing. I didn't take it on purpose though. And I hadn't read it. So actually I didn't do anything wrong. But still, having a letter that belonged to an important man made me feel guilty and uneasy.

Steam rose from the bath as I sat holding the envelope, considering my options. The paper puckered at the corners from the damp heat. Maybe it wouldn't be so bad if I just took a little peek. He threw it away after all. It's not like he'd miss it.

No, I couldn't do that. I shouldn't. This wasn't like poking around in someone's bathroom to see if they had any nice shampoo or Lux soap. This was personal. Confidential. Tomorrow I would take it back to where I found it, discard it in Mr. Winston's trash, and be none the wiser. I placed the envelope on a dry spot next to my satchel and returned my attention to my bath.

Rose-shaped soaps floated around me, perfuming the air with the sweet smell of flowers. I reached for one and it felt slightly gritty. When I took a closer look, I saw that its waxy pinkness was dotted with dark specks. It wasn't just the soap; they were everywhere, those nasty pinpoints—floating atop the bubbles, gathering at the waterline on the sides of the tub. Somehow, even though I'd washed off after the Solstice last night, tobacco dust still clung to me. Aunt Etta sure was right when she said everybody in Bright Leaf lived and breathed tobacco.

# Ten

I sat up in bed at the sound of a light knock on the door. Ruth, the same maid who had greeted Aunt Etta and me a few days earlier, came in with a breakfast tray.

"Good morning, Miss Maddie," she said as she placed the tray on the table by the window and handed me a telephone message.

It was from Frances and said that despite her high fever, Aunt Etta had slept through the night in relative comfort. I should try my best not to feel anxious. I let out a big rush of air. That was good news.

The message also said that Frances would meet me at Aunt Etta's house on her lunch break today and fill me in further. And the best news of all, that Anthony would be joining me for the 8:30 A.M. appointment at Cornelia's house. The thought of meeting with that grumpy old lady in her own home scared me. People were more comfortable in their own homes. *Home field advantage,* Daddy would have said, and I had a feeling that Cornelia would be even more difficult on her own turf. What a relief that Anthony would be helping me.

I thanked Ruth for the update. I hoped she would stay for a few minutes to chat, but before I could strike up a conversation, she swept out of the room with a wave.

I felt unsteady as I got to my feet. After my bath last night, I had climbed into the welcoming bed to study Aunt Etta's *Dressmaker's Bible.* I intended to prepare for today's appointment, but instead drifted off almost immediately and awoke to the sun streaming in through the bay window, the book open on my chest.

I dressed quickly, grabbed my sewing satchel, and placed the sketches I'd removed from Aunt Etta's book inside before walking downstairs. In the grand foyer stood Anthony, rifling through his bag, looking flashy in a royal blue suit with wide-leg pants pulled up high at the waist. A colorful handkerchief stood at attention in his breast pocket.

"Anthony!" I said hurrying toward him. "I'm so excited . . . and nervous . . . and relieved." I whispered the last part. "Thank goodness you're coming with me to Cornelia's."

"Morning, sunshine! I'm excited too!" Anthony gave me a quick peek on each cheek but remained focused on looking for something in his bag. "I can't say I'm not anxious about dealing with the old broad. Who wouldn't be? Honestly, I'm as nervous as a long-tailed cat in—"

"I know," I said, laughing. "In a room full of rocking chairs."

"All the same, I understand how to deal with all types. Besides, Rose and I are already acquainted, so that should help. Enough gabbing for now. We really should get going."

"Yes, of course," I said. "Frances's note said it's a short walk, but I don't want to be late."

"There it is," he said and closed his bag. "Phew. I thought I'd left my fabric samples at home." He looked at me then as if he'd just seen me.

"Honey, good Lord," he exclaimed. "What happened to you?"

I glanced down at my dress, the same simple white eyelet I had worn yesterday. "I hoped this would be all right."

"The dress is okay, I suppose," Anthony said. "It's your hair that's all cockeyed."

Whenever I fall asleep with wet hair, it's always a bit wild in the morning. I tried as best I could to smooth it with some setting cream and a comb, but it stuck out every which way.

Anthony reached into his bag and pulled out a scarf. "Here," he said, offering it to me. "Wear this on the walk over. It'll tame those crazy curls by the time we arrive."

"No thank you. I'd rather eat dirt than wear a kerchief."

Anthony cocked an eyebrow. "Somebody woke up on the wrong side of the fancy bed this morning."

"I'm sorry," I said to him. I truly was. He was only trying to help. "I just hate to cover my hair."

"Alrighty then," he said, a little uneasily. "Better cover up that attitude before we get to Cornelia's house, though. She won't stand for it."

"I'll work on the attitude—and the Medusa hairdo too," I promised. "Should I braid it?"

Anthony suggested something more grown-up, like a topknot or a low chignon. I nodded, twisting my ringlets into place for his approval.

"Yes, *muuuch* better. Now, I have the fabric samples," he said. "But you have the sketches and patterns your aunt set aside, right?"

"Yes," I said, rummaging around in my bag. "Yes, they're here. Aunt Etta had me grab some patterns when we came over yesterday morning. I haven't had a chance to go through them, but these are the ones she set aside for the wives. And I have her sketches of course."

Anthony said *wonderful,* that between the two of us, we'd impress old Cornelia and Rose too. "You should do most of the talking though, honey," he said. "You're the one who is officially in charge, not me." Anthony elbowed me in the side and chuckled, but there was an edge to his voice. He had far more experience with evening wear than I did, and yet Aunt Etta passed him over to put me in charge. It hadn't occurred to me before, that he might feel slighted, even jealous of my new position. I hoped it wouldn't come between us. He was my one friend in Bright Leaf, and I needed him.

As we walked I told Anthony that I'd learned from Aunt Etta's bible that Cornelia tended to wear the same tailored style every year—a long skirt and fitted jacket. Of course, this year I supposed it would be mauve. I continued, filling him in on the notes on Rose. "Obsessed with Veronica Lake" Aunt Etta had written next to her name. I thought of the slinky, low-cut number that Miss Lake wore in *The Blue Dahlia.* That shouldn't be too hard to execute. I'd been wanting to try a technique I'd read about in one of Aunt Etta's magazines that would do the trick. It was first used by a woman named Madame Grès, who designed dresses for famous people like Grace Kelly and was known for her draping and pleats. I told Anthony about the article I'd read.

"That sounds divine," Anthony said. "And Etta's plans for Cornelia and Rose are almost exactly what I had in mind for them! I'd like to say I'm a genius, but the truth is those two are quite predictable, when it comes to their formal wear, that is. I've worked on their Gala gowns before, always behind the scenes mind you, but I know what they like."

"Oh, that's good," I said, though I still felt jittery. As Anthony and I turned onto the already warm road that Cornelia lived on, I tried to focus on the view around me: the grand homes with lush lawns, majestic trees, and tidy beds of hot pink azaleas.

Anthony talked the rest of the way, explaining how we could "divide and conquer." Unless you were Aunt Etta, I well knew, a month was barely enough time to construct all the gowns. He was relieved when I told him that Aunt Etta had gotten a head start on the most important work, but it wasn't just Mitzy, Cornelia, and Rose; there were other Bright Leaf socialites who needed tending to.

"Oh, you mean the second-tier wives?" Anthony asked. "I helped Etta with those last year." He explained what he meant by *second tier*—that's how he referred to them, as if they were farther away from the stage. These women were married to the less important Bright Leaf executives, and nearly all of them bought ready-to-wear, thank goodness. Still, there were special flourishes to help these cookie-cutter dresses stand out, not to mention alterations so that their gowns would appear tailor-made. Etta was a genius at fitting women who were shorter or taller or skinnier or fatter than the sample size. And she knew their bodies from years of working with them, so she understood what to do to make everyone feel glamorous. We would somehow have to do the same.

"Well, here we are," Anthony said, checking the address on a piece of paper. We had come to a giant dollhouse. At least that's what it looked like to me.

"Wow," I said. I'd never seen another home like it anywhere. "It's not at all what I imagined."

"Me neither," Anthony agreed. "I can't believe that old bag lives here! Look at that gingerbread trim and the stained-glass windows. Aren't those to die for? It's the house the witch in Hansel and Gretel would build if she were sitting on a gold mine."

Most of the mansions I'd seen were white with big columns or redbrick with black shutters—big, bold places that told you wealthy people lived there. But Cornelia's house confused me. Robin's-egg blue with white and red trim, the Victorian was bright and cheerful—welcoming, even. I would have expected something cold and gray like her.

Anthony straightened his jacket and made sure his pocket square looked just right, then cleared his throat and gave me the once-over. "Eyelet is a little young for you, Maddie. All the girls here, the ones around your age, wear blouses and skirts now. But this will do well enough for the moment."

*So much for feeling confident,* I thought. April and the rest of the girls I knew back home all wore eyelet in the summer. I shrugged and made a mental note to be more selective with my outfits while here in Bright Leaf.

I took a deep breath and rang the doorbell, smiling nervously at Anthony.

A petite, elderly maid opened the door and right behind her stood Rose, teetering on a pair of peep-toe heels. It was as if she had been waiting in the foyer for our arrival. I took in her outfit and tried not to stare. The style of her stiff poplin day dress may have been appropriate for receiving morning company, but its lush red color and daring neckline seemed more appropriate for a film siren than for a doctor's wife.

"Well, it's about time y'all got here!" she crooned, her heavy mascara giving her a wide-eyed look. "Mother's in quite a mood." She motioned with her head behind her. "When she heard how sick Etta is, she started calling all over, even her friends in Atlanta, trying to find another seamstress. She was furious that they were all booked though. 'Well, Mother,' I told her. 'It is Gala season, after all. What do you expect?'" Lowering her voice she said, "I sure hope y'all don't bungle things up."

"What are you telling them, Rose?" Cornelia bellowed. "Close that door for God's sake. You'll let in those bothersome horseflies again."

Rose tsked and took a puff of her cigarette. "I hope you've had an extra cup of coffee today, Maddie," she whispered, putting her arm around me. "She's on the warpath."

Anthony and I followed Rose into a large sitting room filled to brimming with antiques, dour paintings of milkmaids and horses, and rows and rows of books. Just the kind of dark and forbidding place a cranky old lady would like. Now, this was more like it.

The woman herself sat on the edge of a wingback chair like an ancient queen, her back straight and her lips pressed into a flat line that was only a heartbeat away from a scowl. I got the feeling she was rooting for us to fail.

"Miss Cornelia!" Anthony exclaimed. "Don't you look lovely this fine morning!" He walked over and reached for her hand, which, to my surprise, she offered. Anthony bent at the waist and kissed the wrinkly top of it.

I stood behind him, waiting for them to finish.

"Good morning, ma'am," I said, offering a half-dip curtsey and bowing my head.

"Good God, child," she said. "Stand up straight. I'm not the Princess Elizabeth."

I felt like an idiot. I had no idea how to act around these women.

"Well, you are the closest that Bright Leaf has to royalty, Miss Cornelia," said Anthony. "And I'm not talking about a figurehead either," he continued, turning to me. "Miss Cornelia here practically founded this town, but she's too modest to say so."

A small smile bloomed on Cornelia's face, and I saw for the first time that she must have been an attractive young woman. She had thin, fine features, and a high forehead—a regal presence.

Cornelia rose from her chair, steadying herself by holding the arm.

"Let's get on with it, shall we? I have business to attend to, and I'm sure Rose needs to get back to applying more rouge or having her hair dyed or whatnot."

Rose glanced at us with a defeated look. *Do you see what I have to deal with,* her wide eyes said.

"Yes, let's get on with it," I said in my clearest, most confident voice. I shook off my foolish curtsey and decided to act as if I knew what I was doing. It was a trick Daddy had taught me the first time I had to give an oral book report at school. I tried to practice my speech in front of him the night before the assignment was due, and even though I'd prepared for days, I could barely get a word out. My hands and voice shook so bad that I started to cry. I was devastated. If I couldn't sound right in front of my own father—the easiest audience in the world—what hope did I have for doing well in front of the class?

"Shug, you just have to act as *if*," he said, dabbing at my tears with his handkerchief. "You act *as if* you are confident. Act *as if* you are calm and assured. Act *as if* and so it will be."

*Act as if and so it will be*, I thought.

Cornelia responded with a simple "good," then said, "let's assemble in the dining room. We can discuss designs and you can present your sketches there."

I did my best to tamp down my fears.

"You do have sketches, don't you?" Cornelia looked from me to Anthony and back again. I froze and instead of taking charge like I wanted to, let Anthony answer her question.

"We certainly do, Miss Cornelia," Anthony said.

"We have sketches and all the latest fabric samples and patterns. Maddie has worked with Etta on Gala gowns for a few years now. It's become her specialty. You're in good hands. You'll see."

The blood drained from my face. I wouldn't say that Gala gowns are my specialty by any means, and here was Anthony raising their expectations.

We followed the women into the dining room; Rose pulled out a chair for me.

"Here, darlin,' you park your caboose right here next to Miss Rose."

Something about the way she referred to herself as "Miss Rose" put me on edge, as if a mere pronoun wasn't enough for her. My mother would do that too, look for little ways to set herself apart and above, put you in your place. *What place would that be?* I had always wanted to ask.

"I'm curious to see what you two dolls have planned," said Rose. "But I brought my ideas along this time." She pointed one red fingernail to a leather portfolio. "I have at least ten pictures here from *Photoplay* and even more from *Screen Book*. I'm leaving nothing to chance." She tapped an inch of ash from her cigarette onto a dish on the table.

"That's *not* an ashtray," Cornelia snapped.

"Oh, for goodness' sake," said Rose. "Who can possibly tell what's what around here? Everything in this old mausoleum looks like an ashtray!" Rose sashayed into the adjoining room and returned with a heavy crystal ashtray that she placed in front of us with a defiant little thud.

Difficult women indeed. Aunt Etta wasn't kidding.

"Well, I, for one, am tickled pink that we'll be sewing for you lovely ladies," said Anthony. "I am just dying to see what's in that folder. But why don't we start with the basics? Maddie, let's begin with the patterns you brought. Then we'll look at the sketches and we can go from there."

I slipped my hand into my satchel to retrieve the patterns and realized I'd forgotten to return the envelope to Mr. Winston's study. I quickly shoved it into my bag's inner side pocket and pulled out the stack of patterns. As I arranged the rectangular bundles on the table, I saw, to my horror, that I'd brought the wrong ones.

Each package was topped with a sketch of the finished garment you could expect to make if you followed the pattern inside. But only one of the drawings showed ladies dressed in evening gowns. They were lovely, that's for sure—two sleek blondes in silver and gold numbers that would have suited Rose nicely. But the other patterns—all of them—featured coats and heavy-duty day dresses, drab garments suitable for housewives and factory workers. The one nearest to Miss Rose showed a pattern for a sack dress made from grain bags, a clever innovation that had become popular after we joined the war in Europe. Fabric was scarce, and the colorful bags made a fashionable substitute for ladies who couldn't afford better. But Rose and Cornelia *could absolutely* afford better.

I tried to spirit the bundles away before either of the ladies got a good look, but it was too late.

"Oh, my lands," Cornelia said, sputtering through a fit of hearty laughter, "I'm suddenly having so much fun!" She was in a state of near apoplexy. It was as if one of those stern old paintings had come to life before my eyes. I'd never seen anything like it.

Rose was affronted. "Why in heavens would you put this thing next to *me*?" she hissed. "How could you think I'd ever wear such a cheap cracker dress?" She shook the pattern in my face. "Don't you know who I am?"

Cornelia continued laughing. "It appears the child knows exactly who you are, my dear."

"Mother!"

Rose tossed the pattern on the table and reached for another, this one for women's uniforms.

"Maddie, I'll have you know that I am a doctor's wife, not some white trash factory drudge!"

Her comment fell like a stone. Cornelia stopped laughing. Anthony and I were silent.

Momma would call people who lived behind the paper plant back home white trash, but it was a dirty insult, and Daddy made sure those words never left my mouth. Momma liked to say those families were too lazy and shifty to hold a regular job, but even she wouldn't have talked bad about the men and women who worked on the Bright Leaf line. Everyone agreed that factory work was a respectable way to earn a paycheck.

Anthony cleared his throat and quietly took out a stack of fabrics held together with a large silver ring. He looked a bit defeated, his "light," as he called it, dimmed by Rose's snide comment.

"I'll have you know that there is plenty of honor in field and factory work," thundered Cornelia. "Self-sufficiency, a sense of pride in one's contributions to the community—these are virtues to be valued. The pampered life of an idle housewife, now that's another matter entirely."

Rose stubbed out her cigarette, staring into the ashtray as she ground the butt down to the filter, over and over, far longer than necessary.

"Why don't we put these away," Anthony said evenly, gathering the patterns and placing them on the floor, "and take a look at the sketches instead." He nodded to me and I retrieved the pages I'd brought from Aunt Etta's book from my bag. I placed them on the table for the ladies to examine—on the left, a short jacket with shoulder pads and a tulip-shaped satin skirt for Cornelia. On the right, a clingy, floor-length gown with a plunging neckline and ruching to further accentuate the bust for Rose.

The women were silent for a few moments. "This one would be lovely in silver," Anthony said, pointing to the gown for Rose and flipping through his ring of fabric samples.

"Hmm," Rose replied, leaning over to study the drawing. "I like the dress, but I'm surprised you're suggesting silver. Don't y'all remember I just wore silver for the Solstice?" She took the ring of fabrics from Anthony and flipped through. "Is this gold lamé?" she asked, holding the shiniest sample against her cheek. "Oh, yes this is more like it. I just have to have this. So glamorous!" She left behind a smear of porcelain face powder, her very own holy shroud. "But can you add a side slit to the dress? On second thought, how about a high slit on each side. Why would I want to hide these gorgeous gams?" She laughed as she positioned her legs to the side of her chair where we could get a good look, her toes pointed like a ballet dancer. Anthony nodded, writing down quick notes.

Cornelia rolled her eyes then leaned up in her chair and peered over at her sketch. "The garment is fine. Etta knows what I like. It's the execution in her absence that I'm concerned about. And where are the ideas for my hat?"

I froze. Aunt Etta must not have gotten to thinking about Cornelia's hat yet.

"What about a pillbox," Anthony offered, eyeing me uneasily. "Or a turban. Those are oh so chic."

Cornelia turned to me sharply. "Well . . . did you bring ideas for my hat or not?" she asked. "Do you have anything at all to contribute?" Before I could answer, she pivoted to address Anthony. "If the girl has no ideas, why is she even here?"

I cleared my throat and sat up tall. *Act as if,* Maddie, *act as if.*

"I have ideas," I said. "I have plenty of ideas." All three of them stared at me expectantly. I felt Anthony willing me to say something smart.

"For instance," I said shakily, "why not make your skirt into a flowing pair of wide-leg trousers that appear to be a skirt, but are far more comfortable? If we leave the design as it is, it will be pretty, but you'll have to suffer a bit for the look—especially if we line the interior of the skirt with enough crinoline to define it properly. You'll have to wear a bulky tulle petticoat that will feel scratchy all night long. I wouldn't recommend it if you have sensitive skin. Now, if you're still set on a traditional skirt, we might try reworking the lower half of the dress into a fitted column—though, of course, that change would require you to wear a special girdle to maintain the long line. And we all know how painful a strong girdle can be." I tsked, growing more confident as I held their attention. "For my money, the trousers are the smart choice. Why should men be the only ones to dress in comfort at parties?"

Cornelia studied me. I feared I'd overstepped, misread her, and embarrassed myself by suggesting she dress like a man. But she nodded, almost imperceptibly at first, then with a more pronounced bend in her neck.

"I like that," she said. "I do indeed like that very much. But, make sure that the fabric you've chosen dyes well," Cornelia warned us.

"Mauve again?" Rose asked glumly, lighting another cigarette.

"Yes, the orders for mauve dye are starting to roll in from the women in my bridge club, as well as the more mature ladies on the hospital committee," she said. "As I've told you many times, Rose, I shall wear mauve exclusively until I've hooked every woman in town over the age of fifty. Then on to the next trend from Paris."

So the mauve-only outfits were part of a business venture, not some cockamamie obsession. Aunt Etta did say that in addition to her tobacco holdings, Cornelia owned textiles mills across North Carolina. I didn't know that she sold dyes too. It was a brilliant idea, especially since all the ladies looked to Paris trends. Now that I thought about it, purple was highly coveted and difficult to find. The old lady knew what she was doing. I saw Cornelia differently at that moment, and she stared right back at me, unflinching. After a few long seconds, she scooted her chair back and stood. "We're finished here." She waved her hand dismissively toward the sketches and fabrics and began to make her way to the door.

"Thank you so much," Anthony called after her. He and I got up and began to gather our things. "I'll get right to work on a hat design for you, Miss Cornelia," he promised.

Cornelia stopped and turned around, pausing a moment before she spoke. "Have the girl design a suitable hat. I'd like to see what she can do."

The girl. She'd called me *the girl* again, but she wanted me to design her hat.

"Yes, ma'am," I said brightly. I couldn't help but

grin from ear to ear. I'd pleased this impossibly difficult woman and recovered from the awful misstep with
the patterns.

Rose remained seated at the table, eyeing her
mother-in-law as she smoked.

"Oh—I have a book that you may find of interest,
Maddie," Cornelia added. "I'll have my maid bring it
to you before you leave."

I glanced at Anthony, who looked as surprised as
I was.

"Yes, ma'am," I said again. "Thank you. I'll take
good care of it."

"I expect nothing less," said Cornelia, then she left
the room.

# Eleven

W e did it!" Anthony said, beaming at me. We had waited until the house was well behind us before letting our thoughts tumble out. Then we started talking so fast we tripped all over each other.

"Just barely!" I laughed. "I thought I'd faint when Rose started screaming about that awful feed bag dress. Thank goodness you were there."

"Oh my God, her face! She looked like she'd discovered a bee in her banana pudding. Can you imagine Rose in a feed bag dress? Chicken feed would suit her best, don't you think?" It sure felt good to laugh like that. "And your idea about the pants for Cornelia! The old battle-ax ate that right up. Where did that come from?"

"It just popped into my head. I heard her complaining at the Summer Solstice about how her husband always took credit for her ideas. I thought it was about time she wore the pants in the family."

"That's brilliant, Maddie," he said, squeezing my arm. "Fashionable—just like Katharine Hepburn."

As far as I could tell, they were both determined women, both maybe a little stubborn. The choice seemed right, somehow. "Well, at least she'll have a new way to wear her beloved mauve," I said. "But, Anthony, I almost died when you told them I was an expert at Gala gowns!" I gave him a little smack on the arm. "Why did you do that?"

"I had to do it. You can't start a job out on an apology," he said, slipping off his jacket and draping it over his arm. "I thought it would give them a boost of confidence. You too. I was right, wasn't I?" He bumped my shoulder playfully, but it felt more like a thump—one that brought me crashing down to earth.

Anthony was right. I did need a boost of confidence and a heck of a lot more, too. I needed experience. I needed time. How was I supposed to get all those gowns ready for the Gala? How would I deal with all those rich ladies who were used to everything being *just so*. I felt good about my skills—the skills that I had anyway. But I wasn't sure if I could pull this off. I wasn't sure at all.

"Cornelia doesn't like anyone, you know." Anthony

was chattering on like a magpie. "Not one single person other than Mitzy, and that includes her own son. Except she wants *you* to make her hat. Not to mention she gave you that book like you two were old school chums."

"She did, didn't she? I was so surprised. It didn't make a lick of sense to me, especially since yesterday she had called me a 'mere child,' and today she kept referring to me as 'the girl.'"

"I wouldn't have believed it if I hadn't seen it with my own two eyes," Anthony continued. "I doubt it'll last though. She'll turn on you in an instant if she doesn't like her outfit."

Momma could be like that. Sweet as sugar one minute, vinegar the next.

I gulped. "Sure will be a lot of pressure, that's for sure. I mean, I've never done anything like this before."

"You can do it, Maddie. I saw the formal gowns you made last summer and Etta bragged about how well made they were."

"She did?" Aunt Etta always encouraged me, but she wasn't quick with a compliment.

"She sure did. She also said that you were a real talent, that you would surpass her one day."

"Wow," I said. "I wish she would have told me that. I mean, it's not like—"

"Maddie, do you hear yourself? *It's not like this . . .*

*it's not like that . . .* So what. Settle down to the task at hand. Don't let your mind swirl around like that. Let the work take over. Focus on the job. You can do this, Maddie. You can. Repeat after me: 'I can do this!'"

"Okay," I said, taking a deep breath. "I can do this." A smile formed at the edge of my mouth. It felt good to say that, so I tried again, louder this time. "I can do this!!"

"That's my girl," Anthony said, giving me a hug. "You are going to make Cornelia a hat that will be the envy of the whole county."

Gosh! The hat. "Oh, Anthony, you don't mind my making it, do you? I mean, I don't want you to feel—"

I didn't get a chance to finish my sentence.

"Are you kidding? Honey, no! That's one less thing I have to worry about. I'll have my hands full with Rose."

"Well, she shouldn't be too much trouble, should she? She doesn't seem nearly as difficult as Cornelia."

Anthony took the handkerchief from his vest pocket and wiped his brow.

"Rose isn't as obvious about it as her mother-in-law," Anthony said. "But she's a real pill in her own right. I've known her for almost three years now," he continued. "And she's changed a lot since she married into money."

*Married into money.* Exactly what Momma is trying to do.

Anthony explained that he first met Rose when he was working the Miss Bright Leaf pageant of 1943. That year, several of the girls who were competing—all of them who went on to snag tobacco executive husbands themselves—had hired Anthony to alter their gowns and style their hair during the contest. He was willing to do it for next to nothing, since it would give him the experience he wanted, and these young women didn't have much money, so the arrangement was perfect.

Rose had come here from Mississippi because she had heard about all the jobs available for women. She wanted to earn enough money to get her to New York. That's what her dream was, according to Anthony, to go to New York.

Rose, poor thing, stuck out like a sore thumb at her first Miss Bright Leaf pageant, he said. *Like a hayseed in a haystack.* She'd won a handful of local pageants near her itty-bitty hometown in Mississippi, but the Bright Leaf competition was a big step up.

"Not many girls who'd been crowned Miss Mule Day Queen of New Raymond, Mississippi, would dare take on the finishing school princesses who go out for the Bright Leaf title," said Anthony. "But Rose is more than just gorgeous. She's a spirited little thing and she elbowed her way in front of those moneyed little hellcats in a heartbeat. Of course, they all hated her on sight."

"Not you?"

"I may be many things, sugar plum, but a hellcat is not one of them," Anthony said. "I admired her. I looked at that young lady and could tell she came from nothing. I'm talking *nothing,* like dirt poor, same as my family before daddy became a tailor. Her father ran off when she was just a baby, leaving her momma with four kids to feed."

I thought of all the years I had had with my father and felt grateful. Aunt Etta was right. No matter how bad you have it, there are always people worse off. I just never imagined Rose was one of them. I tried to picture this glamorous woman as a poor little girl, barefoot with a dirty face like the field laborers' kids I'd seen playing with sticks near the crop.

"Rose had big dreams. She came back the following year and won the Miss Bright Leaf title. She placed in every competition she entered—beauty and grit will do that, you know—and saved all her winnings for a big move. That girl was Broadway bound, I tell you. Then Dr. Hale spotted her with that crown on her head, waving from the back of a convertible in the Bright Leaf Thanksgiving parade. And once she got wind of his family money, that was that."

"What do you mean, *that was that?*"

"She was set," he said. "Dr. Hale's family has more money than the Vanderbilts. I mean, he's a respected doctor who inherited his father's seat on the board and a big piece of Bright Leaf Tobacco to boot. Rose saw her ticket out of poverty, and she took it."

"She never made it to New York City?"

"No, she surely did not. Oh, maybe for a visit, but certainly not to live and work. She chose a life of leisure over adventure."

"Maybe she fell in love with him," I said.

Anthony turned to face me, hands on his hips. "Honey! Have you seen that man? Believe me, the only thing he's got that Rose wants to love on is that big fat bank account."

I wasn't sure about this whole marriage business, but to marry *just* for money?

"You know what they say," Anthony continued. "A woman who marries for money and a man who marries for beauty are both equally robbed in the end."

I let out a bark of laughter and wagged my finger in his direction. "You are a troublemaker."

"Oh, c'mon. Tell me he doesn't look like Rumpel-stiltskin."

"Well, from the sounds of it Rose sure has spun straw into gold," I admitted. "But people fall in love for reasons that have nothing to do with looks."

"Maybe, but Dr. Hale isn't exactly mister personality. He's not even a nice person."

"What do you mean?"

"Well, he's plenty friendly to the fancy people in town. But if he can't use you to climb the social ladder, you're no better than dirt to him."

I patted the outside of my satchel, thinking of the envelope with his name on it.

"But he's already rather successful, isn't he?"

"Yes and no. He's a rich doctor, but his older brother was even more successful. More handsome too." Anthony chuckled. "August—short for Augustus Jr.—was destined for greatness. At least that's what everyone said. He planned to take over for his father at Bright Leaf Tobacco Headquarters, and rumor has it that Cornelia is the one who cultivated his business sense. He was fiercely loyal to her and planned to give her a prominent position on the Bright Leaf board of directors. But he died in an automobile accident, on his way home from a Christmas party of all things."

"That's terrible," I said. How senseless and unfair it seemed.

"You'd think that losing one son would make Cornelia closer to the surviving one," Anthony said. "But that doesn't seem to be the case. I've never been in the same room with Dr. Hale and his mother, but I've heard you can cut the tension with a knife. It's kind of sad, actually, the way he tries to please her. Likely she resents him getting his father's seat on the Bright Leaf Tobacco Board, the seat she wanted. He's not even a businessman, although he is helping Mr. Winston with the advertising for the new cigarette for women."

"I saw him on a poster at the factory, and in some magazine advertisements at the Winstons'."

"Yeah, his face is plastered all over, the wives too. Doctor knows best and all. He probably believes this is his chance to finally impress his mother, show her that he is the kind of businessman August was destined to be. I'll bet he'd do anything to make her proud, but what do I know? Half of what I just told you is gossip and the other half is rumor." Anthony shook his head and laughed to himself.

"I saw Rose on the poster with Dr. Hale," I said. "And yesterday, in the Winston's parlor, I saw a whole magazine article about Mitzy."

"This whole advertisement thing is going to Rose's head, if you ask me. Her chance at fame, I suppose."

Anthony said that he couldn't fault Rose for marrying to escape a hard life. Hell, many of the women he knew had done the same. It was the way she had started to look down on people who didn't have money that upset him.

"She's completely forgotten where she came from," he said. "Did you hear her?" He held his hand up like he was smoking a cigarette and stuck his leg out, pointing his toe like a dancer, mimicking what she had said.

It shocked me too, the words she had used. But Anthony seemed to take it real personal.

"Maybe she just got flustered and forgot herself?"

"Oh, no," Anthony insisted. "Rose *forget herself?* That would be like you forgetting you have red hair. She meant every last word of it. Rose hates to be reminded of her old life. She never talks about her family or her past. I suspect she sends money to her mother and brother and sisters once in a while, but who knows? She's sure never invited them to visit her in Bright Leaf. Not once."

"She cut off her own family just because they're poor?"

"Appearances are everything around here, honey. Rose isn't so different from the other tobacco wives. Deep down, I doubt that any of 'em give a hoot about the have-nots, unless it makes them look good that is. Rose is just honest about it."

I opened my mouth to protest, ready to argue that Mitzy's new school proved he was wrong—not to mention that she offered me, a stranger, a place to stay without batting an eye. But Anthony raised his hands to slow me down, as if he already knew what I was going to say.

"Yes, yes," he said. "I know, the wives do all kinds of volunteering in their fancy clothes. Charity work for families in need too—especially Mitzy. But pay attention and you'll see that it's all about her. She acts like the perfect wife and pillar of the community, but she's no saint."

Anthony's words hit me hard.

"And I'm sorry to say that your aunt's other rich customers have not a thimbleful of respect for people who struggle either. You'd think that the wives would at least feel some sympathy for the factory workers in this town, but none of them have any idea what the girls are going through right now."

"What do you mean?" I asked.

"The conditions at Bright Leaf are terrible for the women right now," he said.

"I thought the women were excited to have those jobs," I replied.

"They were, at first." Anthony said that they all understood that factory work was hard, that the women knew what they were signing up for. What was terrible was how the conditions were getting worse and worse now that the men were returning.

"The Bright Leaf bigwigs are intentionally mistreating the women so they'll quit," he said. "They need them to make sure MOMints production comes off without a hitch, but with the men starting to come back, they want the women out so the men can have their jobs back."

"But aren't there enough jobs for the women *and* the men?"

"I guess not. The bosses are hoping most of the ladies will leave, so they don't have to be the 'bad guys' and fire them, but that's already starting too."

He told me the story of a woman who worked in Sorting whose husband had been killed in action. "She was a hard worker, never missed a day, and never left early. When she found herself on her own with her two kids, she asked to move up. Everybody thought she was a shoo-in, but the bosses let her go. Said they didn't need another supervisor and fired her, just like that."

"That's awful," I said and swatted a mosquito hovering near us.

"She really needs the money because her youngest boy has to have an expensive operation," Anthony said. "Poor thing was born with a hole between his mouth and nose." I'd never heard of such a thing.

"Gosh, that's terrible. Why would they fire her like that when she was doing such a good job and needs to provide for her family?"

"They don't like ambitious women, honey. Few men do."

I thought of Momma and how her only ambition was to find another husband. Rose too. She had wanted to be an actress but settled on playing the part of the doctor's wife. I didn't understand it. I could never give up my sewing. Not for anybody.

Anthony continued. "What's even worse is that the girls are so proud of the work they've done. When they saw that poster in the break room and heard about the big advertising plan, they had an idea. They could be in the advertisements. Like Rosie the Riveter, but for MOMints. Made *by* women *for* women."

"That's so smart," I said.

"Isn't it? Well, Mr. Winston nipped that in the bud."

I thought of what Mr. Winston had said to Mitzy over dinner. *You let me worry about production, and you focus on selling MOMints with that pretty little face of yours.*

Not worry about production? Women *were* production. They had made the cigarettes. Shoot, they had kept the company afloat the past five years. Why couldn't they be in the advertisements? And why couldn't Mitzy worry about production if she wanted to?

Mr. Winston acted like he was protecting his wife, but really he was looking out for himself. He didn't want to improve things for the women at the factory. Just the opposite in fact. He wanted to get rid of them.

**The sun** beat down on us while we waited at the bus stop. Anthony was due for uniform fittings at the factory—some of the men had returned from overseas and needed new jackets and pants. *Poor things lost half their weight fighting over there,* he'd said. Anthony and I would catch the crosstown bus just down the road from the Winstons' and he'd hop off near the factory while I continued on to Aunt Etta's house to meet Frances and pick up my suitcase. The tar road gave a little underfoot, softened up in this wilting heat. I pressed it with my toe and breathed in the turpentine smell. I liked it. The sweet piney smell that inspired our state nickname, the Tar Heels. It was made from pine gum, a gift of the land, just like tobacco.

Anthony removed his fancy vest and stuffed it into his satchel as the bus creaked to a stop right in front of us. "I'll have to change clothes at work. Can you imagine if I wore this at the factory?" He laughed, pointing at his high-waisted pants.

We settled into seats near the front and rode quietly. The silence was a relief. I loved Anthony, I did, but he

could be a bit much. It tired me out to be around someone who *talked your ear off,* as Momma would have
said. I smiled recalling all the ways Momma described
talkative people. *He could talk the legs off a chair, the
hide off a cow, the gate off its hinges.*

"Maddie, honey." Anthony snapped his fingers. "I
have to get off here." That was quick.

I swung my legs into the aisle to let him out. "I'll see
you the day after tomorrow," he said, scooting past me.
"We'll get going on the gowns, and evening trousers
for old Cornelia." He winked and gave a quick wave as
he bounded off the bus.

My satchel felt heavy in my lap, heavier than usual.
Then I remembered the borrowed book from Cornelia. Sitting back, I took a deep breath, then removed
the book from my satchel. The crisp brown butcher
paper crinkled when I opened the neat package. The
title of the hardback cover was a mouthful: *Wielding
Power from the Pedestal: The Hidden Role of Southern Women in Enacting Civic Change from 1880–1930.*

I skimmed the table of contents and flipped
through the pages. It was well worn, with handwritten notes in the margins and passages underlined in
black ink. On the inside front cover, Cornelia's full
name—Cornelia Witherspoon Hale—was written in

the same neat cursive I saw at the exhibit the other
day. I read the preface.

The story of iron-willed Southern ladies is not the
one I originally intended to tell. Some years ago,
as I was contemplating my next academic project,
I came upon the idea of writing about the unsung
heroes of the growing progressive political movement that we are witnessing today in the American
South. My assumption, naturally, was that I would
plunge into my research and identify a handful of
forward-thinking men, all of whom had brought—or
were continuing to work toward bringing—more
modern, tolerant, and broad-minded viewpoints
to our traditionally conservative region. Instead, I
found something else: in examining thousands of
personal and public records of reform movements
in the South, I discovered that many of the most important advocates for change on the local level were
women or groups of women—and that this trend of
activist women began well before our better halves
won the formal right to the vote in 1918.

As Southern men, we have long accepted the
idea that our mothers, wives, and daughters are, at
heart, "proper ladies" rather than political animals.
We like to imagine that most of them prefer to let

the stronger sex do the talking in the public sphere. But, as my research reveals, the reality of Southern women is quite different from the myth. The pages of this book will demonstrate many of the ways in which our women embrace change and use their considerable advocacy skills to push us ever forward, even if circumstances require that they do so largely behind the scenes.

I expected a book about fashion or millinery, one that would help me construct the perfect formal wear or hat for Cornelia. But this book wasn't for Cornelia's outfit at all. It was for me. It was written by Professor Harland P. Goodwin from the University of Virginia, and on the leather-bound cover, five women stood on the steps of an imposing building with white columns and an American flag. They wore long white skirts, jackets, and sashes that read VOTES FOR WOMEN.

The first chapter included personal accounts from women in their own voices. A woman named June Grayson from Lubbock shared her story of how she and her women's club had applied pressure on their husbands—many of them influential congressmen—to force all twenty-one Texas congressional representatives to vote for the Fair Labor Standards Act of 1938. Thanks to these women, the act passed, and as a result, employment of children under the age of sixteen was now prohibited in manufacturing and mining on a national level.

Then there was the story of Eunice Greenley, who enlightened women in church basements about the disparity in education, the almost completely one-sided emphasis on men, which limited options for women. She rallied the women in her Bible study group and together they lobbied for girls to receive their high school diplomas, just like boys.

These women were strong and determined. *Feisty,* Daddy would have said. Most of the ladies were married, but given how they made their way through life, I got the sense that there wasn't a husband hunter among them. It was news to me that women had been working behind the scenes, making things happen as far back as the 1800s. Women's clubs and church groups had always seemed awful boring, but that was before I knew they talked about more than roses and Bible verses. This was thrilling. Like discovering hidden heroes. Heroines, I should say. And even more thrilling was the fact that Cornelia thought I should read this. She saw something in me, I realized in that moment.

When the ride got bumpy, I glanced around to see where we were. We'd crossed into the south side of town, not far from Aunt Etta's house. Better not miss my stop.

"A Seat at the Table" the next story was titled. My eyes went wide as I read about a determined old woman who refused to take no for an answer when she wasn't allowed to attend community meetings in her hometown. The mayor who ran the biweekly meetings in his office, meetings open to any and all male citizens of Sacramento, California, didn't permit women to darken his door. So what did Alma Ray Brearly do? She sat herself down right outside the mayor's officer and didn't budge until she was invited to sit with the men at the long oak table inside. There was a photograph of her, this tiny but fierce women, sitting in a lawn chair in front of the building, a peaceful look on her face and her pocketbook in her lap.

*Knowledge is power,* she had argued. *And conversely, the withholding of knowledge is an act of oppression.*

I was so caught up in the book that I nearly missed my stop. "Sir," I blurted out. "This is where I get off, sir."

The driver caught my eye in the rearview mirror and slowed to a stop. It was Ed, the same man Aunt Etta had spoken to about his sick wife the first day we went to the Winstons'. Lord, how things could change in the space of a week.

"Wish your aunt a speedy recovery for me, would

you?" he said. He must have noticed my surprise at his knowing Aunt Etta's business. "My wife's back in the hospital and saw them bring her in."

"Oh," I said. "Thank you. I'm sorry to hear about your wife. I haven't talked to my aunt yet, but hope to soon."

"They limit calls at Baptist, especially for new patients. Got to let them get their rest."

"That makes sense," I replied. "How is your wife doing?"

"She's having a rough time of it," he admitted. "But she's a real trooper. She can't wait to get back to work. Can you believe that?"

"Wow," I said. "I guess that's a good sign."

"It's unnatural if you ask me," he tutted. "Women working like that, but it makes her happy."

"Well, that's good," I said. "Bye now."

It made me feel a little better, knowing patients couldn't take calls. I felt awful I hadn't spoken to Aunt Etta yet. I couldn't wait to tell her how well things went with Cornelia this morning, if she was feeling up to talking, that is. I made quick work of the short distance to Aunt Etta's house. Once inside, I pushed aside the curtains above the kitchen sink and opened the window. I poured myself a glass of water and my stomach grumbled when the ice-cold liquid hit it. The house was strangely quiet without Aunt Etta here. For a split second, I imagined that this was my house. The clock and breakfast table, the neatly folded yellow dish towel and silver coffeepot. The workroom downstairs and screened-in side porch, my own bedroom and bathroom too. It all looked different as I considered what it would be like to own your own home. The thought of it was exciting and terrifying at the same time, like walking on a tightrope with no net below.

I shook off my pondering and decided to make coffee for Frances. I measured two heaping tablespoons of grounds, added water to the pot, and plugged it in.

While the coffee brewed, I went downstairs to pull together all the things I would need from Aunt Etta's workroom. I carried everything upstairs and made a pile next to the door so it would be easy for Isaac when he came to pick me up.

After a few minutes, the percolator stopped its gurgling. Just as I went to pull a mug from the shelf, Frances blew through the front door.

"Frances!" I raced to greet her, throwing my arms around her neck.

"Maddie May, oh honey, it's so good to see you," she said, dropping her handbag to return my embrace. We held each other real tight for what felt like several minutes, the way people do when someone's sick or died.

"It sure smells good in here, Maddie May," Frances said, breaking the silence.

"I made coffee," I said. "Why don't you sit and I'll pour you a cup."

"What a treat," Frances said, smiling as she settled herself at the table. "I'm not used to being waited on."

"How is she, Frances? I've been so worried. Please, tell me everything."

Frances checked her watch. "I know you've been worried sick," she said. "I don't have much time. I'm on my lunch break and have to get back to the office soon. But I'll tell you what I know, honey."

I scooted closer to Frances. I was all ears.

"The coffee's good, honey. Thank you." She set down her mug and looked me right in the eye. "I'm not gonna sugarcoat it, Maddie. She's quite ill. But Dr. Hale assured me that once the fever breaks, she should be through the worst of it." I hung on Frances's every word. "As long as her lungs stay clear."

"What do you mean?"

"Measles can lead to pneumonia, especially in adults," she said. The blood drained from my face. Mitzy had said that's what David's mother died from. And she was much younger than Aunt Etta.

"Maddie May," Frances said, placing her hand on top of mine. "Etta's getting excellent care. The nurses keep the head of her bed raised so pneumonia doesn't set in, and they get her up and moving at least twice a day. And God forbid, if she *does* get pneumonia, there's a new medicine that can cure it. It's hard to get, but the doctor already mentioned it as a possibility."

I let out the breath I'd been holding. There was a treatment, something new that could help. It was going to be okay.

"Goodness," Frances said, noticing the clock. "I'm sorry, honey, but I have to get back to work. I'm taking a shorter lunch break so I can leave a little early and visit Etta today." Frances stood and collected her handbag.

"Why don't I meet you at the hospital later?" I suggested, standing and following Frances to the door. "I can come visit with you."

"I wish you could, Maddie May, but I'm afraid that's not possible," she said. "Only adults can visit. Measles spread like wildfire among children."

"I'm not a child," I snapped, then caught myself. "I'm sorry, Frances. I didn't mean to be rude."

Frances smoothed a curl at my forehead. "You're right. You're not a child, and if I made the rules, you'd be visiting Etta every night. But it's out of our hands, Maddie May. The best thing you can do for Etta right now is exactly what you're doing, sewing for the wives."

"All right," I said. "I can do that." Frances was right. I needed to keep my purpose in mind.

"That's my girl," Frances said, tweaking my chin. "Ah, I almost forgot." She reached into her purse and pulled out a brown parcel. "This is from Etta. Read these instructions carefully," she added. "Every last word or your aunt will tan my hide."

"Absolutely, I will. Thank you." I smiled and held the door as she left. "Bye." She turned at the end of the walkway and blew me a kiss, and I did the same back.

I returned to the kitchen and cleaned up the coffee. Then I opened the parcel to find three pages of instructions and an unused light brown moleskin journal. Tucked inside the first page was a short note that read: *Maddie, Etta wants you to have this now —Frances*

Aunt Etta had promised to buy me my own journal when she deemed me ready to create my own designs. I flipped through the crisp, blank pages and brought the soft leather to my nose. I felt giddy, like I'd graduated from apprentice to real seamstress.

I put down the notebook and unfolded the instructions. They must have been dictated by Aunt Etta. I imagined her telling Frances what to write, insisting that she not miss anything in that surefire way of hers. I felt a wave of comfort and appreciation for my smart, talented, strong aunt. I placed the moleskin and Aunt Etta's instructions in my satchel, intending to go downstairs to collect my suitcase when something caught my eye. The envelope I'd accidentally taken from Mr. Winston's office, with big red letters stamped right there on the front: CONFIDENTIAL. Something private from one powerful man to another. I pulled it out of my satchel and stared at it. I held it up to the light and stared some more. Lord, was I curious. Especially after everything Anthony had told me about Dr. Hale and the Winstons earlier.

There was only one thing to do. I had to take a peek. *Knowledge is power,* I'd just read in Cornelia's book. Maybe I'd learn something.

A thrill ran through me as I removed the letter and unfolded it.

<u>**FROM THE DESK OF ROBERT S. HALE, MD**</u>

*May 18, 1946*

*Dear Richard,*

*May I once again thank you for your patience with the matter at hand. As I told you over the telephone, I have endeavored to learn all that I can about the* maternal smoking study and its findings without drawing attention to our concerns. Its conclusions are rather alarming, I must say, although they remain contained, within small circles of specialists in Sweden, where the research was conducted.

I had hoped that the study design itself would fall short of acceptable standards, rendering it unreliable, but that is regrettably not the case. Its design is quite sophisticated, I'm afraid, using multiple logistic regression analysis to estimate the odds of an infant death or a low-weight birth for mothers who smoked. In other words, the science is credible, which means that it will eventually be published in medical journals and likely spur additional studies elsewhere.

The most concerning results include the following: nearly twice the risk of miscarriage, infant death, or low birth weight; five times the risk of crib death within the first six months of life; and increased risk of congenital malformations including cleft lip and palate.

I find these results difficult to believe myself, but given the study's sound design, it will gain traction and medical publications will give it credence. If I had to bet my hat, I'd say we have a year, perhaps two, before medical

reporters, and eventually daily newspapers, here
in America become privy to this information.
Perhaps conducting our own studies to show
that MOMints are safe is advisable, although it is
quite costly and takes considerable time if done
properly.

I fully appreciate how much is riding on the
MOMints business, Richard. As you are well
aware, I have much at stake myself. This is indeed
a troublesome wrinkle, and I fear we are up
against it. I loathe being the bearer of bad news,
nevertheless, I'm hopeful that we can address this
matter and get on with the next big success for
Bright Leaf Tobacco.

*Sincerely,*
*Robert*

At the bottom of the letter were notes written by a
different, firmer hand, the phrases in bright blue ink,
exactly the same ink I used to write down the hospital
number.

**_Best defense is a good offense_**

**_Conduct our own "studies"_**

*Doctor recommendations (women trust doctors, they know best)*

*Talk to Elizabeth—pictures of wives (most attractive ones) in advertisements and newspapers*

**Americans trust Americans (we know our cigarettes, not foreigners)**

**<u>Big advertising and promotion plan</u>
(P. T. Barnum?)**

**<u>Board meeting (discuss plan)</u>**

I reread the letter again, and again, then once more, even more slowly. Certain phrases jumped out at me— *miscarriage, infant death, crib death, malformations, cleft lip and palate.*

It was terrifying. Unbelievable, really. That something as natural as tobacco could be bad for you. That it could hurt babies and even kill them. It couldn't be right. Every mother I knew smoked, and plenty of them had healthy babies. Maybe they smoked different cigarettes in Sweden. They couldn't have tested Bright Leaf tobacco over there. It was grown only here, in North Carolina.

The more I studied the letter, the more I realized that something else troubled me. It was the way Dr. Hale put things—not just what he said, but what he didn't say. He never said *I'm concerned about this, we need to test MOMints right away to make sure they're safe for mothers.* In fact, he made it sound like they *might* test the cigarettes, but it would take *considerable time if done properly.* Why would you not do it properly? And did they even have time? The letter was dated May 18, just a little more than a month ago.

I took a deep breath and stared off in the distance.

Then I went back to the letter, focusing this time on the handwritten notes below. They'd obviously been written by Mr. Winston. The beginnings of a plan. A plan that would include conducting *our own "studies."* But the word *studies* was in quotes, suggesting that maybe it wouldn't be a real study. I thought too about Mr. Winston's emergency board meetings, about Mitzy asking what was wrong. *Nothing I can't handle,* he'd said.

I felt sick to my stomach and furious with myself. Why did I have to go and read this? And what was I supposed to do now? So much for knowledge being power. I didn't feel powerful at all. Just confused and scared.

# Twelve

"M a-a-ddie, sweet-h-e-art," Mitzy singsonged as I entered the Winstons' front door. Ruth disappeared quickly down the hallway after letting me in, leaving me with Mitzy right inside the entryway. She wore mint-green wrist-length gloves and carried a forest-green clutch, as if she was on her way out.

"I expected you hours ago, dear," she said, glancing at the grandfather clock to our left. "Why, it's nearly dinnertime. Where were you?"

"I'm sorry, ma'am," I said. "It took me longer than I thought to gather what I needed from my aunt's house."

"Oh, that's right," she said. "You had to stop at Etta's. I completely forgot."

I was used to Aunt Etta needing to know my whereabouts, but not a rich lady I barely knew. I wondered if she expected me to ask her permission every time I left her home.

"I'm glad you caught me on my way out, Maddie. I want to have a little talk with you before I head over to the Gala venue, dear. We're having it at the Elk Wood Inn, like always, and I'm off to select some new menu items for this year's event." She smiled at me warmly.

My mouth went dry and hands tingled, like when your foot falls asleep. *I want to have a little talk with you.* When adults said that, it was usually bad. I ran through the possibilities. Maybe Aunt Etta took a turn for the worse. Maybe Momma was in trouble. Maybe Cornelia and Rose complained about me, changed their minds and didn't want me to sew for them. Or what if . . . dear God, what if Mr. Winston noticed the envelope I'd taken?

"All right," I managed with a weak smile.

"Let's go into the parlor, shall we?" she suggested. "You can put those heavy-looking bags down and we'll have our chat."

I followed Mitzy down the corridor, her shoes click-clacking in time with my beating heart.

Once inside the parlor, she placed her clutch on the coffee table and pointed to an armchair. "You can put your things there," she said, then sat on the sofa and patted the cushion for me to join her.

I hesitated.

"Maddie, darling. I'm not going to bite you! I'm going to congratulate you!"

"Congratulate me? Whatever for?" I asked.

"Your appointment this morning, of course." She patted the top of my hand with hers like I was being silly. "You were quite a hit with Cornelia and Rose," she said. "That's no easy feat, dear."

"News sure travels fast around here," I said. I forced myself to smile, as if the Bright Leaf gossip grapevine was a good thing.

"Lightning fast." Mitzy laughed. "Everybody knows everybody's business in Bright Leaf, dear girl."

I swallowed so hard I was afraid she could hear it. My satchel sat right there on the armchair, not two feet from Mitzy. I'd hidden the letter from Dr. Hale deep in its inner pocket, along with my money, cigarettes, and treasures. I stared at it, willing it to keep my secret.

"Maddie, are you all right? You seem distracted." She frowned.

I snapped to. "Yes, Miss Mitzy. I'm fine. I'm sorry. I was just thinking about the gowns. About all the sewing to be done," I said.

"Well, as I was saying, you can take your dinner in

the room where you'll be sewing, if you'd like. I'm sure you're just dying to get things organized, especially with all your appointments tomorrow with the other wives."

The other wives. I wondered if you could tell just by looking that they weren't Bright Leaf royalty—not like Mitzy, her sister, and closest friends. I wondered if you could tell they were rich, but not wealthy. That they had money, but weren't swimming in it.

"Did you hear me, sweetheart?" she asked. "About Ruth bringing up dinner. She'll bring it at six thirty. That should give you a few hours to get settled."

"Yes, ma'am," I said, as casual and polite as I could muster. Really, I was dying to be alone, to let down my guard and stop my head spinning.

"I must admit I was a smidge nervous for you to take over for Etta, but I trust her implicitly. *If Etta believes she's up for the job, I do too.* That's what I told myself. But when I heard how pleased Cornelia was this morning, well, my confidence just went through the roof." She raised her gloved palms and looked to the ceiling with a flourish. "Now all that's left is to do all the work," she said with a giggle.

Only someone who didn't have a mountain of work to do would find that funny.

"I'm no Aunt Etta," I said, "but I'll do my best."

"You're much too modest, Maddie," she said. "And with that young man assisting you, what's his name—?"

"Anthony," I said.

"Yes, Anthony. I believe Rose knows him from her pageant days. He's . . . um . . . he is, isn't he?" With that, she fluttered her hand in front of her face. "They're so good at this sort of thing!" she trilled brightly.

How was I supposed to respond to that?

"Oh, forget I said anything. I just know that between the two of you . . . well, I'm sure you'll rise to the occasion." She checked the cuckoo clock behind her and retrieved her clutch from the coffee table. "I have to go. I'm running late, but let's see now . . ." She was talking a mile a minute. "The most important thing is directions to your workroom. Just take the staircase near the kitchen to the third floor and you'll see a long hallway straight ahead. At the very end of the hall, you'll find your workroom. Actually, let's call it your studio. Doesn't that sound professional? *Studio.*" She let the word hang there for a moment. "I just love that, don't you?"

"I do." I thought of the only other studio I knew— Aunt Etta's. I couldn't let her down.

She leaned in like she had a secret. "Now don't tell any of the other girls that Etta started on my gown months ago. Do you know she always gives me first choice of the latest fabrics?" She giggled again, touching my arm. "Anyhow, it's just fit and finish for me. One less thing for you to do!"

One less thing. Yes, please.

"Now, for the big surprise: I got a new Singer sewing machine! It's the latest, fresh out of the shop window! While I was out to lunch with Ashley earlier, I saw it on display at Piece Goods Fabric Store and thought, *Yes, I must have this!* And I couldn't help myself. I also picked out a selection of notions and new fabrics, to give you a greater selection to work with. Won't that be fun? I hope it will do." She beamed at me, her hands clasped together.

*A brand-new Singer?* Aunt Etta had used her trusty old model as far back as I could remember, and it was the only machine I'd ever used. I hoped I could figure out any new bells and whistles on this more modern one.

"That's so kind of you, Miss Mitzy," I said. "I can't thank you enough. Truly."

"Oh joy," she said, clapping her hands together and standing to reward me with a big smile. "Anything for my Maddie."

I grinned back, hoping she couldn't tell how uncomfortable I was. *My Maddie.* She hardly knew me. It was all too fast and familiar. She'd been so kind to me, so generous, but maybe I was just another charity case. Maybe her generosity to me was just another way for Mitzy to feel good about herself.

"I'm sure you want to see the studio and get started while the ideas are fresh in your mind," Mitzy said, tapping her temple. Then she squeezed me quickly and tucked a few curls behind my ear. I instinctively reached up and untucked my hair, letting it fall against my cheek.

She blinked several times, bristling slightly. "You have such a lovely face, Maddie sweetheart," she said. "You really shouldn't hide it."

"Thank you, ma'am." I didn't dare tell her that I prefer my hair to look more natural.

"Oh—another thing. Enough of this ma'am talk," she said. "It makes me feel awfully old." She scrunched up her nose and shook her head. Her hair, arranged in a perfect victory roll, didn't move when she did. I bet she used Hair Net Spray, like in the advertisements in *Vogue* magazine.

She paused, then said, "Actually, why don't you just call me Mimi. That's what David calls me. It's almost like 'mommy,' but not quite." She laughed stiffly. I worried for a moment that she might say more, but she just blew me a kiss and flounced out of the room.

Mimi?

Almost like "mommy"?

Gosh, I didn't even call my own mother "mommy" and I sure as heck didn't need another momma.

**The steps** leading to the third floor were steep, and there were far fewer of them than in the sweeping staircase to the second floor. Feather fan ecru wallpaper lined the walls, its busy pattern playing tricks on my eyes. It seemed to shimmer and shift, as if alive. The ceiling was low, giving me the strange sensation that I was growing taller, like Alice in Wonderland. I made my way down the long narrow hallway excited, nervous, and very unsure of this new world I had found myself in. It was all so strange. I wouldn't have been surprised to find a Cheshire cat waiting for me.

The door stood open in a shaft of afternoon sunlight. I put down my satchel and bags and looked around. The studio was every bit as dazzling as the Princess Rose Suite. The ceiling, instead of being flat, was pointed, like a church steeple. A large, round window looked out onto the Winstons' backyard, flooding the space with light. And there, on an enormous table in the center of the room, sat the new Singer sewing machine in bright, confident red. Not one, but two dress forms stood next to the table. Nearby shelves displayed the many tools of the trade. It was obvious Mitzy had gotten more than just a selection of fabrics.

I saw that Isaac had brought up the garment bags and materials I'd gotten from Aunt Etta's, including her ivory-handled dressmaker's shears for cutting fabric *only.* "You'll make those duller than a butter knife," she'd complained after I'd trimmed a paper pattern with them that one time. Her portable sewing box was here, and next to it sat a pink basket filled with brand-new, unopened things. I picked up button cards, rows upon rows of snaps and fasteners, and packs of needles in every size imaginable. Some for hand sewing and others for the machine. There was a seam ripper, two tape measures, and a classic tomato pincushion with the little strawberry attached. It was filled with emery sand so you could push your pins in and out for quick and easy sharpening. Mitzy must have bought out the whole notions department at Piece Goods. I just hoped nobody else in Bright Leaf wanted a needle and thread.

On the far side of the worktable sat still more materials: hooks, eyes, and loops (the expensive Peacock-brand ones), pearl-head pins—much easier to spot at a hem or a dart than cheap metal-topped straight pins—standard scissors, tins filled with rainbows of thread in different gauges, and dozens of new and unopened patterns. Lined up against the far wall were the bolts of fabric, arranged by color from stark white cotton to black lace.

Nearly everything necessary was here. All I needed was a bin for fabric scraps and small round weights—two-inch disks were best—to hold fabric in place while I cut out the patterns. I ran my hands along the rolls of satin, silk, and chiffon, delighting in the abundance of it all. But then was quickly hit with a stabbing feeling of guilt. It didn't seem right that some people had so much and others had so little.

For the past few years, I'd rounded up metal buttons and snaps, bobby pins and paper clips, and taken them to the scrap drive. Momma donated some of our pots, pans, and spoons. Daddy tore down our chain-link fence for the cause. Even the poorest of the poor in the Holler gave what they could. But fabric rationing and metal shortages—just like sugar—didn't seem to apply here.

I understood it was the way of the world, but it didn't seem fair. Being around all this luxury was making me feel uneasy, but then I remembered it wasn't mine, that this was all just borrowed finery and I had a job to do. I collected myself and opened my satchel to retrieve Aunt Etta's instructions. I could feel Dr. Hale's letter in the inside pocket practically burning a hole through the fabric. I should get rid of it. Throw it away or burn it. That was the safe thing to do. But something told me not to.

I read the three pages of Aunt Etta's notes again carefully, then read them twice more. I arranged all the tools and notions as Aunt Etta had always showed me. *Mise en place* was the very first lesson she'd taught me—putting in place everything that I would need, like a chef preparing to cook a meal.

Next, I removed the gowns from their garment bags and arranged them on the rack. The first thing I pulled from a hanging bag was Mitzy's nearly finished gown: a canary-yellow chiffon with exquisite pearl beading around the sweetheart neckline and all along the forearms of the full-length sleeves. It was light and sunny, just like the lady herself. For Cornelia, there were two sets of muslins, both two-piece jacket and skirt combinations from previous years that we could use for reference. There were fabric swatches for Rose and two patterns, both for slinky gowns with slightly different bustlines.

Mitzy's sister Ashley had two options, both ready-to-wear gowns—simple, smart princess sheaths, navy with subtle cream accents, that would need next to no altering. In the last bag, I discovered a treasure trove of ready-to-wear gowns in the most popular summer colors, all generously cut for easy tailoring. What a relief! There was so much to work with, so many gorgeous pieces that would just need fit and finish. It was still a great deal of labor, but far more manageable than I had anticipated.

When I'd returned all the gowns to their protective bags, I sat down and placed on the small table my new journal, the instructions, and Aunt Etta's *Dressmaker's Bible* with the appointment details for meetings with the *second-tier* wives, as Anthony called them. I glanced at the schedule that had been set weeks ago by Aunt Etta then put it aside. First, I would map out my plan for the tobacco wives. I cracked open my new moleskin to the second clean page, leaving the first page blank, as I always did.

I paged through the *Bible* and saw that each woman had her own page with a "TW," short for Tobacco Wife, written in the upper-right corner. The page included the wife's name, measurements, and notes.

Rose: "38, 22, 36 Accentuate the bust" Of course she'd want to accentuate the bust. I practically didn't need that note. "34–24–34 Sensitive underarms—watch seams"—that was Mitzy's instruction. "True size 8 but prefers size 10, generous bias cut. Comfort over vanity. No hats"—Ashley. And finally, "True size 6. See client's notes." A sheet of fine stationery attached to the card read "No beading. No sequins. I loathe lace. Feathers are preferred for hats, but no goose or duck." I laughed at the guidelines for Cornelia. She knew what she wanted and she spoke her mind. I stifled a yawn and poured myself a glass of water from the pitcher on the table.

I'd focus on ideas and sketches for Cornelia first. The lines for her trousers flowed from my pencil easily, smoothly. I always used Dixon's graphite. They were inexpensive and got the job done, didn't smudge either. After making quick work of three slightly different trouser designs, I turned my thoughts to the hat.

*No turban*

*Fascinator (too common?)*

*Breton (too casual for evening?)*

*Cloche?*

*Tilt? Cartwheel tilt.*

I circled *cartwheel tilt*.

I'd need an assortment of feathers, ostrich maybe. I'd seen gorgeous ostrich hats in the last two issues of *Vogue*.

At some point, Ruth slipped in with my dinner, freshly carved turkey, roasted small white potatoes, and a ceramic bowl filled with the tiniest strawberries.

I paused for a few moments to show her around the room, and she told me that she had one fancy dress at home, a midnight-blue viscose with a sequin appliqué of a palm leaf draped over the left shoulder. She helped me move the clothing rack closer to the worktable before leaving me to eat and continue with my to-do list.

I alternated between taking notes and bites of my meal until I'd polished off every last mouthful. As I was jotting down my thoughts, I heard footsteps in the hallway and turned to see David standing in the doorway, one hand in his pocket and the other holding a cigarette. He wore a jacket and tie, his hair neatly combed.

He knocked, then asked if he could come in.

"Gosh, David. Of course," I said. "Please, how are you? I mean, *please come in*. How are you?" Suddenly I was a bumbling mess.

"I'm fine, Maddie. And you?"

"Yes, fine, thank you."

He stepped into the room and looked around. "Wow." He surveyed the surroundings. "This looks great. Like a professional dressmaker's shop." He smiled and looked at my hand. I was still holding a pencil, poised above my journal.

"You're a lefty," he remarked.

"I am," I said.

"Me too!"

"Really?"

"May I?" he asked and took the pencil from me. He wrote his name–David Jackson Taylor. Then he asked how I spelled my full name. *M-A-D-E-L-I-N-E*, then middle name *A-N-N*, and last name *S-Y-K-E-S*.

He handed the pencil back to me. "I like that. That's a beautiful name."

"Thank you," I said, my heart fluttering when his hand touched mine.

"My father tried to get me to switch to my right hand when I was little," he said, taking a puff of his cigarette. "He kept putting a pencil in my right hand, made me throw a ball with it too. It didn't end well." He laughed.

"Why would he do that?"

"I don't know. He said something about left-handedness being feminine."

"I never heard that before. My father said left-handed people were creative, clever."

"I like your father's approach better than my father's," he said, motioning to an empty plate from my tea service, as if asking permission to tap his ash there.

It wasn't ideal, but there was no ashtray in sight.

An oversight, surely, in a Bright Leaf house. "Sure," I agreed, nudging it closer to him.

As he raised his head to blow smoke in the air, I noticed a scar at the base of his chin, just a tiny white line.

"How are you really doing, Maddie?" he asked after a moment of silence. "With all this"—he motioned around the room—"and your aunt being sick, on top of everything else you're dealing with."

"Oh, I'm fine. I was thrown for a loop with Aunt Etta being in the hospital and having to take on her most important work, but I'll be fine."

"Maybe your mother could come help you," he offered. "Does she sew?"

A bark of laughter escaped my mouth. "No," I sputtered. "No, she's busy trying to find a—" I caught myself before saying too much. "She's just needs time to herself right now. It's hard to explain."

"Try me," he said.

I sighed. "I try not to think about it, actually. The way she deserted me. And I haven't talked to anyone. About how I'm a girl with a dead father and a mother who doesn't want to live with her anymore. No one would understand that one-two punch." I couldn't believe I had said all that. What was wrong with me?

"No one?" he asked, leaning in so close I could see

the gold flecks in his eyes. "Ahem." He pointed to himself.

Of course. His mother died when he was just a baby, and his father left him for months on end to work.

"You understand," I said.

"Yes, Madeline Ann Sykes," he said, nodding. "I understand."

# Thirteen

The chairs were right where David and I had left them yesterday, close, their arms almost touching. Time flew by as we had talked last night. About our parents, about his plans for college and after, about our shared hatred for Jell-O salad. Being with him felt right and familiar, but thrilling too, like I'd opened a hidden door inside myself. I wanted to replay our conversation in my mind, to turn it around and around like a record on a phonograph. But I had work to do, and the first of the *other wives*, as Mitzy had referred to them, would be arriving soon. I wished Anthony was here, but he wouldn't be able to join me until later. Today's appointments were all on me.

Aunt Etta's notes about Mrs. Anna Rebecca Ashworth were sparse, saying only that she was a delightful young mother and that I should expect her to be late.

Sure enough, nearly forty minutes after the appointed time, Anna Rebecca blew into the workroom like a cheerful tornado. She was very tall with a halo of sand-colored ringlets and striking clear blue eyes in a shade an artist might use to paint a tropical sea. And she was not alone. She apologized, said that her nanny was sick—*measles, just like Etta, I'm afraid*—and hoped that her boys wouldn't be in the way. The four of them, all towheaded and under age seven, filed in like naughty ducklings, each wearing the same red gingham playsuit and identical devilish smiles. We spent the first few minutes searching for the baby of the group, who had hidden himself under a huge pile of tulle without anyone seeing where he'd gone. Once we'd found little Beau and busied him and his brothers stringing buttons on an endless piece of thread, I asked Anna Rebecca what she had in mind for her gown.

"Oh, I don't know," she said. "It's been ages since I felt like a girl. Lately, Etta just keeps it simple for me— easy silhouettes, everything in stiff navy fabric because it hides jam fingerprints and diaper cream stains . . . you know what I mean."

I pulled a dress from the ready-to-wear options. I held it up and noted its features: balloon sleeves cuffed at the elbow, belted waist, and a floor-length, hip-hugging skirt. "The silk faille feels light but is actually quite heavy and stain resistant," I said cheerfully. She was my first appointment on my own and I wanted to please her.

"This works nicely," said Anna Rebecca. But as I reached for my measuring tape, I caught a glimpse of her sighing deeply instead of smiling. She was satisfied—but not happy—with the dress.

"What if we went in a different direction?" I asked. "This is your big night off from jam and diapers, isn't it? And you have the height and figure to carry off nearly any style, so I'd love to put you in something fun!" I'd spotted just the thing earlier and it would be beautiful on her. "How about this?" I said, pulling a divine gown with an off-the-shoulder bodice and full, ruffled skirt. "This gown is similar to what Rita Hayworth wore in *Cover Girl*. The aquamarine silk illusion is beautifully deep, and it matches your eyes exactly."

Anna Rebecca blushed at the comparison to Rita Hayworth.

"But can I pull it off?" she wondered, biting her lower lip. "I just loved that movie, but she's terribly glamorous in that scene."

"You're a woman who can do lots of things," I said. "There's no harm in feeling frivolous and pretty for a few short hours. What do you say?"

"All right, let's do it!" said Anna Rebecca, clapping

her hands. We smiled at each other, conspirators for a moment. Then I took some measurements and scheduled time for her final fitting. As she gathered up the boys to leave, I prayed that the rest of the consultations would be as fun and as easy.

My triumph didn't last long. Aunt Etta's notes had warned me to stay on my toes with Mrs. Bernice—"Babe"—Holborne. It turned out to be good advice. Babe had blunt-cut bangs and pencil-thin eyebrows shaped in an angry arch. She asked for a custom, sleeveless gown of black satin with a high neck and a daringly low back. When I suggested that we consider a lighter color for a more summer-y look, she drew in a deep breath through her nose.

"I need a seamstress, not an opinion," Babe said. "Can you be a seamstress?" I was shocked but recovered quickly enough to promise that I could be a seamstress—and a very good one at that. Babe nodded, but the set of her jaw told me there was trouble ahead. She huffed when I asked if she had a preference for duchess or antique satin, and when I asked if she preferred a blue black or a true black, I thought she'd pitch a fit. I nearly made it through the session, but when I told her I had her measurements from Aunt Etta, she insisted that I take them again. When I did, she accused me of pinching her. "That is *it*," she said. "Really. That is just the last straw. I'm not putting up with all this rigmarole. I'll have a gown flown in from New York. Or I'll wear something already in my wardrobe. The affront!"

My heart sank as I watched her gather her handbag and go. I tried to tell myself that it wasn't my fault, that she was just itching for a fight, but it was hard to take. I'd only tried to please her. I resolved to do better with my next customer.

Mrs. Eleanor Finch was somewhat nicer but no easier to please. A bottle blonde with a stubborn streak, Eleanor had her heart set on an apple-green gown with a scalloped peplum and a matching scalloped mini-cape. I had an emerald-green dress with a scalloped peplum, and when I suggested making a mini-cape to match or constructing a custom gown and cape in one of the other green fabrics I had—sea foam, perhaps— she turned up her nose. "I'd prefer a vivid green. Sea foam is rather mild in comparison."

I offered to keep searching for her preferred color, but all she gave me was a weak "I'll think about it," which left me feeling defeated.

Still, she was nicer than that Mrs. Holborne, and she did tell me to wish Aunt Etta a speedy recovery. All of the ladies said this in some form or other—*give Etta our love, tell her this too shall pass*—but some of them seemed more bothered by her absence than others. I'll bet Aunt Etta would have come up with a solution for Eleanor, convinced her to go with another color, or knew where to quickly get her hands on apple green.

There were only two tobacco wives left that afternoon: Mrs. Jacqueline Patwin and Mrs. Allyson Littlefield. They arrived together at 4:00 P.M., arm in arm and giggling. I liked them immediately. The women were shaped very differently—Jacqueline was like a slender vase while Allyson was buxom up top—nevertheless, they insisted on custom royal blue gowns of the exact same design. I tried to steer Allyson toward a style with more structure so that her bust would be comfortable and supported. But she was firm about wanting to match her friend. I wondered if there was some construction method or invisible corseting technique I could use to make the dress work equally well for each woman. I wished I could ask Aunt Etta. Perhaps Anthony would know.

After the ladies left, I collapsed in a chair by the window and shut my eyes, spent from a full day of appointments. It was a good tired, a proud tired, despite losing one customer.

"Hey, sunshine!" A voice startled me out of my half-asleep state. There was Anthony, breezing in, both arms full.

"I must have dozed off," I said, rising out of the chair. He placed his hunter-green carryall on the table, and I took the other bag, a large tote, which was surprisingly light. I set it on the table next to his sewing carryall and stifled a yawn.

Anthony straightened his vest and wiped his brow with the back of his hand. "Will you look at this!" His eyes sparkled as he scanned the room. He slowly walked around the studio, taking in the new sewing machine, the bolts of fabric, the ready-to-wear works in progress, and spools of thread arranged like the colors of the rainbow.

"Good Lord. Is that a new Singer?" he gasped, staring at the sewing machine in the center of my worktable. "In fire-engine red. Just like your hair, honey. Aren't you the lucky girl? First you win over Cornelia and now you're sewing with a machine that would make Etta jealous."

Anthony was joking, but I could tell that my good fortune made him uneasy. Maybe he was the one who was jealous.

"May I?" he asked, noticing my open journal of sketches. Of course he was welcome to look at them.

"These are fabulous," he said, flipping through and stopping on my drawings of Jacqueline's and Allyson's gowns.

"Do you really think so?"

Seeing the sketches through his eyes, I had to admit that they did look professional. "I'm beginning to feel more confident," I told him.

"As you should," he said, turning his attention to the hanging dresses I'd pulled earlier. "Who is this sassy off-the-shoulder number for?" he said, lifting the aquamarine dress.

"Oh, that's for Anna Rebecca."

"The one with those three little rascals?" he asked, raising his eyebrows. I wondered how he knew her. "She's a former beauty queen, you know," he said before I could ask.

"The very one," I said. "Seems to be up to four rascals by now—although who knows? When she was here, there were too many small bodies in the room to keep proper count."

"This gown is quite glamorous. I'm surprised she asked for this."

"She didn't," I said. "I sensed she was longing for something different, that she'd enjoy feeling beautiful and daring for an evening. I encouraged her to go in this direction."

A smile crept across Anthony's face. "Look at you." He tapped my arm. "You're a natural, Maddie. You have a dressmaker's talent and a personal touch with clients. That's important too. It's not all about the sewing."

The thought of dressmaking being about more than sewing struck me as funny, but Anthony was right. In my short time filling in for Aunt Etta, I'd noticed that listening, really listening, to the women made all the difference. It's why I suggested pants for Cornelia and something more glamorous for Anna Rebecca. I knew how to read them, get a sense of what they thought and felt. *Mind your own business*, Momma always said when I made observations about people. She made like my nosiness was a weakness, but maybe it was a strength.

"Thank you," I said. "But that won't matter if their gowns aren't finished. Now that I've started, I realize how much there is to do. "

"That's why I'm here," he said. "We'll tackle it together, honey." He removed his vest and laid it on the worktable. "Oh, now *this* I must see!" he said, noticing Cornelia's hat base across the room. "It's the custom block for Cornelia's head, isn't it?"

"Yes," I said. "The very one."

Anthony stroked its smooth surface. "I bet this brainless hat block is a lot more human than the woman herself." He laughed.

I snickered with him but felt a little twinge nonetheless. "I don't think she is as terrible as people make her out to be," I said. "Maybe she's just misunderstood."

Anthony turned around and put his hands on his hips. "Well, listen to you," he said. "Defending old Cornelia." He paused a moment, studying the hat block from every angle. Or maybe he was studying me. "What are you planning for her?"

"I was thinking a cartwheel, but not just an ordinary cartwheel, a chic tilt with clean, strong lines. I'm leaning toward these two for the base." I held up both swatches. "This one may be too stiff, though," I said, handing both to him. "It needs enough give that I can stretch it across the base to stiffen and set. That's the trickiest part— blocking it with just the right amount of tension so it holds its shape but doesn't stress the weave at the crown."

"I agree," he said. "This one feels like the proper weight, but good Lord, there are so many to choose from." He walked over to the fabric bolts lining the far wall and ran his hand along the colorful columns, stopping at the sateens and satins.

He lifted a sturdy rectangle of gold lamé from the row, "Might as well go ahead and pull this for Rose's 'showstopper,'" he said with a wink. He handed it to me for the worktable then turned back to the other metallics. "Oh, my word! This is capital D-i-v-i-n-e." He removed an emerald- green lamé roll and unfurled it on the table. "It's the shade of Gene Tierney's eyes."

He sighed. "Rose should go with this instead of gold, don't you think?"

"It is gorgeous," I said, rubbing it between my fingers. "But she seems dead set on gold."

"What does she know? This is much more striking. It's also in keeping with her role as one of the advertising models for MOMints," Anthony added. "And Dr. Hale will love it."

Dr. Hale.

I had tried to forget about the letter, but it kept creeping into my thoughts. If there was anyone I could trust in Bright Leaf, other than Aunt Etta and Frances, of course, it was Anthony. And he knew more about the Winstons and Dr. Hale than I did.

"When did the MOMints advertisements start appearing?" I asked. "The poster with Rose and Dr. Hale at the factory. When did that go up?"

"Hmm . . ." Anthony said. He continued gazing at the green fabric. "Right around Memorial Day, I guess. Yes, it was definitely that weekend because I had to work on a holiday, *again*." He rolled his eyes, replaced the green fabric bolt, and removed bundles of patterns from his bag.

The date on Dr. Hale's letter was May 18. Memorial Day was a week or so after. Did that mean the advertisements were made before the letter from Dr.

Hale? Or were they quickly made after? If doing a study took a long time, like Dr. Hale said, how could they have done a real study in just a week? I felt like Nancy Drew, trying to piece it all together.

"Do you know I haven't had a holiday off since last Christmas?" Anthony continued. "I'm thankful for the overtime, I am, but, honey, please. Everybody needs a break once in a while, right?"

I half-heard him, too deep in my thoughts to answer. I needed to tell someone. I couldn't keep living with this churning around in my brain. Anthony could help me figure it out.

"Anthony," I said. "I need to tell you something." He pivoted to give me his full attention, abandoning the patterns on the table.

"What is it?" Anthony said.

"I saw something," I said. "Something that I shouldn't have seen." I gestured to the chairs by the window and sat down.

Anthony brightened, taking a seat. "Do tell! Something scandalous, I hope."

"It's not like that," I said. "It's not funny, either. Can you keep a secret?"

"Lord no, honey! You know I can't." He laughed. "I just told you a whole heap of gossip yesterday and there's more where that came from."

"I'm not fooling around, Anthony," I said, shaking my head. "Oh, forget it. Never mind."

"Come on now, honey. I'm only teasing. Of course I can keep a secret *for you.*"

But could he? Suddenly I wasn't so sure. I bit my lip, as if that would help me make my decision. Anthony was my friend, but how could I rely on someone so loose-lipped? I couldn't take the chance.

"It's . . . it's . . . just something I saw at the Solstice," I said. I had to think fast. "Some younger boys were stealing cigarettes from adults' bags when they weren't looking."

"Shoot, is that all?" he said. "I thought you had something big to tell me by the sounds of it."

"Well, you know me," I said. "I don't have quite the thirst for gossip that you do, but I thought I'd pass it along."

"Honey, that little tidbit wouldn't quench anyone's thirst. Next time you have something to tell me, make sure it's *really* something."

A knock at the door startled us. "Oh, hello, Ruth."

"Afternoon, Miss Maddie, Mr. . . . is it Anthony?"

"Sure is, sweetie," Anthony said with a wink, and Ruth smiled at him.

"Miss Mitzy wanted me to remind you 'bout church on Sunday. Said I was to give you notice so you can plan your work," she said. "She goes to the early service, the one that starts at eight. Says she'd like you to join her."

"Oh, right. Of course. Thank you, Ruth," I said, thinking I should go but how it'd been months since Momma and I had stepped foot in the Lord's house. Momma wasn't feeling too church-like after Daddy died.

As Ruth excused herself Anthony whistled and said, "You'll have to tell me all about Presbyterian Church, honey. I'm dying to know about the ladies' hats. Be sure to wear your best dress or you'll stick out like a sore thumb."

"I'm flattered that Mimi wants me to go to church with her," I said.

"Mimi?" Anthony blanched.

"Yes, she asked me to call her that." I blushed. It sounded silly once I'd said it aloud.

Anthony shook his head and started in on me. "Maddie, darlin . . ." he said, tentatively. "I know you're new to all this and you sure are doing great being thrown in with all the wives and their world, but just remember, this is their world."

I was about to get all indignant, to ask Anthony what he meant, but I knew.

"Now, I'm sorry to say, but I won't be able to help you until Monday. You're on your own for the weekend, although, I guess Sunday you'll be otherwise occupied anyway," he said, then peeked out the door to make sure Ruth was out of earshot. "I'm needed at Factory One. The supervisors who met their quotas last month are getting special patches, a reward for cranking out the most cigarettes. And"—he lowered his voice to just above a whisper—"I told my sister I'd take the bus home with her after a secret meeting of women factory workers on Saturday night. They're thinking about striking. Threatening to stop production if their demands aren't met."

"Really?" I said. "Where is the strike meeting?"

"It's after the late shift in an old drying barn behind Factory One. Why?"

I thought of the book from Cornelia, the stories of women gathering behind closed doors to change things for the better. Its pages spoke to me when I'd read them yesterday and even more so after today's appointments. With each fitting, my confidence grew. It felt good to be like those women at the factory, to be productive, to be needed. But, if Anthony's gossip was to be believed, Bright Leaf Tobacco wanted to take that away from them.

"I'd like to go," I said.

"Really?" Anthony seemed surprised. I was a bit surprised myself. I'd never considered doing anything like this, and I wasn't sure how Mitzy would take to it if she found out, but I was curious.

I cleared my throat. "Yes. I'm a working woman myself," I said. "Maybe I could learn something."

"You have a point there, honey," he said. "Just be careful not to let the Winstons know. And be sure to tell me everything."

"Of course," I said. Although I couldn't tell him about my other reason for going to the strike meeting. I wanted to know more about MOMints and Mr. Winston, anything that might help me make sense of the letter from Dr. Hale. More than wanted—I *needed* to know.

# Fourteen

It was a funny thing, my friendship with Anthony. So different from the way April and I got along. She and I had been friends for such a long time, we could finish each other's sentences. *Two peas in a pod,* Momma liked to say. We went to the same school and knew all the same people, and we didn't have any secrets from each other. I wanted to tell Anthony about the letter, to share it with him line by line. Surely he could tell me what to make of it, to help me understand what it all meant. But I just didn't feel I could trust him with this information. Not until I had a better idea of what I wanted to do.

These were the thoughts going through my mind as I stood in the Winston's foyer on Saturday evening waiting for Anthony to arrive. He had insisted on giving me a ride to the strike meeting, which confused me,

260 · ADELE MYERS

because he said he was taking the bus home later with his sister. He was all secretive and giggly about it when I pointed that out and asked whose car he was driving. I knew his mother had an old Plymouth—I saw it once when she dropped him off at Aunt Etta's—but I'd never seen him drive it himself.

I stepped into the parlor to check the cuckoo clock. It was nearly eight thirty and the meeting started at nine. It'd be another ten minutes until Anthony arrived. I started toward the window to watch for him but noticed an ivory and gold telephone on an end table. I should call April! Why hadn't I thought of it earlier? I'd been dying to tell her about everything that had happened since Momma had pulled me out of bed in the middle of the night.

Mr. Winston was at headquarters preparing for a big board meeting, and Mitzy had turned in early for the night again. She'd said I could use the telephone if I needed to, and I could sure use a good talk with my best friend. I had enough time before Anthony was due to arrive.

I dialed the familiar number, WNC-0311, and held my breath. The line rang five times before someone picked up.

"Jenkins residence," April's little brother shouted into the phone.

"Henry," I said softly. "Henry, it's Maddie. Is April there? I need to speak with her."

"What?" he bellowed. Henry was April's only sibling. He was five or six years old now and spoke with a cute lisp.

"Henry, could you please put April on the phone?"

"She's not here and Momma's taking a bath," Henry said. "Bye, Maddie, Momma's callin' me." I could hear April's mother's voice in the distant background. "What did I tell you about playing with the telephone, Henry?" Then there was a click as Henry hung up the phone.

Disappointed, I puffed out my cheeks and released a rush of air. I got up and went to the window and, a couple minutes later, saw headlights at the end of the Winston's driveway.

I hurried outside and down to the parked car, but as I got closer I couldn't believe what I saw. There was Anthony perched in the driver's seat of a noisy, bright green John Deere.

"Where did you get a *tractor*?" I asked, taking in the sight of my friend sitting proudly behind the wheel.

"It belongs to the factory. One of the supervisors asked me to pick it up from the service station on my way in tonight. Isn't it a hoot?"

I chuckled and shook my head. Anthony always managed to make me smile.

The dim of early evening surrounded us. Lightning bugs winked here and there, a slight breeze brushed my ear. I climbed into the high cab and felt the cool metal seat on the backs of my legs. It felt pleasant in the warm evening air.

Anthony pumped the gas and the tractor sputtered to a start. He threw it into gear and we lurched forward, our heads jerking back and then coming to rest. A flash of riding the Ferris wheel with David crossed my mind. I wondered when I'd see him next and whether I should say anything to Anthony about our conversation the other night. He'd probably tease me. Worse, he'd warn me not to get too close, to remember my place.

As we rumbled down the smooth paved road, the cicadas chirping and massive trees rustling overhead, it felt like all was right in the world. Every sight and sound was a marvel, a beautiful gift from above. I looked over at Anthony to share the moment but his expression was serious. His eyes were fixed straight ahead and he slowed his speed to a crawl as we got on the main road, checking his side mirror over and over. He was a terrible driver.

"Are you okay to drive?" I asked him. The way he white-knuckled the steering wheel made me nervous.

"Of course," he said, glancing at me several times. "Why? Why wouldn't I be?"

"Never mind," I said and turned my attention to my surroundings.

When I arrived in Bright Leaf about two weeks ago, the tobacco fields were thick with leaves as big as elephant ears. Now the rows of plants stood stripped bare, only their sad skinny stalks and small clusters of wilted red flowers at the top still standing.

"They harvested," I said.

"They sure did," he replied.

We rode in silence. Anthony was so focused on the road that he wasn't as chatty as usual. I was thankful for the quiet. The anticipation of tonight's meeting and what I'd discovered in that envelope weighed on me. What would Mitzy do if she found out that I'd taken her husband's private letter? And what if Mr. Winston somehow discovered that I was fraternizing with the female factory workers, the women who were causing *all that trouble* for Bright Leaf Tobacco? He'd have me fired, and then the wives wouldn't have gowns. Aunt Etta would be so upset and disappointed in me. This was a terrible idea, I suddenly realized, going to the strike meeting. I couldn't help myself though. I wanted to hear what the women had to say and try to make sense of what I'd read in that letter.

The dangers that Dr. Hale wrote of scared and saddened me. How could our beloved tobacco be *bad*?

264 · ADELE MYERS

Tobacco farming and manufacturing fueled the whole state of North Carolina from top to bottom. The town we were driving through had been built on tobacco money, and so was every school, church, and store I'd ever seen. Our fathers, and their fathers before them, made cigarettes. Those who didn't work the land or the line worked in paper, packaging, or transport. Not to mention all the maids, waitresses, and shopkeepers who did the other jobs that kept Bright Leaf going, fueling the industry. Aunt Etta liked to joke that nicotine ran in our veins. I looked over at Anthony, gripping the wheel and squinting to see the road as darkness closed in. Where would he be without Bright Leaf Tobacco Company? Where would any of us be?

"We're almost there," he said, pointing to the tall, lit-up headquarters building in the distance.

"What will it be like? I asked. "The meeting, I mean."

"I'm not sure. It's the first meeting like this that I know of." He paused. "I'm dying to know what they say and what's going to happen with the women's jobs. What they do affects me too. Not to be selfish, but if they lose their jobs, it'll cut my business in half."

As we wheeled onto the street leading to the factory, a fat raindrop hit my arm, then another and another. By the time we parked next to the warehouse, the sky had opened up, the dark clouds overhead releasing buckets of water as we ran to an awning outside Factory One. We scurried under and Anthony checked his pocket watch.

"You'd better go," he said. "It's already five minutes 'til nine." He pointed to a dirt path beside the building where we stood and said to follow it to the end. "Walk down the hill and you'll see the barn in the distance. It's about a hundred yards."

"Okay," I said, but I felt uncertain.

"You can't miss it, honey," he assured me. "It's the only drying barn back there. Now skedaddle." He gave me a quick peck on each cheek and ran back toward the tractor.

I followed the dirt path and carefully made my way down the steep hill, as instructed. My feet slid on the wet grass, and I nearly fell more than once. Far in the distance, light filtered through the frame of a closed door. I could barely see the barn itself, the way it blended right in with the pines. As I neared, I saw that it didn't have even one window, and the outside looked like a giant patchwork quilt, where somebody had stuck whatever lumber they could find any which way. Each piece was painted a different green. In some places a metal sheet had been hammered over a plank or two.

When I got even closer, a fireplace facing the outside became visible, a flue, right under a beat-up overhang. I knew that farmers kept the flues running day and night during curing, filling the sealed inside chamber with smoke to give the tobacco that sweet taste and signature Bright Leaf yellow color.

I dashed under the overhang, my clothes soaked through and stuck to my now-chilled body. My hair hung heavy, and my feet squished when I wiggled my toes inside my shoes.

As my eyes adjusted, I saw old tractor parts and dented-up, rusted buckets littering the ground outside the barn. Cigarette butts, smoked down to the nub, were scattered everywhere.

I pushed my way just inside the door and was surprised to find a packed room, filled with women milling about. The ceiling must have been two stories tall, and up near the top shriveled bundles of tobacco hung from thick beams. A dusty wooden bench ran along the four walls, and the air smelled of stale tobacco and mold.

"Can I have your attention?" a woman's voice carried above the din. "We're going to get started."

Women continued to pour into the crowded room. We were packed so tight I could feel hot breath on my neck.

"Attention!" shouted the woman.

Everyone began to settle in, some taking seats on the bench that encircled the room. I sidestepped along the wall and found an out-of-the-way spot to stand. The rain continued to beat down outside, peppering the tin roof with relentless pings. Thunder rumbled, and a curtain of water ran down the sloped roof, soaking the women just outside the door. They pushed their way into the barn, like cattle fleeing a prod. I looked around and saw there were as many Black women in the room as white.

"Move in, y'all," said the same voice that had called us to attention a moment before. She was standing on a crate, a short, plump strawberry blonde with a pale complexion who looked more like she belonged in her momma's kitchen than leading an uprising. "There's room back here." She pointed to the corners behind her.

The latecomers didn't move. They bottlenecked near the doors and greeted each other instead of listening, but when a loud, shrill whistle pierced the air a hush fell over the crowd. The short blonde had stepped down to clear the way for a stunning older woman with dark brown skin.

"I respectfully request that you ladies fill in the empty spaces at the back of the barn," the woman said, pointing to the rear of the room. I blanched at the sight of her hand. She was missing two fingers. Her hair was pulled back in a tight bun at the base of her neck, and shiny flat waves framed her face at her temples. She introduced herself as Sadie, and she seemed to be in charge.

Someone brought over another crate, and the short blonde, Margaret she said her name was, climbed up on it, the two of them now visible above the crowd. They waited until the cavernous space was thick with silence before calling the meeting to order.

Margaret spoke first. She said that the National Labor Relations Act meant that businesses were obliged to recognize and bargain with their workers.

Sadie explained. "This has been the law for over ten years now. It's time we catch up," she called out to the rafters. "If we organize, they must consider our demand for job security." Her voice was strong, carrying through the barn as the women around us stomped and cheered. Above the noise, one of the women on the floor objected.

"We ain't got no job security," a white woman hollered. "They already giving our jobs back to the GIs."

"Well, that's the thing about this law," said Margaret, reading off a paper in her hand. "It gives us the right to do three things: to organize into a trade union, engage in collective bargaining, and take collective actions such as strikes."

A grumble caught fire in the room. "Why the bosses gonna bargain with us?" a Black woman huffed from the rear of the crowd. "Especially my people. You're crazy if you think this law's gonna protect us. Bright Leaf Tobacco *is* the law in this town."

Sadie motioned like she was patting the air, gesturing for everybody to quiet down. "Now listen," she said. "Shhh. Please," she urged everyone. "Do you want to keep your jobs or don't you?"

Yeahs, hell yeahs, hoots, and hollers erupted from the crowd.

"All right, then," she continued. "Listen up, ladies. This is our chance. Our only chance to keep our jobs. Now is the time, and we must seize it." She peered around the room, scanned every corner to make eye contact with each and every person. You could have heard a pin drop. "Bright Leaf Tobacco needs us right now," she continued. "We have leverage, but not for long."

I didn't understand what she meant, and from the looks of the other blank faces around me, I wasn't the only one. Sadie must have picked up on our confusion.

"Leverage is the ability to influence situations or people so you can control what happens," she explained. "Like a lever. A force that's applied to an object." She paused a moment to let that sink in. "Don't you see?

If we stop work, MOMints production stops. And if MOMints production stops, the bosses lose money. A lot of money. That's our lever, our *leverage*." A wave of ahs and uh-huhs rippled through the barn.

"That'd serve 'em right, greedy bastards," a woman next to me whispered.

"Money talks," another shouted.

These women. They cussed and shouted and didn't give a damn. They talked like men, and I liked it. "Damn right!" I said. It was more of a quiet statement than a shout, but it felt good.

"Now is the time, ladies," Sadie continued. "Bright Leaf Tobacco can't run without us women on the line. But our time is running out. The men are returning, and they'll take their jobs back. The bosses will fire every single one of us."

"They can't do that," someone shouted.

"You wanna bet?" came another voice. "They can do anything they want. Just ask 'em!"

"What we supposed to do, then?" a petite blonde to my left asked.

"We use our collective power to influence the bosses while we can. But we have to stick together. All of us. Blacks and whites," Sadie said.

Margaret nodded. "They're controlling us by seg- regating us, pitting the Blacks and whites against each other. They pay us white women a slightly better wage than the Black women," she said. "Which makes y'all angry at us."

"'Course it does! It's not fair!" a rail-thin Black woman shouted, followed by another chorus of "yeahs," an angry energy rumbling and spreading through the room.

"Ladies, please," Sadie said. "Hear us out. They may pay the whites a better wage, but they keep y'all in check by telling you that if you strike, the Black women will step in and work for less." She paused for a moment before continuing. "Don't you see what Mr. Winston and the rest of them are doing?" Sadie's eyes narrowed, her voice strong and clear. "They're turning us against each other. Coming up with plans in their big board meetings to control us. It's the fat cats running Bright Leaf Tobacco we should be angry at, not each other."

You could almost see the thoughts of the women shift, like gears clicking into place.

Goose bumps popped up on my arms. I knew Mr. Winston was in charge, but hearing her call him out like that made me shudder. Suddenly, I felt guilty, like staying at the Winstons' house had made me the enemy or something. What if someone called *me* out and asked me to leave? I surveyed the crowd for familiar faces and spotted the ashy blonde I'd seen in the break room that day. I averted my eyes, hoping she hadn't seen me. Two Black women nearby looked familiar too. I decided I'd better leave before someone recognized me. As I inched my way toward the door, I looked up and drew in a sharp breath when I saw her. She wore an oversize trench coat and a rain bonnet, but there was no mistaking her for someone else.

Ashley. Mitzy's sister, standing on the far side of the barn.

My heart quickened. If the Winstons were aware I was part of this, who knew what they would say or do. I sure as heck didn't want to find out. I looked down and began inching my way toward the door.

Sadie was handing out flyers with a list of demands and asking for a show of hands, for volunteers to help. The women around me wouldn't move out of my way, all jostling to get noticed or talking to each other about whether they should get involved. I had to practically force my way through the crowd until a burly lady smoking a cigar saw my plight and hollered. "Let red through for God's sake!" She shouted so loud that everybody within earshot turned to look at me, everybody including Ashley.

Dammit!

When I finally made it through the large doors and stepped outside, sure enough Ashley emerged right behind me. Though the rain had almost stopped, the temperature had dropped a good ten degrees. My clothes were still damp, and I felt like a wet cat standing there, exposed and silly.

"Maddie, isn't it?" Ashley said, lighting up a cigarette. "Etta's niece?"

"Yes, ma'am," I said. "I was just here to—"

She interrupted me before I could finish. "No need to explain," she said. She held the cigarette in her mouth as she tightened the belt on her coat. She took a long draw and blew smoke out as she squinted into the darkness. "The rain lightened up, but it's still coming down. Do you want a ride back to my sister's house?"

"Um, thank you for offering, but I can take the bus. I was planning to take the bus," I stammered.

"I pass by Mitzy's on my way home anyway. I'll drop you off," she said, letting her cigarette fall to the ground and grinding it out with her toe. "I insist."

I dutifully followed her a different way than I'd come. Her white sedan sat on the shoulder of a dirt road behind the drying barn, not up near the factory where Anthony had dropped me off earlier.

When I opened the passenger door, I was surprised to see how immaculate her car was; it didn't look like the automobile of a mother of two young, and I suspected, messy boys.

"My clothes are wet," I said, before sitting. "I don't want to ruin your seat."

"It's fine," she said, waving me to get in. "This car has seen far worse than a damp dress. If my boys haven't destroyed it yet, you certainly won't."

"All right," I said, lowering myself into the bucket seat. She didn't laugh or call me sweetie or even smile. Mitzy would have gone overboard to make me feel comfortable, but her sister didn't. I couldn't tell if she was angry or this was her usual self. She hadn't said much when I first met her at the Solstice, and she was helpful but not overly talkative when she drove Aunt Etta home that night.

"Your husband's car is so nice," I said, running my hand along the raised stitching on the door panel.

"It's my car, not my husband's," she said. The car turned over once and hummed to a start. "Not many women in Bright Leaf can drive, let alone own their own cars," she added, glancing in the side mirror before pulling out. "But I enjoy driving." I thought of Momma, how much she loved being behind the wheel. I wondered where she was and what she was doing at this moment. Ashley's hands expertly spun the wheel as we veered from the dirt road onto a wide, paved one, and I saw that her nails were neatly trimmed and free of nail varnish.

We rode in uncomfortable silence for a time. I longed to fill the quiet, to calm my racing mind, but thought it best to say as little as possible. How could I explain why I was at the meeting? Maybe I could say that I had come to drop off patches, that I got lost and ended up in the wrong building.

I peeked at Ashley. She'd removed her hair bonnet and her brown shoulder-length hair hung smooth and straight as a stick. What was I going to say when she told her sister that I was here tonight? And would they tell Mr. Winston? He'd be furious. God, how disappointed Aunt Etta will be if he asks me to leave. What a mess I'd gotten myself into it.

After a few more minutes, Ashley broke the silence. "You may be wondering what I was doing here tonight," she said, glancing from the road to me and back again. Here I was, so worried that she'd interrogate me, that I hadn't actually considered why *she* was there.

"Oh," I said. "Um." *Think fast, Maddie.* "Um, is it because you work for the company, same as the other women who attended?"

"Yes, partly," she said, her eyebrows knitting together as she tucked her hair behind one ear. "I'm not on the line, of course. But management would still love to push me out, along with the other girls. How did you know about my job anyway?"

I told her that I had seen her name on the plaque at the Summer Solstice exhibit. "And Miss Mitzy talks about your work," I said. "She's so proud of you."

"Really?" Ashley said, a lilt in her voice. "That's nice to hear. I'm sure she talked Richard into giving me the position in the first place. He handed me the job the minute I asked for it, but his feelings about a 'female auctioneer' are clear enough. It just kills him to have a woman in such an important, high-profile position."

She rolled down her window and went on to explain that she had new opportunities now and felt an obligation to make sure other women did too. Partly she attended the meeting for herself, but she was lucky: she had resources, family money, and connections. Most of the women employed by Bright Leaf Tobacco didn't have any of those things. For them, it wasn't about seeking independence or happiness. It was about survival.

"Even so," said Ashley, "it would be a waste of breath to try that argument on Richard. He just wants things to go back to the way they were before the war. He didn't foresee how temporarily empowering women would complicate matters for him. And he'd be outraged if he thought I was siding with the 'enemy.'" She paused for a moment. "I don't mind ruffling Richard's feathers on occasion—in fact, I quite enjoy it. But he'll never listen to me. Mitzy's the only one who has a chance of changing his mind about women in the workforce, but even she hasn't had much luck. It takes leverage, like Sadie said earlier. Men won't change unless they have to."

I hung on every word Ashley said. Her quiet confidence, the way she talked about challenging Mr. Winston and changing things for women. It was inspiring.

"Could you hand me a cigarette?" she asked, gesturing with a tilt of her chin. "There, in the glove box." She pushed in the lighter, and I retrieved a pack of MOMints for her. I slid one out and handed it to her. The lighter popped out, and I held it to the business end.

"I'd like to keep it between us," Ashley said after taking a long draw on the cigarette. "The fact that I was at the meeting." She paused a moment and blew the minty smoke above her head, filling the car briefly with gray haze before it raced out her open window. "Mitzy knows how I feel about women's rights and I'll tell her eventually about tonight, but for now, can you keep it confidential, Maddie?"

"Of course," I replied. "I understand."

"Excellent," she said.

Relief washed over me as I rolled down my window. It didn't seem she cared about what I was doing there, and she certainly was not interested in bringing it up with her sister. I'd dodged a bullet, that's for sure.

"You know," Ashley said, "when I was your age, I never dreamed that I could be an auctioneer. It just didn't seem possible. At the time, women who wanted to work could be nurses, teachers, or beauticians. If those jobs didn't suit you, you took the conventional route: courtship, marriage, children." She paused for a few moments, drew on her cigarette, and then shook her head almost imperceptibly. "It's wonderful, it is," she said. "Being a mother. But no one tells you what it's really like, how much of yourself you give up."

I shifted in my seat, curious.

"I love my husband," she said, glancing at me and returning her eyes quickly to the road. "Silas is a good man—he's trying hard to understand why I want to work when I don't have to, especially now that the war is over, even though I can tell it doesn't make sense to him. Of course, I adore my boys. Motherhood transforms you in miraculous ways. But just like marriage, it does come at a cost."

She continued, sharing how she felt orchestrating the auction, holding the attention of the expansive warehouse and powerful men, adjusting her chant at just the right time to close a sale—it took focus and skill, but also something more. There was an art to it that was deeply satisfying.

"Every woman should have the opportunity to work," she said. "Men would have us believe that it's too difficult, that we're weak, but it's actually just the opposite." She took a last pull on her cigarette and then extinguished it in the ashtray.

"I think I know what you mean," I said. "Taking over for Aunt Etta has been challenging. I didn't think I could do it at first, but I surprised myself. It feels good to be good at something."

"Exactly," she said, giving the steering wheel a little slap with the heel of her palm. "That's exactly what I mean." Ashley glanced in the rearview mirror as she pulled to a stop down the street from the Winstons' house. "Keep at it, Maddie. That feeling of satisfaction, knowing you can take care of yourself. That's something no one can take away from you."

I smiled and thanked her for the ride, then opened the car door, letting the misty night air envelop me.

# Fifteen

You're positively drenched!" Mitzy tutted as I stood soaked on the entryway carpet. "Where on earth have you been?"

"Oh, I . . . um . . . I rode over to the factory earlier with Anthony. He had some uniforms in need of repair and was going to give them to me. But it turns out . . ." Mitzy squinted and tilted her head, listening but not believing, I feared. I was a terrible liar. I prayed she didn't pick up on the tremble in my voice.

"Well." She sighed. "You should not be worried about factory uniforms with the Gala just weeks away. You tell him that." She shook her head and peered at my shoes. Hopefully she didn't notice the musty, smoky smell coming off me after being in the barn.

"Let Ruth take your soggy shoes, Maddie, and why don't you go upstairs and get cleaned up. I couldn't sleep and have been looking for you." She smiled, her cheeks rosy. "I have a surprise."

"A surprise?" I repeated.

"You'll see. I'll be up in a bit to show you."

Show me? Gosh, I'd had enough excitement for one night. I wanted to be alone with my thoughts, to take a nice long bath and mull over everything I'd seen and heard. What Ashley had said to me. The women at the meeting. They sparked something in me with their passion, with their profound sense of fair play. It was like when you hear a singer, a really good singer, and he hits a note so pure you can feel it in your own body. Something important happened to me tonight and I wanted to savor it.

I padded upstairs in my stocking feet and went straight to the bathroom inside my suite, slipped out of my wet dress, and hung it over the tub. I dried off and wrapped my damp ringlets in a towel, then reached for a fluffy white robe.

I heard Mitzy's voice after a few minutes had passed.

"Knock, knock. Are you ready for your surprise?"

"Just a minute," I shouted. I removed the towel from my hair, tightened the robe and opened the bathroom door. There stood Mitzy, beaming, holding a half dozen dresses in her arms as if they were a sleeping child.

My eyes went wide as she explained that she had

pulled a collection of her favorite dresses out of storage. Several darling options for church tomorrow, and two stunning gowns for the Gala. Aunt Etta made one of them for Mitzy's sweet sixteen and designed the other for her debutante ball.

"Oh my gosh," I said, taking in the two gowns as she hung them in my closet. "Aunt Etta made these for you? They're beautiful, but I couldn't possibly wear your special dresses. What if I accidentally damaged them?" I hadn't until that moment thought that I would be attending the Gala.

"Nonsense! They're just wasting away in my closet. Nothing would please me more than for you to enjoy them. I'm sure Etta would be delighted as well."

I wasn't so sure about that. It was awfully nice of Mitzy, incredibly so, but it didn't feel right. I tried to protest, but Mitzy wouldn't hear of it. They're wallflowers, she had said, just waiting to be worn again. Maybe so, but these were hardly the clothes of a shrinking violet. The dress she'd given me for the Summer Solstice, the beautiful light blue she'd bought at a boutique in town, was a simple silhouette—conservative and elegant. But these gowns were daring pieces made for a far more adventurous person. I thought Mitzy's childhood dresses would have the low hemlines and boxy shapes popular when she was younger. These looked like clothes from the prohibition era, something a rebellious flapper might wear.

The first dress was sleeveless and was made of a flawless midnight blue silk. It had a skirt that would skim the bottoms of my knees, a dropped-waist bodice, and a tall, cloud-like collar made of see-through illusion fabric. There was a proud stiffness to the collar so that it could be propped up and manipulated to frame the wearer's face and neck. Aunt Etta had taken great pains to sew hundreds of translucent beads in a geometric pattern around the hem of the skirt.

The second dress was made of a similar silk, this one in a delicate, pale rose color. The full-length gown featured a plunging v-neckline and a deep cowl in the back. The draping was simply exquisite. Even on the hanger, the silhouette was stunning. The care that went into the gown's construction was evident. The body-hugging bias cut, its A-line skirt with a slight flare. It was just divine.

"What do you think?" Mitzy asked. She stood behind me and squeezed my shoulders as I stared at the rose-colored gown, lost in thought.

"It's exquisite," I said. "Both of them are, though I don't know if I'm brave enough to wear either one." I looked away from her bright-eyed gaze. "I guess I'm surprised too. Your style has changed so much."

"They are a little unconventional, but I was much more of a trailblazer back then. I see that you're smitten with the blush, so let's try that first, shall we?" Mitzy motioned me toward the bathroom where I could undress. We left the door open a crack so that I could talk to her while she stood just outside.

"I'm curious," I said as I removed my robe. "What made you choose these silhouettes in the first place?"

"Looking back now, it seems silly," she began. I could hear the smile in her voice. "When I was a girl, I was absolutely consumed by flappers and suffragettes. They were so free and outspoken—glamorous, of course. As the years passed, I continued to idolize that Zelda Fitzgerald look and then later was drawn to the styles the Hollywood starlets favored. Of course, my parents were scandalized when I insisted on these daring dresses, God rest them. But they always did let me get away with murder. Ashley, too. I mean, you should have heard the way we talked in those days!"

I stepped into the rose-colored dress, carefully pulling it over my hips. "It's hard for me to imagine you being badly behaved," I said.

"Oh, I wasn't really, not in the traditional sense," she said. "But our political opinions about women were pretty shocking at the time, and we didn't much care who knew it." She laughed again, remembering.

"Ashley is quiet. Not shy, mind you. Just quiet. People get those two mixed up all the time." Mitzy was right. Everyone thought April was shy, but she wasn't. Not in the least. April had plenty to say and wasn't afraid to say it, but she didn't waste her words. She didn't suffer fools, either. I could see how Ashley might be like that. "My sister barely says anything at all, except when she's working. But she'll give you an earful on women's rights if the mood strikes her. I—on the other hand—I'm done with all of that."

"Done with all that." I repeated under my breath. It struck me as sad, that this woman who seemed to have everything had given up her opinions.

I glanced at myself in the mirror, then slipped out to show Mitzy the dress. I was surprised by how beautiful I felt—and how comfortable. The neckline wasn't nearly as plunging as it had seemed at first. I should have known that Aunt Etta would find a way to please daring young Mitzy and her parents too. The gown was sophisticated, but not at all risqué. Even so, I wasn't sure I could pull it off.

"Oh, don't you look gorgeous!" Mitzy gasped as I stepped into the room. She adjusted the bodice and led me over to the full-length mirror to inspect the result. "That color is gorgeous on you. Do you love it?"

I did. In fact, I had never felt more beautiful. I held

my hair up with one hand as I pivoted to take in the back of the dress. The draping fell perfectly, halfway down my back, giving the gown a daring, yet elegant sophistication.

"I don't mean to pry," I said, turning to examine the front more closely. "But what happened to make you change?"

"Oh, it's hard to explain," she said after a beat. "I think it goes back to when Mr. Winston contracted polio. I wasn't much older than you are now when he fell ill. Suddenly the life I'd planned wasn't possible."

I didn't have much sympathy for Mr. Winston. Not anymore. "That must have been very difficult for you," I said, turning to face her.

"It was," she replied. "I planned to go to college, in Georgia, which was unusual for girls at that time. But I couldn't leave Richard. Then my mother was diagnosed with cancer."

"Oh, that's awful. I'm so sorry."

Mitzy had talked about college that first day I came here with Aunt Etta. She'd also compared herself to me on more than one occasion. My ambition reminded her of her own, she had said. But I didn't see it. I didn't feel like we were alike at all.

She removed a slim cloisonné cigarette case and her

favorite pink-and-gold lighter from a pocket hidden in her silky paisley dress. I made a mental note to experiment with a similar pocket design for Jacqueline's and Allyson's gowns.

"Georgia is lovely." She sighed. "Have you ever been?"

"No, I haven't," I said, admiring her pale pink nails as she flicked the flame to life. "What's it like?"

"Oh, it's captivating. I saw the most beautiful hybrid tea rose in Georgia," she murmured, a faraway look in her eyes. "They grow the most divine peaches you've ever tasted in your life. I hope you'll have the chance to see it one day."

"I hope so too. I've never been outside North Carolina," I admitted.

Mitzy blew smoke into the air. "You know, my mother never traveled outside North Carolina either. We had the means, mind you. And I tried desperately to get her to tour the University of Georgia with Daddy and me, but she refused."

I frowned.

"My mother lived a rather sad and solitary life, even though she had a husband who loved her and two daughters who adored her. It troubled me greatly as a girl. She spent her days thumbing through travel magazines in our parlor—ironic, isn't it? An armchair traveler who whiled away the hours drinking her precious gin and tonics."

I was shocked. Mitzy's mother sounded more like my mother than the perfect housewife I'd imagined her to be. Maybe Mitzy and I had more in common than I thought.

She walked over to the bay window with a sigh. "I vowed that I would live a big, full life," she said. "I was going to visit the places in mother's magazines. I was going to study and be bold and take advantage of all the new opportunities for young women."

Turning, she gazed across the room toward me, one thin arm draped across her waist with the other elbow resting on it like a shelf.

"Then I'd start my family," she said, taking a deep draw on her cigarette. "I would be the perfect mother—devoted and attentive. I certainly wouldn't drink. Well, except for my brandy, which doesn't count. But life demanded other things of me . . ." She trailed off quietly.

I wanted to ask what she meant but didn't think I should.

"Anyhoo," she said, her tone turning more upbeat, "I channeled my energy into caring for Richard. Then for my mother, before her death. Caring for her fulfilled me, really it did, but in a surprising and altogether different way. Giving what you didn't get for yourself, well, it can be soothing. Healing, I suppose. I had a sense of purpose. But then Mother died, and Richard adjusted, and he didn't need me as much. In fact, he seemed to resent me when I tried to help him. Men like to believe they're the strong ones, you know."

Momma liked to say that too. I thought it was just something she'd made up.

"He's so focused on the business now. I hardly—"

I don't know what made her stop talking, but she did, quite abruptly.

"Oh, would you listen to me, blathering on and on! Would you like to try on the other dress?"

"It's surprising," I said carefully. "To me, it seems like you have the perfect life, that you have everything."

"We all have troubles, dear," she said, squeezing my hand. "They just come in different wrapping paper. But don't you worry about me. I've managed just fine. Keeping busy. Busy as a bee. That's the secret. A busy person doesn't have time to be unhappy! I've discovered so many ways to occupy myself and feel some semblance of purpose. And when I have my child"— she blushed—"hopefully, three children—two girls and a boy—then all will be right with the world."

# **Sixteen**

Maybe it was because I'd barely slept, but walking into church the next morning felt like floating through a vivid and disturbing dream. The piercing sun was too bright. The insistent birds too loud. Even the music coming from the sanctuary bothered me. Then there were the women, a steady stream of them, fussing and fawning over Mitzy. Her dress and hair, her lipstick, her gloves. Everything was flawless, everything divine. Where did she find that royal blue fascinator— and that bag? *And who is this with you?* they inquired, batting their eyes. As if they didn't already know, hadn't already heard through the gossip mill.

I'd been collecting clues about Mitzy since my arrival in Bright Leaf about two weeks ago. She was fashionable, had an incredible eye for detail, and loved to host. Mitzy was a devoted wife and a generous woman.

In fact, until last night I might have said she was too devoted, too generous. I saw things differently now. This beautiful life she was living was not as it seemed. Her cheerful facade masked pain and disappointment.

Her attentiveness to her husband, her caring for David ever since his mother died, and her tremendous charity to the town of Bright Leaf . . . it was about more than keeping herself busy. It was an offering, a way to give to others what she had been missing herself. Another woman might have become bitter with her mother's indifference and her husband's illness, but Mitzy soldiered on, covering up her heartache.

And that heartache, that deep longing for a child. She had tears in her eyes when she told me that being a mother was the single most important thing to her. It was, she said, what she was meant to be. I felt a true swell of feeling for her then, and I had reached out to hug her, to show her I appreciated her, to let her know I cared.

I thought of all this as we walked into the grandest place of worship I'd ever seen. How hard it must be for her to keep up appearances amid these chattering women. Mitzy was as busy as a bee, she had said. But did she know that she was Queen Bee? It was as plain as day to me, the way these ladies looked up to her, envied her too. I saw it at the Solstice as the wives vied

292 · ADELE MYERS

for her attention, giving her compliments, letting slip a tidbit of gossip. Anything to get her notice. I saw it here too, with the flutter of a gloved hand and the tilt of a head just so. They were all painted lips and curled lashes, pastel pocketbooks, and flower-trimmed hats. They called each other *sweetie, honey, darling, dove, precious,* and *sugar.* In some ways they were pale versions of Mitzy, replicas trying to match the original. But in other ways they were all alike, these tobacco wives. They were all so determined to be happy.

Mitzy and I took our seats—front and center, a few rows from the pulpit. Ashley waved from where she sat, at the far end of our row, and I noticed a few of the second-tier wives sitting behind us with their husbands. As we got settled, one of the women I didn't recognize leaned in close, her smile so wide I could see every tooth in her head.

"Is this Etta's niece I keep hearing about?" she cooed. "I was so alarmed when I got the news that your aunt was feeling poorly. How is she, dear?"

"She's improving," I said. "Thank you for asking, ma'am."

"The ladies are all very concerned about how their dresses will fare this year without Etta's able hand," she said. "Oh, and about her health of course."

I smiled politely as she peppered me with questions

about my sewing and reported that her Bible study group was praying for Etta's swift recovery. Thankfully the trumpeting organ pipes interrupted the missus busybody, and she scurried off to her seat.

We rose and Mitzy opened a leather-bound hymnal to the appropriate page, the paper almost sheer, onionskin thin. She handed it to me with a warm smile before doing the same for herself.

> *Crown Him with many crowns,*
> *The lamb upon the throne:*

I knew this one.

> *Hark! How the heav'nly anthem drowns*
> *All Music but its own!*

I glanced around the sanctuary and scanned the balcony. Almost every seat was filled. There must have been at least two hundred people here, all finely dressed, lining the smooth mahogany benches decorated with intricate carvings. I closed my eyes and let the music fill me.

> *Crown him the Lord of Heav'n:*
> *One with the Father known.*

*One with the Spirit through Him giv'n*
*From yonder glorious throne.*

I liked the feeling of grace I got inside a church. The flicker of candles against the majestic ceilings, the way the colored light cut through the stained glass windows. Everything soothed my soul, even the voices singing off-key. Especially the off-key ones, actually. There was something humble about the little squawks and missed notes. You could hear the effort in them and they felt all the more precious because of that. If I closed my eyes, it was almost like I was back home at First Baptist. The same smells and swell of feelings.

*Adored and magnified*
*Crown Him with many crowns*

Mitzy tapped my arm. "Scooch down, dear," she said, squeezing in to make room for Mr. Winston and Dr. Hale. She must have been happy to see her husband. She told me he never liked to miss church, but this morning he had a meeting that couldn't wait. He had important things to discuss with Dr. Hale. We should run along ahead, he said, and he'd try his best to make it. Mitzy told me this and, as if anticipating my question, then casually mentioned that we'd see

David after the service, that he would be going with friends.

I slid as far as I could across the bench as Mr. Winston and Dr. Hale lowered themselves onto the seat with a creak and a thud. Out of the corner of my eye, I watched as Mr. Winston pushed on the side of his knee and forced it to bend, like unlatching a ladder. He did the same thing on the other side and heaved his dead legs under him with his hands. I tried not to stare at the metal braces affixed to his shoes. Mitzy offered him her hymnal, but he shook his head and removed a cigar from his coat pocket. He didn't light it, but its musty smell filled our row as he held it between his teeth.

I felt an odd mix of pride and embarrassment sitting with the Winstons. They were North Carolina royalty and I was in their court. Yet I felt sorely out of place, an imposter just pretending to belong. I looked the crowd over more closely. A white-gloved hand waving like a windshield wiper caught my eye—Anna Rebecca surrounded by her husband and her four boys. Cornelia sat on the aisle near a side exit, holding her purse in her lap, as if she were about to leave. Rose sat next to her, examining her nails. I wondered if she was annoyed that her husband sat next to Mr. Winston instead of next to her. She was all decked out for the occasion, with an enormous burnt orange hat that set the woman behind her scowling. A crow of a woman, dressed all in black, perched several rows up to my left. When she glanced behind her, her thin angry eyebrows in full view, I realized it was Babe.

"You can't please everyone" Momma had told me years ago, and it was the best piece of advice she had given me. Some people just don't want to be pleased. They like to carry a fuss around with them as if it were an umbrella. Looking at Babe, I was surprised at how relieved I felt. I had plenty of work to do and I was doing it the best I could. Now I didn't have to worry about satisfying this woman who was determined not to be satisfied. A blessing in disguise is what it was.

Dr. Hale leaned across Mr. Winston to whisper something to Mitzy, which made her giggle. He grinned in my direction, revealing that he had his mother's striking gray eyes. My breath quickened and I felt a bolt of panic thinking about his personal letter hidden deep in my sewing satchel.

My thoughts ping-ponged. I could make out a word here and there—*righteous, deception, witness, atone*—but nothing the preacher said made much sense. I tamped down my guilty thoughts and turned my attention to the sermon just as a stampede of well-dressed children thundered down the aisle. Solemn and fidgety, they were doing their best to behave.

If it weren't for their fancy clothes, these boys and girls might well have been at our Sunday school in the Holler. It had always been a task to get me there. I'd rather be out swimming or riding my bike, not in church being told to sit nice with my hands in my lap. I hadn't minded so much at first, not when I was told it would be like school, only instead of arithmetic and geography there'd be stories called parables. I had really liked the Good Samaritan and the one about the mustard seed. The lessons were simple, black and white rules that said *do this, don't do that.* They were easier to follow when you were little, though, when the lines between right and wrong didn't move. Things didn't seem so straightforward once I got older. Like the time when Mrs. Briggs, our Sunday school teacher, said we'd go to *h-e-double l* if we cussed, and I pointed out that *h-e-double l* itself was a cuss word. She didn't like that one bit.

I watched as the children plunked themselves down in front of the amused preacher. He was the same man who had led the prayer at the Summer Solstice, but instead of his brown suit, he wore an ivory robe.

"Oh I just love when they end the service with the children's lesson," Mitzy whispered. "Aren't they darling? Reverend Butts is just wonderful with them."

"Yes," I agreed, stifling a laugh. The children must have a field day with his name.

"Who can tell me," said Reverend Butts, once the children got settled, "what a sin of omission is?"

A boy's plump hand shot up. He was perspiring and huffing as he answered. "A sin is when you tell a fib or you're greedy and you eat all the chocolates."

The reverend chuckled. "Yes, dear boy, those are indeed examples of sin. I think we've all been guilty of eating more than our share of our favorite sweet, haven't we?" The adults tittered and nodded. A few of the ladies patted their waistlines. "Thankfully the Lord forgives our greed and gluttony," he added.

"But I'm talking about a different kind of sin, young man. A sin of omission." He forced the word out in a bluster, as if he could convey the meaning by sheer force of will.

I crossed and uncrossed my legs, fixed my eyes on a carved wooden leaf on the pew in front of me.

"When we think about sin," he continued, "we often think of something we did. Eating the chocolates, as Matthew said. But there's another kind of sin that occurs when you don't do something."

A tiny girl gasped. "You can get in trouble for doing nothing?"

"Ha-ha. No, dear, not exactly. Let me explain. Isaiah 56:1 tells us 'This is what the Lord says: Maintain justice and do what is right, for my salvation is close at hand and my righteousness will soon be revealed.' And James 4:17 describes the sin of omission in beautifully simple language—'So whoever knows the right thing to do and fails to do it, for him it is sin.'"

I shifted in my seat and bit my lip.

Then he asked for a volunteer to help him demonstrate how sins of omission separate us from God, from others, even from ourselves. Reverend Butts handed a pair of horseshoe magnets to his young volunteer and told her to hold them together. They clicked right into place.

"You can feel it, can't you . . . the way the magnets connect? They are now one, strong. The magnets are drawn to each other as if by force, just as God draws us in with his grace. Now, turn one of the magnets around and try to put them together." The little girl struggled to connect them.

"Something's wrong," she said, baffled by the invisible field that kept them apart. "It doesn't work."

"No, it doesn't," he said, catching the adults' eyes. "The magnets, in this case, are like us when we don't do the right thing. We are separated from others; it creates a sort of tension. When you know the right thing to do, and you don't do it, you are distanced from the Lord, and from those you love. You can no longer connect." He let his words sink in, then took the magnets from the girl. "Thank you, dear."

"For it is not *only* what we do," he bellowed, raising his arms and beholding all the parishioners, "it is what we do not do, for which we are accountable. All rise."

The organ started up and everyone joined in a short closing hymn. I attempted to join in but I felt sick to my stomach and slightly dizzy.

"May I be excused?" I asked Mitzy as soon as it ended and the parishioners began to mingle.

"Of course, dear, there's a ladies' room right down that hallway, next to the Sunday school wing."

"Thank you."

I hurried through the crowd, anxious to hide myself in a stall and gather my thoughts.

"Maddie!" It was David, grinning as he stood with a group of boys and girls. "Come meet my friends."

"Oh, hi, David. Um, sure."

Nine or ten of them stood there, studying me. Four boys and the others were girls, including the beautiful Vivien I'd met at the Summer Solstice. I sensed a sneer from her as she examined what I wore. It wouldn't have mattered to her that I had selected a lovely Bermuda cloth floral among Mitzy's dresses. This girl could detect a hand-me-down from a hundred paces.

"This is Caroline, and Lilly, and Alexandra, and Chloe, and Madeline," David said. Another Madeline. I smiled at her and the other girls too. "And you met

Vivien at the Solstice," David said. He pointed his thumb at the four boys. "These four jokesters are Niko, Zachary, Noah, and Renn." The tallest of the fellows elbowed David in the ribs with a chuckle.

"This is Maddie, everyone," David said. "She's a seamstress, and a talented one at that. She's filling in for her Aunt . . . Etta. You might know of her," David said.

"Oh, my mother just loves Etta's gowns," one of the girls said. "Says she's Bright Leaf's best. The only game in town."

Vivien changed the subject, bringing the attention to herself. "As I was saying, I hope I'll see you, David, at the Fourth of July celebration." I could practically feel the breeze as she batted her lashes at David.

"I'm not sure yet," David said with an easy smile.

"Are you going to see the fireworks, Maddie?" one of the other girls asked.

"I don't know. I hadn't thought about it. I have a lot of work to do."

"I do too," David said. "My college paper is due in a month." It went quiet, and I felt them staring at me. What was I supposed to say?

"Say, Maddie, do you have a minute?" David asked. "I wanted to ask you something about your work."

"Sure," I said, relieved that he'd filled the awkward silence.

302 • ADELE MYERS

"Excuse us for a moment, would you?" David said to his friends.

"Okay, see you around."

"Bye."

"Nice to meet you, Maddie."

David led me down a long hallway into what must have been the choir room. Rows of empty chairs, two dozen of them at least, sat in a half moon facing a piano and music stand.

What could David possibly have to ask me about sewing? He answered my question before I could ask. "I don't really need to ask you about your work," he said with a sly grin. "Unless asking you to take the night *off* from work counts, that is."

"What do you mean?" I asked.

"The Fourth of July. Taking off on the fourth of July. When Chloe asked you about going to the fireworks, you said you had to work. I plan to be working on my college paper, but I had an idea. What if we both take a break that night and celebrate the Fourth together?"

"I don't know," I said uneasily. "I have fewer than two weeks left before the Gala."

"Come on, Maddie." He grinned. "Please? We could meet up at the Winstons' and then head over." He explained that Mitzy always had a small get-together for her sister's birthday, which was on July fifth. Every year, Mitzy served her favorite cake and the family toasted Ashley before dispersing to enjoy the festivities.

David was clearly a catch, as Momma would say. It wasn't just that he was handsome and rich and came from good stock, which are the things she says are important. He also had a quiet calm about him and a quick wit. He was kind and thoughtful.

He watched me expectantly, hopeful.

"All right," I said. "It's a date."

# Seventeen

Sewing had always been a surefire way to save me from my churning thoughts, to quiet the voice that made me doubt myself, but when I returned to my studio after church I felt defeated by the sight of so many unfinished gowns. There was Ashley's navy sheath, Anna Rebecca's bodice and skirt, and the look-a-like gowns for Jacqueline and Allyson too. And, of course, Cornelia's hat. Her outfit was nearly finished, thankfully, and Anthony would be handling Rose's gown, but I still felt overwhelmed by all the tasks before me.

I sat for a moment to compose myself, then came up with the idea of tidying my workspace. I could manage that while I waited for Anthony to arrive. I started with the patterns and sketches, organizing them into orderly bundles. Then I neatened up the fabrics and put my scissors and chalks away. I did my best, but even these simple tasks felt slow and labored, like I was wading through mud.

"Honey, what have you been doing?" Anthony exclaimed when he finally breezed in. "I thought you'd have those matching gowns finished, steamed, and ready for pickup. And why is Cornelia's hat still on the base? You better shake a leg if we're gonna finish all this."

"You did not just tell me to shake a leg!" I said.

"I did indeedy. I'd shake both of them if I were you."

"Well, you're not me, Anthony. I am me. And I need help, not a lecture."

Anthony's eyes flew open like I'd smacked him across the face.

"Well," he huffed, tilting his chin and smoothing the side of his hair.

"I'm sorry. I'm so sorry," I said. "I didn't mean that. I'm just tired and worried about Aunt Etta and . . . and . . ."

"And . . . I forgive you, but just barely," he said. "Let's stop fussing and get down to business. It'll be all right."

We agreed to keep things light and focus on the job at hand. We had only ten days until the Gala and the pressure was mounting.

Cornelia's hat base needed redoing. The tricky job of stretching it across the hat block was the most challenging step, and I'd never done it myself. With Anthony's help, I knew we could do it, but it took several tries. It was a fussy job and everything had to be just so. We messed up three times and collapsed in a fit of giggles when, on the last attempt, the fabric slipped from Anthony's fingers as we pulled in opposite directions and he went flying like a ragdoll, landing on his rear.

"Did I split my pants?" he asked. "I sure hope not. I don't have time to fix my own clothes with all this"—he gestured to the gowns around us—"and the extra uniform work at the factory."

I assured Anthony that his pants were still intact and offered him a handkerchief to wipe them off.

"Speaking of the factory," he said as he dusted himself, "I heard all about the big meeting. Apparently the two women who organized it delivered their demands to Mr. Winston and they threatened to strike if they didn't get a response from Bright Leaf Tobacco by the day of the Gala. They're supposedly assembling a group of female workers to attend the event in their uniforms instead of formal wear," he said. "And word has it that if Mr. Winston hasn't given them what they want, they'll announce the strike at the party. Can you imagine?"

"Anthony! I can't believe you didn't tell me this sooner." I was astonished that my loose-lipped friend hadn't shared this news right away. "My goodness, can you imagine what Mitzy would think if that happened?"

"I know," said Anthony. "It would be an absolute disgrace for her. Hopefully Mr. Winston comes to his senses in time. It's just not right the way he allows the girls to be treated."

I nodded my head in disapproval and we both returned to our work in silent contemplation. Anthony stitched pearls at the neckline of Mitzy's yellow chiffon dress while I guided Jacqueline's hem through the sewing machine. After a rocky start with the new Singer, I'd finally gotten the hang of it. I finished, released the foot pedal and needle clamp, and pulled the royal blue satin away from the throat plate.

"How's your momma, Maddie?" he asked after a while. "Have you heard from her at all?"

I let out a gasp. "Oh gosh, Anthony, I can't believe I didn't say anything. Yes, I finally did hear from her! She sent a postcard. Frances saw it when she collected Aunt Etta's mail and called here yesterday to read it to me."

"Ooh, do tell!"

"Would you believe the picture on the card was of the Grand Ole Opry, of all places?"

"The Grand Ole Opry!" he repeated. "What on earth is she doing there? I must say, I have always wanted to see it myself."

"Apparently she met a rich music producer from Nashville," I said, hanging Jacqueline's gown on a padded hanger. "I can't say I'm surprised. She didn't say too much about what she's doing or when she'll be back, but I did learn that she at least didn't sell our house."

Anthony tilted his head and looked at me quizzically.

"When I tried to call a few weeks back, the telephone was disconnected. She forgot to pay the utilities," I explained. "But she said I 'shouldn't worry.' Easy for her to say. She doesn't have school in the fall. Who knows if I'll be going back to Pine Mountain High."

"That must be hard," Anthony said. "Not knowing when you're going back or what you're going back to." Anthony snipped an errant thread from Mitzy's gown. "I have to say, though, I'm selfishly thrilled that you're here. And can you imagine what Etta would have done if you weren't?" That hadn't occurred to me, that me being here turned out to be good luck for Aunt Etta.

"I was so angry at first," I said. "When Momma just up and left me. But I feel different now."

"Oh?"

"Well, it's hard to put into words, but I'm not in such a hurry to leave Bright Leaf."

Anthony clapped his hands together. "I would be over the moon if you stayed!"

"Oh . . . I wouldn't stay forever," I said. "I couldn't."

"The Lord giveth . . . And the Lord taketh away."

"Silly, I do have to go back to school in the fall."

"What's stopping you from skipping your last year and staying in Bright Leaf? I didn't finish school. Why should you? You're all grown-up and already sewing gowns for the finest ladies of Bright Leaf." With that he gave my shoulder a squeeze.

Anthony may have been a gadfly and a terrible gossip, but he was true blue, a real friend. I felt awful about the way I'd spoken to him earlier.

"I suppose it's possible," I admitted. Lots of girls my age didn't finish high school. "But I want to graduate with my class. I've worked hard and I want that diploma."

"Smart girl," he said. "Of course you do."

"For now, it's nice to be here, to be of use," I said. "It feels good, you know—to be needed?"

"I do know," he said, then got quiet for a moment. "Oh, I nearly forgot!" Anthony rushed for his sewing carryall, then carefully removed a fistful of feathers from his bag. "Do you have a vase? Or an empty water glass or something? If these feathers aren't handled with care, the shaft will crease and they'll be ruined."

I poured out a few stray buttons from a Ball jar and set it on the table in front of him. He placed the ostrich feathers inside, quill side down so that they stood upright like flowers.

"These are gorgeous, Anthony," I said, admiring the bouquet of ink-black plumes. "So elegant. They're exactly what I wanted for her hat. Now I just have to find time to cut away the excess fabric, sew the brim, and add the head ribbon and all the trimmings."

He sighed. "You'll do it. I know you will," he said as he stood up. "Now I'm afraid I have to skedaddle, honey. It's getting late, and I have to be back at the factory first thing tomorrow morning. But I'll see you in the afternoon, and the day after that and the day after that." He gave me a peck on each cheek and left in a whirl of air kisses.

With Anthony gone and the satisfaction of some good work behind me, I decided to take a well-earned break, but a knock on the door sounded just as I sat down.

"Maddie, dear," Mitzy said, opening the door slowly, as if she might be interrupting.

"Miss Mitzy!" I scrambled out of the chair and quickly scanned the room. Thankfully I kept a tidy workspace and all was in order.

She wore a red-and-white-striped coat dress with silver buttons down the front, and a white eyelet pique collar, and moved with grace as she walked around the room. This was the first time she had stopped by the *studio* and she wanted to *see absolutely everything,* she said.

"Oh my goodness," Mitzy cooed. "Look at those gorgeous feathers." She crossed to the table and placed a rectangular brown paper package next to the ostrich plumes so that she could run her hand across their downy soft tops.

I showed her Cornelia's nearly finished hat and she nodded approvingly, agreeing that the feathers would be perfect. Then she walked over to the gowns and began examining them.

"Why are there two royal blue dresses that look almost identical?" she asked, comparing the dresses for Jacqueline and Allyson.

"Miss Jacqueline and Miss Allyson asked for matching dresses," I said, joining her next to the rolling rack. "They insisted, in fact."

Mitzy scrunched up her nose. "Hmm," she said, bringing her forefinger to her lips. "I'm surprised that this was what they wanted. None of my friends would dream of wearing the same dress as another woman, but who am I to judge? You'll have to suggest that they vary their accessories, Maddie. One should wear gold jewelry. Gold is lovely with royal blue. The other should wear a pop of color. A bold, complementary shade. Perhaps a bolero shrug in vivid red or bright pink."

The thought of adding another item to my long list of evening wear to finish made my stomach clench. "Thank you for the suggestion," I said, managing to stretch my mouth into a smile. I hoped Mitzy wouldn't notice if I didn't make the shrug. Who knew if Miss Jacqueline or Miss Allyson would even want one.

I braced myself for more "helpful" suggestions as Mitzy inspected each dress and questioned me about the wearer and work left to be done. After she was satisfied with my updates and designs, she suddenly remembered that she had things to do and excused herself.

On her way to the door she stopped at the table in the corner and tapped her forefinger on the brown package she'd brought. "Cornelia wanted you to have this." She winked.

As she opened the door, she said in a serious tone, "You're doing a fine job with the gowns. Keep up the good work, Maddie."

I was pleased to have Mitzy's praise and approval. Seeing everything through her eyes, I realized how far I'd come. I sat down at the table, smiling to myself, and ripped open the paper of Cornelia's package to discover a book, *A Room of One's Own* by Virginia Woolf. As I started to leaf through the brand-new pages, a letter fluttered onto my lap.

*Dear Maddie,*

*This essay by Virginia Woolf is based on a series of lectures that she delivered at two women's colleges at Cambridge University in October 1928. It should be required reading for every young woman, and therefore I have purchased this copy for you.*

*I hope that you will take to heart what you read here, and in the book that I loaned to you. You were too quiet during our meeting. Only when prompted did you assert yourself.*

*You must use your voice, Maddie. Take ownership of what's yours. Speak up for yourself as soon as you enter a room, otherwise, men will drown you out. Share your ideas confidently and claim your place in this world.*

*Oh, and design a hat for me that will be the talk*

*of the Gala. I have a feeling that it will be the first*
*of many.*

*Sincerely,*
*Cornelia Hale*

Intrigued and flattered, I began reading the curious book. This Mrs. Woolf spoke of war and jealousy
and of all things—soup! But mostly she talked about
women, about the history of men's opposition to
women's emancipation, and about how a woman must
have money and a room of her own if she was to write.
I had no notion of writing a book—reading was quite
enough for me—but as I looked around the room, not
quite my own, I thought about how money and space
were allowing me the privilege of my work. How it
was *my work.* What a wonderful realization that was.
I wanted to thank the English lady who had written
this. I wanted to thank Cornelia too. I may have been
out of school for the summer, but these lessons were
golden.

As I continued reading, a cross-stitch sampler
hanging in Frances's living room came to mind. She had
made it during the summer when I was ten because Aunt
Etta was teaching me to cross-stitch at the same time.
My samplers were neat and meticulous, and I was able

to complete three of them before my visit to Bright Leaf ended that year. But Frances only ever sewed the one. She was terrible with a needle and thread, and Aunt Etta and I teased her relentlessly about her slow progress and lopsided work. Still, she wouldn't give up. She said she liked the quote too much to abandon it. I could picture the sampler now, framed in oak over Frances's mantelpiece, the wobbly stitching picked out in green against a bright white background: WHEN THE STUDENT IS READY, THE TEACHER WILL APPEAR.

I thought of my own teacher, then. My dear Aunt Etta. She had been in the hospital for nearly two weeks now, so surely she'd be going home soon. I couldn't wait until then though. I'd waited long enough. I needed to talk to her. To see how she was doing and tell her not to worry, that I would take care of things for her, that all she had to do was concentrate on getting well. That was the right thing to do, and I should've done it sooner. I walked down to the parlor and picked up the phone to call the hospital.

A nurse answered, her voice proper and starched as I imagined her uniform to be. "Ward eight," she said. "This is Nurse Baxter speaking."

"Yes, um, hello. Nurse? My name is Maddie Sykes. I would like to speak to my aunt Etta, please. Etta Sykes, that is."

"Last I checked on her she was sleeping. She shouldn't be disturbed."

I needed to think fast. "Please, nurse? I'm my aunt's only family and she's there all alone. I don't want her to think that I've forgotten her."

"Well, that's kind of you, miss, but your aunt needs to rest." There was dead air for a moment, and I thought Nurse Baxter might have hung up, but then she said, "Tell you what. Let me go and check on her, and if she's awake and feeling up to it, I'll see if I can bring her here for a moment. But only a moment, mind."

"Thank you so much. Thank you!"

The nurse was gone for what seemed like ages, but then I heard Aunt Etta's voice on the phone. She spoke more softly than usual, and her voice was a little raspy, but it was my aunt all right. I could have cried, it was so good to hear her.

"Maddie, honey. Hey there. It's so good to hear your voice. I wish you could come visit. They're awful strict here though, aren't they? How are you?"

"How am I? Aunt Etta, you're the one in the hospital. I'm the one calling to ask after you."

"Thank you, sweetheart." I could hear the smile in her voice. "My fever broke last week, but truth be told, there were a couple of scares. Probably why the doctors are keeping me here still. But I'm doing better, and I don't have the need to sleep as much. I've just been feeling a tightness in my chest. I'm sure that's nothing. I'm hoping they'll let me out of here in the next few days. But enough about me. Is everything all right with you at the Winstons'? How are the preparations going for the Gala? I want you to tell me all about it."

I did, mostly. I told her about how kind Mitzy was to me, about the fittings for Rose and Cornelia, and about how I'd set up the workroom just like she'd taught me. I didn't want to bother her with news of how Babe had stormed out, so I told her that Anthony and I were working well together and that she shouldn't worry about anything.

Surprisingly, even though I was telling her only the bright side so that she wouldn't fret, as I went through the list of everything, I started to feel better about the mountain of work at hand. I was beginning to believe that I might pull this off after all. "Oh, and you'll never guess what I came up with for Miss Cornelia—"

Just then I heard the nurse's crisp voice.

"All right, now. It's time to get back to bed. You're not going to get better in this drafty hallway."

"Maddie, dear. I have to say good-bye. You look after yourself, do you hear?"

With that, the phone went dead.

# Eighteen

*A small gathering of family and friends.* That's how
Mitzy had described her sister's Fourth of July
birthday celebration. It was anything but.

When I walked downstairs on the afternoon of the
party, I came face-to-face with a dozen young people
I understood to be the tobacco kids. At least that's
what Anthony had called them. These youngsters had
the same look of wealth and status as the wives. One
little girl was wearing an elaborate smocked dress with
puffed sleeves, and another wore a sundress constructed
of hard-to-find floral seersucker. Another, about my
age, was wearing an outfit I swore I saw in one of Aunt
Etta's *Vogue* magazines. I loved the ensemble Mitzy
had set aside for me. It was perfect for the Fourth, a
full navy skirt with a red and white polka-dot bodice.

Mitzy marched us all through the house toward the

salon, where wide double doors opened like a gaping mouth onto the back porch. The rose garden, buzzing with wasps, stood off to the right. A string quartet filled the air with a staccato tune from a platform out on the lawn. Young children chased each other in circles around the white tables, and some of the older folks had already found seats and filled their plates with cantaloupe balls and tiny sandwiches with the crusts cut off. I saw Cornelia sitting at one of the tables. She raised her champagne flute in my direction when I caught her eye and may have even smiled.

A waiter in a white jacket handed me a frosty glass of Cheerwine. It was impossible to get during the war, but there was plenty here. I took a sip and sighed when I tasted the familiar sweetness of the black cherry fizz. I hadn't realized how much I'd missed it. Looking around at the gathering, I found it hard to believe that there'd even been a war. Red, white, and blue balloons marked the chairs at both ends of the longest table on the lawn. Off to the side, near the quartet, sat a smaller table with a chocolate cake under a glass cover. Ashley stood next to the cake, giving two little boys a talking-to. One crossed his arms and glared at her while the other one laughed and ran off. She noticed me approaching and leaned down to say something to her son. He couldn't have been more than four, with big brown eyes and hair so blond it was almost white.

"Hi there," I said, bending down to his level. "What's your name?" I asked, but he wasn't much interested in me.

"Carter, where are your manners? Say hello to Miss Maddie," said Ashley. "She's Miss Etta's niece. You remember, the lady who sews for me."

"Hello, Miss Maddie," he droned in the way prompted children do, his eyes never leaving the chocolate cake.

"Momma, can I have the first piece-a your birthday cake?" He squinted as he looked up at his mother.

"No, sir," she said. "You can wait your turn like all the other little boys and girls. Anyway, this isn't my birthday cake. Aunt Mitzy would never serve a plain brown cake at a party."

Carter stuck out his bottom lip, then got distracted and scampered off to join a game of duck, duck, goose.

"This isn't your birthday cake?" I asked.

"It's for Richard," Ashley explained, tucking her hair behind one ear.

"For Mr. Winston?" I didn't understand.

"Yes, that's right."

"But it's not his birthday."

"Exactly," said Ashley, pursing her lips and giving

me a little wink. "Richard prefers chocolate, you see. If he condescends to come to a birthday party—and he's usually too busy, mind you—he expects chocolate cake."

"Oh," I replied, lowering my voice to match her quiet tone. "Does everyone always do exactly what he wants?" I knew my question was rude, but I never would have dared to ask had we not had that conversation in her car.

"Mitzy certainly does," said Ashley, taking a sip of her lemonade. I thought that was all she would say, but she continued, even more quietly.

"Mitzy may take things a little too far, but she's not much different from the others. We've all been taught that our husbands call the shots. God forbid we should ever have an opinion of our own—and if we do, we'd better keep it to ourselves. I mean, it's right there in the marriage vows, isn't it? 'Love, honor, and obey.'"

I nodded, unsure of how to respond. Ashley covered her lemonade with her hand, deterring a hovering wasp. When she reached over, I saw that her dress was big on her, gaping under the arms. *True size 8 but prefers a 10*, I remembered from her note card. *Comfort over vanity* it said.

"Did you ever notice, Maddie, that men are asked to speak different words than we are during the wedding ceremony? Husbands don't have to *obey* anyone. They only have to 'love, honor, and cherish.' How's that for getting off easy? It's sad that so few of them even manage to hold up the simpler end of the bargain."

I glanced around, wondering if Ashley's husband was one of the men in shirtsleeves playing croquet near the rose garden, or maybe one of the important-looking executives clustered together at the far end of the lawn. There was a collection of men there, holding highball glasses and wearing nearly identical summer suits. I didn't know much about her husband except that he'd been called up to fight right at the very beginning of the war and had only recently returned home from Europe.

Ashley had gone quiet now and was looking over my head, all around the lawn. Searching for her sons, I bet. Across the way, Mitzy stood on the terrace, waving at Ashley to join her.

"Come on over here now, Ashley," she called. "We're about ready to cut the cake!"

Ashley flashed me a strained smile then made her way through the throng of happy guests, all nodding and smiling indulgently at her. She climbed the three flagstone steps to the outer edge of the terrace, where Mitzy had rolled out a three-tiered pink cake with white sparklers. The string quartet shifted gears and started to play the familiar refrain of "Happy Birthday to You."

"Happy birthday to Ashley and America!" one of the men standing with Mr. Winston shouted, raising his glass.

As I took a sip of my Cheerwine, my eyes landed on David, who appeared to have been watching me from across the lawn. A slow smile emerged as he removed his straw fedora and began walking in my direction. I felt a little shiver at his reaction, a nice one. Then I had a flash of the jitters as I imagined myself spilling my cherry red drink all down Mitzy's beautiful dress. Thankfully, a waiter took the glass out of my trembling hand as David approached.

He kissed me on the cheek before speaking, lingering a bit longer than a peck—his lips soft and his skin slightly rough, sandpapery, where he must have missed a spot shaving.

"You look lovely," he said, holding my gaze.

"You don't look so bad yourself." I wasn't sure if that was the right response, but I'd heard an actress say that in a movie. "There are so many people here. I thought it was supposed to be a small party."

"By Mimi's standards, this is a small party," David

said with a grin. He took a sip of his lemonade and tipped his head toward Mitzy, who was approaching us. "Here comes the hostess herself."

"There you two are!" Mitzy gushed as she sidled up to us. "Are you heading into town for the fireworks soon?" she asked as she handed each of us a slice of strawberry cake with a scoop of vanilla ice cream.

"Actually," David said. "I had another idea, if Maddie is interested. It's a quieter spot, with a better view of the fireworks. You can see the covered bridge we talked about. Remember? You promised."

Mitzy scrunched up her nose. "A dusty old bridge? That's not very festive, David."

"That sounds interesting," I said, relieved that I wouldn't have to mingle with David's friends, to put on airs all night, surrounded by rich kids. I wouldn't have to deal with that flirty Vivien trying to woo David either.

I took a bite of cake; it tasted exactly like fresh strawberries, not too sweet.

"Well, all right then," Mitzy said. "You two have fun." She grinned before excusing herself to *make sure every last one of my guests has a slice of this divine cake.*

David polished off his cake and ice cream, and a waiter took our plates. Porch lights flickered on and a group of children, assisted by one of the fathers in shirt-sleeves, lit sparklers on the lawn, their faces alternating between terror and delight as the white sparks crackled.

David replaced his hat and offered me his arm. "Shall we?"

I threaded mine through his, and off we went, across the lawn and around to the front of the house. We walked down the drive together, the crunch of the gravel under our feet. It was ordinary yet extraordinary, walking beside this handsome boy, the late-day sun slipping below the horizon, and the weight of the air at that moment. If this was a dream, I didn't want to wake up.

We walked arm in arm for a good long while, way past the houses and onto the paved road that turned to bumpy dirt when we got closer to the tobacco fields. Occasionally David would point out something in the distance—an old tree revered for some reason or another, a spot where a landmark once stood. Mostly we were quiet, the type of comfortable quiet neither of us felt the need to fill.

I could see our destination coming into view. The top of the covered bridge forming a graceful peak at the field's edge, its red walls faded from decades under the hot sun. We turned down a narrow dirt road, where on either side of us were knee-high tobacco stalks as far as the eye could see. That's when David started coughing. At first, the coughs were small and polite. But the deeper we went into the fields, the worse it got. His eyes watered and his chest rattled, followed by a deep bark then wheezing as he tried to get air in and out.

He let go of my arm, held up one finger, then took a pack of cigarettes from his pants pocket. He lit one up and sucked on it.

"Are you okay?" I asked.

"Yes." He nodded. "These really help." He shook the pack in my direction. "Would you like one?"

"No, no thank you," I said.

"You sure?" he asked.

"Yes. I don't think that smoking—"

David coughed again. Louder and longer than before. "Don't worry, I'm not contagious," he said with a playful little croak.

"It's not that. I just—I don't smoke anymore . . ."

"Really?" He tilted his head to look me in the eye. "Why is that?"

I didn't know what to say. I felt like I could trust David, maybe even tell him about the letter, but I was enjoying the moment too much. I didn't want the world to intrude, so I shrugged my shoulders and hoped he wouldn't press further.

"How can you live in North Carolina and not smoke?" he asked, reaching for my hand. "The whole state is built on tobacco," he continued, as though I needed reminding.

"Yes, I know." That was exactly why the letter made me feel sick.

He nodded ahead. "The covered bridge is a great example of that. This very bridge made it possible for Bright Leaf to export. Without a way to cross the river, we'd have been a small-time operation."

He seemed so proud. The bridge was impressively long, at least a quarter of a mile from end to end, and covered from the elements with a peaked wooden ceiling.

"It's a bit dusty and old," David said, slapping the side of it. "But doesn't it have nice bones?" He gazed up at the cat's cradle of beams. "The frame, I mean." He turned to me. "I'm boring you. I'm sorry."

"No, not at all," I said. "It reminds me of constructing a corset. The supports are called bones, steel and spiral ones." I squinted up to admire the rafters. "That's interesting," I said, pointing to a curved beam. "That curved beam there would be like the spiral ones you use for the curved sides at the waist of a corset. Straight steel ones are fine for the sides and back, but they'd buckle at the curved seams. Same principle here with the bridge, seems to me."

David stilled and studied me, a half-smile on his face.

"What?" I said, wiping my cheek. "Do I have something on my face?"

"No." He laughed, coming closer. He stood right in front of me and brushed an errant curl from my forehead.

A few breathless moments passed between us before he gently drew my face to his. I was transported—me back home at the quarry, standing atop its highest rock wall, my toes gripping its gritty ledge as I considered the still turquoise water below. I swam there every summer, but had never been brave enough to jump from the highest point.

Then David's lips touched mine, and it was as if I'd stepped off. Release, fear, joy, astonishment as my body pierced the surface and shot deep under, the water ice cold at the bottom, then warming as I came up up up to take a glorious breath.

We hung there for a few seconds, our mouths so close they were practically touching, smiling at each other. A car approached in the distance, and we stepped out of the bridge to let it pass. David intertwined his fingers through mine as the driver tipped his hat, his car kicking up gravel as he drove by.

David squeezed my hand. "Maddie, Maddie, Maddie." He sighed. "You're really something." I'd only ever kissed one boy, Peter Piercy, and that was back behind the school on a dare. There was no comparing that kiss with this.

"Follow me," David said. "This is what I wanted to show you." He directed me around the corner to a makeshift ladder that led up to the top of the bridge. "Great view of the fireworks."

"I'll bet."

"Ladies first," he said.

"In this?" I motioned to my skirt. "I don't think so, David Taylor. You first."

He laughed. "Of course."

We climbed the rungs and found a spot near the peak, which wasn't as steep as it appeared from below. We sat on the sandpapery slope, our knees bent to steady ourselves, and took in the twinkling lights in the distance. I shivered, a slight chill running through me. David draped his arm around my shoulder, and we huddled close. Then, as if on cue—pop, pop, hiss. An explosion of red, white, and blue rained down. A pause and then another pop, pop, bam overhead, white ones like dandelions bloomed and disappeared in the sky. A bottle rocket swooshed high, and faraway cheers erupted as it went off with a deafening bang.

David looked like a little boy, his face open and full of wonder as we watched the sky light up above us.

"What happened to your chin?" I asked, running my finger across the thin white line.

"That battle scar?" he said, rubbing it with his thumb. "I decided to experiment with my father's razor . . . when I was five."

"Oh my gosh, David," I said. "Thank goodness it wasn't worse."

"Yeah," he said. "I learned my lesson and didn't try again until I was fourteen. That time Mr. W taught me." I pictured Mr. Winston helping a young version of David glide a razor across his face and was thankful I hadn't told him about the letter. I knew David and Mr. Winston were close, but the fact that they shared such a meaningful rite of passage gave me pause.

When the fireworks became fewer and farther between, we heard a grinding rumble coming from the opposite end of the bridge.

"Uh-oh," David said, squinting in the distance. "Looks like a flatbed, a fully loaded one."

An enormous truck barreled toward us, its red cab barely visible, its headlights on full bright.

"Should we get down?" I asked, my breath quickening.

"Too late now," David said, his eyes darting first to the truck, then to me. He wrapped his arm around me tighter. "S'all right. We'll be fine."

The bridge rattled beneath us as the truck neared, its gears grinding as it entered, then thundered out the other side. David and I whipped our heads around to watch it go. It carried at least a dozen hogsheads on its long back, lying on their sides like logs. The giant barrels of tobacco were filled to the gills and tied down with thick rope. I held my breath as the driver came up on the sharp turn ahead, but he hugged the curve without a hitch.

Relieved, I glanced at David. "I thought the truck might tip right over," I said.

"No." He shook his head and pulled me closer. "It would take a lot more than a little bend in the road to bring down a load of tobacco."

# Nineteen

It wasn't like Mitzy not to greet her sister, not when Ashley had come here for her final fitting. She'd taken supper in her room last night too. I hoped she wasn't feeling poorly, not with the Gala just days away.

I looked around the parlor, the same room where I'd first assisted Aunt Etta and Mitzy just a few weeks ago. It felt different now, transformed. I'd almost asked if the walls had been painted or the drapes had been replaced, but I knew that it was me, and not the room, that had changed. My confidence had grown with each appointment, with each fitting and alteration. I'd been tentative at first, unsure of who I was and what the wives would make of me. But now I spoke up and offered my opinions. And I realized that watching what was going on around you wasn't a bad thing at all, not when you could put what you saw to good use.

"I don't even need to try it on," Ashley said, biting her fingernail as she examined her outfit. "It looks perfect to me."

"Are you sure," I asked. "Don't you just want to—"

"Really, I can see what a good job you've done. I know it will fit. I'm going to check on Mitzy and will be back to collect it in a few minutes. Thank you, Maddie. For all you've done. Etta would be proud of you."

I hoped my disappointment didn't show. I was looking forward to spending more time with Ashley. Our conversations had been eye-opening, and I wondered what she might say if we had a chance to talk more while I fit and finished her dress.

I learned that women tended to share more of themselves when they stood on a seamstress's platform. Now that I was working more closely with the wives, I noticed how they opened up like flowers as they studied their reflection, contemplating what they saw.

I was tidying up my little work area when muffled voices prompted me to peek out the parlor door. Three slow figures were shuffling down the hall—Ashley and

334 • ADELE MYERS

Ruth supporting a panic-stricken Mitzy. She had her hair pulled back and not a stitch of makeup on her ghostly face. She walked as if she might break.

"Should I call Dr. Hale?" Ruth asked.

"Yes," Ashley said, holding on to her sister. "I'm taking her straight to the hospital."

"I was praying it would stop," Mitzy whispered. "It was just a little at first. But then this morning, the pains started."

"It's probably fine, Mitzy, but it's best to have Dr. Hale check you and the baby to make sure."

The baby. Mitzy was expecting. My hand flew up to cover my mouth. How could I not have realized? She hadn't been "feeling herself" lately. At the Solstice party she'd had to sit down and rest, and then later it must have been Mitzy I saw getting sick behind that Buick. The signs were all there. I can't believe I had missed them all.

I stepped into the hallway to join them. My palms were clammy, my jaw slack.

Mitzy gave me a meek smile. "Maddie, I wanted to tell you about the baby under pleasant circumstances," she said apologetically. "I almost shared the news with you when you were trying on my gowns last week, but I wanted to be sure before I said anything." She paused and shook her head.

"Mitzy, you don't have to explain," Ashley said. "Maddie, can you help? Hold these."

She pushed two handbags into my arms and guided her sister to the staircase.

"Do you have any more appointments today?"

"Not until late afternoon," I said.

"Good," Ashley replied. "You can help me get Mitzy to the hospital. Ruth, after you phone Dr. Hale, please clean up Mitzy's room and bathroom. She'll want fresh linens when she comes home." Turning to me, Ashley said, "I'll call Richard and tell him we're taking Mitzy to the hospital."

"Oh!" Mitzy said. "Please, Ashley—don't do that. He's so very busy and there's nothing he can do. Let's wait."

Ashley considered this. She took a deep breath and nodded. "Okay, Mitzy. But I'm going to call him after you've seen the doctor."

"Thank you," she said, her voice low. Then, "I'm sorry I made such a mess." Poor Mitzy, offering up her apology like she'd done something wrong.

Everyone assured her that any mess was the last thing she should worry about now.

Once we'd made it to Ashley's car, we helped Mitzy lay down across the backseat and elevated her legs. I sat in the front passenger seat as Ashley sped us across town, rolling through stop signs, passing cars left and right.

"Easy on the bumps," Mitzy said, wincing.

"Sorry," Ashley said. She kept glancing in the rear-view mirror, sweat beading at her temples. "Maddie, you follow me when we get inside. Since you're with us, it's fine for you to come along to the maternity floor. If you can carry our things, I'll help Mitzy."

I nodded, then stared at the road ahead.

The doors of the maternity ward at Baptist Hospital opened into a vast, rectangular room. Identical metal beds lined the stark white walls, almost all of them oc-cupied by pregnant women. Each had her nightstand and privacy curtain, many of which had been pushed aside to reveal the patients and their swollen bellies. The women chatted with their neighbors or read or tended to their sewing, something to pass the time. Not all of them, though. A blonde with dark circles under her eyes held a mewling infant to her breast as a nurse tried to guide the reluctant baby. The woman beside her lay on her side moaning, her legs pulled up under her. A little farther down, a young lady, not much older than me, sobbed into her cupped hands as two nurses removed a bloody sheet from beneath her. It was a shocking and strange sight, the display of such high and low emotions in one room. I averted my eyes from the ones suffering. It didn't seem right for me to witness their pain.

"Oh, there he is," Ashley said.

Dr. Hale entered the ward, lowering his surgical mask and removing a pair of gloves, which a nurse took and scurried away.

"Mitzy, Ashley. Come over here." He motioned with his hand, as if guiding a driver out of a parking spot. "Let's get you to an exam area, shall we?" he said, taking Mitzy's hand between his palms. "Agnes," he shouted, "take Mrs. Winston to number five. No, ten. There's more privacy there at the end."

Ashley helped her sister slip out of her coat and handed it to me. "Wait here until I get her settled," she said.

Dr. Hale stood with me as the sisters followed a nurse behind the curtain across the room.

"Feel free to take a peek in the nursery," he said to me. "They say we're having a baby boom in this country. I can attest to that," he added with a smile. I peered through the glass where rows upon rows of tightly swaddled infants squirmed and slept. Some of the babies were in baskets. Others were in glass boxes with lightbulbs shining on their delicate, tufted heads.

A match struck just behind me, the smell of sulfur and then smoke as Dr. Hale lit a cigarette. He looked over my shoulder. "Those are incubators," he said, pointing. "The premature newborns must be kept at a slightly elevated temperature. Keeping their bodies warm for them means they can use their calories to help their underdeveloped bodies grow."

I took in the tiny bundles. Their heads reminded me of fuzzy peaches and looked every bit as delicate. Most babies were chubby little things, but these newborns had strangely lean faces, which made their eyes look enormous. "What is that on their noses?" I asked.

"That's surgical tape. It keeps their feeding tubes in place. You can hardly see them from here, but each baby has a thin feeding tube that runs from the naso-pharynx directly into the stomach."

"Their mothers don't feed them?" I asked.

"No, they don't have the sucking reflex yet, and even if they did, we don't want them using up energy eating."

It was sad and unnatural. And there were so many of them.

Ashley joined us at the window. "The nurse said she's almost ready," she reported, glancing at the lines of infants in front of us. "There are so many more incubators than when Carter was born," she said.

"Yes, there's greater demand now," said Dr. Hale. "I personally think it has less to do with the baby boom and more to do with the fact that so many of you ladies entered the workforce." He tsked. "Soon enough, we'll get you all back home where you can focus on a woman's real job, getting our next generation here safely."

Ashley and I exchanged a look. The nurse cleared her throat then waved us over. Dr. Hale removed a small tin from his jacket pocket, snuffing out his cigarette and closing it with the butt inside. We followed him to Mitzy's bed.

"Excuse us," Dr. Hale said, then swished the privacy curtain around Mitzy so we couldn't see what was going on. We could hear it, though. Every word.

"Let's see about you and that baby, shall we?" the doctor asked. From the bottom of the curtain I could see Mitzy raise her legs onto the bed. "Get a pillow for her feet," Dr. Hale snapped at the nurse. "And a Pinard horn."

"Tell me what happened, and when it started," he said. I could hear the crinkle of cotton. Whether it was Mitzy's blouse or a bedsheet, I couldn't tell.

"It started last night, the bleeding," Mitzy whispered. "But only a little. Then this morning . . . well this morning there was even more and then the pains started." She paused for a moment. "Just like before."

There was silence for a moment, then Dr. Hale said, "Heart rate is a bit elevated, but that's to be expected.

Now, Mitzy, take deep, slow breaths." I could hear a slight tap as he positioned and repositioned the stethoscope. "Mm-hmm. Sounds good," he said.

"Now, let's check on baby's heartbeat," he said. Then came the cheerful jingling of Mitzy's charm bracelet.

Please let the baby be okay, I prayed. Please let the baby be okay.

"You'll feel some pressure," he warned.

I held my breath, wondering what Dr. Hale had heard. Next to me, a pregnant brunette shook her head and exhaled a steady stream of smoke from her crimson lips. She wore full makeup and a baby blue nightgown. It was then I noticed the trails of smoke drifting toward the high ceiling from nearly every bed. Worse was the stench of mint wafting over from the nurses chatting nearby. Suddenly, I couldn't catch my breath. I glanced around the room, frantic, the mix of antiseptic and minty smoke sickening me.

Dr. Hale pushed aside the privacy curtain and handed the Pinard horn to the nurse. He motioned for us to come closer, raised his head and smiled broadly. "A perfectly normal, strong heartbeat," he reported.

"Really?" Mitzy said, her voice high and shaky. "Are you sure?"

"Indeed I am," Dr. Hale assured her. "We'll do a

full exam and keep a close eye on you, but I suspect you've simply overdone it again, Mitzy."

"Oh, thank God. Thank God," Ashley said, leaning over to hug her sister.

"Yes, well, not getting enough rest can disrupt the female hormones, you know," Dr. Hale said. "You ladies are delicate and need to treat yourselves as such."

Ashley scowled at that.

"We've discussed your schedule before, Mitzy," the doctor continued. "It's simply unreasonable for someone with your history to be doing all that you're doing. I want you to reduce your activity *drastically.*" He pulled a small notepad and pen from his breast pocket and began to scribble something. "You'll take two tablespoons of Miss Molly's Soothing Syrup at bedtime every night. Once a day, you'll apply a vegetable compound liniment to your abdomen. Nurse Agnes will give that to you." He nodded at the young nurse who was assisting him. "I know a rest cure isn't possible with the Gala so soon, but try to take it easy and keep yourself calm," he said. He tore the page off the pad and handed it to Mitzy. "Do you have some MOMints with you? Those will help. Agnes!" he called, snapping his fingers at the nurse. "Bring Mrs. Winston a pack of MOMints."

*No!* That's the last thing she needs. My heart beat

wildly in my chest and I broke out into a cold sweat. How could he suggest that she smoke cigarettes knowing what he knew? Unless . . . I studied his face. He looked so proud, gazing down at Mitzy, as if he had saved the day. He spoke with conviction when he said MOMints would help her, but it was impossible to know whether he was telling the truth or lying underneath that smug grin.

"Thank you ever so much, Robert," Mitzy said, wiping under her eyes with the pads of her middle fingers. "I don't know what I'd do without you." She sighed. She promised that she would get plenty of rest. "I'll do whatever I need to do. I couldn't cope with another loss," she whispered and shuddered slightly.

"Good," Dr. Hale said. "Let's get that baby here safe and sound."

He turned to Nurse Agnes. "Get her a blanket," he said. "And give me those." He reached for the MOMints and lit one for Mitzy.

# **Twenty**

It pained me to leave Mitzy at the hospital, but when Ashley dropped me off at the Winstons' house, I dashed right up to my studio. I prayed Anthony would be there.

"Anthony!" I gasped as I rushed in. I was relieved to find him at the worktable, though I'd forgotten he'd be there.

"Good lord," he said, backing away from the dress he'd been working on. "You scared the bejesus out of me, Maddie." He cut his eyes behind me as he spoke out of the side of his mouth. "And probably our guest too."

I spun around to find David standing near the small table where I ate and worked on sketches. "What are you doing here?" I snapped in surprise. David flinched at my rudeness. "Oh, I'm sorry," I said. "I just . . . I didn't expect you to be here."

"Obviously not," David said, with a tight laugh. "I came by to see you and was catching up with my old acquaintance while I waited."

"David, do you remember how we used to skip stones down at Windsor Pond during your father's fittings?" Anthony chuckled. "I still can't skip more than three times, but David always—"

"Anthony!" I spat. "We don't have time for you two to reminisce!"

"Gosh, Maddie," he said, his eyes wide. "What's wrong? I've never seen you so upset."

I couldn't catch my breath. The air wouldn't come fast enough. I felt panicked. Hemmed in. I fanned my hands in front of my face in an attempt to calm down. Anthony led me to one of the chairs at the small table and placed a glass of water in front of me.

David sat next to me and rested his hand on my back. "Are you all right? What on earth has happened?"

"No, I mean yes, I'm okay." I paused. "It's not me I'm worried about."

Anthony removed the pink measuring tape from around his neck and placed it on the table. "Is it Etta? Your mother?"

"No, no." I shook my head. "It's Mimi. She had a scare with the baby this morning. I've just come from the hospital."

"Baby?" David pressed. "She's expecting again?"

"What do you mean, *again*?" asked Anthony.

"She lost a baby last fall, right before it was supposed to be born," David said. "She was devastated."

Oh God. This was even worse than I thought.

"Is she okay?" Anthony asked. "What about the baby?"

I held my face in my hands and closed my eyes. "Dr. Hale says they'll be fine as long as Mimi stays off her feet. He's keeping her under observation overnight. Just as a precaution."

"Well, that's good news," David said. "Isn't it?"

"Yes," I agreed, raising my eyes to meet his. "But that's not all." I stood and retrieved my sewing satchel from behind the bolts of fabric. I couldn't keep this to myself any longer. Something had to be done.

"David . . . Anthony . . ." I said, my voice quivering. "I need to show you something. I need your help."

I removed the envelope from my bag and gave it to David, my hands shaking.

He took it, tentatively, "What is this?"

"Just read it. Please."

He rose from his seat and leaned back against the

wall as he took in the letter. Confusion crossed his face. "Where did you get this?"

I explained how I found it in Mr. Winston's study. "You were with me," I said. "It was an accident . . . I mean, I just grabbed it from his trash can to write down the hospital phone number. Later, I discovered that it wasn't just a discarded envelope, and when I read the letter inside, I knew something wasn't right."

"First of all," David said, "this is confidential. You shouldn't have read it. And second, Mr. W and Dr. Hale are two of the most upstanding men in Bright Leaf. If they are involved, there is no reason to be concerned."

I flinched at David's response. How dare he reprimand me for reading it, and then jump to the conclusion that there was nothing to worry about?

"But look what it says," I insisted. The paper rattled in his hand as I pointed to the part about infant death and low birth weight. "*This* doesn't concern you?" I said, jabbing it with my finger. "Look right here." I grabbed the letter from David and held it up for Anthony to see. "Dr. Hale says right here that 'the science is credible.' Credible. The science that smoking causes infant death is credible."

David stared blankly at the letter.

"Well?" I shouted, pivoting from David to Anthony and back again. "Am I the only one disturbed by this?"

Anthony cleared his throat. "Why don't we sit down and read it more carefully," he suggested.

David ran his hand roughly through his hair. "Okay, yes, let me read it again."

The two of them sat at the small table by the window, huddled over the letter. I paced as they read and re-read it. I'd practically memorized the whole thing I'd gone over it so many times.

"Well?" I said.

"Well, it does say here at the bottom 'conduct our own studies,'" Anthony offered. "Bright Leaf are American cigarettes, not the foreign ones that were tested."

"Yes," David agreed. "Mr. W's notes clearly lay out a plan. They're taking care of it, Maddie. I really think you're overreacting."

*Overreacting?*

"You're wrong," I said. "You're too quick to give them the benefit of the doubt. You've got to read between the lines. Dr. Hale says that studies are expensive and take time. This letter is dated May 18; that's only a month and a half ago. Do you really suppose they conducted their own study in six weeks?"

"I don't know, Maddie," David admitted. "But Mr. W is like a father to me and Dr. Hale has been taking care of my asthma since I was little. It's hard to believe they would do anything to hurt anyone, especially Mimi. We should at least give them the benefit of the doubt."

"Why?" I protested. I was the girl who cried wolf. Something was terribly wrong—terribly wrong and nobody would believe me. "Why should they get the benefit of the doubt? Because they're rich men? Because they're powerful?"

Anthony looked positively stunned that I would speak to David this way.

I went on.

"What about the women? What about the babies? You didn't see what I did. Mimi was distraught, terrified."

The heat in the room had become unbearable. I strode over to the window.

"And you should have seen all the babies—tiny babies, smaller than dolls. Dozens of them lined up behind a glass window, skinny little things with tubes going down their noses. Born too early. Who knows how many of them will survive. Just like Mimi's baby last fall. Do you know that Dr. Hale *told* her to smoke MOMints? At the end of the examination, he lit one for her and told her they would help her relax. He practically prescribed them."

My fingers strained to raise the pane of glass, to let

in some air, but my hands slipped, and I scraped them on the rough wood. "Damnit, damn," I hissed, examining the now-ragged fingernails on my right hand.

"Maddie, there is just no way Dr. Hale would deliberately put Mimi at risk like that," David said.

"How do you know?" I demanded. "How do you know for sure?"

"This is ridiculous," David said. "The three of us standing around here talking in circles. I'll talk to Dr. Hale. Find out about this study in Sweden and the one he refers to here. I'm sure this is all just a misunderstanding."

Anthony and I looked at each other. "I don't know," he said. "Isn't MOMints Dr. Hale's big claim to fame? I mean, he's the one who helped the chemists at Bright Leaf develop the mint formula."

"That's right," I said, seizing the moment to create an ally. "Dr. Hale and Rose are the stars of the national ad campaign, too. This is all so suspicious. He has a lot to lose if MOMints fail."

"She's right," Anthony said. "He has too much to lose. We have to find out what this letter means without giving away that we've seen it."

"How exactly are we supposed to do that?" David asked. I was trying to read his tone, but he wasn't giving much away.

I walked back to the window and frowned before noticing the metal bracket that stopped it from opening. It wasn't stuck; it was locked. I released the gold latch with my thumb and lifted the glass as far as it would go. I filled my lungs with a huge breath of fresh air.

Then I turned around to face my friends.

"David," I asked. "Don't you think it's time you saw Dr. Hale for a follow-up appointment?"

# Twenty-One

D r. Hale's private office was far more welcoming than the sterile halls of Baptist Hospital. Buttery leather armchairs instead of hard wooden seats. Hunter green walls instead of hospital white. A vase of fragrant lilies sat atop the oak coffee table, along with a figurine of a doctor holding a newborn upside down by its feet. Fashion magazines decorated every flat surface, as did sterling silver ashtrays, each of which contained a fresh pack of MOMints and a book of matches balanced against its lip.

"He'll be right with you, David," said the receptionist. Lucille was an older woman who wore her graying hair in a chin-length bob, a pencil tucked behind one ear. She smiled as she held up a lollipop from a glass jar. "When you're done, I'll have your favorite waiting right here, David." She looked over to me. "This child used to be just crazy for the green apple ones. When he was a toddler, nothing else would do. So I always put them aside, just for him." Lucille winked as if she had just shared a juicy secret. David smiled sheepishly.

Dr. Hale appeared in the doorway. "David, my boy. You nearly missed me. I have an early dinner date, and I was on my way out when you rang." He raised an eyebrow at the sight of me. "Well, hello there. I didn't expect to see you again so soon." I smiled at him as did David.

"Well, you'd better come on back, I guess," he said, holding the door open with one hand and waving David in with the other. "What's this *emergency* that couldn't wait until tomorrow? Does it have something to do with courting this pretty young lady here?"

I was mortified by Dr. Hale's crude joke.

David chuckled uneasily. "Would you mind if Maddie came back with us?" he asked. "This concerns her too."

"My," Dr. Hale said, "you two have gotten cozy." My face burned at the insinuation. I only hoped that I could keep my cool, that David and I could indeed pull this off. "It's a little unusual, David, to have a young lady in the examination room. But the decision is yours. The world sure is changing."

"Yes, sir," David said. "Thank you."

Once inside the exam room, Dr. Hale patted the table for David to hop up. "What seems to be the problem?"

"It's something new, actually," David said. "I had a terrible attack a few days ago. It was on the fourth of July, the worst one ever. Maddie was with me that night and witnessed it. She insisted I come see you."

I stood just inside the door, holding my clutch with both hands in front of me. I nodded and looked concerned.

"It was frightening to see David like that, Dr. Hale, and to see Miss Mitzy in her state earlier today. It was so reassuring the way you cared for her. I just felt we'd all sleep better tonight knowing you had checked out David too."

"Quite right," he said, placing the stethoscope in his ears. "I do have a calming effect on my patients. Now, David, let's have a listen to those lungs before we talk. I want to see if I detect anything new in your condition, without being prejudiced by your observations." He lifted his chin in my direction. "Or those of your lady friend," he said with a wink.

David untucked his shirttail. The paper crinkled beneath him on the examination table.

"Should I step outside for this part?" I asked, moving a little closer to the door.

"No, no," David said. "Please stay."

"He won't need to undress," Dr. Hale said, placing one hand on David's shoulder and the other beneath David's shirt on his back. "You're welcome to stay."

Still, I looked away and studied the wall to give them some privacy. A large framed photograph, another advertisement featuring the MOMints logo in the bottom corner, leaned against the wall. It was the largest one I'd seen, the size of a card table, featuring a carefully arranged group of women and children captured in vivid color.

"Grand, isn't it?" Dr. Hale said. "Feel free to take a closer look, young lady. I'll be unveiling this particular advertisement at the Gala." He turned his attention back to David, this time placing the stethoscope on his chest. "Deep breath," he said and paused to listen.

The photograph was truly spectacular, like something out of *Life magazine*. That was only fitting, Dr. Hale explained, as the new ad would appear in all the big national magazines, to coincide with the rollout of MOMints across the country. The women were arranged on an emerald-green lawn, some standing and some seated on bright white chairs with their legs delicately crossed. A magnificent oak, its gnarled knots and thick trunk attesting to a long life in Bright Leaf, provided a dappling of shade.

At least a dozen children, blond and dressed all in

white, surrounded the women in the foreground. One of Ashley's boys sat on her lap; the other stood nearby, as if at attention, his sweet, chubby arms stiff at his sides. All the women wore shades of green—MOMints green.

Mitzy looked absolutely stunning in a flowing tea dress. Rose donned a dreamy polka-dot peplum dress with white piping. She held her MOMints cigarette aloft, her eyes wide and her lips a fiery red. Cornelia wore a two-piece kelly-green suit and a sour expression, her only dissention a hint of French mauve in the flowers on her hat. The other wives, the ones who I had fitted and counseled in my workroom, stood behind Mitzy, Ashley, Cornelia, and Rose, the pecking order as evident in this photograph as it was in life.

"Fit as a fiddle," Dr. Hale reported. "Your lungs sound clearer than usual, my boy." I pivoted from the photograph and returned my attention to them. "Likely it was excitement that caused the trouble." Dr. Hale replaced the stethoscope around his neck and leaned back against a cabinet. He had removed his tie from earlier, and his gray eyes glinted as he observed David thoughtfully.

"What a relief," David began, fumbling a bit to rebutton his shirt. "I thought for sure that I'd need a treatment, but I feel like I can breathe easier just hearing you say my lungs are clear."

"Good then," Dr. Hale said, removing his pocket watch from his doctor's coat. "So we're done here."

"Wait," David said. "Since we're here, I wanted to ask you about something. Something related to my asthma that I overheard, actually—in the executive lunchroom a few weeks ago."

"Certainly, my boy," he said, replacing his pocket watch.

"Well, I was eating by myself that day, just reviewing some accounting statements Mr. W asked me to come by and help with, when two men I didn't recognize sat at the next table."

I hung on David's every word, leaning in, as if willing him to lie convincingly. We'd practiced several times on the way over.

"I wasn't eavesdropping. But their voices were so loud," David added. "I couldn't help but hear their conversation."

"Ha!" Dr. Hale exclaimed. "I bet they were salespeople! Every salesman I've ever met is a born gossip. They're like women that way."

David laughed with him. "So," he continued, "these two men were drinking whiskey and smoking cigars. They were celebrating because the younger man's wife was in the family way, and both of them were toasting her and the new baby to come. But the older man lowered his voice and asked if the younger one had heard anything about some medical studies the Bright Leaf directors are all up in arms about." David paused for a beat and then went on.

"The younger man shook his head—hadn't heard a thing. Then his friend revealed something very disturbing. It was so strange and upsetting I can recall the exact words he used." David looked to me for encouragement. I nodded for him to continue. "He said, 'I don't want to speak out of turn, but I suggest you get your girl to quit cigarettes pronto if you don't want your kid to end up with shriveled lungs. There are too many babies born with breathing trouble in this town, and the scientists are starting to think it's because our wives are smoking too much.'"

Dr. Hale's face turned to stone. He didn't utter a word. David pressed ahead, just as we had practiced. "Is that what happened to me?" he asked, in a small voice. "Do I have asthma because my mother smoked too much?"

Dr. Hale eased into a wide smile.

"Absolutely not," he declared. "No, no no," he said, all bluster and relief. "I'm familiar with all the latest scientific research about tobacco. As a Bright Leaf board member *and* a doctor, I am always careful about keeping up with new peer-reviewed studies relating to cigarettes. I take my obligation very seriously," he said.

"Oh, I know you do, Dr. Hale," David agreed.

"There's a lot of quackery out there, especially in Europe. Surely they have better things to do," he explained. "But I've reviewed it all, and I assure you, I've never read a single legitimate study that connects juvenile asthma with exposure to cigarette smoke in the expectant mother." Dr. Hale looked back and forth between us, as if to underscore his confidence. "In point of fact, my personal research tells a very different story. I don't need to remind either of you how invested I am in MOMints, do I?"

We shook our heads.

"Well, it may interest you to know that the whole idea for that product originated with my own patient data—notes I've been keeping for years about the kinds of supplements that quash anxiety in new mothers. It just so happens that, in preparation for the nationwide launch of MOMints, I've enlisted one of my colleagues over in Rock Hill to work with me on a more formal study of our obstetrical and postpartum patients. It's been a very exciting project—and a serious one. The protocols I designed are airtight, and I'm happy to report that the results have been very favorable indeed.

All of my theories have been quite borne out by the findings."

Dr. Hale gave me a kindly smile.

"So, knowing what I do," he continued with a wave of his hand, "we can dismiss David's noisy salesman as an ignorant rumormonger, and nothing more."

David grabbed my hand and expressed how relieved he was by this news. I couldn't tell if he was still acting or not.

"I'd love to see your findings, once you've compiled them in a paper," said David to Dr. Hale. "The research sounds fascinating."

"Well, I'm flattered by your interest, my boy," replied the doctor. "Richard tells me you've decided on a career in business, but perhaps we'll make a physician out of you yet! Or perhaps, like me, you'll do both jobs at once." He winked again at David as he moved over to a file cabinet in the corner and slid open a drawer. "My Rock Hill colleague and I are just about to submit our written conclusions to the *National Journal of Obstetrics*. Now, mind you, this isn't the final draft of the study," said Dr. Hale, pulling out a black leather-bound portfolio. "But it does set out the case that mint and nicotine have a calming effect on expectant mothers. Why don't you have a read while I wash up," he suggested. "I need to leave shortly—don't want to keep Mother waiting." He handed the portfolio to David and smiled. "Take a look and then we can all forget the silly conversation you overheard."

I was glad he didn't rush us off. I wanted to see the study with my own eyes.

David and I pored over the article, reading and re-reading the findings and the conclusions as quickly as we could. Then we noticed the dozens of issues of the *National Journal of Obstetrics* that lined Dr. Hale's bookshelves. We flipped through one of the issues and learned it had an impressive circulation of thirty thousand readers.

After ten minutes had passed, Dr. Hale returned.

"See there?" he said, extending his hand for the portfolio. "It's solid science, my boy. Nothing to worry about." The knot in my stomach had loosened entirely, and I stole a glance at David. I hated to admit it, but he and Anthony were right. Was I ever relieved. I hoped they would forgive me for being so harsh earlier.

"Thank you," David said. "It was very kind of you to share it with us."

"Of course, son. I'm always here to field questions. Now don't forget to sign the register out front before you leave, so Lucille can bill your father for today's consult."

David shook the doctor's hand and walked out into the hallway while I took one last look at the MOMints advertisement.

"Perhaps you'll be featured in one of my advertisements one day," Dr. Hale said as we stood admiring it.

"Oh," I said, blushing. "I don't know about that."

I turned to Dr. Hale and extended my hand.

"Thank you very much," I said, grasping his palm firmly. "I'm awfully grateful to you for speaking with us like adults. Not everyone places so much value on the concerns of young people."

"You are more than welcome, Maddie," he said, returning my handshake. "I quite enjoy discussing my practice with young people like you and David. Few possess the intelligence and maturity to process my professional conclusions. But the two of you certainly do. Why, you practically ate up the findings in my study like a pair of medical students!"

"Did we?" I asked, feeling proud of myself. "It's probably because you laid out the patient evidence you collected like a story, with a beginning, middle, and end. It was so reassuring to see proof that you conducted a real study. I feel silly now for overreacting to your letter about smoking hurting babies."

**I followed** David's path through the hallway and found him in the waiting area at Lucille's desk, a lollipop in his mouth and a pen and clipboard in his hand.

"There you are, Maddie dear," Lucille called as I approached them. "I was worried David would eat all of my treats before I had a chance to offer you one!" She held up the jar and shook it in my direction. "Can I interest you in a Concord grape? Or are we going to let David single-handedly keep Charms Candy Company in business?"

We all laughed a little, but before I could reply that I wasn't one for lollipops, Dr. Hale appeared in the doorway.

"Maddie, before you go, could I have another word?" He stood, holding the door open for me. "I should share something with you about your aunt's progress."

"Oh! Yes, of course," I said. I'd been so worried about Mitzy and distracted by our conversation about the studies, I hadn't even thought to ask him about Aunt Etta. "David, you don't mind, do you?"

"Of course David doesn't mind," tsked Dr. Hale. "A gentleman always waits for a lady. Young man, I suggest you put even more of your good manners to use by walking Lucille to the bus stop while I chat with Maddie. The walk there and back should only take you twenty minutes at most."

"No need for that, Dr. Hale," Lucille said. "The boy shouldn't have to go out into this heat just for me."

"Nonsense, Lucille. The sun is already setting, and I don't like the idea of you walking alone in the twilight, especially with that hip of yours. The fault is mine for holding you so late, but I'm sure David here will help me redeem myself." The doctor chuckled—a little awkwardly—and the rest of us followed his example.

"It would be my pleasure to escort her, sir," David said, his smile genuine. Lucille, who was obviously delighted by this turn of events, made quick work of grabbing her handbag and her cane. As they exited the office arm in arm, David turned back to me and smiled.

"Sit, please," Dr. Hale said as we entered his office. He motioned to a pair of high-back chairs as he took a seat himself behind his stately desk. On a nearby credenza sat a framed photograph of Rose gazing into the camera, a coy smile playing on her lips.

"Ahem," Dr. Hale began, folding his hands. "So, Maddie, I wanted to speak with you about Etta's condition. As you know, she's been improving, but what you may not know is that she has been battling pneumonia—a lung infection—in not one, but both lungs."

The room was spinning at this news. That's what David's mother had died from. Why hadn't they told me? Was I such a child that nobody could tell me the truth?

"I had no idea," I said. I was frightened and angry. Mostly, I was scared. "Why didn't anyone tell me?"

"I suppose they didn't want you to worry," he said. "She is under my care after all."

"Thank goodness for that." I sighed. "It's a relief to know she's in such good hands."

"Yes, I expect your aunt will make a full recovery . . . with the right treatment that is."

I sat up taller and scooted to the edge of the chair. "Treatment, sir?"

"Well, I've started her on a promising new therapy called penicillin. It's far superior to the sulfa drugs we used to prescribe for these types of dangerous infections. In fact, many consider it a miracle drug."

"Oh, that's wonderful," I said. "Thank you so much."

"But, there's a problem, Maddie," he said, furrowing his brow. He paused, as if choosing his words. "Some *obstacles* to overcome if we want to continue treating your aunt with penicillin. You see, it was first mass-produced for our troops overseas—to treat battle wound infections and the like. Although it's becoming more widely available, supplies for the general public are limited. If a doctor, like myself, wants to acquire it for his patients, then that doctor must use his considerable influence, his relationship with the manufacturer, to obtain the medication."

"Oh," I said. "But I thought you said you have been able to get it, that Aunt Etta's being treated with it now."

"Yes," Dr. Hale replied, leaning up in his chair and placing his hands in a steeple on the desk. "She is being treated with it—for now."

"*For now*, sir?"

"Well, there are issues of supply and demand. You're a clever girl. I'm sure you understand that. I may be able to continue that treatment," he said. "Assuming, of course, that's what you want."

"Oh my gosh, yes, sir—of course!"

"Good," he said, smiling and nodding. "Good." He paused a moment and tapped the gold-toned Rolodex perched on the corner of his desk. "Because you must understand, Maddie: I'm doing your aunt a favor, and by extension, I'm doing *you* a favor. I can't do things like this for all my patients, and I have to be certain that you trust my expertise and judgment implicitly."

"That goes without saying, sir."

"Does it?" Dr. Hale's question hung in the air a moment, then he pressed on. "We would be a team, Maddie," he said. "You and me."

"Okay." I nodded, unsure of where this was heading.

"And teammates have to trust each other," he continued. "Wouldn't you agree?"

366 · ADELE MYERS

An alarm bell sounded. It wasn't just his tone, although there was that, it was his question. *Wouldn't you agree?* That's what people say when they're trying to get you to do something wrong. I was startled, but my mouth was way ahead of the rest of me, and I heard myself replying "yes, sir," before I could process the warning.

"Good," he said. "So I trust that you will hand over the letter that I wrote to Richard."

The letter.

But how?

Then I realized. What an idiot I had been! My own words reverberated in my head. *I feel silly now for overreacting to your letter about smoking hurting babies.* My God, how could I have been so stupid?

A surge of panic shot through my body. "I'm not sure what you're talking about, Dr. Hale," I stammered.

"We both know that's not true." He was smiling, but his eyes were hard. "You obviously read my private letter to Richard. God knows how someone like you could have gotten your hands on it, but it's clear that you did."

"I . . . um, I . . . I'm sorry." I tried to press the waver out of my voice.

"You should never have read my private correspondence." He raised his voice.

I glanced at the door. It was just me and Dr. Hale in the now empty office. I had no choice but to somehow convince him that I no longer had the letter.

"I haven't . . . I haven't seen it," I said. "I mean, well, I have *seen* it, but I don't have it. It was an accident. A stupid accident. I didn't even read the whole thing," I lied. "I accidentally saw it in the trash, but I don't have it. Honest."

He studied me for a moment, calculating. "All right," he said. "But if I find out you're lying to me or if you dare breathe a word of this to anyone, you'll be very sorry."

Not ten minutes ago, I had believed everything he said. David and I both had fallen for his phony study story, and now here he sat threatening me.

"And I mean *anyone*, do you hear me? Not a word to your aunt or David or Mitzy. And if you do decide to talk, no one will believe you. I'll make sure of that. And I'll also stop treating your aunt. As teammates, you understand . . ."

I swallowed hard and squeezed my clutch. "You would stop treating Aunt Etta?"

"The access to penicillin, it's a perilous thing you understand. It's entirely possible that supply would dry up. Dry up like the Winstons' hospitality and your business here in Bright Leaf."

So there it was. Dr. Hale's real purpose in calling this private meeting. I set my jaw and found the courage to look him in the eye, mirroring his hard gaze.

"Why, it's even possible," he added, "that if you talk out of turn, the Winstons will decide to terminate your aunt's services—and her special friend's too, for that matter."

The way he said "special friend" made me feel like I was going to be sick. This wasn't fair. Aunt Etta and Frances didn't deserve to be punished. They had nothing to do with any of it.

"I imagine it would be difficult for them to start over somewhere new. They're not fooling anyone, you know. We turn a blind eye to them in Bright Leaf because of Etta's history with Mitzy, but I doubt their kind will be tolerated elsewhere."

*Their kind. Tolerated.* I had an urge to reach across the desk and slap the good doctor into the middle of next week. But I just sat there, mute and expressionless, trying to take in the enormity of my predicament.

"So, Maddie. Do you understand?" Dr. Hale pronounced every word slowly, his volume pitching louder with each syllable.

I couldn't manage to form a reply. I just sat, staring at him, stunned.

"Do you?" He was shouting at me now. False patience and kindness replaced by rage. "Do you have any idea who you're dealing with, young lady?" he bellowed, banging a closed fist on his desk. A vein on his forehead bulged and pulsed. "I'm an influential man in this town. A powerful man. Tell me—what are you? Just a slip of a girl with no pedigree—a child who needs to know her place."

"Robert!" A booming voice behind me startled both of us. "Who on earth do you think you're talking to like that?"

I spun around to discover Cornelia, standing in the doorway. She couldn't have had more of a presence if she were six feet tall.

"Mother," said Dr. Hale, the fire and venom of the last thirty seconds evaporating into thin air. "What are you doing here?"

"You were supposed to come to my house for an early supper, Robert. After an hour of watching the roast grow cool, I decided to come here and collect you myself."

Dr. Hale looked at the ground as she continued. "But never mind all that. How dare you speak to my protégée in such a nasty manner?"

"Your *protégée*?" he sneered.

"I know talent when I see it."

"Honestly, Mother. My directions to this girl are

none of your affair. If you're smart, you'll stay far away from this."

A growl of disapproval was her only response to her son, and before I realized what was happening, she reached for my arm and pulled me to my feet.

"Let's go, Maddie," she bellowed.

Dr. Hale called out to me as we walked back across the room. "Maddie," he said, "I trust you'll do the right thing."

Cornelia gestured for me to head into the reception area, and as I did, I heard her stop and turn back, as if remembering something. "Oh, and Robert," she said, in her most regal and haughty drawl, "you may want to inform your *wife* that the white lilies she chose for your waiting area do not belong in a doctor's office. They signify death, my darling. Not good for business."

**The Cadillac** sat idling outside the office. When Cornelia's driver saw us approaching, he rushed to open the rear door for us.

"Go ahead and slide in, girl," Cornelia said, pointing to the empty backseat. "You'll join me for supper. I'll get to the bottom of this."

I lowered myself onto the wide leather bench, my mouth dry and my fingers tingling.

"He's always been a bully," Cornelia snorted, settling herself onto the seat next to me. "A lot of puff and blow but no substance." Her driver shifted the car into gear, and she asked me what I was doing here in the first place.

"David!" I cried out. "I forgot. David came here with me. Oh, please, wait! We can't leave him." I explained that David was walking Lucille to the bus stop.

"We'll pass the bus stop," Cornelia said. "We can easily pick him up there."

"Thank you, ma'am. That's very kind of you."

"Both of you will join me for dinner. It will give you plenty of time to explain what just transpired inside. My Robert rarely goes on the attack unless he feels threatened. Which leads me to ask, what do you have on him, my dear?"

The thought of sitting at Cornelia's elegant dining table, sharing a meal and dodging questions, seemed impossible. David had no idea how I'd messed things up for us, and I certainly wouldn't be able to tell him within earshot of our hostess. I needed to get out of here. Not to go to my room at the Winstons'. Not to go to my room at Aunt Etta's. I wanted to go back to the Holler, to my cornflower-blue bedroom and Momma, unpredictable as she was.

"Would it be okay if I roll down the window?" I asked.

372 · ADELE MYERS

"Yes, it's quite stuffy in here," she agreed, lowering the glass on her side too. "But don't think you've fooled me by ignoring my question."

There wasn't the smallest hint of a breeze, even with the window down. I was beginning to feel closed in, trapped, like I couldn't breathe, when we came upon David and Lucille at the bus stop. Cornelia instructed her driver to stop.

"David," I said, speaking through the open window. "Miss Cornelia has invited us to her house—for dinner."

He leaned in and gave Cornelia a little wave. "That's very kind of you, ma'am, but Miss Lucille's bus is late and I don't feel as if I should leave her here alone. You go on without me."

I looked David straight in the eye, willing him to understand the predicament I was in.

"What a gentleman you are, David Taylor," Cornelia said, smiling at him. "Another time then."

Cornelia gave directions to her driver to continue. After a few moments, she turned to me. "He's a fine young man, that David," she said. "Mighty fine. I credit Mitzy with a lot of that."

"Yes, ma'am," I said, happy to change the subject from Dr. Hale. "Miss Mitzy sure is fond of him."

"You know, Maddie, there are few things as important as the person you decide to go through life with."

I was mortified. Why was everyone pushing me into David's arms? "Oh, but Miss—"

"I know, I know. You don't share the same social station in life. But the two of you have something much more important in common—integrity, character."

"Thank you, ma'am," I said. I wondered what she would think of my character if I exposed her son.

"You're young yet," she continued. "You've got a good head on your shoulders, Maddie, and I know you won't rush into anything. So many of the young girls around here act as if the *getting* married is what matters. Heck, anyone can make a match. It's making the right match, spending your life with someone who shares your values, that's important. *Marry in haste, repent at leisure,* the saying goes. You just take your time and make sure you understand that the choosing goes both ways."

"Yes, ma'am. Thank you, ma'am. I'll remember that."

"Good," she said, and patted my hand. "Now, about that ruckus in my son's office."

That again. She wasn't going to let up until I told her what happened, and we'd already passed the Winstons' house. I had to do something.

"Miss Cornelia," I said, pivoting to face her. "I appreciate your invitation to dinner and I promise to tell you what happened, but it will have to be another time. Right now, I really need to get back to my sewing. I have a lot of work to do before the Gala and only so many days to do it. I can walk back to the Winstons'. It's not far from here."

"I admire your dedication, Maddie," Cornelia said. "But walking, at this hour?" She frowned.

"Yes, ma'am. I'll be fine." She looked at me appraisingly for a few long moments.

"I'm almost finished with your hat," I offered. "I think you're going to like it."

She cocked one eyebrow. "Very well then. But I won't hear of you walking there after dark. I'll take you myself."

"Oh, no, Miss Cornelia, you've gone to enough trouble. I couldn't impose."

"Maddie," she said, turning her steely eyes on me. "Do you really think that I'm going to take no for an answer?"

With that the car turned around and headed to the Winstons'.

# Twenty-Two

I gave Cornelia a tight smile and a small wave as I opened the Winstons' front door. I just went right in, not even bothering to knock. No one was here except probably Ruth, and she wouldn't care. Mitzy was still at the hospital, and Mr. Winston's car wasn't here. Maybe he went to see Mitzy or was at his office in town. The heavy wooden door shut behind me with a clunk and I leaned my back against it to catch my breath.

The events of the last hour tumbled over me and through me. The look in Dr. Hale's eyes when he threatened me, when he threatened Aunt Etta! I couldn't believe anyone could be so sinister, let alone a doctor. To think that he held my aunt's life in his hands—Mitzy and her baby too.

How I wished I could talk to Anthony and David right

now. But Anthony was at the factory, and who knew when David would be back from seeing Lucille home.

Aunt Etta was in danger—imminent danger—and there I was, working merrily away on those damn dresses. I had no idea. My eyes welled up, a stormy mix of fear and shame and fury. But this was no time to cry. I had to think and think hard. I wiped away a tear with the heel of my hand and straightened my dress. *Pull yourself together.*

I walked into the parlor and sat on the sofa, staring into the middle distance. Everything was out of focus, unclear, just like my thoughts. How could I live with myself if I didn't tell Mitzy what I had uncovered? All the other women too. They needed to know how dangerous smoking was.

Dr. Hale's words echoed in my mind. *I'll make sure that no one believes you,* he'd said. He was right, of course. I'd be fooling myself to think Mitzy would trust me over her longtime doctor and friend. Even if she read the letter, he could trick her just like he'd tricked me and David earlier. It was hopeless; my word against Dr. Hale's.

I reached across the coffee table and poured myself a glass of water from the pitcher. Gosh, the water was warm. Likely it had been sitting out all day. I walked across the room, intending to replace it with fresh water from the powder room faucet, but stopped dead in my tracks. There, on the credenza underneath Mitzy's wedding portrait, sat a manila folder and a stack of MOMints advertisements.

I flashed back to that day in this very room, the morning Aunt Etta fell ill. Mitzy accidentally handed me that folder along with magazines to help me pass the time. *Oops,* she'd said, taking it back. *That's just Richard's boring old plan.*

I was in deep. No point pulling back now. Without thinking anymore about it, I looked inside the folder and removed a two-page, typed document. It was an advertising plan, Mr. Winston's, dated one day after the letter from Dr. Hale. I sat in the chair closest to me and began reading.

May 19, 1946
Notes for Board Meeting

## MOMints Advertising Plan

Use wives in advertisements and newspapers (ELIZABETH to help with this)

Our competitors use famous
actresses (Claudette Colbert,

Barbara Stanwyck, Joan Crawford)
to promote their brands. We'll do
the same with our local celebrities.
Select wives with the most desirable
appearance and social standing.
Use their likenesses and words
(we'll provide) to the best advantage
in advertisements. Only young
married women of childbearing
age should be displayed, with the
exception of Cornelia. (Her standing
in the community is invaluable.
Must include her in all group
photographs.)

Doctor recommendations (women trust
doctors, they know best)

Dr. Hale will vigorously and
confidently recommend MOMints
in advertisements. Entice smokers
from other brands: MOMints are
less irritating. MOMints are trusted
by more doctors. Women put their
confidence in doctors and will believe
whatever they say. Use official

language so they feel safe and
protected with MOMints.

## Conduct our own "studies"

The public likes to know that they
can count on the products they buy.
There's no better way to earn the
customer's trust in your product than
to point to research that proves its
worth.

Time is of the essence. A study of
women smoking MOMints is not
feasible, however, our "studies" and
"science" will rely on promoting the
benefits of the mint oil in MOMints: a
winning, credible story.

Ladies have used mint in tea
and whatnot for generations. Our
advertisements will claim that
MOMints cigarettes have all the
properties of mint that our ladies
desire: it calms the nerves, helps
with hysterical tendencies, relieves

indigestion, masks bad breath, controls the appetite to keep them slim before, during, and after their interesting condition. (This will please the husbands too!)

Best defense is a good offense. Don't wait for studies to come out to address them. We must influence what women think and feel. If we stress the benefits in advertisements, their opinions will be formed before negative news emerges.

P. T. Barnum lessons

We know from sending free cigarettes to the troops that once they start, they'll gladly pay for more. Now's our chance to get the women waiting for the boys to return home. They've missed their men, want to start families as soon as their husbands arrive and MOMints will help them do it. Give away free MOMints at the Summer Solstice and Gala Fundraiser—once

our ladies get a taste, they'll want
more.

## Americans trust Americans

We know our cigarettes, not
foreigners. If ladies hear from Bright
Leaf Tobacco now, they'll believe us
and not be swayed by others who
don't have America's best interest at
heart. Women who smoke MOMints
are proud Americans, Dr. Hale is a
trusted American doctor. This is what
our patriotic, God-fearing ladies need
to hear.

My mouth fell open as I took in the details of this advertising plan. A pack of lies was more like it. I glanced around the room, afraid I'd be found out.

This was it. The proof I'd been looking for. Proof that Dr. Hale didn't conduct a real study. Proof that Mr. Winston went forward with MOMints in spite of the dangers. Proof that they didn't warn Mitzy or any of the other women, that they cared about no one but themselves and their success.

These despicable men deliberately deceived women—including their own wives and mothers—to make sure they wouldn't believe the damaging research when it did come out. *Americans know our cigarettes, not foreigners. Doctor knows best.*

I glanced at the stack of magazines. The one on top, *Life* magazine, featured the photograph I'd seen in Dr. Hale's office. Mitzy and the other wives, holding court, smiling as they held their MOMints cigarettes aloft.

I gritted my teeth. They didn't just deceive the women, they *used* them to sell the damn things. I had to see Aunt Etta. Tonight. Right now. I had to tell her what I'd uncovered and show her what I'd found. I shoved the plan into my satchel and tried to catch my breath.

I had no idea how sick Aunt Etta was, and it pained me to think of upsetting her in her state, but I had no choice.

I knew that telling Mitzy was the right thing to do, but first I had to get my aunt's blessing.

# Twenty-Three

"Hello," I said to the nurse on evening duty. "I'm here to see Etta Sykes. I believe she's in room 224." I was hoping to get the nice nurse I had spoken to on the phone, but this one—Nurse Casey—was all sharp edges. Her voice was snappish, her response to me curt, as if words themselves were in short supply.

"Only adults are allowed to visit patients," she said.

"Yes, I understand that, but I received special permission from Dr. Hale." If he could lie, well, then I could too.

"Dr. Hale?" she repeated, looking at me sideways.

"Yes, he called earlier," I said. "Left a message with a nurse . . . Baxter, I think it was."

"Well, it's highly irregular," she said. "Let me see if there's any notation on her chart."

Shoot. This nurse was all rules and regulations. No way was she going to let me in.

Just then, a doctor came tearing around the corner.

"Nurse Casey," he said. "Room 297. Now. The patient is in distress."

"Yes, doctor," she said, without looking up. Nurse Casey took off down the corridor after the doctor. I knew enough not to question my good luck, so I seized my chance and took off in the opposite direction.

I don't know what I expected when I entered room 224, but the sight of Aunt Etta with tubes running from her nose to a torpedo of an oxygen tank gave me a start. I double-checked the number on the door, hoping I'd stumbled on the wrong room. But there was the quilt Aunt Etta had made for Frances, and on the bedside table, one of Aunt Etta's favorite sewing lamps, a warm glow in a cheerless room.

I inched closer, terrified as much by the silence as I was by the hissing of the oxygen. I studied Aunt Etta's face. Her long eyelashes, the touch of gray around her hairline. Her cheeks weren't so plump or rosy as I'd remembered them, but the love I felt seeing my beautiful aunt made my heart swell. She looked so peaceful I didn't want to wake her. But then her eyes fluttered open.

"Maddie, honey!" Her face lit up.

Oh, the relief that swept through me. I flew to her bedside and buried my face in her chest. She felt different, smaller, the bones of her back hard and sharp where she was usually soft, but her embrace was strong as ever. I clung to her for dear life. I didn't ever want to let her go.

"How did you get in, honey?" she asked. "It's like Fort Knox around here."

I settled myself on the edge of the bed, clasping her hands in mine. Instead of her usual stylish pincushion, she wore a white bracelet on her wrist, her name written in a careful hand.

"Oh, I persuaded the nurse that a short visit from your favorite niece wouldn't do you any harm. In fact, it might just do you some good."

Aunt Etta looked skeptical, but she gave me a wry smile as if to say, *your secret's safe with me.* She loosened my hands so she could adjust the tubes in her nose. They were held in place by white tape on her forehead.

"How are you feeling, Aunt Etta?" I asked, watching her chest rise and fall.

"I thought I was getting better," she said. "That I might even be going home, but I've got an infection in my lungs. They just gave me some new medicine that's supposed to help, but I guess they're stuck with me for a little longer around here." She smiled. She was trying to put me at ease, but it was clear that she was very sick.

"Aunt Etta, why didn't you have Frances tell me what was going on? I would have come right away."

She patted the top of my hand. "Oh, honey, there was nothing you could have done. They wouldn't even let Frances visit until a few days ago. I didn't want you getting all keyed up about me and being distracted from working on the gowns. What are you doing here now anyway, and at this hour? Tell me honestly."

"It's a long story," I said, trembling. "I don't know where to begin." I wondered if I should lead up to the whys and wherefores of it all, if I should start by telling her how it's been staying at the Winstons'. But all that seemed like a bluff—it wasn't what I'd come for.

"I'm afraid I've gotten myself into some trouble. Well, not me, Miss Mitzy is the one in trouble, but really it's Dr. Hale who should be. It's his fault. Mr. Winston too. They're in cahoots, and they're not doing anything to protect the babies."

"Babies? Maddie, slow down," Aunt Etta squeezed my arm. "What in heaven's name are you talking about?"

Then it all came tumbling out. How I'd unintentionally found the letter. How suspicious Dr. Hale's words were. How I desperately wanted to talk to Aunt Etta about it but didn't want to worry her. How I decided to keep it to myself, to forget about it. But I couldn't, not completely anyway. Then Mitzy. Mitzy, who had already lost a baby, was expecting again and had a scare. When I got to the part about how Dr. Hale had threatened me I could see the anger coloring Aunt Etta's face. She was madder than a wet hen. Of course she was. I had betrayed her trust and interfered with her clients and her business. I was such a child to think that she'd take everything I told her at face value.

I paused to catch my breath and something behind me caught my attention. It was Frances. She stood with her mouth hanging open just inside the doorway, a glass in one hand and in the other, a pitcher of water spilling out onto the floor. She straightened it and let out a little yelp.

"Frances," Aunt Etta said. "How long have you been standing there?"

"Long enough," Frances said, wiping up the puddle with a nearby towel.

She placed the pitcher and glass on the side table. "Maddie May," she said. "Come here, my girl." I stood, waiting for the fallout, but she wrapped her arms around me and hugged me so tight I thought I'd burst.

I'd tried so hard to hide what I knew, to forget about the letter, and carry on with sewing, to get the job done. It had been a relief to tell Anthony and David about finding it, but they didn't know the full story yet, and they weren't family. I hadn't let my guard down, not really. Not until now.

I sobbed in Frances's arms for a few moments, then returned to my spot next to Aunt Etta. She gently raised and repositioned her legs so that Frances could sit facing me at the foot of the hospital bed.

"Tell us exactly what Dr. Hale said, Maddie." Aunt Etta shifted to sit up taller. "Threatened you how?"

"Well, the thing is," I said. "It wasn't so much me he was threatening as it was . . . *you*."

"Me?" Aunt Etta said.

"Yes," I began. "Dr. Hale said that he wouldn't continue your treatment with the new medicine for your pneumonia."

"That son of a—" Frances huffed. "That little milquetoast of a man. Never liked him. Never did."

"And that's not all. He said that Miss Mitzy wouldn't have any use for me . . . or you, Aunt Etta. That none of the wives would. He'd see to it that Frances would lose her job too."

"How dare he try to intimidate you, Maddie," Aunt Etta said. "And to threaten me, and Frances? Well, that I would not have expected from a man who styles himself as a pillar of the community. He certainly isn't the principled man his brother was. Cornelia's right about that."

Frances's mouth twisted in disgust. "There was a time when I used to feel sorry for him," she said. "It was downright pitiful watching him try to fill his brother's shoes. But this? I didn't think he was capable of something like this."

"I'm scared of what he'll do," I said. "I'm terrified. But I don't think I can live with myself if I don't warn Miss Mitzy. She's been so good to me, and she desperately wants to have a baby. I have to tell her she's endangering her baby, don't I?" I searched both of their faces for the answer. "I want to give her the letter, but I won't do it without your blessing."

I tried to calm down, but I was a swirl of emotion.

"It's a lot to take in, Maddie," Aunt Etta said. "That study. Whether smoking is safe. It's true, I have heard rumblings about people's lungs. Though that kind of talk is coming from way overseas, not here. But nothing about babies. Not a word."

Frances nodded in agreement, patting Aunt Etta's quilt-covered legs.

"I haven't paid it much mind," Aunt Etta continued. "Haven't wanted to. Truth is, I've tried not to think about it too deeply. North Carolina *is* tobacco, the tobacco capital of the South. It's our pride, our livelihood."

"Um-hum," Frances said, shaking her head again.

Panic rose in my chest. I thought Aunt Etta would agree with me. I hoped she'd be proud of me even. Now I wasn't so sure.

"But I'll be damned," Aunt Etta said. "If I'm going to look the other way when powerful men in this town are deceiving our women and possibly putting mothers and babies in danger."

"So you agree that I should tell Miss Mitzy?"

"Agree?" Aunt Etta said. "I insist."

Frances nodded.

"But what if you can't get the medicine you need?" I asked. "And you lose your jobs like he said? What will you do?"

"Honey, Dr. Hale's not the only doctor in North Carolina, and Bright Leaf's not the only town with jobs. If it actually comes to that, we'll start over somewhere else. We could head farther east, to the coast. Frances has always loved the Outer Banks . . ."

Her words hung in the air, the only sound our breathing and an occasional beep down the hall, a nurse's footsteps quietly passing the door.

"But you've lived in Bright Leaf your whole life. So did your mother and your mother's mother. Won't that be hard for you? And . . . . risky?" I asked. "If you have to start over somewhere new and—"

Aunt Etta and Frances let their faces fall blank without registering any sort of surprise. But Frances's cheeks turned five different shades of red. She opened her mouth as if to speak, then closed it without a word.

Why did we have to stay silent about the important things, to look the other way?

The three of us embraced, bound together by what we couldn't acknowledge. Frances sniffled a little, and I closed my eyes, breathing in the familiar, powdery scent of Aunt Etta. After a few moments, we loosened our hold on each other, and Frances removed her now-foggy glasses and wiped her eyes.

"Maddie," she said, turning to me, her eyes bright and clear. "You have our blessing." She replaced her glasses and smiled. "Your father would be proud, Maddie May."

# Twenty-Four

An open pack of MOMints sat on top of my dressing table. I stood in front of the mirror and picked up the green box, brought it to my nose. I had an urge to light one, breathe in the minty smoke, even with all I knew. But I didn't. Instead, I stared at the cigarettes as if they were a friend who had betrayed me.

I reflected on my conversation with Anthony and David this morning.

They agreed, as I knew they would, that I had to tell Mitzy about the letter and the cover-up as soon as she returned from the hospital. David took it especially hard. His face had turned white as he compared Mr. Winston's plan to the letter from Dr. Hale. Once it sunk in, he looked dejected but resolute. Of course I had to tell her, he had said.

Sadness hung in the air as the three of us had stood

looking at the documents in my studio. It felt like a death, a loss. We'd not only lost our trust in the man who ran Bright Leaf and the doctor who was supposed to take care of its citizens; but we'd also lost something more personal and precious. We'd lost our beloved tobacco.

That's what was going through my mind as I stepped into the hallway. From downstairs, I heard the unmistakable din of voices.

"Don't worry, dear, Ruth will see me upstairs." I could just make out Mitzy's high-pitched tones from the foyer. I smoothed my dress and made my way toward Mitzy's bedroom. "Why don't you and David have a drink before dinner," she said.

I opened my satchel and removed the letter and plan, then changed my mind and stuffed them back inside. I'd tell her first, then I'd show them to her. Less of a shock, that way. Less of a confrontation.

Footsteps approached and Mitzy entered the hallway, looking down, her lips pressed tight, her brow furrowed. I'd never seen her face arranged like that. Ruth followed closely behind her, carrying her handbag. When Mitzy saw me she snapped back to cheerful.

"Maddie, sweetheart!" she said, crossing to where I stood outside her door. "So good to see you, dear. Are you waiting for me?" I forced a smile, tried to act natural. Mitzy embraced me for a few moments, then drew back, placing her hands on the sides of my face and looking me in the eye. "You look a little ill, dear. I do hope that the hospital wasn't too upsetting for you," she said. "Seeing me like that. You know . . . and those poor little infants in the incubators. It almost breaks your heart, doesn't it?"

It was just like Mitzy. She's the one who had been in the hospital, but it was me she was worried about.

"It does," I agreed. "But I'm so happy that you and the baby are all right. And I'm so excited for you, Mimi." At first it had seemed silly to call her Mimi, now it seemed silly to hold back. If she wanted me to call her Mimi, where was the harm in it? "Congratulations!" I said, glancing at her tummy.

"Thank you, dear. To say I'm relieved . . ." She looked down, as if speaking to her stomach, one hand placed gently over it. "Well, you know . . . Why don't you come in, have a seat with me?"

I followed her into her bedroom and we sat down in her private sitting area. She glanced at me, looking as though she was about to say something, but my face must have given me away.

"What's wrong, Maddie?" She placed her hat on the table. "You look positively ashen."

There was no good time, no perfect moment to tell her, I realized, and I could no longer hide what I knew.

"You're not ill, are you, sweetheart?"

"No," I said, my voice cracking.

"It's not your aunt, is it?" she said, squeezing my hand. "She's getting the very best treatment that Bright Leaf has to offer."

"No." I released my hand from hers. "It's not that. I'm glad that she's getting the right medicine . . . for now."

"What do you mean, for now, dear? Dr. Hale will make sure she gets all the appropriate care—the best— until she's back to her old self."

"No," I said. "He won't."

Mitzy flinched. "What do you mean by that? What is it, Maddie?" Her voice was lower now. Cautious.

I shook my head and fought back tears. "He won't after I tell you . . . after I show you what I found."

"Maddie, whatever are you talking about? Out with it."

"I want to, Mimi. But I'm not really sure how to begin." I clasped my hands to keep them from shaking. "I don't want to upset you," I said. "I know you need to stay calm because of the baby. But there's something I need to tell you, and it can't wait any longer. It's a big secret—one that affects you, and a lot of other people too." I was crying now, out of anger and frustration more than anything else. "I just hope you'll understand that I'm only trying to do what's right."

"Maddie. You're scaring me. What's wrong?"

I shook my head, unable to continue.

"Sweetheart, you can tell me anything. You know that." She extended her hand across the table. I nodded and took it in mine.

"That's better. Just relax and take some deep breaths first." I scrubbed the tears from my eyes and filled my lungs several times. While I worked to compose myself, Mimi got up and retrieved a pack of MOMints from her handbag.

I gasped. "No, Mimi. The baby!" I couldn't let her light it.

"The baby?" she repeated, alarmed.

"Dr. Hale . . . he doesn't want anyone to know," I said. "What he's so desperate to hide that he threatened to stop Aunt Etta's treatment." I stood and reached for my satchel.

"What in the world?" Mitzy sputtered. "What in the world are you talking about?"

"Read this," I said, handing over the letter.

I paced back and forth as she read. I hadn't thought much beyond this moment. Telling her was only the beginning though. What would happen next? And how soon would Dr. Hale take his revenge?

"Where did you get this?" Mitzy asked.

I unburdened myself then, sharing every last detail.

"Tell me exactly what Dr. Hale said," she said, her face pale and her eyes distant.

I looked down and swallowed hard.

"At first, he dismissed our concerns as nonsense. David and me, that is."

"David knows about this?"

"Yes, we went to Dr. Hale's office together. Dr. Hale was a good sport about all of our questions when he thought we were only asking him about rumors. But when he realized we'd seen his letter he dropped the act and threatened me."

Mitzy's mouth fell open a touch. "How do you mean, he threatened you?"

"He said that if I told anyone about this he'd stop taking care of Aunt Etta, and that you and Mr. Winston would kick me out of your house," I said. "He also promised that the wives wouldn't want Aunt Etta to sew for them anymore. She'd lose her job and Frances would too."

"He can't do that," Mitzy said.

"That's what he said, and he seemed like he meant business. I didn't know what to do because I was afraid no one would believe me. If you just read the letter, you could interpret it to mean that Dr. Hale and Mr. Winston had done their own study. But—"

"But what?" she asked, her face stern.

"But then I remembered the advertising plan." I removed the document from my bag and handed it to her. "It's all there, I'm sorry to say. A whole plan—proof—that they covered up the smoking study."

Mitzy tossed the unlit cigarette she'd been holding onto the side table and studied the pages. She covered her mouth with her hand at one point and cussed under her breath, "Damn him." Her face turned crimson as she reread the letter, then compared the two documents. "Well," she huffed, folding them and pressing them firmly in her hand.

"I'm so sorry," I said. "I never meant for any of this to happen. But I had to tell you."

"You did the right thing, Maddie," she said. "And now I will too."

# Twenty-Five

"Richard!" Mitzy shouted. "Richard, where are you?"

Ruth dashed out of the kitchen, wiping her hands on her apron. "Where's Richard?" Mitzy demanded.

"In the dining room, ma'am," Ruth said. Her face was wary. "He and David are having a drink."

"Richard!" Mitzy called. I followed her close behind as she rushed into the dining room. Mr. Winston and David were seated at one end of the table—Mr. Winston's end—sipping beverages from short highball glasses. When David saw the two of us barreling into the room, he lifted his chin, offering me a small, grim nod.

"Elizabeth, my peach, why are you bellowing so? You're supposed to be resting, darling. Doctor's orders."

"What is this, Richard?" she said, her hand shaking as she waved the letter in the air and approached him. "What study is Robert talking about and why are you covering it up?"

"Well, now." Mr. Winston chuckled. "I can't see anything without my spectacles." He reached into his shirt pocket and pulled out a pair of wire-rimmed reading glasses. "Let's see what we have here," he said, taking the letter from Mitzy's hand. He didn't react in any obvious way, but after what felt like several long minutes, he lowered his glasses and peered over them at Mitzy. "Where did you get this, Elizabeth?"

"It doesn't matter where I got it," she replied, studying his face. "What matters is what it says." Her face flushed and sweat beaded at her temples. "Is this letter connected to your advertising plan?" She held up the pages of his notes. He averted his eyes, just slightly. Then hers went wide with alarm. "It *is*!" she shouted, snatching the letter out of his hand. "You designed the plan after Robert told you about the risks and dangers. You are deliberately trying to cover it up, Richard! You knew, and you didn't even warn me? How dare you!"

"Now, calm down, dear. There's no use getting yourself all worked up." He patted the air with his hand. "Sit down, darling. Please, let's be reasonable."

"Reasonable? I will *not* be reasonable!" She shook

the letter at him. "How could anyone be reasonable after seeing this? I'm supposed to be reasonable knowing that you've been hiding *this* from me?"

"Elizabeth, darling. *Hide* is a strong word. Why would I alarm you with an unsubstantiated study from some foreigners, especially in your condition? I know how dramatic you can be. I didn't want you to overreact. I just wanted to protect you." *Overreact.* There was that word again. He smiled and glanced at David, perhaps hoping for his approval. But David wouldn't meet his eye.

"All I've ever wanted was to be a mother," she said. "How could you keep your knowledge of such damaging information from *me*, Richard? How?"

He pulled his drink closer to himself and twirled the ice around with his finger but said nothing.

"What do you have to say for yourself?" she shouted.

"Elizabeth, please," he said. "Calm yourself. We don't know how credible this foreign study is. It could all just be a bunch of foolishness. There's probably nothing to worry about."

Mitzy crossed and uncrossed her arms, her gaze fixed on him.

"It says right there in the letter," I said, my voice small. "Dr. Hale himself says that it's credible research." I caught David's eye, and he nodded his support.

Mr. Winston looked at me, as if realizing I was there for the first time. "Stay out of this, girl," he growled. "This is none of your business."

Mitzy clutched the documents tightly in her trembling hand. I thought she might shout at him or storm out of the room, but she spoke quietly and slowly, each word separate and clear.

"How could you keep this from me, Richard? How could you do this when we've already lost a baby?" Her voice caught in her throat. Her eyes welled up.

He stared into his drink and rattled the ice.

"Richard!" she snapped. "I asked you a question."

"Yes, you did," he said. "A dirty, dirty question. How could you accuse me of keeping something from you when there's nothing to it, Elizabeth? It's a foreign study. It's got nothing to do with Bright Leaf Tobacco, no bearing on our business at all."

"How do you know that, Richard, if you didn't test Bright Leaf the way they tested their cigarettes?"

"Why on God's green earth would I do that? Why would I go looking for trouble, Elizabeth? That you would take the word of some foreigners over your own husband. I mean, the absurdity of it."

"I can think of another word, Richard—and it isn't absurd, I can tell you that. Think of me. Of your *family*." She said that word with such force, such betrayal. "And what about all the other women and babies? The other wives. The women at the factory." She paused for a second, calculating. "All those babies at the hospital. All those babies lost." Her eyes went wide. "*This* is why so many babies are being born premature," she shouted, shaking the papers. "*This* is why women at the factory are miscarrying. *This!* Not the fact that they're working, that we're not resting enough. How dare you—you and Robert both—blame us for losing our babies. How dare you make us think it's somehow our fault that our babies are dying, when you knew about this study. Don't you want to know if Bright Leaf Tobacco is dangerous? What if they're right? What if I lost our baby because of your goddamn cigarettes?"

Mr. Winston looked down at his now empty high-ball and clenched his jaw.

"You want to know if our *goddamn cigarettes* are dangerous, Elizabeth?" He pushed the glass to the side with the back of his hand and leaned up in his chair. He placed his forearms on the table, staking his claim.

"Let's talk about *goddamn cigarettes*. Let's talk about how they paid for this table, and those chairs, about how they keep the lights on," he said, pointing to the ornate chandelier overhead. "How they provide jobs for half the state of North Carolina." He cleared his throat, his voice rising. "What about the workers, you ask? I'll tell you about the workers, Elizabeth. They have *work*," he spat. "They have jobs, good-paying jobs. They have food to put on their tables, and schoolbooks for their children. They have roofs over their heads. Medicine when they're sick and warm beds in the winter."

He slapped the table with his hand, startling us. "You want to find out if our cigarettes are dangerous? You want to look real closely at Bright Leaf Tobacco, Elizabeth? Let's say we do that. Let's say we do our own study and we find out that they are dangerous. Then what? You think it's so simple? Then you tell me! Is that what we should do? You want to risk having to shut down the fields and the factories, tell the truck drivers there are no loads to haul? You want to take away ninety percent of the paper mill's business, Elizabeth?"

My heart beat wildly as he continued his tirade.

"You want to lose this house and your closet full of glamorous gowns? You won't need them, actually, because there will be no Garden Club or tea parties and Gala Fundraisers. No one in Bright Leaf will have jobs or money to spend, surely nothing to donate."

Mitzy stood rooted in place.

"And worst of all, darling," he said, "you'll lose the

adoration of the town. Everyone in Bright Leaf loves to ooh and aah about how *generous* you are, Elizabeth." He smiled sickeningly when he said the word *generous*. "Elizabeth, that *generosity* of yours is funded by cigarette sales. Those sales fund your day care center, the new school, and every other goddamn thing in this whole goddamn town!"

He struggled to get up from his seat, his face bright red as he fumbled for his crutches. "So, Elizabeth," he said, making his way toward her. "The best thing you can do right now is give me that letter and my plan and forget this conversation ever happened."

I held my breath, waiting for her to refuse or agree to hand over the documents. But she didn't do anything. She just looked at him, looked at him as if he were a stranger.

Then, after a few long minutes, she turned to leave the room. Before closing the door behind her, she pivoted back to him and said, "This is no longer your decision, Richard. It's in my hands now."

# Twenty-Six

**R**uth knocked lightly at my door.

"Good morning, Miss Maddie," she said. "I'll be bringing your breakfast up to your studio. Miss Mitzy said there'll be no meals in the dining room until she says otherwise."

"Is she okay?" I asked, pulling on a robe. "Did she say anything else?"

Ruth twisted and untwisted the tie of her apron.

"Says she doesn't want to be bothered, that if you need anything, you're to come to me."

My heart sank. I felt like I'd done all the wrong things for all the right reasons.

Ruth continued, lowering her voice. "I never seen her like this," she said. "So fired up. She didn't tell me a thing, but I heard plenty last night. When y'all were in the dining room."

"You did?" I whispered, approaching her. "I'm the one who . . . well it's my fault."

Ruth's eyes went wide and she blew out a whoosh of surprised air. "Lord," she shook her head slow, side to side. "I didn't figure this was your doing. It sure is blowing up a storm."

*My doing.* This was all my doing. I buried my face in my hands for a moment, hoping to God I had done the right thing.

Just then, Isaac called out from downstairs. We both turned with a jerk toward the door. "Ruth! Ruth!" Isaac shouted. "Miss Ashley's here."

"I got to go," Ruth said, straightening her apron.

"Ruth," I pleaded. "Please . . . please tell me that everything is going to be all right."

She paused for a few seconds, her hand on the doorknob. "It's not for me to say," she said, shrugging her shoulders. "But time'll tell. Always does."

I dressed quickly. I was spent, wrung out, but still had work to do, lots of work and only two days to do it. On my way up to the studio, I removed my shoes and padded by Mitzy's bedroom where I paused to listen at her door. She was on the telephone, her voice urgent, but I couldn't make out what she was saying. I felt the vibrations of her footsteps, a slight tremble underfoot. Her pacing, the anger and worry. It couldn't be good for her, the stress of it.

As I entered the studio my eyes landed on Mitzy's gown. We'd done her final fitting first, as was Aunt Etta's custom. My heart swelled with pride as she had admired herself in the mirror. She'd loved the finishing touches I'd added—the row of pearls at the sleeve and the delicate beading at the neck. She looked like a walking dream.

I shuddered at the sight of it now, its bodice hugging the dress form and its billowy yellow skirt fluttering slightly. Anthony had left the window open. That's all I needed, for tobacco to ruin her gown, for dust to make its way in here and dirty it, and all the others. I strode to the window and slammed it shut. "Damnit," I snapped.

A creak in the corner startled me. I spun around to see David rising from a wooden chair.

"David," I scowled, then softened. "You scared me half to death."

"I'm sorry." He crossed the room and took my face in his hands, searching my eyes. "Are you all right?"

"No," I said. "I'm not." I wrapped my arms around his neck and let the tears come.

"What happened after I left last night?" he murmured, cradling the back of my head with one hand.

"Nothing," I said, sniffling and pulling back to look him in the eye. I wiped my tears from his nice shirt. "Nothing. That's the thing. After Mimi went to her bedroom and Mr. Winston stormed off to his study, I didn't see either of them for the rest of the night. We haven't spoken this morning. I'm told I'm not to bother her." The words formed a knot in my throat. "All I know is I heard her pacing around her room like a condemned man, talking on the phone something urgent."

"I noticed her bedroom light was on all night. I can see it from the guesthouse."

"David, she's so upset. It can't be good for the baby."

"But knowing the dangers, even if it's upsetting to her, has to be better than the alternative."

"I called Aunt Etta last night after the blowup in the dining room."

"What did she say?"

"That she's proud of me. That I should try not to worry. That I'd done what was needed, it was in Mimi's hands now and she hoped to be out of the hospital next week, God willing."

"Well, that's good," he said. "Isn't it?"

"It will be, but who knows if that will happen when Dr. Hale takes away her medicine," I said. An eddy of ugly words circled my mind like dried leaves, a swirl of emotions I couldn't tamp down. I was helpless against these powerful men. They'd ruin Aunt Etta and Frances, just because they could. Spite was a dangerous thing.

"Try not to get ahead of yourself," he said.

"David, you really think he's going to let this go? He won't. There's no way."

"You don't know that. You don't. But I can tell you one thing, Maddie. If Dr. Hale does follow through with his threats, I will do everything in my power to stop him."

"You will?" I looked up at him.

"What you did was brave and important and right. You had to do it, Maddie. Of course, I'll be by your side, no matter what. But it's not in your hands anymore. It's up to Mimi. She said so herself."

I hugged him tight. He meant it. I could tell, and I admired his optimism about Mitzy, but I didn't feel it myself.

"Don't worry," he said. "She'll do the right thing. She'll protect you and your aunt. I know she will."

There was nothing left to say. I stared at Mitzy's empty dress, then got to work.

I saw very little of anyone in the days leading up to the Gala, I was so busy with the final touches for the wives' gowns. Anthony took on a few last-minute jobs for girls at the factory a couple days before the Gala. A group of female supervisors had been invited to the event at the last minute and Anthony would add some flourishes to their nicest dresses for the occasion. He worried that he was deserting me, but I encouraged him to do it. He needed the money, and I could finish the dresses on my own. I hemmed and pressed, snipped errant threads and reinforced snaps and beads on every last dress. All of the gowns looked picture-perfect from the outside, but finishing the inside is what made the difference between homemade and couture. I made it a point to finish the edges inside each and every dress, just as Aunt Etta would have done.

I was thankful for the work and the distraction from my worries. What would Dr. Hale do when he found out I told Mitzy? Did he know yet? Surely Mr. Winston had told him, but who knows. There were so many secrets in Bright Leaf. I wanted to ask Mitzy, but when she did emerge from her room, she'd smile sweetly and ask how the gowns were coming along, but there was a distance between us. I knew not to bring up what had happened. I let it lie.

Ashley joined Mitzy for meals in her room on more than one occasion, and I tried to time it so I'd run into her, but she didn't have much to say. Just that Mitzy was fine. That she needs time to herself. Everything will be all right. I'd see.

My time at the Winstons' house was ending. I knew that. I'd stay here until the afternoon of the Gala, see to all the final gown fittings and deliveries and then go back to Aunt Etta's after attending the big party that night. After all that had happened, I wasn't sure I should go to the Gala at all, but Ruth said Mitzy insisted. I'd worked so hard and deserved a night to celebrate. I didn't feel much like celebrating, but I'd go. It was the right thing to do.

My last night sleeping in the Princess Rose Suite, I dreamed of my bedroom back home in the Holler. I wondered if Momma was back there now. I'd written her after I got her postcard to tell her about how Aunt Etta was sick and I was sewing the gowns, but I don't know if she received my letter. In my dream, Momma was nowhere to be found. I was alone in our house, my bed now gone, my closet empty, the doorjamb absent the pencil marks and dates showing how much I'd grown. I ran into our living room, frantically searching for Daddy's shoeshine kit, but it wasn't our living room at all. It was my bathroom here at the Winstons' and the tub was overflowing with thick, dark water. The ugly sludge flooded the room, rising up to my ankles as I desperately reached for the valve to turn it off. I woke with a start in the pitch-black, clenching my jaw, my nightgown soaked through with sweat.

Ruth's questions, questions I'd tamped down yesterday when she asked, came to the front of my mind.

*What are you gonna do after the Gala? Will you stay in Bright Leaf? Go back to your hometown? Think you'll keep sewing for the wives?*

I don't know, I had told her. I still didn't. It didn't seem I was much in control of my fate.

There was something about trouble that brought on the *would haves.* If I'd known I might not have a home to go back to, I would have taken one of Daddy's work shirts and breathed it in until my lungs were full of the smell of pine and earth and good hard work. I would have stood in each room once more, touched the wallpaper and twisted the doorknobs. I would have looked it all over and burned it into my brain. I would have. But I didn't.

It was bittersweet leaving the Winstons', saying goodbye to this place. I wanted to enjoy the luxuries here right up until I left—the fresh linens and warm, sweet-smelling baths, the delicious meals, my beautiful studio. And, of course, being close to David. That's what I tried to do. But the more I tried to hold on to everything, the sadder it made me feel. It made me wonder if not knowing you were leaving was a better way to live.

# Twenty-Seven

"Cigars . . . cigarettes? Cigars . . . cigarettes?"
The cigarette girl wore sequined tap pants, a matching green blouse, and a pillbox hat. She was a bottle blonde with a million-dollar smile, the type of girl men got silly over. There were a half dozen others dressed just like her circulating among the guests, each one as pretty as the next, each capable of inspiring a wolf whistle or a *va va voom*. And every one of them carried a mint-colored display box filled with Bright Leaf cigars and cigarettes.

Handsome servers in white dinner jackets lined the grand entrance to the Elk Wood Inn. They held trays of champagne for the ladies and short glasses of dark alcohol for the men. Everyone was bathed in gentle candlelight from the dozens of hanging glass lanterns that came special from New York City. Mimi had taken great care over those lights, as she had over everything else.

It was like a scene from a movie, all glamour and charm. The room seemed to vibrate, alive with the orchestra's upbeat tunes and hundreds of happy guests—dapper gentlemen and ladies in long, flowing gowns—all chatting and drinking. Women kissed each other on the cheek and giggled. Men shook hands and talked a little too loud. I may not have realized it over the last several weeks, what with all the work and worry, but I'd really been looking forward to this night.

All this time I'd been busy with the women's outfits I hadn't given much thought to what the men would wear. Anthony had mentioned that they'd be in their best bib and tucker, but I didn't consider what that would be. Double-breasted jackets weren't allowed during the war, and stiff front dress shirts were banned. The restrictions had been lifted, but apart from some of the older gentlemen who wore tails and white ties, the younger men wore black tie and crisp semiformal tuxedos in exquisite wools and gabardines. They were classic and modern, the perfect complement to the women in their more elaborate ensembles.

There was a group of beautiful women who looked like they had stepped off the pages of *Vogue*. Mitzy told me weeks ago that *influential couples from Atlanta,* that's what she called them, traveled five hours to attend the Bright Leaf Gala every year. Their gowns were exquisite.

I once read that Coco Chanel said "elegance does not consist in putting on a new dress." But, oh! The dresses! Cornelia would be the only one in mauve, but I saw a vibrant shade of purple and more than one scandalous red. All of the women's dresses were floor length, but the necklines and waistlines, the sleeves and bodices, were so very different from each other. I saw a Claudette Colbert look-alike in a sleek beaded gown of ivory-colored crepe. Another woman, just as slinky, wore a black column with a plunging back over which fell a long strand of pearls.

I saw the gowns that I had worked on and felt the thrill of recognition and pride at each one. My work held its own beside the beautiful women from Atlanta. Jacqueline Patwin and Allyson Littlefield arrived together, as they had for their fittings. Their dresses were almost identical, but the women themselves were so different that somehow their dresses looked different too. They were made of the same royal blue fabric, each with a fitted bodice and flared skirt, but I had given Jacqueline a rounded neckline to add some depth to her slender figure. Allyson's neckline was deeper and a little more dramatic, drawing the eye vertically, making her appear taller. The friends were so happy with themselves, giving their outfits the best possible accessory—a confident smile.

This was my first grown-up affair and I would dance and drink champagne, give and receive compliments. But there was more to it than that. More than just the thrill of one dazzling night. As I looked back over the previous days and weeks, I realized that as much as I'd been tending to the needs of the tobacco wives, I had also done something for myself. Something big and important and true. I didn't feel like the Maddie who had been whisked away in her nightgown and dropped off like a parcel in Bright Leaf. I felt more sure of myself, a little stronger and proud. Daddy would have said that I *rose to the occasion* the way I took over Aunt Etta's business. There was an immense satisfaction in a job well done, in doing my best. I could only hope that my best was good enough.

I took a deep breath and tried to steel myself for what was to come.

As I stood at the entrance to the grand hall, the sights and sounds inside assaulted me. The big band's bugle pierced the air and the men's smelly cigars clouded the room. The voices that just a moment ago had sounded cheerful and happy, now sounded forced. I had the feeling that everyone was acting, that I was watching a play, carefully crafted. Almost every single lady was lighting up a new MOMints cigarette as sure as if she'd stepped out of Mr. Winston's advertisement. They puffed and flashed their pearly whites like happily ignorant passengers on a sinking ship.

I thanked the cigarette girl without taking anything from her display box and moved on. Just inside the foyer, three men gathered at a cigar bar, waiting. An elegant gentleman with gray hair wearing a silver MASTER ROLLER pin handled stiff leaves as big as dinner plates behind the butcher block table. He rolled and pressed, rolled and pressed, with precision and care. One impatient-looking man, who kept glancing around the room, looked me up and down then whispered something to the other two. God, what I'd give for a cigarette. But how could I? Not anymore. Never again. I looked away and took a glass of champagne from a silver tray. A sip of bubbly would calm my nerves; Mitzy had taught me that.

Before I could bring the glass to my lips I felt a hand at my elbow as someone gently pulled me to the side. "Hey, sunshine," Anthony whispered. "I was worried you were gonna stand me up tonight. Couldn't blame you if you did, but I'm pleased as punch that you're here. You deserve a glamorous night. And you look absolutely gorgeous."

THE TOBACCO WIVES · 419

"Thank you," I replied, taking a gulp of cold champagne. The tartness burned my throat as it went down.

"And your hair's almost as perfect as when we practiced," he said, walking in a circle around me to get a full view. A few days ago Anthony had showed me how to twist a pompadour in back with a cascade of curls in front, all held in place with a pearl comb. Wearing my hair up was a must, he insisted, when I tried on the dress for him. He oohed and aahed over the elegant draping and said the deep cowl in the back was *simply divine*. I looked so grown-up and sophisticated. *You've come a long way from eyelet, honey.* When Mitzy loaned me the rose-colored dress, she insisted that I borrow her comb to wear along with it. *It's the perfect accessory to show off your glorious hair and it matches the pale pink silk beautifully.* That was well before I told her about the letter, of course. My hair hardly seemed to matter now.

"Hey, you two," Rose interrupted, slinking up behind Anthony. She held a glass of champagne in one hand and a full highball of an amber liquid in the other, her long legs almost entirely exposed by her revealing gown. I flinched at the sight of her. Anthony had handled her final fitting so I wouldn't have to see her after the altercation with Dr. Hale.

"That's quite a drink you've got there," Anthony said, eyeing the nearly brimming-over highball.

"Oh that." She giggled. "I told the barkeep to fill it up to the tippy top. My poor husband's so keyed up," she tutted. "He needs a good stiff drink."

Anthony caught my eye and changed the subject. "You look divine, Rose. I'm so glad you went with the green lamé. Although you would have been gorgeous in the gold too." He lowered his voice. "Yours is my favorite gown, if I do say so myself. It's the most stunning of all the gowns here tonight."

She grinned and took a sip of her champagne. "Thank you, hon. You did a nice job and you did too, Maddie. Mother loves her hat. Where is she anyway?" Rose lifted her chin and strained to see over the crowd. "You know, she's been acting strangely, even for her, and just now she and Ashley said something about a surprise tonight. It's all very mysterious. Have y'all heard anything about an announcement?"

"No," I sputtered, nearly spilling my champagne all down my dress. "No, I haven't heard anything."

"Me neither," Anthony assured her.

"We really should go now," I said. "If you'll excuse us, Miss Rose." I grabbed Anthony's hand and pulled him into the crowd with me.

A surprise announcement.

I didn't know whether to be thrilled or terrified. My breath quickened as I weaved my way through the hum of mingling bodies, Anthony trailing after me. Where was David? I searched the faces for his. Instead of finding him, we were intercepted by Anna Rebecca, who made a beeline to put herself in my path.

"Maddie, oh my word, don't you look absolutely gorgeous." She kissed me on both cheeks and stood back to examine my dress. "That color is gorgeous on you and I love your updo." Anthony mouthed that he would keep looking for David and scooted away.

"I just adore my gown," Anna Rebecca continued, twirling her full skirt and giggling. She glowed with happiness. She really did look like Rita Hayworth in that gown. And the way the light caught her shoulders . . . I couldn't have imagined it better. "You were so right about this dress," she gushed. "My husband can't stop staring. I haven't seen that loopy expression on his face in years!"

"I'm so pleased," I said, laughing and looking over her shoulder. "You're a vision in blue," I added distractedly.

When she finally scurried off, I approached a long table with seat assignment cards arranged in rows and searched for my name. MISS MADELINE SYKES, TABLE TWO, and just below my card, MR. DAVID TAYLOR,

TABLE TWO. Thank goodness. Maybe David had already made his way to our seats.

In the distance, large round tables covered in white tablecloths with grand bouquets of white roses awaited. Each vase of pristine flowers was lined with Bright Leaf tobacco leaves picked at their peak and flash cured to achieve that bright yellow—another of Mitzy's special touches for the evening. The tables flanked an elevated stage where an easel with a covered piece of artwork sat next to a gold-accented lectern. Just off to the side stood Mr. Winston and next to him, Dr. Hale, the two men deep in conversation. They glanced in my direction and my heart skipped a beat. I polished off the rest of my champagne in one long swallow.

"Maddie." It was David. He placed his hand at the small of my back and leaned in close. "There you are," he whispered. I pivoted to face him and he raised one eyebrow. "Wow," he said, stepping back and considering me. "Don't you look beautiful?" Then he corrected himself. "It's not a question," he said. "Maddie, you are beautiful."

"Thank you," I said, my heart swelling. "You're . . . you're really something, David Taylor."

He leaned in, his mouth just a few inches from my ear. "Not just beautiful, but breathtaking," he said quietly. I blushed and scanned the room, savoring the moment.

"I have to tell you something," I whispered finally, trying to appear casual.

"What?"

"Don't look in Dr. Hale and Mr. Winston's direction," I said. "I don't want them to suspect I'm talking about them."

"Of course."

I told him about what Rose had said about the surprise announcement.

David raised his eyebrows and tilted his head. "Really?" He looked out over the tables, now filling up with men and women. "Have you seen Mimi yet? And the others?"

"No, not yet," I said.

A server in a smart dinner jacket approached us. "Do you need assistance locating your table?" he asked.

"We're all set," David said, pointing to the numbered card in his breast pocket with a smile. He took my hand.

We made our way through the maze of tables, pausing for a brief detour to speak with Mitzy, Cornelia, and Ashley. One of the ladies said my name—Ashley, I think—and I smiled, pretending I'd heard whatever she'd said.

We were trying hard to act normal, but David talked

quickly, extra cheerful, unlike his usual calm, reserved self.

"Beautiful hat, Miss Cornelia," he said, winking at me. "It must have been made by a talented seamstress."

"Indeed it was," she said, lifting her champagne flute in my direction. "And I know of at least three women who will be calling Maddie shortly for a pair of these magnificent trousers."

Cornelia seemed pleased, pleasant even. It was surprising, given what she must now know about her son's deception and about the tobacco operation she helped build.

"Maddie, sweetheart," Mitzy said, standing to embrace me. "Maddie, don't you look lovely. Just exquisite. Even more beautiful than when you first tried on the dress." There was something different about Mitzy's hug tonight. She felt stiff, held back, like a drawn bow. It showed in her face too, underneath that ever-sunny disposition, although she was trying hard to cover it. I hugged her back tight, hoping she could feel the swell of gratitude and pride that filled me.

"Thank you," I whispered. "For everything."

She pulled away from me without responding. "Doesn't she look wonderful?" she asked the others at the table.

It was as if I'd said something wrong—like that

familiar pang I got with Momma. One minute she'd be fine, then the next she'd turn on me, like the flip of a switch.

"You do look lovely, Maddie," Ashley said, raising her glass as well. "But even more impressive to me is the fine work you did on all of our gowns. You're a true professional."

I held the words close, hoping I'd earned them. *A true professional.*

A jarring, static tap, tap, tap echoed throughout the enormous hall. The lights dimmed as Rose approached the table, polishing off her champagne as she took her sweet time shimmying into her chair. Meanwhile, David and I retreated to table number two, just as I spotted Anthony in the back of the room with two girls from the factory. He gave me a quick wave and a hopeful look before I dropped quietly into my seat.

"Ladies and gentlemen," a woman's voice rang out. "Let's all give a big Bright Leaf welcome to our own Mr. Richard Winston, president and chief operating officer of Bright Leaf Tobacco."

The applause was thunderous as Mr. Winston hoisted himself out of a chair near the stage and positioned his crutches under him. He smiled broadly but struggled to make his way up the steps leading to the lectern. Dr. Hale jumped out of his chair to help, but Mr. Winston batted his hand away. Chastened, Dr. Hale retreated to his seat with a tight smile. I felt a cautious little smile myself, to see the doctor put in his place like that. It made me hopeful for things to come.

"Good evening," Mr. Winston boomed. "And welcome. Welcome to the most important event of the Bright Leaf social season, our Gala Fundraiser." He cleared his throat and removed his cigar from the side of his mouth, using both hands to support himself on the lectern. "This year, the proceeds from this glorious event will benefit our veterans and their families." The crowd applauded and a chorus of hoots and hollers erupted from the back of the room. "Many of our brave soldiers and their wives are here this evening, in fact," he said, gesturing to the back of the room. "Men fresh from combat and ready to get back to work. Let's give them the hero's welcome they deserve."

"Wilco to that," a man yelled from the back, causing a ripple of claps through the room.

"We could not be happier to have you back, my friend. You, and all the other men of Bright Leaf Tobacco, have made us the success that we are. The ladies have done their best to keep the lights on while you were fighting overseas, but boy are we thankful those days are over. Now, our women can get back home where they belong."

I could see Mitzy at the next table, her lips pursed, her delicate nostrils flared slightly. She was like a boxer preparing to enter the ring.

"Dr. Hale and I have an exciting announcement tonight," Mr. Winston said, glancing at the covered artwork beside him. "So, without further ado—"

But he was interrupted by the abrupt scrape of chair legs against the marble floor. Mitzy stood slowly, drawing the attention of the room. She scooted her chair back into place and began walking toward the stage, carrying a note card, her yellow dress flowing gently around her.

I reached under the table and grabbed David's hand. We laced our fingers together and held tight.

Mr. Winston chuckled anxiously, then glanced at Dr. Hale, who stood ready to join him onstage. A look passed between them.

"Elizabeth," said Mr. Winston, as if speaking to her alone, forgetting the crowd for a moment. "Elizabeth," he repeated, his tone growing serious. Mitzy didn't respond or even meet her husband's eye. She simply kept moving toward the lectern, undaunted.

"Mrs. Elizabeth Winston," Mr. Winston announced as she approached the base of the elevated platform. He gestured to her graciously, as if he had planned the interruption from the start. "Please help me welcome my dear wife to the stage." He reached for her hand as she lifted her hem to climb the steps, but she didn't take it.

"Thank you," she said, without looking at him. "I'll take it from here." He allowed her to take the microphone but did not leave the stage. Instead, he fell back a few paces and hovered by her side.

An excited murmur snaked back and forth through the crowd. No one seemed to know what would happen next. I looked to my left, back to table one, where Cornelia caught my eye and nodded. Ashley sat on the edge of her seat, watching her sister intently, a broad smile on her face. They seemed excited, happy even.

"Good evening, ladies and gentlemen," Mitzy began. "Thank you for joining us here tonight and for your generous support of our veterans." Her eyes flicked to the soldiers in the back of the room. "Many brave Bright Leaf men have fought and served to protect our country," she read from a note card. "And," she paused, "many strong, capable Bright Leaf women have stepped in to keep our economy going strong while the men have been overseas. They too have served." She squinted toward the back of the room, raising her hand, as if shielding her eyes from the sun. "Sadie? Margaret? Where are you ladies? Please, stand." The two strike organizers stood up proudly at the back of the room. "There they are. Sadie Lee and Margaret

O'Shea. Strong, capable women, dedicated factory workers who have kept the cigarette lines running day and night while our men were at war."

I stole a glance at David. *What is she doing?* I mouthed.

He shrugged.

Near the stage, Dr. Hale was wringing his hands. He kept trying to catch Mr. Winston's eye, but Mr. Winston was staring blankly into the audience, his usually ruddy complexion as pale as milk.

"Thank you, Sadie and Margaret, and all of the other women who toil on behalf of our beloved Bright Leaf Tobacco," Mitzy continued, her eyes landing purposefully on tables throughout the ballroom. "Including my own dear sister, Ashley Smith. Ashley, would you stand please?" Ashley stood, practically glowing in her smart navy gown. "And, we must also recognize the tireless contributions of my dear friend Cornelia Hale, who, as all of you know, is one of the founders of the company and of this town. Cornelia is a woman whose vision and business acumen has gone unnoticed for far too long. Cornelia, would you stand up too, please?" Cornelia rose slowly from her chair, her head held high and proud. Rose scowled and mumbled under her breath.

"While we are certainly pleased that our men are returning, we must not minimize the tremendous job that our women have done. They have not just kept the lights on, they have grown our business and even made improvements in our factories."

There were tentative claps around the room.

"To those who would say that 'loyalty is its own reward,' I would respectfully disagree. Loyalty deserves loyalty, and I am very pleased to announce that we will not be returning to business as usual. The women will keep their jobs. In fact, Sadie and Margaret are being promoted to factory supervisors effective immediately. They will join the management team at Bright Leaf Tobacco Operations, and I believe their first order of business will be to finalize a contract for female employees ensuring postwar job security and reinstatement for women who were recently let go."

Applause broke out, mostly among the women seated in the back of the room. Some of the men exchanged panicked glances.

"What about the . . ." I whispered to David, tilting my head toward the pack of cigarettes on the table.

*I don't know,* he mouthed.

"And," Mitzy continued, "for far too long, women have been excluded from the Bright Leaf boardroom. So, I'm also pleased to report that Ashley, Cornelia, and I have been appointed to the Bright Leaf Tobacco board of directors, also effective immediately." Mr. Winston flinched visibly after this pronouncement and approached the lectern, as if to cut his wife short. But instead of stepping aside, Mitzy leaned in closer to the microphone. "Isn't that right, dear?" she asked him.

"Well . . ." he hedged. He knew he was outnumbered when the women rose from their chairs, hooting and clapping wildly, their applause echoing throughout the ballroom. Eventually, the men started to stand up too, until the whole room was on its feet.

"Yes, yes, that's right," Mr. Winston confirmed. "We're grateful to all the little ladies in Bright Leaf and truly value their support." He put his arm around Mitzy's shoulder and glanced at Dr. Hale. "We're so appreciative, in fact, that we're featuring some of our beautiful Bright Leaf wives and mothers in a new MO-Mints advertisement that will appear in all the national magazines." He pointed to the easel and waved for Dr. Hale to come up onstage.

Dr. Hale took the stairs two at a time, practically tripping over himself, a silly grin on his face. When he reached the easel, he pulled back the fabric covering with a dramatic flourish to reveal the photograph of the tobacco wives, then inserted himself between Mr. Winston and Mitzy.

"MOMints will go on sale nationally starting tomorrow!" boomed Dr. Hale, his fist drumming the air in triumph.

"With a percentage of the sales of MOMints going to our veterans," Mr. Winston shouted over the applause. "And to their wives," he thundered, pointing enthusiastically to the back of the room. The crowd erupted once again.

Mitzy leaned forward, as if she might say something more, but then glanced at her husband and plastered a smile on her face.

I stared at her up on that stage, proudly smiling, shoulder to shoulder with Dr. Hale and Mr. Winston. What a coward she was, what a phony. I felt as if I'd been punched in the stomach. I shook my head and closed my eyes.

"Let's everyone raise a glass, shall we?" Mr. Winston said. A waiter rushed to hand him and Mitzy and Dr. Hale flutes filled with champagne.

I tapped David on the leg with the back of my hand. "How could she?" I spat in a whisper, my jaw quivering with rage. "She's not doing anything." He shook his head and squeezed my hand.

"Excuse me," Mitzy interrupted.

I flinched, my breath catching. *Here it comes. Here it comes.*

I tried to catch her eye, craning my neck to put myself in her line of sight, but she wouldn't look my way. She had a glassy-eyed look, not focusing on anyone.

"I'd like to propose a toast," she said, holding her glass high. "To all of you, the men and women of Bright Leaf. Many of your families have worked tobacco for generations. You've tended the fields that your forefathers first tilled so many years ago. Or you've worked the factory line, or taught at Bright Leaf Elementary, or driven delivery trucks across the state." She gestured to tables in the back of the ballroom as she spoke. "Over the last few days, I've thought a lot about tobacco, about what we do here in Bright Leaf. I've come to realize that tobacco isn't just what we do. It isn't just what we sell. It's who we are!"

The room erupted in cheers to that.

"As my husband says, tobacco isn't just a business, it's our lifeblood." She paused for a moment, taking in the crowd. "Please raise a glass and toast with me. To our lifeblood."

"To our lifeblood," a chorus of voices repeated.

I bolted out of my seat, practically taking the table-cloth with me. I couldn't help it. I couldn't sit there smiling, cheering, while she lied to everyone, deceived the women, pretended that all was well. I couldn't sit there and pretend I hadn't been betrayed.

I lifted my skirt's hem and rushed out into the black night, stumbling on the slick cobblestones and nearly falling before righting myself. I stood under an oak around the corner from the entrance to catch my breath. Hot tears rolled down my face, falling on my borrowed bodice. I wished I could take it off, rip it from my body and replace it with my favorite yellow day dress, throw the fancy hand-me-down in Mitzy's face and tell her to take it back. Take everything back.

"Maddie," David huffed, ducking to join me under the tree. "Maddie, it's okay." He reached for my arm.

"No," I croaked. "No, it's not okay. It's anything *but* okay."

Anthony appeared behind David, out of breath. "Maddie," he sputtered. "God, Maddie. I don't know what I expected her to do, but it wasn't that." I just shook my head.

"Maddie, listen," David said, placing his hands gently on my shoulders. "Maybe she's waiting for a better time to get the information out. Maybe she can't do it tonight, but she will . . . eventually."

Anthony nodded in agreement. "Yeah, maybe David's right."

I wiped my cheek with the back of my hand. "No, she won't," I said. "She won't sacrifice the town and her place in it. Did you see the way she made herself the hero? It makes me sick. All those changes for the women—they're wonderful, they are—but she did it to make herself feel better. You watch, she'll be like a saint in this town now. Saint Mitzy, saving the women of Bright Leaf, while lying through her teeth and putting them and their babies—her own baby—in danger."

David stood there, silent. I took a deep breath and, in the stillness, I heard a faint clicking of heels against the cobblestones that grew closer. I squinted into the distance.

"Dammit," I said under my breath. "Here she comes."

David's head jerked around and both of us watched as Mitzy approached, her yellow gown fluttering as she held her hem to watch her feet, carefully crossing the driveway.

"I want to talk to her alone," I said.

David gave me a quick kiss and Anthony squeezed my hand. They greeted her briefly and excused themselves.

"Maddie, darling," she said, smiling at me sweetly. "You rushed out in such a hurry. Are you all right, dear?"

"No, I'm not all right," I said through clenched teeth.

"I hoped that you'd be pleased about the wonderful changes I announced tonight. Ashley and Cornelia were certain that you'd be thrilled. But you seem very upset."

"Of course, I'm upset," I said. "How could I not be upset?" I was trying not to raise my voice, not to make a scene, but it was maddening how calm she seemed. "What about the study and the advertisements?" I asked. "What about the babies?" I glanced at her stomach. "Your baby?"

Her demeanor changed then. Her posture too, as if she were wearing a corset that had just been tightened.

"I'm taking precautions," she said quietly. I realized that I hadn't seen her smoking since the night I gave her the letter.

"Wonderful party, Mitzy!" a boisterous man shouted from a short distance away. He and his date crossed the driveway arm in arm. "Best one yet," she chimed in. "Sorry we have to leave early." Mitzy seemed relieved that the couple spotted us and used it as an opportunity to step out from under the tree.

"Thank you both." She waved and suggested to me that we continue our conversation on the paved road, out in the open.

She faced me and took my hands in hers; her charm bracelet jingled on her wrist.

"Maddie," she said. "I know you're disappointed

and angry. I understand. Really I do. But I did what I could."

I held my tongue. I'd listen, but I wasn't going to let her off the hook.

"Perhaps I didn't handle things exactly as you would have liked," she continued. "But I did what I thought was best for everyone. You're still young, Maddie," she said sweetly, squeezing my hands. "Life is more complicated than you know, especially for women. Sometimes we have limited choices or no choice at all. I hope you can forgive me. I hope that one day you'll understand."

# Twenty-Eight

I flipped on the kitchen light, my eyes landing on Aunt Etta's cat clock. It was nearly midnight. I slipped off my borrowed shoes, poured myself a glass of water, and stood drinking it at the sink. My head throbbed from my conversation with Mitzy and the two glasses of champagne I'd had right after.

I'd held back my tears for the rest of the night, somehow managing not to let on how upset I was. I'd said *hello*s and accepted *thank-you*s from the wives I'd sewed for. I'd pretended to be as thrilled as Cornelia and Ashley expected me to be about their new roles at Bright Leaf Tobacco, about the changes for the female workers. And I was happy for them. But Mitzy's cowardice ruined it all.

On the drive to Aunt Etta's, I turned over David's

promise in my mind. *It will be okay, Maddie.* He'd whispered just before Isaac pulled up to the Inn to give me a ride. *I promise that I will always be there for you. That we'll get through this together.* He wrapped his arms around me and kissed me gently on the forehead. *I'll see you tomorrow,* he said. It was a sweet thing for David to say, but I'd be a fool to think he would always be there for me. How could we possibly be together after everything that had happened? Mr. Winston and Mitzy were like parents to him. How could he stand by me and keep them in his life too? It hurt my heart to think of saying goodbye to David. We'd only just begun our relationship and I could see a future with him. I'd never felt this way about a boy before, but we couldn't be together, not after tonight.

**I took** a sip of my water and placed the glass next to the sink. I walked around the kitchen expecting . . . what exactly? I didn't know. I picked through the stack of mail next to the telephone. Just bills and what looked like cards, get-well cards I'll bet, and the new fall issue of *Vogue* magazine as thick as the Yellow Pages. I flipped through the stack of mail until my eye caught on an envelope addressed to me in Momma's neat cursive. I ran downstairs to my bed and tore it open.

> *Dear Madeline,*
>
> *It's your Momma, writing to check on you. I rang weeks ago but no one answered the telephone. Did you get my postcard? I sent one from Nashville, Tennessee, and that's where I'm at right now. It's nice here. I met a real good man. His name's Johnny and he's a music producer. He's a real important man who works with famous singers at the Grand Ole Opry. He has a big house and works hard, just like your daddy did.*
>
> *Johnny's a good man and he makes me happy. It feels good to laugh again. I'm thinking of moving here—getting a fresh start. I want to bring you here. I think you'll like Johnny and Nashville.*
>
> *I'm sorry for leaving you at your aunt's like I did. I didn't want to tell you at the time, but the bank was fixing to take the house. I didn't know where we would go and didn't want you there when it happened. We had some nice times in that house, didn't we? Well, the good news is I got it back. Johnny talked to the banker and helped me with the paperwork for your daddy's GI money.*

*Men know how to take care of these things. It's all right now and we'll get payments on the regular from the veterans' fund. We won't have to worry about money anymore.*

*I love you, Maddie. I should tell you that more often. I'm sorry that I don't say the right things sometimes. I don't always make the best choices in life, but I do my best. I hope you understand.*

*I'll be down to get you from your aunt's soon. I'll try calling again and we'll make a plan.*

*Love,*
*Momma*

I brought the letter to my nose. Momma always sprayed her letters with perfume and this one brought with it the smell of honeysuckle. I ran my finger along where she'd signed it *Love, Momma* and the whole of the last month welled up in me. I sobbed like I don't think I'd ever sobbed before. Not just crying, but something deeper. A deep cleansing is what it felt like. Like so much let loose in me. So many hurts came to the surface and spilled out in that one good cry. I cried for Momma, for Daddy and Aunt Etta too. I cried about the women at the factory, about that pretty woman's hands, Sadie's missing fingers, and Cornelia never getting credit for her ideas. I cried about the babies, the ones at the hospital, the one Mitzy lost, and the one she was carrying now. And, although I couldn't forgive her for what she did tonight, I cried for Mitzy too. But mostly, I cried because I saw the world differently now. I'd been so sure of what was right and wrong, of who was good and bad. Through my child's eyes everything was so simple, so clear. But life wasn't like that. It was far more complicated. I understood that now. And now that I knew, there was no going back.

# Epilogue
## *1990*

W hen do you have to get back to Bright Leaf?" I asked Mitzy. David still referred to the woman in my sitting room as Mimi, but the name held too much baggage for me.

"I'm in no rush." She sighed. "Now that there's no one to go home to."

"I'm sure the empty house will take some getting used to," I said.

"It's the firsts that are hardest, you know?" she said.

I did know. "Here, let me pour you a cup of chamomile," I said. "While it's still hot."

"Thank you, dear," said Mitzy, settling herself onto the sofa facing me. "It has been rather lonely without Richard at the other end of the table. I'm trying to keep myself busy, though, as always. Speaking of

444 · ADELE MYERS

which, it was very kind of you to let me visit on such short notice."

"Don't be silly," I tsked. "You're always welcome here. But I must say, I was surprised that you asked to see me alone. I was happy to take the afternoon off from work, and I'm sure David would have been pleased to do the same." I sweetened Mitzy's tea with a single cube of sugar, as always.

"I'm sure he would have—he's always been so kind. But I really only wanted to talk to you." She took the cup and saucer from me, her charm bracelet jingling lightly and her nails the same perfect pale pink. She wore her age well, but she was smaller now, diminished by the years. "It was so kind of Frances to come to the service," Mitzy said, taking a sip. "I heard that she drove all that way by herself? Is that true?"

"It certainly is," I said, nodding my head. "Six and a half hours from the Outer Banks to Bright Leaf. Just Frances and the open road. Can you believe she's still driving at her age?"

"She's really something. You know, I always admired her. I always thought of her as an adventurous woman," Mitzy said.

"Me too," I agreed.

"It's still so strange to see her without Etta," Mitzy said, placing the cup and saucer on the coffee table.

"I know. I still catch myself thinking it's Aunt Etta calling when the phone rings after five o'clock. She rang almost every day at sunset after she and Frances moved to the beach. Even at the end, when she was so weak, she rarely missed a day."

"That's our Etta. She loved you so, Maddie. And she was fiercely proud of you too."

"I hate that she never got to see the shop, though," I said. "I'd give anything to have been able to show it to her."

Mitzy leaned over to pat the top of my hand. "It's done so well over the years. Please tell Anthony I said hello. I tell everyone who will listen about your marvelous shop. I only wish you two would open a second location in Bright Leaf. Cornelia's Two, perhaps?"

"Oh." I laughed. "I don't think so. We can barely keep up with one store. There was only one Cornelia, and there's only one Cornelia's Custom Dresses."

Mitzy laughed with me, her nose crinkling up. "She'd love that you named it after her."

"It wasn't as if she offered us much of an alternative," I replied, still grinning. "She practically stipulated it in her will, along with all her other advice for how to best spend the money she left me."

"Well, I'm sure she'd be extremely proud of the business you've built here in Raleigh. The life you've

446 · ADELE MYERS

built. Establishing yourself in a growing city was a wise choice."

"It was—wasn't it? Although I wasn't thinking about growth potential at the time. I just knew that Bright Leaf was not the place I wanted to go after college."

She frowned and looked away.

"I'm sorry," I said. "I didn't mean to say that so forcefully. It wasn't my intention to be cruel."

"No," Mitzy said. "No, I understand." She shook her head and sighed. "Can you believe that you were only fifteen that summer?"

"No," I said. "I felt much older than that."

"You seemed older too," Mitzy said. "You had to grow up fast. Losing your father, and then your mother's troubles. How is she, by the way?"

"She's doing well," I said. "She lives with her husband right outside Beaconville, not far from here. She met him at church. She's gotten very involved in the church."

"Oh, that's good to hear." Mitzy paused for a few moments and shook her head. "You had so much to deal with that summer, Maddie. Far too much for a girl your age."

"Yes," I said. "But I try not to dwell on it. It was all a very long time ago."

"It was," she agreed. "It was, and yet it seems like

yesterday to me. I don't think there's a day that goes by that I don't turn it over in my mind. About whether I did the right thing."

I looked down at my hands and took a deep breath. I'd given up on discussing this subject with her many years earlier, David and I both had.

We tried to talk sense into Mitzy; we tried so many times. But she would always put us off, change the subject, promise to talk about it later. At first, in the days following the Gala, she refused to speak of it because she was expecting. She didn't want to get herself worked up, to risk the baby's health. When she lost that pregnancy, and in the years that followed, when it became clear that she and Mr. Winston would never have children, she still refused to talk about the study and the way that Bright Leaf Tobacco continued to advertise to women. *But the MOMints business is doing so well,* she'd said. *The women at the factory are thriving.* When I saw her at Cornelia's funeral, ten years had passed and still she brushed me off. There was no point rehashing old disputes when Dr. Hale and Rose were gone, living a high-flying life in Atlanta thanks to the runaway success of MOMints and his prestigious new job as medical director at DeKalb Hospital. He'd even received an award from the American Medical Association for his work with expectant mothers. Did I really want to go against him after all this time? And Ashley had made such progress with the Bright Leaf Women in Business Coalition, an organization that she and Cornelia founded before Cornelia died. She was mentoring dozens of women across the state. "We wouldn't want to interrupt such meaningful work," was the way Mitzy put it.

I looked up to find Mitzy gazing at me expectantly, her question about whether she did the right thing hanging between us. She wanted reassurance, I could tell. Her eyes were practically pleading with me to ease her conscience. But I said nothing and took a sip of my tea. Let her sit with herself.

"You've done so many good works, Maddie," she said after a few moments of uncomfortable silence. "Are you're still involved in that . . . what's that group?"

"The American Cancer Society?" I asked.

"Um . . . no, I was thinking of the Junior League." She shifted in her seat and peered into her teacup.

"The Junior League is a wonderful organization," I said. She looked up hopefully, relieved. "But I spend my time and resources volunteering with the Cancer Society and the Better Business Bureau."

"Oh, is that so?" Mitzy's hand shook as she placed her cup and saucer on the table. "The business group must love having a successful businesswoman to help them."

"Actually, they're helping me," I said.

Mitzy looked confused.

"The Better Business Bureau is helping me lobby Congress."

"Congress? My . . . whatever for?" she asked.

"To put an end to cigarette advertising," I said.

I explained to Mitzy how educating people about the dangers of smoking was not enough. I had such high hopes after the surgeon general's report came out, the first on lung cancer. I was sure that the maternal fetal research would follow shortly after. Women would finally be armed with the facts about how smoking affected pregnancy and babies. But it took another sixteen years before the women's report came out.

"Um hum." Mitzy looked so uncomfortable, but I pressed on.

"I was naive. I thought once women knew the risks, they'd stop smoking. But many didn't. They couldn't. Once they started, it was extremely difficult to stop." My pulse quickened and I cleared my throat. "Do you know why it's so difficult to quit?" I asked.

She stared at me blankly.

"Because it's addictive. Nicotine is addictive. The

tobacco companies have known that for decades, but they claim they didn't know. It's coming out though. Have you been following the congressional hearings? They're finally questioning the executives under oath about what they knew and when they knew it."

"Yes, I saw," Mitzy said. "It's very disturbing."

"Do you know what's even more disturbing?" I said. My voice grew louder as I continued. Even after all these years, my outrage was there, simmering just below the surface.

"The fact that tobacco companies, including Bright Leaf Tobacco, continue to target and deliberately mislead women, men, and now teenagers, through advertising. The ban on television and radio ads didn't stop them. They just spent more on magazines, newspapers, and billboards. They still make all kinds of false claims about the wonderful benefits of cigarettes, get people hooked, and then claim they had no idea they're addictive. That's what's disturbing. That is where I devote my energies now."

Mitzy had no idea that I'd started the Truth in Advertising division of the Better Business Bureau. She feigned interest and pride in my *good works*, but she looked shaken. I paused to catch my breath.

"I'm sorry," I said. "I get a bit carried away. I'm extremely passionate about this."

"As you should be." She withdrew a handkerchief from her handbag and dabbed at her eyes. "You have nothing to apologize for, Maddie," she said. "I'm the one who's sorry. I'm sorry I didn't do more. That I didn't truly do the right thing." She paused a moment before continuing. "I wanted to. I did. I planned to make an announcement at the Gala. I stayed up all night, playing it over and over in my mind. I was going to tell everyone about the study. Warn them. But when the time came, I couldn't. I just couldn't find the courage." She shook her head slowly. "It would have destroyed Richard. It would have just killed him. And Cornelia. She would have been humiliated, Maddie, devastated that her son was behind such a fraud. It would have cost so many good people their jobs, their lives, their homes. I didn't have it in me to bring that kind of loss and shame on Bright Leaf."

She reached into her handbag and withdrew a large envelope. "But now that Richard's gone," she said. "Now that so many, many years have passed, I want you to have this." She handed me a manila folder.

"I wasn't completely honest when I told you that Richard had destroyed the letter. I never would have relinquished it to him. I kept it all those years . . . as leverage. You don't think Richard willingly made all those changes for women, do you?" She smiled sadly.

"You take it now, Maddie. You decide what to do with it now."

I took it from her and opened it to find not only the letter from Dr. Hale but also Mr. Winston's advertising plan, over forty years old. Both documents were faded, but legible, the words as clear as they were when I'd first read them so many summers ago. My breath quickened as I turned the pages over in my hands. I skimmed the letter and plan. Despite the decades that had passed, I remembered every single word. Sights and sounds from that summer flashed through my mind. Mitzy's heels and the tinkling of her charm bracelet. The cuckoo clock that startled me in her parlor. The sweet-smelling but gritty tobacco-flecked soaps floating around me in the clawfoot tub the night I discovered the envelope. David running his fingers roughly through his hair, defending Dr. Hale until he no longer could.

"Are you sure about this?" I asked.

"I'm more sure than I've ever been about anything in my life," Mitzy said.

"I'll be obligated to go public with this, Mitzy," I said, holding up the letter. "I'll have to turn it over to the congressional committee."

"I know," she said. "It's why I'm finally coming forward now. Well, that and Richard's death of course. I couldn't bear to see him testify. It's painful enough to watch the younger executives in the hot seat. You know, one of Ashley's sons has to testify."

"Yes, I heard."

I looked down at the papers in my lap. "Dr. Hale will probably have to testify," I said. "After all these years, I'll be back to stir up trouble for him. It could get very messy."

"I've never known you to back away from a challenge."

"I suppose I did always have a fighting spirit," I said, offering Mitzy a wry smile. "I'm wiser now though. I understand that it takes more than wishful thinking to bring about real change. Still."

"Oh, Maddie, you've always been wise. You had a better-developed moral compass at fifteen than I had at twice your age. Shouldn't you be the one to finally bring all this to light? To do what I couldn't?" She gathered her purse and stood up from the couch.

As I escorted her toward the door, we heard brisk footsteps in the foyer. Then a warm baritone voice called out my name. "Maddie, sweetheart, whose car is that in the driveway?"

"David!" Mitzy said, as my husband's face appeared in the doorway. "There you are, you handsome boy. I can still call you a boy, can't I?" David strode into the room and she kissed his cheek, squeezed him tight. He raised his eyebrows at me, noticing the folder in my hand.

"Is everything okay here?" he asked. "Mitzy, I had no idea you were coming today. I thought I wouldn't see you until our lunch next month." David made it a point to take Mitzy to lunch every other month, but he rarely saw Mr. Winston after that summer. He certainly never went back to Dr. Hale's office after he threatened me, and David made some threats of his own when Dr. Hale tried to stop Aunt Etta's treatment.

"Yes," Mitzy said. "That was the way I wanted it. I came to see Maddie. Talk to your wife. She'll fill you in."

She winked at me and waved; she would see herself out. But I insisted on walking her to the door, and before opening it, I wrapped my arms around her. "Thank you," I whispered. Despite her advanced age, she still gave that firm Mitzy hug. "Thank you for doing what you could then. And thank you for doing this now."

She pulled back to look me in the eye. "It's about time, sweetheart. I'm just glad I lived long enough to do it." She squeezed my shoulder and winked at me. "Now get back to that handsome husband of yours."

I returned to the living room, where David stood waiting. "What just happened?" We sat on the sofa, his arm encircling my waist.

I held up the folder. "I'll give you one guess what this is," I said.

"No, it can't be," he said.

"Yes, it is." I nodded.

"I can hardly believe it. I thought Mr. W burned it forty years ago."

"Probably would have if Mitzy had ever given him the chance. But she kept it for herself instead, and for years she used it as a bargaining chip—as a way to force him to make the changes she wanted for the company and the community."

"God." David sighed. "I guess proximity is useful when you're blackmailing someone."

"I suppose," I said, elbowing him a little for the goofy joke. "But she's decided that it should belong to me. *You decide what to do with it now,* she said."

"She *said* that?" David whistled and slouched against the back of the sofa, pulling me along with him. "So what now, Admiral? I'm sure you've already got a fully formed plan in the works beneath all those curls."

"Of course, I do," I said. "But first, I must call Anthony."

"Oh, yes," David said. "He's going to be stunned."

David smiled and squeezed me a little tighter. "And I imagine he'll want to create an extra special outfit for your congressional interview."

"I hadn't thought about that," I said. "That I may have to testify. I was thinking I would just turn over the letter, but that won't be enough, will it?"

David turned serious. "Are you sure you want to do this, Maddie? It could get ugly, really ugly. Maybe even turn people against us. Hurt your business."

"I know," I said. "I told Mitzy the same thing. I'm not exactly thrilled to be courting trouble," I admitted. "And I certainly don't want the shop to suffer after everything Anthony and I have done to make it a success. But I've been waiting for this moment for over forty years, David. I didn't know if it would ever come. But here it is." I held up the letter. "This could really make a difference. Put an end to the ads that lure people in and hook them. But tell me truthfully, how do you feel about it? It will impact both of us, and the kids and grandkids too."

David didn't say anything at first, just stared at me quietly for long enough that it made me nervous.

"What are you thinking?" I asked, trying to ignore the tremble I could hear in my own voice.

David pushed himself off the couch and reached for both my hands to pull me up alongside him. He didn't release his grip once I was on my feet, facing him.

"I was remembering the toast Cornelia gave on our wedding day."

"That was over thirty years ago, honey," I chuckled.

"Well, I still remember every word," he said, pulling me close. I tilted my chin up and rested it on his chest as he continued. "I believe the exact phrase she used to describe you was *a force to be reckoned with. A force so independent and driven to be her own person that I doubted she'd ever get married.*"

"Yeah." I grimaced. "About that . . ."

David laughed and pulled me in tight. "Cornelia was right about most things, but thank goodness she was wrong about that." He paused and gazed at me. "I love that you're still your own person. You're still a force to be reckoned with after all these years."

I rested my head on his shoulder and squeezed him tight. "Well, who else would I be?" I teased.

We held each other like that for a while and I reflected on what I'd said. It was a flip remark—who else would I be—but a deeply meaningful one too.

Who would I be without that summer in Bright Leaf? What if I hadn't lost my father and been dropped off at Aunt Etta's? All the *what ifs* that go into making a life. I smiled now, thinking of how I decided that I would never be dependent on a man like my mother was. I would be like those women in the books Cornelia had given me. I would take care of myself by myself. Life would be easier that way.

But I came to realize that none of us leave this life unscathed. Each of us experiences loss, grief, disappointment. In fact, sometimes our most painful moments and trying times turn out to be the opportunities that bring us more fully to ourselves. That life is best lived when you open yourself up to it, all of it.

# Author's Note

As a girl growing up in North Carolina, I was fascinated by my grandmother's stories about the women she called "the tobacco wives." She was a hairdresser for the wives of the wealthiest, most powerful tobacco magnates in Winston-Salem, NC, in the 1940s, and tales of these wealthy, glamorous women captured my imagination.

Many years later, I moved to New York City after graduating from journalism school at UNC Chapel Hill and found myself compelled to write a short story about the fashionable Southern belles who had dazzled me as a girl. These women seemed even more fascinating when I realized that despite their wealth and privilege, they, like most women in the 1940s South, were powerless in many ways. When my writing teacher at the time suggested that I consider turning the short story into a longer piece—"it feels like there's a novel here," she had said—the seeds of *The Tobacco Wives* were planted.

The seeds of the book "germinated" for many years, over twenty years to be exact. During that time, I built a successful public relations and advertising career, married a wonderful guy from Brooklyn, and had a son. In 2011, I decided it was time. I committed to writing a novel about the wives.

The story grew as I interviewed family members and conducted research. I learned about disturbing factory practices, such as using floor sweepings to make off-brand, reconstituted cigarettes (*recon* for short). I also discovered a dangerous condition that the field workers experienced while handling wet tobacco plants, a form of nicotine poisoning nicknamed "The Green Monster." The sickness was caused by the toxic substance seeping through the workers' skin as they harvested ripe, green leaves.

I drew upon my relatives' deep connections to tobacco, connections deeper than I even realized when I began writing this book. I mined not only my grandmother's stories from her days as a hairdresser, but also my summers spent assisting my other grandmother, who was a seamstress. I learned about my grandfathers' pasts, who both served the wealthy tobacco families, one as a senior executive with Wachovia Bank and the other as a home builder. My great-uncle was a portrait artist who painted tobacco executives and their wives from his converted carriage house studio in Reynolds Village, the former country estate of the Reynolds family. My conversations with him and my parents, who grew up in Winston-Salem, were illuminating. Tobacco permeated all of their lives and they passed along their memories and mementos from the heyday of Big Tobacco, including a charm bracelet from my mother's 1963 prom, engraved with a large gold $R$ for R.J. Reynolds High School and tales from my father about his teenage summers working in a cigarette factory and drying plant.

What struck me most about these conversations was the immense pride that people felt back then about helping to build "the tobacco capital of the South." In hindsight, it's hard to believe that they didn't know about the dangers of smoking, but during those years they truly had no idea. What was it like for them, I wondered, to have such pride in their work and community, only to learn that they were manufacturing products that made people sick, even killed them? How did proud tobacco town executives and workers react in 1950 when medical studies linked smoking to cancer? What would a tobacco wife do if she was the first to know, or better yet, if she discovered her husband had been covering it up? These questions took the book in an exciting direction and spurred me to learn all I could about the fall of Big Tobacco.

*The Tobacco Wives* was inspired by tales from this part of my family's history, but the setting, characters, and events of the story are fictitious. I borrowed from the Big Tobacco revelations that came later, well into the '60s, '70s, and '80s. Two books in particular were incredibly helpful: *The Gilded Leaf—Triumph, Tragedy, and Tobacco: Three Generations of the R.J. Reynolds Family and Fortune* by Patrick Reynolds and Tom Shachtman and *Golden Holocaust: Origins of the Cigarette Catastrophe and the Case for Abolition* by Robert N. Proctor.

As I delved more deeply into the tobacco industry cover-up, I realized what a significant role advertising had played in shaping public opinion. Knowing that damning medical studies would eventually come out, tobacco executives created advertising campaigns to influence and deliberately mislead consumers. Their ads featuring doctors, touting health benefits of cigarettes, and promising product features like weight loss, masked the ugly truths about the dangers of smoking that they knew were coming.

My expertise in public relations and advertising

gave me insight into the strategies tobacco companies employed. I know the power of marketing, how it can shape perceptions and drive consumer behavior. I drew upon my experience in the field to develop Mr. Winston's plan, including techniques like credentialing, target audience insights, and attribution of health benefits to ingredients versus the final product.

While early evidence of tobacco's dangers focused on lung cancer, I chose to write about the impact smoking had on women. The 1940s was a time of social unrest, wartime conflict, and emerging new options for women, a time that some historians say spurred the modern women's rights movement. Setting the book in this period and taking liberties with the timeline and nature of tobacco studies' emergence enabled me to explore themes such as Southern women's role in society, the impact of WWII on the workforce, and the use of women in advertising. Anne Firor Scott's book *The Southern Lady: From Pedestal to Politics, 1830–1930* gave me an invaluable perspective on women's lives and the influence they wielded behind the scenes.

I thoroughly enjoyed traveling back to the 1940s and uncovering the hidden history of this unique place and time and hope that my readers did, too.

# Acknowledgments

I am immensely grateful to my literary agent, Stefanie Lieberman. This book would not have been written without Stefanie's vision, expert guidance, and unwavering support. She and her team at Janklow & Nesbit, Adam Hobbins and Molly Steinblatt, went above and beyond to make *The Tobacco Wives* a reality.

Thank you to my editor, Liz Stein, who blew me away with her insights, ideas, and sharp edits. She made the book so much better and guided the incredible team at William Morrow to bring it into the world. At William Morrow, thank you to Amelia Wood, Emily Fisher, Jessica Rozler, Nancy Singer, Ploy Siripant, Shelly Perron, and Barbara J. Greenberg.

Many thanks to my teachers, fellow writers, editors, colleagues, dear friends, and extended family for believing in me and providing feedback and encouragement:

Alexandra Shelley, Jacqueline Tuorto, Allyson Fisher, Brenda Copeland, Kim Purcell, Geri Mazur, Kara Araujo, Rachel Chou, Galaxy Craze, Nashwa Rafla-Savio, Mara Hatzimemos, Natasha Fishman, Julie McAskin, Melissa Stolper, Ruth Marlin, Shelly Auster, Anna Van Lenten, Susanna Kohn, Donaldson Brown, Justine Lambert, Kate Morrone, Susan Alvarez, Ani Demurjian, Dayna Konko, Maria Becker, Stephanie Mohorn, Brittney Hanlon, Cassi Smith, Kelley Burch, Bethany Erskine, Seze Devres, Margie Lempert, Jenny Fenig, Ilze Thielmann, Dave McDowell, Natalie Reingold, Helen Reingold, Barbara Whitson, Elaine Butler, Wendy Whitson, and my community of CrossFit South Brooklyn coaches, friends, and platform mates.

Special thanks to Dietra Gamar for making this life and this book possible. I am forever indebted to you for helping me find my voice and become my best self.

I am so thankful for my grandmothers, who gave me childhood experiences and memories that fueled my writing. Madeline King Myers, thank you for your unconditional love. You were the kindest person I've ever known, so kind that you never did give me any real dirt on the tobacco wives, so I had to make it up myself. To Elma Menius, who gave me the gift of carefree summers, sewing, and playing UNO. To Cleta Ayers, who taught me how to make biscuits, string beans, and enjoy long walks after dinner.

Thank you to my parents. Jeanie Penland, you were the first person to read to me. My love of reading and writing began with you, and it has given my life purpose and joy. Thank you for that priceless gift. Gordon Myers, you have always encouraged me to pursue my dreams and provided me with the education and resources that made it possible. Thank you. To Kaye Myers, thank you for your support through the ups and downs of my publishing journey. Your belief in me lifted me up when obstacles arose and for that I am very thankful. To my sister, Katie Myers Krier, thank you for your love and encouragement, and for always making me laugh. To my brother, Neil Myers, my first friend, thank you for your support and for always being there for me.

I'm grateful for my writing companion, Chipper, who stayed glued to my side through many months of editing. Thank you for keeping me company and only occasionally breaking my flow with your barking.

Finally, thank you to my husband, Jay, and my son, Niko. You are my favorite people, the best part of every day. I love you.

# HARPER LARGE PRINT

We hope you enjoyed reading
our new, comfortable print size and found it
an experience you would like to repeat.

**Well – you're in luck!**

Harper Large Print offers the finest in
fiction and nonfiction books in this same larger
print size and paperback format. Light and easy to read,
Harper Large Print paperbacks are for the book lovers
who want to see what they are reading without strain.

For a full listing of titles and
new releases to come, please visit our website:
**www.hc.com**

## HARPER LARGE PRINT

# SEEING IS BELIEVING!